# *REBEL LOVE*

Jessie felt Garth's hand lightly caress her back. "I'll come back after the war if you want."

"You might be dead by then."

"I might not."

She turned her head and looked at him with a trace of contempt. "I don't want you to come back. I haven't forgotten what you are."

"But you like me."

"I *tolerate* you."

One dark eyebrow rose in cynical mockery. "Is that what it is between us?"

Her eyes flamed dangerously. "Don't patronize me!"

He reached out and gripped her arm, pulled her back into bed with him. She fell half across him, her hair spilling over his chest. She struggled to get up, but he put both arms around her and held her firm.

"I'm coming back whether you like it or not."

ELIZABETH FRITCH

# WILD SWEET MADNESS

LEISURE BOOKS ❧ NEW YORK CITY

A LEISURE BOOK

Published by

Dorchester Publishing Co., Inc.
6 East 39th Street
New York, NY 10016

Printed in the United States of America

# 1

There was a sudden, terrible explosion, a searing flash of flame. Jessie Morgan buried her head more deeply into the pillow, and her heart froze, seemed to shrivel inside her, but the sounds still came from near and far.

It was a hot, oppressive July afternoon in Gettysburg; it seemed the southern invaders had brought the heat with them. And death and destruction and misery . . .

Jessie's heart gave a mighty lurch. She rolled over on her bed as the staccato fire of rifles erupted somewhere nearby. The fighting had been going on in earnest since yesterday morning, with Union and Confederate troops alike maneuvering for a better position throughout the town. Jessie didn't know who was winning, only the awful, constant noise that shattered the serenity of the home she shared with her widowed mother.

Another blast rocked the foundations of the house. Jessie flew off the bed and ran in a crouch to the window, the irises of her blue eyes dilated with fear. Another terrible roar that ripped at the eardrums resounded, rattling the panes of glass and knocking a framed sampler off the wall. She could smell the acrid stench of gunpowder, hear the triumphant cries of men from somewhere not far away.

Taking a deep unsteady breath, Jessie cautiously rose up to peer out the window. Across the street was a splintered, gaping hole in the side of her neighbor's house. Inside someone was crying hysterically. Gettysburg had been so peaceful until a few days ago, before the hated Rebels had come, a little place no one had ever heard of, a mere dot on the map.

Venting a sigh of desperation, Jessie turned away from the window. She was tired; she hadn't slept at all last night, despite the let-up in the fighting. She knuckled her eyes and shuffled over to the pier glass in the corner, wishing the noise outside would cease. She gazed at her image in the mirror, and a trembling shock coursed through her. Instead of the pert, comely face she was accustomed to seeing, a stranger stared back at her. The high cheekbones and forehead were the same, the nose still as straight as ever, but there were bags under her eyes. Bags, at nineteen! And the clear, wide-set blue eyes looked murky and red. Her dark chestnut hair, drawn back in one long braid, hung limp and forlorn.

Always before Jessie had considered herself to be passably attractive—some even said beautiful. Now she looked like a harried slattern, drab and dull and as jumpy as a cat. Damn those Rebs! And damn General Meade for not sending them packing back to Virginia right away!

Movement at the door startled her, and Jessie turned in alarm. She gave a soft moan of relief. It was only her mother, Hattie Morgan.

"There isn't much in the house to eat," the older woman said.

Jessie gaped. "Surely you don't want me to go out and get something!"

A touch of mirth clung to her mother's lips. At forty, Hattie Morgan's features had resisted the ravages of time. Her blue eyes were friendly and warm, her face aristocratic, a legacy perhaps from her birth into a wealthy southern family. Soft-spoken, frail and birdlike, yet strong, Jessie knew her mother's loyalties were being sorely tested during the last few days. Hattie had married a Pennsylvania merchant and come north, but her roots were still back in South Carolina. For Jessie's part, she *knew* where her allegiance lay—right here in Gettysburg with the Union Army.

"I'm going down to the cellar for some pickles and canned tomatoes," Hattie said.

Jessie glanced nervously toward the open

window, where puffs of smoke still billowed from the cannon shot. "I'll come with you."

She followed her mother out of the bedroom and into the small parlor. All the reports spoke of most of the fighting going on in the outskirts of town, but no one could convince Jessie of that. Still, for the moment, the firing around the house seemed to have abated.

"Why did they come *here*?" Jessie asked suddenly.

"Maybe it's as far as they got. Maybe they wanted our food and cattle and pigs. They say the Confederacy's running out of supplies."

Jessie uttered a scornful grunt. "Let 'em all starve."

"You've got relatives down south."

"Ones I've never met. They might as well be on the moon now." Her mouth curled in disdain. "They're all so rich—with their fancy plantations and fine horses. Papa *worked* for his money."

"And a good thing he did, else we'd both be taking in sewing and washing to keep us in food."

"Johnny Reb might fix that for us anyway." Jessie ground her teeth in growing impatience. "I *wish* I knew what was going on out there."

A sudden knock at the door startled Jessie. She froze, her eyes wide, her heart pounding. Maybe it was General Lee himself, come to pillage and plunder! She cast a nervous eye at her father's musket hanging over the fireplace. It wasn't loaded; besides, it had such a powerful kick, it had knocked her off her feet the few times she had fired it.

Fear prickling her spine, Jessie glanced timidly at her mother. "Should we answer it?"

She and her mother looked at one another with shared discomfort for a moment. Then, finally, Hattie shrugged and stepped toward the door.

Jessie threw a frantic glance in the direction of the kitchen. A butcher knife? A frypan? She could see the headlines now: JESSICA MORGAN KILLS GENERAL LEE SINGLE-HANDEDLY. The only problem was, she didn't think she could kill *anyone*, even if her life depended on it.

By now, Hattie had reached the front door, and Jessie shrank back, put a hand to her mouth and squeezed her eyes shut tight. But instead of a cry of alarm, Hattie greeted whoever it was warmly.

Jessie opened her eyes and blinked in dumbfounded surprise. It wasn't the loathesome General Lee. It was two tattered and tired-looking Union privates. Jessie sagged with disappointment. Had she really *wanted* it to be General Lee?

"Ma'am, I wonder if we could please fill up our canteens." One of the men—a youth who looked hardly old enough to shave—extended a battered canteen in Hattie's direction. "It's mighty hot out there."

Hattie stepped aside and ushered the pair inside. "We have plenty of water—unless one of your cannonballs put a hole in our well."

Jessie studied the two soldiers curiously as they followed her mother into the kitchen. She trailed along, faintly amazed. Were these two gawky youths an example of the kind of men defending the town? They weren't any older than herself, if indeed as old.

"What's the latest news?" Hattie asked.

"Don't rightly know," one replied, filling his canteen from the pump at the sink. Hattie offered him a glass, and he drank it down in three swift gulps. "Things seem to be quietin' down some around town. But I hear there's heavy fighting in the peach field down by the Emmitsburg Pike."

"Lotsa casualties," the other added, taking his turn at the pump. Jessie caught a whiff of an unwashed body and nearly gagged. "Some of our men are up on Little Round Top."

The taller of the pair corked his canteen and slung it over his shoulder with a miscellany of other odds and ends. Jessie noticed a toothbrush—of all things—poked through a buttonhole in his dirty tunic jacket. His gaze went shyly over Jessie, then settled on a heaping bowl of plums on the counter. "Would you mind?" he asked hesitantly.

Jessie shrugged indifferently, then offered him a plum and one for his companion.

"Take them all," Hattie said. "We've got more."

Jessie winced as filthy hands with broken fingernails emptied the bowl. Plenty, she thought bitterly. What the birds hadn't gotten to, the soldiers had made target practice of.

The two youths thanked them both effusively and started to leave by the back door. One turned back and gave them a look of warning. "Two ladies like yourselves—be mighty careful. There's Rebs hereabouts, and we might not always be around to protect you."

Jessie gave him a tightly puckered smile. If these two were the kind of men Abe Lincoln had in his regiments, it was no wonder the north had been losing the war!

She watched the pair leave, strangely disconcerted. "They weren't what I expected."

"They're only boys," Hattie said, locking the door.

"That's what I *mean*!"

Hattie smiled reassuringly and put an arm around her daughter's shoulder. "Come on. Let's go get those things from the cellar."

Jessie shot a wistful glance at the empty bowl. Still, she supposed it was for a good cause. If those two *were* all Abe Lincoln had, then she wished them well. And if what they said about the casualties were true . . . She shivered involuntarily. The hospitals—*everything*—must be filled with them. There would be much to do once the Rebels pulled out—*if* they ever pulled out. With this unhappy thought, she snared a lantern and match and began to descend the cellar steps behind her mother.

The stairs were steep and made of old

wood; they creaked and groaned with each footstep. Jessie made her way down in darkness, then set the lantern on the table to strike the match. She could smell something quite different from potatoes, onions and apples—something sweet and metallic, a strange, unpleasant odor.

The lantern flared; the room was bathed in light. She heard her mother's sharp intake of breath and turned to look. Jessie's face went white with shock, and the breath froze in her throat. She wanted to scream, then wanted to vomit.

Lying on the floor in a pool of blood was a Confederate soldier. His uniform was torn and a bright red kepi lay off to one side. His face was against the floor, as drawn and pale as that of a corpse; he was unconscious, laboring to breathe. The upper portion of his left sleeve was a shredded, torn mess; blood stains seeped into the gray material, far darker than the red piping of his shell jacket.

Jessie cringed back and raised the palm of her hand as if to ward off some unseen enemy. "A dead Reb—in *our* cellar!"

"He's not dead." Hattie bent and carefully rolled him over onto his back. She felt his throat for a pulse, lifted one eyelid. She turned to Jessie, her eyes dark with concern. "Run up and get some water. Add a little whiskey to it."

"But, Mama, he's a Reb!"

Hattie raised a brow impatiently. "He's a man!"

Casting one last apprehensive look over her

shoulder, Jessie fled up the steps and into the kitchen. She nearly dropped the glass, spilling some whiskey on her skirt. She ran a trembling hand across her face, fear and confusion playing alternately over her features. What was he doing in their cellar?

When she went back downstairs she discovered her mother had tied a clean strip of linen at his shoulder as a tourniquet. For the first time Jessie noticed a number of jars had fallen from the shelves. Her gaze traveled upward to the trap doors leading to the backyard. The bolt was unlatched; he must have managed to get in that way. A haversack was lumped on the floor, its contents spilled.

"The water!" Hattie reminded her peevishly.

Snapping out of her wonder and shock, Jessie knelt at the soldier's side. Her mother raised his head while Jessie held the glass to his lips. At first the liquid trickled down over his chin and stubbled cheeks, then finally he began to drink. He took a few sips and started to cough, and his eyelids fluttered briefly.

"Enough," Hattie said.

Jessie set the glass aside. "What are we going to do with him?"

"I don't know."

"We can't go out and find a doctor in all this fighting." Jessie's mind whirled with confusion. "I wish those two soldiers would come back."

"They'd only arrest him, and he'd probably die."

"He might die *here*! I don't want a Reb dying in our cellar!"

Hattie's eyes clouded with indecision, and she bit her lip. "Let me think."

Jessie glanced away, then turned her attention to the unconscious soldier. Black hair, wet with perspiration, straggled over his forehead. He sported an equally black mustache, and several days' growth of beard covered his cheeks. But his chin was strong and the lean lines of his face almost handsome, even in his obvious pain.

"We'll have to get him upstairs," Hattie finally said.

Jessie gasped, scandalized. "What?"

"We'll take him up to your room."

Jessie shook her head, completely baffled. "We can't! We'll never get him up those stairs." She put up her hands in a gesture of helplessness. "Besides, we could be arrested or something for . . . for helping the enemy."

Hattie dismissed her daughter's protest with an impatient wave of her hand. "He's not our enemy now. He's just a poor sick boy. And he needs our help."

Jessie struck her forehead with the heel of her hand, and a wild look of exasperation came over her. "Must be your southern blood."

"Must be." Hattie lifted the soldier's head once more, and Jessie held the glass for him. He drank deeply this time, and when his eyes opened, they were glassy, like gray ice. "It's all right, son," Hattie said, brushing back a damp lock of his hair. "Can you stand?"

He tried to speak, but the words were garbled. Nevertheless, with Hattie's and Jessie's help, he struggled to a sitting position, then to his knees. His face twisted in agony, and he reached for his shoulder.

Hattie took his hand away. "Just try to stand. We'll worry about that later."

Laboriously, the soldier stood. He swayed a moment, and Jessie feared he would collapse. He tottered and hung on to her like a drunk, his head down, gasping. With both she and her mother supporting him, Jessie slowly started up the steps. It was a slow, painful progress; he was heavy and too tall to lean comfortably on either woman. If he loses his balance now, Jessie thought dismally, we'll all go down.

But he didn't. Laboring for breath, pale and contorted with pain, he reached the kitchen with their assistance. In the cellar it had been cool and quiet; upstairs, it was hot, and gunfire could be heard once again. Jessie thought of what they were doing, and she had to fight off an overriding panic.

"Just a little farther now," Hattie told him.

The soldier mumbled an unintelligible reply, but Hattie's voice, with its faint southern lilt, must have been reassuring to the man. He seemed to redouble his efforts to walk, and Jessie silently thanked God when they reached her bedroom.

They maneuvered him to the bed, and he flopped down crookedly like a sack of potatoes. Hattie rearranged his booted feet while Jessie sorrowfully took note of the blood quickly staining the patchwork quilt she had worked so long and hard to make.

"Close the window and curtains," Hattie said.

"But it'll be stifling in here."

"Better hot than to have some nosybody looking in."

"Nobody's out but soldiers."

"That's exactly what I mean."

Thrusting out her lower lip in a pout, Jessie did as she was told. At least the sounds of gunshots and the roar of the cannons lessened with the window shut. She turned back to her mother, heaving a disheartened, helpless sigh. "Now what?"

"I'll need more clean rags. And that bottle of carbolic from the kitchen."

Jessie left the bedroom, glad to get away. She gathered up more pieces of torn sheets from the box in the cellar, then locked the bolt from the inside; for the present, she didn't want any more Rebs dropping in un-invited. Curious, she gingerly picked up the haversack and cap and took them back upstairs with her. These she left in the kitchen while she found the bottle of carbolic in a cupboard.

Jessie swore, letting her breath out in a hiss. Helping the enemy! And when she returned to her room her irritation increased. Hattie had removed the soldier's tunic and blouse and was carefully examining the wound. Jessie's mouth thinned into an angry line. A southerner in her bed and seeping blood on the quilt. She had often speculated on what it would be like to have a man in her bed. But not this . . . this Reb!

"Get some towels," Hattie said.

Jessie did as she was told, silently fuming at this sense of betrayal to her country. If she *had* to help someone, better it would be one of those pimply faced privates who had come earlier. She still wished they would return. At least one burden would be off the Morgans' hands. Still, she couldn't deny there was a sense of excitement and intrigue to it all.

She returned with the towels and placed them under the soldier's left arm as she was instructed. She couldn't look at the wound; the glimpse she had of shredded flesh and blood sent her stomach raging.

"The ball's not here," Hattie said. "Must have passed clean through the fleshy part of his arm. I'll hold it open while you pour carbolic on it."

Jessie swallowed hard. "I can't. I'll throw up."

Hattie sighed impatiently. "You've beheaded chickens and skinned rabbits before."

"But he's a man!"

A wryness touched the expression on Hattie's face. "I'm glad you're finally beginning to understand that."

Jessie realized her protests were useless; her mother was adamant. She eyed the open wound cautiously. Gorge rose to her throat; she tasted bile and took a deep breath to keep from vomiting. But she managed to uncork the bottle. She dribbled a few drops onto the torn flesh; the liquid bubbled, mixed with the man's blood. At Hattie's direction, she poured more into the wound. The soldier cried out in pure agony, thrashed a moment, then fell into deep unconsciousness.

Jessie fought back an impulse to gag, then poked the cork back into the bottle's neck. "I'll never be a nurse. And think of all the men who'll be like him—and worse—before this is through."

Hattie was rewrapping the arm with strips of cloth. "I've thought about that a lot since yesterday. At least we've got only one to tend to."

"But he's from the wrong side."

"He has no side anymore."

Jessie grunted, unconvinced.

"Take off his gunbelt and stow it under the bed," Hattie said. "We'll have to hide his uniform."

Jessie fumbled to unbuckle the holster; the gun was a huge, heavy thing with the name STARR printed on the barrel. His, or one he had stolen from a Yankee? She stuffed it under the bed, along with his blouse and shell jacket.

"I'm going to take off his trousers," Hattie said.

Jessie stood paralyzed with shock. "Mama!"

"I'm not asking you to stay. You can go down and clean up the blood in the cellar."

Jessie grimaced at the thought.

"Then, tonight, you can sneak out and see if the hens have stopped laying in all this racket. We'll need the eggs. Maybe we can trade with old Mrs. Webster for some milk from her cow."

Jessie trudged from the bedroom. As she reached the kitchen, another burst of cannon fire almost tore through her eardrums. She jumped and pressed her hands over her ears as renewed fear stirred in the pit of her belly.

Then she saw the haversack and kepi lying on a chair. Who was he? Where did he come from? Did he have a name? She felt so hopelessly frustrated, she didn't know whether to cry or scream.

I wish they would all go home—Union and Confederate alike—and leave us alone and in peace again!

# 2

"He didn't move all night," Hattie said.

Jessie sat at the kitchen table, brooding into her coffee. "The least you could have done would have been to put one of Papa's old nightshirts on him."

"He's wearing underdrawers. Anyway, I had enough trouble getting him undressed."

"You know we'll never be able to tell anyone about this. We'd be outcasts for the rest of our lives."

"Depends on who wins. We might end up singing 'Dixie' and bowing to Jeff Davis."

Jessie looked appraisingly at her mother. "You'd like that, wouldn't you?"

"No. But you know how hard it's been for me to take sides in this. My family's in South Carolina and Georgia—my life is here in Pennsylvania." A faint, sad smile played around her mouth and eyes. "I used to write to my sister Peggy Sue before . . . Haven't heard from her since right afer Fort Sumter, over two years."

"If Papa was alive, I bet he'd be a colonel or something. Maybe General McClellan's right-hand man."

Hattie's lips twitched in a faint smile. "Your papa fought in Mexico when you were a baby. He didn't like war. He'd be right here tending his store. I miss him something awful, but I'm glad he's not here to see what the country's doing to itself."

Jessie drank some coffee, bit into a stale biscuit, then washed it down with more coffee. "I saw Mrs. Webster's boy this morning when I went for the milk. He says the Rebs mostly have the town, our men command most of Taneytown Road and east. He wants to join."

"He's only fourteen!"

Jessie shrugged. "I'd probably join, too, if I wasn't a woman."

"You can't stand the sight of blood."

"True."

Jessie studied her mother thoughtfully for a moment. Being an only child, and especially after her father's death three years before, she had a special bond with Hattie Morgan. Until then, Jessie had had a relatively easy life; at sixteen, she had quickly had to learn responsibility. Someday, she wanted a husband and children; for now, she would stay and help her mother. Besides, all the eligible men had gone off to fight.

Ben Morgan had left them fairly well off. He

had been as shrewd in business as he was in saving his money. They owned their modest house and an acre of land, and by living wisely—if not too frugally—they had enough to get by. Jessie had briefly toyed with the idea of teaching school, but that would have meant four more years in the female academy, which she loathed.

"There's beef stew I can heat up if he's ever able to eat it," Hattie said. "Would you like to go look in on him? I'm curious about him, anxious to go through his knapsack."

Jessie shrugged and rose from the table. The kitchen was already warm; it promised to be another hot day. All the same, she refilled her coffee cup and took it into the bedroom with her. The soldier lay on his back on the bed, the sheet pulled up to his waist. His chest, matted with dark hair, rose and fell evenly with his breathing. A thin sheen of sweat coated his torso.

Jessie pulled up a chair and sat down, staring at him. "Mister, you could get us into a pack of trouble."

His mouth seemed to curve into a slight smile. Astonished, Jessie leaned closer to him. "Are you awake? Can you hear me?"

But there was no answer; his face settled back into an expressionless mask. Hattie had bathed him, and at least he smelled better than their two visitors yesterday. Jessie examined him again, more intently this time. His shoulders were broad and well muscled, his belly flat and lean. His features were angular and pleasing, and he had a narrow, bladelike nose. Jessie smiled with a faint melancholy. A pity he was a Reb. He was certainly a fine specimen of manhood.

Jessie released her breath in a heavy sigh. There was no sense sitting here; he was out, and it appeared he would be that way for some time.

Just as she was about to rise, she heard a knock at the back door, and her mind froze with fear. A sinking terror deepened within her. What would happen if this man was found here—in her bed!

Hattie dashed into the bedroom, nearly skidding halfway across the floor on the rag rug. "Hide this!" She tossed the haversack and kepi at Jessie, then darted back out.

Jessie stood staring foolishly at the canvas sack and red cap, then stuffed them under the bed with the soldier's other things. She scowled darkly at his unconscious form; then, fear regaining its hold on her, she closed the door as she left.

She stood quietly outside the bedroom, listening, her heart hammering in her chest. But as she recognized a familiar voice, Jessie felt herself go almost limp with relief. It was only Mary Purcell, the woman whose house had been struck by the cannonball yesterday. Composing her features, Jessie walked calmly into the kitchen.

"The hole's really a blessing in this heat," the woman was saying. "More ventilation, you know."

Hattie nodded noncommitally. Evidently she hadn't asked the neighbor in, for they were both standing half in and half out of the kitchen. "At least no one was hurt."

"But the cat's missing." Mary Purcell wore her graying hair piled high on her head and wrapped tightly in a bun, held in place by several tortoiseshell combs. Her age was indeterminate, though she was older than Jessie's mother. She was broad in the shoulders and hips, gave the impression of bursting good health, of strength and vitality. Ordinarily, Jessie enjoyed the woman's high spirits, but not today. Not until Johnny Reb was safely out of the Morgan house. The older woman turned a bright smile on Jessie. "They say the Rebs are pulling out of town to the south."

"Maybe they've decided to go home."

"That'll be the day." She hesitated, obviously waiting for an invitation inside. When none came, she tugged at her apron and turned to leave. "If you see the cat, bring him home. Do you know those soldiers had the nerve to steal the clothes right off my line?" With this, she marched down the steps and out the gate.

Jessie glanced at her mother, her brows drawn together in a worried frown. "I thought for sure we'd been found out."

"She'll never suspect a thing."

"She doesn't miss much that goes on around here."

"At least for the time being we're safe."

Hattie seated herself at the kitchen table. "Do you really think the Rebs are leaving town?"

"I hope so." Jessie flung herself into a chair and frowned peevishly. "And I hope our guest can leave soon too."

"Which reminds me . . ." Hattie reached into her pocket and extracted several letters bound with a red ribbon. "I was just going to look at these when Mary showed up." She untied the ribbon and handed an envelope to Jessie.

Jessie peered at the name: Captain Garth Bodine. So that was his name, and a captain too. The return address was a place called Magnolia Hall in Charleston, South Carolina. Jessie stared at the stamp—a likeness of Jefferson Davis—and scowled.

Hattie stared at her own letter in disbelief, then threw back her head and laughed. "I don't *believe* it! Uncle Claiborne!"

Hattie's eyes glittered with excitement. "*My* uncle. Or second uncle or whatever." Her hands fluttered nervously as she opened the letter and quickly scanned the contents. Her blue eyes grew larger with each passing second until she exhaled a tremendous breath. "That soldier in your room belongs to Uncle Claiborne and Aunt Delia."

Jessie's mind tried to absorb this incredible fact. "You mean he's related to us?"

"He must be a distant cousin of some kind. Look here—" She held the letter for Jessie's inspection. "It even mentions Peggy Sue."

Jessie's face twisted with wrath and frustration. It was bad enough, the way things were now. But to have this Garth Bodine turn out to be a cousin! Jessie swore softly.

"We can't turn him out now," Hattie said.

Jessie groaned in mock pain. "I might have guessed that. But who *are* these people? I never heard of them."

"They were the rich relations. Somewhere back, we're connected by grandmas. Mine married the poor side."

"But what'll we *do* with him?"

Hattie sighed dolefully, her eyes hooded in thought. "I spent most of last night tossing and turning over that question. That was before we knew which side was winning. But if what Mary Purcell says is true . . ."

"Then he's our prisoner."

Hattie shook her head grimly. "He's our cousin, and we've got to do for him no matter what. Wouldn't you hope the same if you had a brother or husband fighting down south?"

With a defeated sigh, Jessie threw her hands up in the air. She could understand her mother's reasoning, but that didn't make it any less distasteful. He might be kin, but he was still a Reb.

A moan from the bedroom startled Jessie out of her thoughts. Both she and her mother jumped up at the same time, as if knowing intuitively their patient had to be kept quiet for the present.

Garth Bodine came to, feeling as if he were

fighting his way up to consciousness though thick layers of gauze. Pain roared through his shoulder and arm, and a low, keening groan escaped his lips. He twisted his head to one side, saw his left shoulder securely wrapped in white cloth, and questions, one after the other, raced through his mind. His hazy gaze traveled over his surroundings. It was a bedroom, obviously occupied by a woman; a red calico dress hung over a chair and there was a myriad of bottles and brushes and combs on the dressing table.

The door burst open, and Garth turned his head. His neck and shoulder muscles throbbed, but he was able to focus on two women. "Hush!" one of them ordered. "Do you want somebody to find out you're here?"

Garth squinted to focus more clearly on the speaker. She was young and short with a mane of chestnut hair flowing down to her waist. She was scowling, and blue eyes sparked at him.

The other woman—older but bearing a resemblance to the younger—approached the bed. "I know it hurts, Captain Bodine, but try not to cry out."

Garth felt fright and pain and confusion. "Where am I? What is this place and how did I get here?" His tongue felt thick and uncoordinated, too large for his mouth. He was powerfully thirsty.

"You're in Gettysburg, and you've been shot."

His mind swam with gruesome images, and

he groaned with a combination of pain and recollection. An image returned of his men at their cannons, of Garth directing them. Then there was a tearing pain in his arm, and that was all he could remember. But the pain lingered.

"Could I have some water?" he asked.

The older woman glanced at the younger, who left the room. "I'm Hattie Morgan." She approached the bed, a warm smile on her face. "And that's my daughter, Jessie."

"How long have I been here?"

"I'm not really sure. We found you yesterday afternoon in our basement."

Garth had a vague memory of crawling and crouching through bushes after his gun emplacement had been evacuated, of hiding from Yankee sharpshooters, of a trap door in a backyard. But it hurt too much to think about it.

Jessie returned with a glass of water and wordlessly handed it to her mother. Hattie helped him raise up a little, and, ignoring the pain, he drank greedily. The water soothed his parched throat.

"Could you manage a little soup?" Hattie asked him.

He winced as he settled back against the pillows. "I think so." God, how his arm ached. He clamped his teeth on his lower lip until the pain subsided. He wished he could sink back into mindless oblivion again, to a place where pain and thought were absent. He wondered briefly how General Pendleton was faring, if more ammunition for the artillery had arrived, and realized he was too weary to care.

"I haven't been able to get a doctor in to see you," Hattie told him. "Truth is, I haven't tried. I suppose they're all pretty busy. But I couldn't find any bullet when I dressed your wound."

"Why are you doing this? I mean, we invaded your town."

A flash of humor brought a sparkle to Hattie's eyes as Jessie returned with a steaming bowl. "You'll have to excuse me for doing a little prying into your things," Hattie said. "But I was curious about you. It seems we're distant cousins."

Garth blinked in surprise. "Cousins?"

Hattie helped lift his shoulders while Jessie propped the pillows behind his back. He couldn't hold the bowl in his left hand, so Hattie held it for him while he spooned hot soup into his mouth. Pain hammered through his arm, but he ignored it. He was ravenously hungry.

He listened while Hattie explained what little she knew of their relationship. Jessie leaned against the dressing table, her arms folded across her chest, scowling at him.

"Does she talk?" Garth asked Hattie, inclining his head toward Jessie.

"Too much sometimes."

Annoyance flickered across Jessie's face. "Of course I talk. But not to Rebs."

"But we're cousins."

"I never even heard of you before today. And cousin or not, you're still a Reb."

Garth finished his soup and studied Jessie. She was slender and graceful with shapely curves beneath her plain cotton skirt. Her blue eyes sparkled, and that magnificent fall of chestnut hair fascinated him. What a pity she couldn't be more friendly. Under different circumstances ... He wondered what she would look like if she smiled.

Hattie set the empty bowl aside. "I'd better have a look at that arm now."

Garth shuddered. He had visions of the operating tents, the endless amputations. He didn't think he could live with just one arm.

Hattie carefully unwrapped the outer bandages, but blood and tissue stuck to the inner strips of cloth. Needles of pain pierced Garth's skin, roared up his arm and down to his wrist.

"Get the carbolic, Jessie."

Grumbling sourly, Jessie picked up a blue bottle and approached the bed. She looked nauseated, her face as gray as ashes. Garth didn't blame her; he couldn't bear to turn his head and look for himself.

"This will sting," Hattie cautioned.

Sting! The pain that shot through him was like a burning knife. A gasping cry of pure agony escaped from his throat. Darkness swirled around his head, and he gave himself up to black unconsciousness.

"I don't want him in the house." Jessie

picked the last of the meat off a chicken leg and tossed the bone onto her plate. "He's our enemy!"

Hattie frowned in sharp displeasure. "I realize how you feel about the war and the Confederacy, but we can't just throw him out."

Jessie's mouth curled in scorn. "Couldn't we get the sheriff or somebody in authority to come and take him?"

"He's our cousin." Hattie drained the last of her coffee and toyed with the cup handle. "And even if he wasn't, I couldn't turn him out. He seems like a nice young man."

"A lot of nice young men are killing our nice young men."

Hattie didn't reply; her brow puckered in a thoughtful frown. Jessie glanced surreptitiously at her mother, for the first time noticing the tiny lines around her eyes and mouth, a few strands of gray mingling with the sable hair.

The deep rumble of an occasional cannon could be heard in the distance, but there had been no sounds of battle nearby all morning. Jessie sat sullen and brooding, her shoulders hunched forward, her head bent. She hated the Rebs in their gray and butternut uniforms, carrying their damnable rifles and hauling their deadly cannons with them. So far, the war had been fought on Rebel territory—in Virginia and Tennessee and Mississippi, places far removed from Pennsylvania. But now they were here in

Gettysburg, creating havoc and death and misery.

Jessie felt the war was stupid. If the southerners wanted their own country in which to keep slaves, let them. To her, the issue wasn't worth fighting and dying over.

And men *had* died—men from her own community, killed in places like Manassas and Antietam and Fredericksburg. Young men just beginning life or men with families—they were all dead. She shuddered to think how many more would lose their lives after the last three days of fighting right here. The Confederates had come at last, and one of them was sleeping in her bed.

It was intolerable! Even if he was distantly related, Garth Bodine was her enemy. She felt frustrated and angry, and broke the chicken bone in half with a loud snap. The thing that galled her most was that she found the man exceedingly attractive. His ruggedly masculine features, his broad shoulders, massive chest . . .

She quickly pushed aside her disquieting thoughts. But it had been ages since any young man had been around; they were all off to war. She had been almost too young to understand the intimate relationships between men and women when the fighting broke out. Now, at nineteen, she was extremely curious to learn for herself what life was all about.

"He needs a doctor."

Hattie's voice brought Jessie out of her

thoughts. "Why? He was conscious and reasonably alert for a while earlier. You've done the best you can for him. When he wakes up again I think we should just send him on his way."

Hattie raised a stern brow with disapproval. "That's not a very charitable attitude to take."

"How can I be charitable when he's a Reb?"

"If he wasn't our cousin, I'd probably do just what you suggest. But I can't just put him out of the house like a stray cat. He'd be arrested."

Jessie's breath came out in an exasperated sigh. "You're too kind-hearted. He came here of his own free will. He knew the risks. How many of our boys are rotting in prisons down south?"

"I don't know. I only know in my heart what I have to do. He's staying until he's well enough to get back home on his own."

Jessie's mouth thinned in grim resignation. "If the Rebs keep winning like they have been, this might *be* his home before too long."

# 3

Jessie walked briskly along York Street, her eyes flickering with uneasiness. It was late afternoon, and heavy clouds massed overhead, making the air humid and oppressive. There were few people about, and those she saw were Federal soldiers, much to her relief. But there was a sick sense of anticipation in her throat, making it hard to breathe normally. Cannons boomed in the distance; there were reports of a cavalry battle being fought out on the Hanover Road, east of town. Other rumors spoke of a dreadful charge led by the Confederates against the Union forces along Seminary Ridge. But the town, at least for the moment, seemed almost deserted.

There were signs of the fighting, to be sure. Broken windows, bullet holes in brick walls, an out building smashed by a cannonball. Jessie shivered, despite the sticky heat, and wished Doc Brooks didn't live so far away. She was the only woman out on the streets, and at any minute she expected a horde of men in gray uniforms to come sweeping down upon her.

The unreality of her predicament was almost comical. Fetching a doctor for an injured Reb!

Hooves and the creak of wagon wheels from behind distracted Jessie's thoughts, and she turned around. It was an army ambulance, drawn by two slow-footed mules and driven by a haggard, weary-looking soldier. As the conveyance passed, she gazed disbelieving into the open end. Men were laid out on the wooden boards with not even a bit of straw to ease the bumpy ride. Their faces stared back at her in beseeching misery. White teeth gleamed from a pulp of tissue. One man, his body twitching spasmodically, had a slack jaw, a lolling tongue. Eyes bulged, faces were flushed, lips were pressed together in grimaces of pain. And everywhere there was blood.

A wave of sorrow swept through Jessie, an indescribable sadness gripped her. She looked after the ambulance with eyes that were haunted and grief-stricken. And she was on her way to help a Reb!

She paused at the white picket fence surrounding Dr. Cornelius Brooks's house and office and hesitated. For a fleeting instant she was ready to turn away and go back home. But she pushed open the gate and marched up the walk to the porch.

The doctor answered the door himself after a long wait. Age was beginning to sag his round cheeks, leaving jowls and pockets under his eyes; his head was as bald as a pigeon's egg. His suit was disheveled and stained, his normally good-humored face grim and distracted.

"What is it, Jessie? Is your mother sick?"

"No. It's ... it's my cousin." Her voice dropped into a husky whisper, and there was an audible tremor when she spoke. "He's been shot. We wondered if you could come take a look at him."

Cornelius Brooks twisted his pudgy hands in nervous consternation and glanced away. "I'm so busy. I don't know where to begin. I've been working three days straight. There aren't enough army surgeons for all the wounded. I only stopped home for a bite to eat and more supplies."

"Oh." Jessie tried to look properly distraught. In a way, she was; the sooner Captain Garth Bodine was treated, the sooner he could leave.

Dr. Brooks' face softened with compassion, and he gently put a hand on her shoulder. "I'll come over as soon as I finish here. Say half an hour."

Jessie managed a weak, uncertain smile. "Thank you, Doc."

"I'm always available to you and Hattie." He turned to reenter his house, muttering to himself, "Terrible day. Those poor boys."

Jessie stepped off the porch, her mouth twisting into a sullen curl. Why should Dr.

Brooks waste his time on a Reb? Still, some of what her mother had said earlier had sunk in, and Jessie struggled with a feeling of guilt. Garth Bodine was a man, after all, *and* and her cousin. She supposed he deserved medical assistance the same as the Yankees.

She glanced up at the gathering clouds once more, hoping it would rain. It might cool the temperature, might even send the Rebs back home and leave everybody in peace. Another cart was approaching, this time a flat-bed wagon, and she stepped up onto the board sidewalk out of its path. As it neared, Jessie shuddered in nightmarish horror.

It was piled with bodies, in all manner of positions, as if they had just been dumped in willy-nilly. Ghastly, contorted dead faces gazed out at her. One man's mouth was open in what appeared to be an eternal scream, his head twisted around grotesquely so it almost seemed it was on backward.

A strangled cry of denial escaped Jessie's lips; a heaviness pushed at her chest until she felt she couldn't breathe. She stumbled back, fought for balance, then ran.

Garth forked a heaping pile of scrambled eggs into his mouth and smiled at Hattie as he chewed. She was seated at his bedside, soft-spoken and reserved. Her brown hair was pinned up in an almost severe bun, and a tiny pair of spectacles rested precariously on the bridge of her nose. There was a resemblance between mother and daughter, but Jessie possessed a far greater beauty.

"My father mostly raises horses," he told her. "But he gave a lot of them to our army at the beginning of the war."

"He supports the Confederacy?"

"Probably as much as Jeff Davis himself." Garth ate more eggs and drank some milk. He was hungry, despite the occasional dizziness that swept him. His arm was a steady, leaden agony, but by balancing the plate on his lap, he was able to eat reasonably well using his right hand. "He'd have joined up himself if he wasn't so old. My sister probably would have, too, if the army took women."

"Is she married?"

"Loretta?" He gave a faintly derogatory laugh. "She thinks she's too good for any man. But just between you and me, I think she's scared to death of becoming an old maid. She's twenty-two already."

"It's just as well she isn't married—with the war and all."

Garth finished his eggs and was tempted to ask for more. But this woman had already shown him so much kindness. It still amazed and dumbfounded him that they were distantly related, a coincidence he could never have conceived of. He hadn't even known he had relatives in the north.

"I met your father once," Hattie said. "At a Fourth of July picnic. I was just a little girl. He was already a grown man."

"And probably just as pompous as he is now."

Hattie peered curiously at him.

Garth felt his face redden slightly. "We often don't get along. It's not that I'm lazy, but I never really took an interest in running the plantation or spending time socializing at our town house in Charleston. 'Course, he doesn't run the plantation himself anymore. He has overseers."

"And slaves, I suppose."

"Yes. We have slaves."

"Are they happy?"

Garth shrugged, then winced as pulsating pain radiated down his arm. He wished Jessie would return with the doctor. Besides, he wanted to see her again, even if she didn't hardly talk to him and never smiled. "I don't know if they're happy or not. They're well cared for, everything they need is given to them—food, clothing, housing."

Hattie pursed her lips, a tight frown settling on her face. "Maybe I've lived in Pennsylvania too long to remember. Anyway, we didn't have enough money to own any slaves."

Garth hoped Hattie would drop the subject; it made him feel uncomfortable. It was bad enough that he had been part of the invading army and now felt utterly miserable in Jessie's bed. He didn't want to discuss politics with his Yankee cousin.

He drank more milk, then regarded Hattie circumspectly. "How did your husband die, ma'm?"

"The doctor said it was his heart. He just worked himself to death. That was three years ago. I sold the store, and Jessie and I have enough to get by on."

"Jessie—is she affianced by anyone?"

"No."

Garth suppressed a secret smile, but it quickly evaporated. Jessie was barely civil to him. "I'm surprised—a pretty girl like that."

"The war." Hattie gave a long, despairing sigh. "All the eligible young men seem to have enlisted. The ones left—" She shrugged deprecatingly. "They aren't worth looking twice at."

The back door banged shut with a resounding slam. Garth heard footsteps and turned to look to his left, wondering what kind of doctor Jessie had brought with her. But there was no doctor, only Jessie standing in the bedroom doorway, her face pale, her fists clenched into knots at her sides. She stood there a moment, scowling in barely contained fury, then took several steps toward the bed. She knocked the plate off Garth's lap with an angry sweep of her hand; it crashed against the wall and shattered.

"*Damn you!*"

Garth's expression clouded. "What did I do?"

"I saw dead bodies!" Jessie's eyes swept briefly to her mother, who looked startled, then back to Garth. "A whole wagon full of them. Men *you* killed!"

"I didn't kill anyone." Garth's voice was low; he hesitated, swallowed, and added gently, "I was never able to get off a volley before I was shot."

Jessie's eyes were as bright as diamonds as they blazed at him; she crossed her arms across her breasts. "And then ended up in *our* basement!"

Hattie exchanged an uncomfortable glance with Garth. She rose from her chair, went around the bed, and began picking up the broken pieces of crockery. "Is Doc Brooks coming?"

"Yes." Jessie's mouth tightened in grim displeasure. She glared frostily at Garth. "But I don't know why!"

Garth lifted a hand limply in helpless apology. "I'm sorry about what you had to see, Jessie. But I've seen it before too. My side."

"*Sides!*" The contempt in her voice was unmistakable. "Why does there have to be a war in the first place?"

"It just happened." Garth studied Jessie appraisingly. There was a classic purity to her profile; the strong chin, the clean jawline, the prominent cheekbones. Her blue eyes sparkled like crystal when she was angry. For a moment, looking at her, he almost forgot the pain in his arm.

Jessie gave him a look of guarded disgust. "And when the doctor gets here, be sure not to say 'ya'll' and things like that. You'll give yourself away."

For all her anger, Jessie didn't seem ready to turn him in as an enemy yet. He suppressed a faint smile. "I'll try."

Jessie threw him a scalding glare. Catching up her skirts, she wheeled and stalked out the door.

Garth drained the glass of milk and shook his head. "I get the feeling she doesn't like me."

Hattie flashed him an apologetic smile as she gathered up the last piece of broken plate and prepared to leave the room. "You have to understand. I'm a southerner, born and bred. My sentiments are divided. Hers aren't."

Garth watched Hattie disappear, then settled back on the pillow. His arm throbbed, but at least the pain wasn't as great as before, and his mental faculties seemed more alert. He sighed and closed his eyes, conjuring up a picture of Jessie in his mind. Her expressive mouth, her flawless skin, the chestnut hair that swept to below her waist in thick, cascading waves. She was a joy to behold, utterly feminine. She filled his mind with fantasy.

A faint smile quirked at the corners of Garth's mouth, and he let himself drift toward sleep.

Jessie stifled a growing unease as she entered the bedroom behind her mother and Dr. Brooks. Garth was dozing, and the room was dim, a combination of the late afternoon shadows and the heavy cloud cover massing overhead. She had known the doctor all her life—he had helped deliver her—but friendship was nothing when it came to political loyalties.

Hattie touched Garth's uninjured shoulder gently. "Dr. Brooks is here to see you."

Garth stirred sleepily and stared up into the unfamiliar, sagging face of the aging physician. Jessie closed her eyes and inhaled sharply. All he needed to do was open his mouth and say something with that horrid, lazy drawl of his. To her relief, Garth merely smiled.

"I've seen hundreds of gunshot wounds in the past couple of days." Brooks pulled up a chair and seated himself, placing his bag on the bed. "Hattie tells me she doesn't think yours is too serious."

Garth shook his head negatively. Jessie released her breath from between clenched teeth. Maybe these southerners had more brains than she was willing to give them credit for. Maybe he wouldn't speak. Idly, she wondered if she and her mother could be sent to jail for helping the enemy. A sudden coldness of dread crept up her spine, and she walked over to the window, chafing her arms.

She barely listened to the doctor's comments, though indeed it did sound as if the Reb wasn't mortally wounded. She heard Doc Brooks' muttered "superficial" and "not troublesome at all." To these remarks, Garth only said yes or no, for which she was thankful.

She did hear his groan of pain when the doctor put in a few stitches. During this, Jessie kept her eyes steadfastly focused out the window, where ponderous black clouds rolled across the sky. She hoped it would rain and cool everything off; maybe even wash the stench of battle out of the air. The town had been quiet all afternoon; only a distant rattle of cannon could be heard from time to time.

"I'll leave you some laudanum," the doctor said. "You might have trouble sleeping with those new sutures in there."

Jessie turned slightly and saw Doc Brooks gathering up his instruments and stowing them away in his bag. Garth was in obvious pain, and she felt an unexpected twinge of sympathy. His handsome face was drawn into a grimace, his neck muscles corded tight. But in spite of it all, he caught her eye and gave her a rakish wink. Jessie scowled in annoyance.

Hattie handed the doctor his dusty top hat. "I really do appreciate this."

"Think nothing of it," he said, hefting his satchel. He peered at Garth and smiled charitably. "It's a grand thing you're doing for our country."

Jessie made a face as if she had swallowed something bitter.

Hattie ushered Dr. Brooks out of the room. Jessie stood staring at Garth, who was trying to examine the fresh bandage on his biceps. Her gaze strayed from the drooping black mustache and strong chin to his chest. It was well muscled and covered with a soft thatch of dark hair. Her eyes wandered lower to his navel, and she felt herself blush. She quickly averted her gaze from the top of the bedsheet and met Garth's amused look. Her cheeks flushed hot with embarrassment, and her eyes flickered nervously around the room, avoiding his.

"Do you want some laudanum now?" she asked, but her voice came out in a squeaky kind of croak.

"I suppose."

She approached the bedside table, picked up the brown bottle and spoon. "At least you didn't give yourself away."

"It's my neck."

"It might be mine too."

"Not necessarily. By the way, who's winning?"

"I don't know!" She gave an impatient toss of her head, measured out a spoonful and held it to his lips. He made a face; she thought he was going to spit it out. His expression of discomfort gave Jessie a sense of triumph, and a faint smile played about the corners of her mouth.

Garth's gaze darkened on her with disturbing intensity. "I like you much better when you smile."

Jessie's mouth tightened into a grim line. "And I'll like *you* much better when you're gone from here."

Jessie sat in the parlor, tapping her foot to the rhythm of the rain. It had begun over an hour ago; lightning slashed viciously, thunder growled like a waking bear. It was well after nine, but she couldn't sleep, a fact

she attributed to sharing a bed with her
mother. Another reason she wanted Captain
Garth Bodine out of the house. Jessie wasn't
used to sleeping with anyone; she had slept in
the same bed all her life. The Reb had
managed to totally disrupt her life in the
span of less than two days.

She let her gaze drop to Mr. Dickens' novel,
but she couldn't get interested in it. She
yawned hugely and glanced at the clock on
the table. Groaning silently to see that it was
almost eleven, she set the book aside and rose
from the overstuffed chair.

Rain beat against the roof and windows as
she made her way to the rear of the house,
carrying the whale oil lamp. She paused by
her bedroom and frowned petulantly. Out of
curiosity, she pushed open the door and
quietly entered.

Garth was sleeping deeply, evidently from
the effects of the landanum. A yellow flash of
lightning flickered against a leaden sky, illuminating the room. Garth's tanned complexion looked starkly white, but the grimace of
pain Jessie had seen earlier was gone. His
face was serene, handsome, strong, despite
the dark stubble of beard that stained his
cheeks.

Jessie crept closer to the bed and stared
down at the sleeping man, her enemy, her
cousin. She could almost forget he was a Reb,
looking at him now. She continued to stare at
him, her taut expression slowly softening to
pity, and she felt a warm rush of sympathy.

She brushed back an unruly lock of black hair from his forehead and tiptoed out of the bedroom.

# 4

Rain fell in sheets that slashed at Jessie as she dashed across the yard to the safety of the back porch. She burst inside, nearly spilled the gallon jar of milk and shook the water off her shoulders.

Hattie glanced up from her mending, her eyes dark with disapproval. "You're soaking wet."

"I don't care!" Jessie's eyes were bright, feverish, excited. She placed the container of milk on the table and whipped off her dripping shawl. "The Rebs are gone!"

Hattie sucked in her breath, stunned. "Gone?"

Jessie nodded vigorously. "It's all over town! I don't know why they went, but General Lee packed every one of 'em up and off during the storm last night."

Hattie shook her head, her gaze clouding

with confusion. "I don't understand it. I thought the Confederates were winning."

"They lit out—scared!"

"*What?*" From the bedroom came Garth's deep, resounding voice. "Did I hear you right?"

"Oh dear." Hattie set her mending aside and hurried toward the bedroom. Jessie followed, barely able to contain her glee.

Garth was struggling to sit up, his face wrenched with pain. Hattie helped him prop up the pillows. "Jessie says your army's gone."

"In *full* retreat," Jessie added smugly.

Garth's eyes widened in stunned disbelief. "That's not like General Lee. What happened?"

"I don't know. All I know is what I heard. Your Rebs are gone." Jessie's eyes flashed with satisfaction, but the gleam left them quickly and a dark frown marred her smooth brow. If the Federal authorities were indeed back in charge in Gettysburg, then Garth was a dreadful liability.

Uncertainty flickered in his expression. "I should leave—be with my regiment."

"You're in no condition to go anywhere," Hattie said sternly. At his feeble attempt to rise, she pushed him gently back to the pillows. "If you walked out this door right now, you'd be arrested in a matter of minutes. And you'd never mend in those prisons at Elmira and Camp Douglas."

Jessie sneered in contempt. "I hear the southern prisons are no bed of roses for our boys."

Garth flopped weakly back on the pillows, his eyes reflecting fear and conflicting emotions. "I don't know what to do." He shook his head despairingly. "And I don't understand my army. Unless they ran out of munitions or something. We're not quitters."

"Of course you're not," Hattie said.

"Neither are we," Jessie muttered, throwing a glare at him. "But you know you're a big problem for us. If the authorities learn you're here . . ." She let her words trail off and punctuated them with a shudder.

"They won't," Hattie said. "That's the least of my worries."

Jessie gave a low grunt of derision. She stomped out of the room, her shoes squishing from their recent soaking. Then, remembering that all her clothing was still in her own room, she marched back in and over to the armoire.

"I'll fix you some hot sausages," Hattie was saying. "Good Pennsylvania Dutch sausages. And Jessie traded some of our eggs for fresh milk."

"Oh, I always thought she went around looking like a drowned kitten." There was just an edge of a smirk in Garth's tone.

Jessie's eyes blazed beneath his mocking gaze. She picked up a pair of dry shoes, slammed the armoire door, and stormed out of the room again.

Jessie was lacing up her shoe when she heard a knock at the back door. Her mind flew to Garth, and a new wave of fear broke over her. They would all be arrested, not just him. She felt a sick sensation in the pit of her stomach and took a deep swallow of air.

When she reached the kitchen, trying to force her features into some semblance of composure, she was relieved to see the caller was just their neighbor, cheery Mary Purcell.

"Smells good," the woman remarked, nodding toward the sausages sizzling in the skillet. A question flickered across her round face. "A late breakfast?"

"Sort of," Hattie murmured. She shot a quick, helpless glance at Jessie, then looked back at the woman. "Come in for a spell. Jessie, get us some coffee."

Jessie turned to the pot on the stove, tension coiling in her stomach. As long as Garth Bodine was in the house, she preferred not to have company. Her hands shook so badly when she placed the cups on the table, hot coffee sloshed over the rims and onto the saucers.

Mary eyed her with undisguised curiosity, then smiled with grim understanding. "It's all the noise and the fighting. It's got everybody upset."

Jessie forced a distant smile to her lips and crept back to stand by the warmth of the stove. She stole a glance toward the hallway, but all was silent from the bedroom.

"What brings you out in the rain?" Hattie asked.

"The hospitals. They need all the help they can get. So many wounded, sick boys." She fluttered her pudgy fingers in a melancholy gesture, then picked up her cup and drank. "I thought maybe you and Jessie might like to volunteer your time."

Jessie groaned inwardly in frustration. They already had a wounded soldier on their hands. Suddenly realizing the sausages were burning, she quickly turned the links over in the skillet with a fork.

Hattie coughed politely. "Well . . . I don't know. Jessie and I have sort of a predicament here ourselves."

"Oh?" Mary's brows shot up, and she leaned forward eagerly in her chair.

"My cousin's here with us," Hattie said.

Jessie tilted her head back and rolled her eyes. She felt like screaming.

"Cousin?"

"He was wounded the other day. Jessie and I have been looking after him," Hattie explained.

"The poor boy." Mary clucked her tongue solicitously. "I hope it isn't serious."

"Not very. Dr. Brooks thinks he'll be up and around in a day or two."

"*Then* you can help out. Or maybe you and Jessie could even take turns." She flashed a hopeful look at Jessie.

Jessie managed another smile and busied herself dumping the overcooked sausages onto a plate. She knew Mary wouldn't give up. She was active in every charity in town, and the hospital was one of her favorites.

The woman finished her coffee, heaved her bulk to her feet, and adjusted her apron over her ample stomach. "Any time—just stop by the hospital and sign up. As soon as they can, they're going to ship the most seriously wounded cases off to Philadelphia and Harrisburg."

Hattie rose and ushered the woman to the door. It was still pouring buckets. Mary flipped a heavy scarf over her head and shoulders, then turned back to Hattie, one eyebrow quirked in mild curiosity. "I didn't know you had any relatives in the war."

"He's just a distant cousin."

"Give him my regards. And tell him to mend soon."

Contempt and derision twisted Jessie's features, but she couldn't agree with the woman more. A silent prayer for Garth Bodine's speedy recovery whisked through her mind as she poured another cup of coffee from the pot.

Hattie closed the door and turned to Jessie. She exhaled a gusty sigh of relief.

"You're just as scared as I am," Jessie said.

"Nervous."

"Scared." Jessie took a knife and fork from a drawer and laid them on the plate with the sausages. "I want him gone!"

"He will be soon."

Jessie grunted doubtfully. "And you know Mrs. Purcell—she's nosy. She's liable to want to visit him."

Hattie shrugged helplessly and returned to sit at the table. "There's nothing much we can do about it. Or about helping out at the hospital."

Jessie shuddered. She didn't like the sight of blood. Garth was bad enough, but after seeing all those injured men in the ambulance yesterday. And the corpses... She shuddered again.

"Take him his breakfast, will you?' Hattie requested.

Jessie turned to look at her mother, a complaint ready on her lips. But the words died in her throat. Hattie was staring with dark, brooding eyes into her coffee cup, her shoulders hunched, a worried frown creasing her brow. She suddenly looked twenty years older than her age, and even more tiny and frail. Jessie shook her head disconsolately, and, without a word, carried Garth's breakfast out of the kitchen.

He was sitting up in bed, staring blankly at the ribbons of rain running down the windowpane. His eyes were dull, his face tight with emotion. Jessie realized they were all living in a state of fear of one kind or another, and the thought both saddened and angered her.

Garth turned his head and looked at her. "Who was here?"

"A neighbor. Mama told her you're here, but not where you're from."

Brief annoyance and concern flickered across his features. "I reckon you can't keep me a secret for long."

"*I reckon.*" Jessie looked at him with imperious contempt. "Can't you talk normal?"

"I *am* talking normal."

"For a Reb." She thrust the plate at him. "Sorry we're out of grits and gravy this morning."

Garth gazed down at the black, charcoal-like links of sausage and grimaced. "If these are your famous Pennsylvania Dutch sausages, I reckon I'd rather have grits and gravy." His gray eyes glittered tauntingly. "Don't they teach you Yankee girls to cook?"

Jessie tossed her head with a show of arrogance. "I can cook—and good!"

Garth studied her skeptically. "What happened here?"

"*You* did!" Jessie set the cup on the bedside table and gave him an impatient, disgusted look. "If I wasn't so upset you'd give yourself away, I'd have paid more attention to what I was doing."

"Don't worry about me."

"I won't." Her expression hardened, and a scowl formed on her brow. "I'm more worried about me—and Mama, and the trouble you could get us all into!"


Jessie paced around the parlor, twisting her hands fretfully, vaguely uncomfortable. A bit of afternoon sunlight peeped through the clouds, and the humidity had risen with the brief cessation of the rain. Hattie had taken the opportunity to go out to sign them both up for duty at the hospital and see if there were any groceries left in any of the stores.

Jessie paused at the window, seeing a squad of soldiers in blue walking up the street. She thought of Garth and bit her lip anxiously.

Bored, frightened, and unnerved, she made her way down the hallway to her bedroom. He might be a Reb, but at least he was somebody to talk to. But when she entered the room she found him sleeping, the bottle of laudanum uncapped on the table beside him.

She recorked the bottle and let out a long, tired sigh. She didn't look forward to helping out with the wounded; the idea sickened and disgusted her. Even if those she would tend to were her men, she would rather stay here with Garth. Granted, he could use a bath and desperately needed a shave, but at least his wound was covered and hopefully healing.

She regarded him with quiet gravity, finding her eyes wandering again to the broad shoulders and magnificent chest. The mat of hair fascinated her; her father's chest had been devoid of hair. In truth, every well-defined muscle and tendon in Garth's upper torso intrigued her.

Tentatively, she reached out a hand and let her fingers brush against the hair on his chest. It was soft and coarse at the same time, crisp to the lightest touch, and her senses filled with an unfamiliar excitement. She allowed the flat of her palm to brush over the downy thatch, her gaze moving to his face. It was finely chiseled, with a prominent chin and straight nose. Dark, sooty lashes rested against his cheeks; his lips were full and softly curved in sleep. He was good-looking and appealing, no matter which side of the war he was on.

Her cheeks coloring hotly at the train of her thoughts, she took her hand away and gently drew up the sheet closer to his neck. Strange sensations coursed through her body, alien and unsettling.

But across her mind's eye danced a vision of those Federal soldiers on the street, and she remembered Garth's own gray uniform, shoved under the bed, along with his knapsack and gun. Curious, she got down on her knees and pulled out the haversack, stifling a sneeze at the dust that came with it. She was suddenly eager to learn more about this handsome, mysterious cousin of hers. She knew nothing of him—his age, his home, even if he was married.

The knapsack contained little to give her much information. There was a razor and a thin sliver of soap, the bundle of letters her mother had gone through, a bowie knife, a battered tin cup, plate, and utensils, several pairs of socks, and a small leather pouch. She opened it carefully, discovering a handful of gold coins and some crumpled bills. She studied the money curiously, faintly disdainful of the image of Jefferson Davis tht gazed unseeing back at her.

Dissatisfied with her search, Jessie replaced all the items in the haversack and pushed it back under the bed.

Garth remained quiet, listening to Jessie's breathing, watching her dark head move beside the bed. Her lovely, almost perfect face was framed by thick strands of chestnut hair tumbling over her shoulders. Her eyes were soft, expressive, and endlessly blue. It had been her touch that had awakened him, but the feel of her fingers caressing his chest had been so unbearably exquisite, he had continued to pretend to be asleep. Unless he was imagining things, the beautiful Jessie Morgan was as attracted to him as he was to her, even if she did profess to hate him.

He wanted her. It didn't matter that they were distantly related. Even first cousins married quite often, and Jessie was far removed. The fact that she mocked him didn't daunt him; it made her all the more appealing. And her attitude amused him, made him quick to return her snide remarks with ones of his own.

She was examining his revolver, so large in her small hands. "Are you planing to shoot me?" he asked.

Jessie jumped, then stared at him with startled, wide eyes.

He chuckled softly. "What are you doing down there?"

"Looking." A hot blush suddenly suffused her cheeks, and she peeked shyly at him. "How long have you been awake?"

"Just a minute or two," he lied.

Her face relaxed, and she looked distinctly relieved. She shoveled the revolver and holster back under the bed and got to her feet, dusting off her skirt. Garth liked the way her blouse fit her, the way firm, young breasts pressed against the soft material. He felt a stirring of desire that even the steady, low ache in his arm couldn't banish.

"How are you feeling?" she asked.

The question surprised him; she had never seemed terribly concerned for his welfare before. "Better."

"Good." Her eyes left his, straying to the window. "Then maybe you can leave us soon."

"Maybe." He reached out, touched her wrist gently. Her gaze slid curiously over him, but she didn't pull her hand away. "I'd like us to be friends, though. As long as I'm here."

"How can I be friends with a Reb?"

"Try not to think of me as that. Think of me as your cousin."

She drew her hand away, folding both hands together in front of her. "Are you hungry?"

"A little."

"I can fix something for you, but there isn't much in the house. Mama's gone out to try to find some food—if your people didn't wreck everything."

Garth remembered the disaster of the sausages earlier in the day and wasn't especially eager to try any more of Jessie's cooking. "A glass of milk would be fine."

She nodded curtly, turned, and left the room. Garth watched her, admiring the flow of her hips under her long skirt. He wasn't making much progress with her. Granted, he was in no condition to do much more than talk, but a smile from her once in a while would be nice. He sighed despairingly.

When she returned with the milk he took it from her and drank gratefully; it washed the bitter taste of the laudanum away. He turned a quizzical eye on her. "Have you heard any more news about this morning?"

She shook her head; dark tresses whipped about her slim shoulders. "Nothing. But I would like to know something about you. After all, you might end up putting us all in jail."

"What do you want to know?"

"About this family I never knew I had—your family."

Garth shrugged and began relating the details of his life to her. In the next half hour, while she sat quietly in the chair beside the bed, he found himself telling her of the plantation, the town house in Charleston, his father and mother, Claiborne and Della Bodine, even some charitable words about his sister Loretta. Through it all, Jessie sat listening quietly, the expression on her face inscrutable, her lips pressed together in consideration.

"Why did you join the army?" she finally asked.

"It was expected of me by my father." He gave vent to an exasperated sigh. "Like everything else."

"You don't get along with him, do you?"

"Not especially. He wants me to be just like him."

"And how's that?"

Garth's mouth twisted into something like

a smile. "A bit of a bully, I reckon. A rich bully who enjoys hobnobbing with the big planters and the politicians."

"And you don't enjoy that? I thought that's all you Rebs ever did."

His eyes crinkled with amusement. "I'd rather stay home and work the horses."

"You don't *seem* like the kind of man who would want to fight in a war."

"I'm not." He shrugged in resignation. "But I suppose I'm no different from anyone else about defending what's his."

She looked at him, her eyes questioning. "You're not married?"

"Another of my father's regrets. No."

Garth thought he detected a subtle change in her face, but her expression was still unreadable. He studied her carefully, trying to fathom what was going on in her mind. She seemed uncomfortable under the intensity of his gaze and glanced away.

He reached for her hand once more. "Now that I've bared my soul to you, couldn't we have a truce? At least until I'm able to leave?"

She gazed down at his hand. He did the same. Hers looked so small and fragile under his tanned, callused one. "I suppose," she murmured.

"It would make things a lot easier for both of us."

"Yes."

"Friends, then?"

From beneath her lashes she thoughtfully regarded him. "Not friends. But a truce."

Garth squeezed her fingers lightly, and she withdrew her hand.

Jessie crept silently into the bedroom behind her mother, expecting to find Garth asleep. But he wasn't. He was still reading the newspaper, going over and over again every detail of the battle, of the Confederate army's abrupt retreat, of the casualties, of the captured. His face looked strained and worried, as if a battle all of his own raged inside him. Jessie recalled their conversation, his honesty and openness with her, and for an instant she felt sorry for him. Despite what he was, something had subtly changed inside her in the last few hours, and her irritation at him had evolved into a tender concern.

How must *he* feel, being in so alien a place, with only two women to share his secret? If the danger to the Morgans was great, it was far more serious to him.

"There's ham steak and potatoes for supper," Hattie said. "I'm afraid there isn't much in town. Probably won't be for a few days."

Garth glanced up absently. "Anything is fine with me."

"No more laudanum?"

He shook his head. "My arm doesn't hurt too bad—only when the stitches pull."

"Doc Brooks wants me to check it for infection and change the dressing. Do you mind?"

"No." Garth laid aside the paper and

gingerly held out his arm to Hattie's inspection.

Jessie moved to the window, not wanting to view the mangled arm for herself. It had begun raining again, and, despite the time of year, it was very dark outside. Someone had boarded up the crater in the side of Mary Purcell's house.

"I'd like to write home," Garth said. "Tell my family that I'm all right and temporarily separated from my regiment—if there's any of them left."

"I think you should. I'm sure they're worried."

Jessie heard Garth's soft groan of pain as the bandage was removed; no doubt there was dried blood sticking to it.

"There's no redness or swelling," her mother said. "And that's what the doctor told me to look for."

"Reckon I won't lose my arm after all."

The idea appalled Jessie. To think of such a healthy, totally masculine man without an arm . . . Still, no doubt in the last three days many had lost much more than that. A wild surge of conflicting emotions swept through her. She wondered why she persisted in blaming Garth personally for the carnage that had taken place. He had enlisted in his army because it was expected of him. If she were a man, she supposed she would have done the same thing for hers.

"You can turn around now, Jessie," Hattie said with no small amount of amusement. "I don't know how you'll manage at the hospital."

"Neither do I." She approached the bed, eyeing the fresh bandage on Garth's arm grimly. "I'll probably faint."

"Take smelling salts with you just in case."

Jessie frowned with distaste, then her eyes shifted to Garth. "I'll write that letter for you if you can't."

He looked faintly surprised. "I'd appreciate it."

Hattie's eyes went from Jessie to the newspaper, and finally settled on Garth, grave and somber. "I got a feel for the mood in town today while I was out. You'd be in a fine kettle of fish if you were found out. Jessie and I talked it over and we decided it would be best to destroy any evidence of who you really are. I think we should burn your uniform."

An incredulous light entered Garth's eyes. "Burn my uniform! But then I won't have any clothes."

"I still have a lot of my husband's things. Ben was a big man like you. I expect they'll fit."

Garth's scowl betrayed his uncertainty, but he sighed in resigned acceptance.

"Do you have any papers?" Hattie asked. "A commission? Something from your army?"

"Nothing. Only my letters from home. I suppose you should burn those too."

Hattie nodded firmly. "It's for your own protection." She gathered up scissors, bandages, and cotton packing. "Jessie?"

Grumbling fretfully, Jessie got down on her hands and knees for the second time that day and reached under the bed. She pulled out the gray shell jacket embroidered with red piping, the soiled trousers and the battered red kepi.

Garth gazed ruefully at them. "Is there anything in the pockets?"

Jessie fumbled around, dug out a tiny ball of twine, several bills, a jacknife, six coins and a watch. "Nothing much." She deposited the items on the dresser, her nose wrinkling at the gamy odor of the clothes. "When did you have a bath last?"

"In some river in Virginia."

Jessie gave a shudder and left the room. Despite the mugginess, her mother had the stove stoked up; it was like a steambath in the kitchen.

"At least when he leaves town he won't be going as a soldier."

"And I hope it's soon," Jessie said, handing over the grubby things to her mother. "I'll go back and get the letters."

Jessie returned to the bedroom and retrieved the bundle of letters from the haversack. She was conscious of Garth's eyes on her, studying her every move, and it evoked a sensation in her that was both pleasurable and unnerving.

But when she came back and seated herself by the bed with paper and pencil, Garth turned reflective as he dictated the letter to his mother. During the lulls while he was thinking what he next wanted to say, Jessie surreptitiously studied him, looking at him through shuttered lids.

His face was purely masculine and ruggedly handsome, but his eyes had a kind of grave melancholy in them. A cowlick of dark hair flopped across his forehead. The thought that he was very attractive came to her mind again, but she put it determinedly aside.

"I guess that's all," he finally said and released a heavy breath.

Jessie studied his face, trying to read his thoughts. "You miss your family."

"I miss home."

Jessie lifted an eyebrow in mild surprise. "Not your mother and father and sister?"

"My mother, yes. Certainly not Loretta."

Jessie's eyes became sharp with curiosity. "Your sister sounds almost fascinating."

The amusement that flashed in his eyes was sardonic. "She'd likely consider that a compliment. The truth is, she's . . ." He broke off, embarrassed. "Never mind. Maybe you'll meet her someday."

"I doubt *that* will ever happen."

"You never can tell."

Jessie set the letter on the bedside table. "I'll mail it tomorrow." As she stood up, the pencil dropped from her hand and fell onto the blanket on the other side of Garth. When she bent to reach for it his arm curved behind her neck. Before she realized what was happening, he drew her face down to his, and his mouth sought and found hers. His fingertips brushed the side of her throat, and her skin seemed to respond of its own accord, tingling under his casual caress. His lips were soft and gentle, warming her whole body, and for an instant, Jessie gave herself over to the kiss.

Then she wrenched free and pulled away from him. She caught her breath in outrage, and sparks of indignation flashed in her eyes. "You're supposed to be sick!"

A sparkle of deviltry brightened his eyes. "I'm not sick—only a trifle incapacitated at the moment."

Her blue eyes fairly snapped at him. "Not *too* incapacitated, it seems."

His gaze wandered over her in open admiration. "I couldn't resist."

Jessie held a biting retort on the tip of her tongue as her mother entered the room.

"Supper's almost ready. Did you get the letter finished?"

"Yes," Garth replied. "Thanks to Jessie."

She bristled slightly, but she was almost as vexed at herself as at him. She had been totally unprepared for Garth's kiss, and she was fighting the trembling that rose inside her, trying to stop it. The trouble was that she knew the butterflies in her stomach weren't just from anger.

"After you eat," Hattie was saying, "You might want to give yourself a sponge bath. And maybe Jessie could shave you."

Jessie rested a smoldering gaze on him for a long moment. "I might cut his throat."

Garth's mouth quirked dryly, and he chuckled in amusement.

Hattie glanced from one to the other in confusion.

# 5

Jessie sipped her coffee at the kitchen table.
From the bedroom, she could hear the low
voice of Dr. Brooks as he examined Garth.
Outside, birds sang in the trees and the
chickens squawked in the yard. She sighed,
wishing it wasn't Monday morning, the
morning she would have her baptism at the
hospital.

She drank more coffee, her head bowed in
thought, her brow furrowed. She had avoided
Garth yesterday, entering the bedroom only
when her mother was present. She didn't
want to be alone with him, to be tempted. The
sensation of his warm mouth on her lips continued to linger, along with the feel of his
arm around her. In that instant when he had
kissed her she had realized she was filled
with an abrupt desire, something that fired
her mind, made her wish her body could find
a way to satisfy it. And now she was pur-

posely avoiding him, determined not to let him think anything he did or said made the slightest impression on her.

She shut those thoughts out of her mind as Hattie and Dr. Brooks entered the kitchen.

"He'll be back to his old self in a couple of days," the doctor said, scratching his hairless pate. "I told him he could get up today, if he takes it easy."

Jessie nodded noncommitally. She would be inordinately glad to see Garth Bodine gone from the house. Not only was he a Reb, now he was beginning to confuse her, making her mind whirl with doubts and conflicting emotions. He was likable and charming and glib, and the boyish quality about him only seemed to emphasize his virility, his potent sexuality. Jessie's thoughts tumbled wildly; she felt almost threatened by him in some way.

Dr. Brooks looked at her expectantly. "Ready?"

"Yes." Jessie rose from the table, unable to keep the apprehension she felt about her nursing duties out of her expression.

"It won't be so bad," Brooks said.

"I suppose not." Besides, she thought, working at the hospital might keep her mind too occupied to think of Garth and the undeniable way she was drawn to him.

"Do you have your smelling salts?" Hattie asked her.

Jessie nodded. "In my pocket."

"I'll be along with your dinner in a few hours," her mother said.

Jessie inclined her head in acknowledgment, then preceded Dr. Brooks out the door. After a morning among the wounded she doubted she would have much of an appetite.

Federal soldiers seemed to be everywhere as Jessie walked alongside the doctor. The streets were full of civilians as well, shopkeepers sweeping their stoops, carpenters and bricklayers making repairs on the buildings that had been damaged. Gettysburg appeared to be almost back to normal until they reached the railroad station near the town square. There, Jessie saw ambulances unloading patients into waiting boxcars, like so much cattle.

"Do you think they'll come back?" she asked.

"The Rebs?" Dr. Brooks seemed amused. "We licked 'em, didn't we? Why should they come back?"

"I don't know why they came here in the first place."

Brooks flashed her an indulgent smile. "Probably because we're the first town over the Maryland border." He reached into his pocket, withdrew a twist of tobacco and bit off a chunk. He chewed for a moment, his cheeks bulging, then spoke again. "You can be very proud of your cousin." He spat, chewed reflectively. "We all can. Those brave boys in blue."

Scorn twisted Jessie's lips, but at least she received some comfort in knowing that Dr. Brooks didn't suspect.

When they reached the hospital and

climbed the stone steps Jessie steeled herself for the worst. A cold feeling of dread washed over her. Inside, cots filled every available space, and all were occupied by men. The harsh smell of lye, the sweet stench of blood, and other unpleasant, unidentifiable odors invaded her nostrils. A pitifully weak voice cried out for help, and a shiver crawled across Jessie's skin.

Dr. Brooks took her elbow to steady her. "It's all right. That was just from one of the operating rooms."

Jessie stared up at him, her eyes wide with dismay. "I won't . . . ?"

He shook his head, giving her a kindly smile. "You're only here to help comfort the men. Talk to them, help feed them, bathe a fevered brow."

A twinge of uncertainty plucked at her as Jessie watched a thin woman approach them. Her hair was gray and cropped short, her neck scrawny and wrinkled. There were harsh lines on her face and no kindness in her eyes. "Another one?" she asked, almost in a bark.

Dr. Brooks nodded. "This is Jessie Morgan. Hattie's daughter. Jessie, this is Dorothy, our head nurse."

Jessie managed a tight-lipped, hesitant smile, but the woman only scowled, scrutinizing the long chestnut braid hanging down Jessie's back nearly to her waist. "At least you had the sense to get that mane of hair out of the way." She thrust a white apron into Jessie's hands, gesturing abruptly. "Come along."

Gnawing at her lower lip, Jessie glanced helplessly at the doctor and trailed after the woman.

"Nurse Johnson!"

Dorothy stopped quickly and looked around; Jessie nearly collided with her back. A young army surgeon was beckoning to her. Jessie followed to one of the cots on which a youth lay, the twitching grimaces he tried to control indicating he was in considerable pain.

"I'll need some help setting his leg."

Nurse Dorothy Johnson eyed Jessie critically. "Well, Miss Morgan?"

Jessie swallowed the lump forming in her throat and nodded obediently. "Yes, ma'm."

With another skeptical look, Nurse Johnson marched away.

"Just hand me those splints," the surgeon said. "Then the bandages."

Without a word, Jessie picked up several lengths of thin wood. The surgeon had already ripped up the soldier's trousers, and his right leg was twisted grotesquely. Thankfully, Jessie thought, there was no blood. In horrified fascination, she watched as the surgeon grasped the leg and gave it an artful twist. She heard the sickening snap of bone popping into place, felt nauseated and weak. The injured soldier uttered a high-pitched shriek.

Jessie fumbled to hand the surgeon the

splints and bandages. She glanced at the
soldier, seeing the pain contort his face into a
hideous mask. Despite the nausea fluttering
in her stomach and at the back of her throat,
she once again blamed Garth for this poor
boy's pain.

Garth sat alone in the Morgans' parlor,
drumming his fingers on the thigh of the
trousers that had once been worn by Ben
Morgan. The house was oppressively silent,
save for the incessant ticking of the clock.
Jessie was still off at the hospital, and Hattie
had left at noon, after fixing him something
to eat. His arm was in a makeshift sling,
fashioned from one of the women's old petticoats, but since the doctor had removed the
stitches, Garth was in very little pain.

His gaze was drawn back to the newspaper
lying atop the ottoman, and his forehead
creased in an unhappy frown. If what the
press said was true, this summer was quickly
turning into a disaster for the Confederacy.
There was little doubt that the battle of
Gettysburg had been a Union victory, despite
heavy losses for the north. In three days of
hard fighting General Lee had been unable to
dislodge the Federals from their positions,
and Garth felt shamed by his army's retreat.

But coupled with the loss of Gettysburg,
the great bastion of Vicksburg, on the
Mississippi, had surrendered to the Union
the very next day. After two years of constant
victories the combined losses of Gettysburg
and Vicksburg had smashed the image of

southern invincibility. Garth felt that the curtain was beginning to close on the Confederacy.

He scrubbed his face with his palm. He felt he should be back with his regiment only as a sense of honor and duty to his country. But after so many days in bed he realized he was still too weak to travel. Even with the small amount of walking he had done today, his leg muscles felt stiff and sore. Besides, in truth, he would rather stay here for a while. He truly enjoyed Hattie's company, even if she did nick him several times when she shaved him, and Jessie . . . The mere thought of her made his blood run hot in his veins. With her sparkling blue eyes and long dark hair, she had the kind of beauty that could make a man forget he had good sense.

He mentally sighed, wondering if she would ever change her attitude toward him. She was not unfriendly at times, but neither was she open to him. But she *had* returned his kiss the other day, if only for a moment. And the way she sometimes looked at him when she thought he didn't notice . . . Garth was certain she was as drawn to him as he was to her.

Restless, he rose from the chair and walked over to a table where a grouping of several daguerreotypes sat. One was of a much younger Hattie and—Garth presumed—her husband. He picked up another and held it to the light to get a better view. It was of three people—Hattie, Ben, and Jessie. The photograph was perhaps five years old, and Garth marveled at how this fourteen-year-old adolescent had transformed into the ripe, alluring young woman Jessie was now.

A sharp rap sounded at the back door, and Garth felt a quick twinge of alarm. He nearly dropped the photograph when he placed it back on the table. Who would be calling now? Certainly neither Jessie or her mother would knock. His heart gave a fearful lurch. If he answered, would he give himself away? Painfully, he thought of his lazy drawl and concluded it would be better not to go to the door.

He waited, a trapped and haunted look in his eyes. But the knock came again, louder this time, and a woman's voice called out, "Young man, I know you're in there!"

The neighbor woman, he decided, for the voice was familiar. Indecision and uncertainty raced through him, but at last he relented. She *did* know he was here. Hopefully, his speech wouldn't betray him.

A frown of anxiety on his face, he made his way into the kitchen and hesitantly opened the door. The woman stood on the stoop, smiling broadly at him, a plate of cookies held in one hand.

"I'm glad to see you're up and about," she said, and sallied past him into the kitchen. She set the plate on the table and turned to give him another warm smile. Her round, amiable face was dominated by a pair of lively brown eyes that belied her age. "I brought some goodies for you—help build up your strength."

"Thank you, ma'm."

"I'm Mary Purcell, in case you didn't know."

"Garth Bodine." He extended his hand and shook hers gingerly.

She eyed his sling with some amusement. "That's a lovely petticoat you're wearing."

A flush rose under his deeply tanned skin, but he couldn't keep from grinning at this friendly, likable woman.

"Sit," she said, flinging out a hand. She plumped her bulk down on one of the chairs.

Garth cautiously took a seat at the other. "Hattie and Jessie are at the hospital." He was relieved the words came out easily, with no trace of his Carolina ancestry.

"I know. That's why I thought I'd stop by and keep you company. We can eat cookies and have a nice chat."

Garth managed a falsely cheerful smile and picked up a cookie. He took a bite and chewed thoughtfully.

"I should have brought over some more milk," she said. "I declare, those two old cows give more milk than a whole herd."

"I reckon we still have some." He groaned inwardly at his choice of words, but Mrs. Purcell seemed not to notice.

"How are the cookies?"

"Fine, ma'm. Mighty tasty." What he really longed for were some of the Bodines' cook's gooey, sugary pralines. "Did your cat ever come back?"

She nodded. "Just as fat and lazy as ever. How's your arm?"

"Better. The doctor says I just lost a lot of blood."

"What unit were you with?"

Garth nearly choked on the cookie. "I . . . uh . . . The artillery, ma'm."

"Who was your commander?"

Garth felt despair settling over him. "I don't rightly recall, ma'm. I must have gotten a bump on the head. Truth to tell, I don't exactly remember a whole lot."

Mary Purcell studied him carefully, her interest sharply curious. She smiled knowingly at him. "I knew it! You're one of Hattie's kin from down south!"

A look of intense, contained desperation entered Garth's features. He felt like crawling under the table. He glanced apprehensively at the woman, the color completely drained from his face, but he said nothing. The cookie he had eaten felt like a lump of hot wax in his throat.

"You might as well admit it, young man. I have no intention of informing the authorities."

Garth stared at her in vague bewilderment and disbelief. "You don't?"

She gave him a kindly smile. "Why should I? You can't help where you were born. Besides, Hattie's my dear friend, and I wouldn't do that to her."

Garth could only stare at her in silent dismay.

She looked at him with an inquiring frown. "Where *are* you from?"

"Charleston." His voice came out in a kind

of wheezing croak. "In South Carolina."

"Oh, I know where it is. Fort Sumter and all that."

Garth frowned in studied puzzlement. "You're really not going to turn me in?"

"I'm really not," she said, rising from her chair. "Eat your cookies and forget we ever had this talk."

With that, she was out the door. Garth stared after her for a long time in stunned silence. Still, deep worry nibbled at his mind.

Seated on the settee in the parlor, Jessie stared across the room at Garth, her mouth twisted in agitation. In the glow of the lamps, his lean, chiseled face looked drawn and tense; he was staring off into space, his eyes clouded with concern. Occasionally, a muscle twitched in his jaw; sometimes he cracked his knuckles.

When she and her mother had come home from the hospital he had told them of his surprise visit from Mrs. Purcell, of his inability to conceal his identity, of the woman's conclusions. Right now, Hattie was next door, talking to their neighbor. But at any minute Jessie expected there would be a knock at the door and a troop of Federal soldiers. She felt a cold stab of fear between her shoulder blades.

Garth blew out a wearily grim breath. "I've got enough money to buy a horse. I suppose tomorrow I'd better do just that and get the hell out of this town." He rose stiffly and walked to the window, peering out into the deep twilight through the curtains.

"Maybe she won't tell," Jessie offered hopefully, but there was a grain of doubt within her. "She's nosy—nosy and sharp as a tack. But she's very fond of Mama and me."

"She's a Yankee—a Yankee with a hole in the side of her house."

"It's boarded up now. Besides, you didn't put it there."

Muttering something unintelligible, he paced several times back and forth across the room, his left arm cradled in that ridiculous sling. Jessie gazed at him with considerable interest, her blue eyes full of speculation. He had broad shoulders and a powerful chest, a slender waist and long, muscular legs; the clothes looked much better on Garth than they ever had on her father.

Garth wasn't ready to travel yet; she knew that. Besides, there were no doubt scores of Union patrols between here and Virginia. And in truth, she wasn't so sure she was as eager to see him go as she had been a day or two ago. She would be less than a woman if she didn't find him physically appealing. The problem was that she no longer felt nearly as strong nor as immune as she had in the past.

He sank back into the chair, put a hand over his eyes and cursed softly. "I don't suppose you have anything to drink?"

"There's whiskey."

"Could I have some, please?"

Jessie went into the kitchen and fetched the bottle and a glass from a cupboard. Outside, horses' hooves trotted in unison up the street, and she involuntarily stiffened. She managed to fight down the fear and returned to the parlor, gnawing her lower lip. This waiting was intolerable!

She poured two fingers into the glass and handed it to Garth, lingering by his chair. He slugged back a huge mouthful of the whiskey while she regarded his roughly planed features. One wave of black hair flopped over his forehead, and he pushed it back with a brush of his hand. She was almost painfully aware of his proximity, of his smell, the heat of his body. He was indeed a magnificent male animal, his magnetism almost overwhelming. But she continued to hold herself aloof, refusing to give in to those delicious sensations his mere presence caused within her.

"I think I need a sip of that," she finally said.

He passed the glass to her, and she drank. The liquor scorched her throat and stomach, and she nearly choked.

"Loretta finds iced mint juleps more to her taste," he remarked dryly. "I expect you would too."

Jessie returned the glass to him and refilled it. She had no idea what a mint julep was, but if it tasted as bad as the whiskey, she wasn't interested. She felt the soft caress of his gaze and flushed, turned and flounced back to the settee.

The back door opened, and Jessie's blood ran cold. A ball of panic spread through her body and caught in her throat. She had visions of a dozen angry troopers ready to take them all off to jail.

Unable to still the turmoil and worry within her mind, she glanced up and saw it was only her mother. She exhaled a long, trembling breath of relief.

Garth stood and faced her, an eyebrow raised in silent inquiry.

Hattie waved her hand. "Mary's assured me she has no intention of informing on you. Actually, she said she rather liked you." She eyed the whiskey obliquely, and a ghost of a smile flickered across her face. "I think we could *all* use some of that right now."

# 6

Jessie sank back in the tub and let the warm
water caress her skin. She absently ran the
sponge over one arm, then closed her eyes
and sighed contentedly. Outside, the
chickens clucked in the yard, a dog was
barking somewhere nearby and the late afternoon traffic on Liberty Street seemed to be
heavy. Feeling exhausted and emotionally
wrung out, she luxuriated in the scented
water, sought to make her mind go blank.

It had been nearly a week since that
horrible day when Mary Purcell had come to
call on Garth. So far, nothing had
happened—no soldiers banging on the door,
no sheriff, no one. Garth's secret seemed
secure with the woman. In fact, Mary visited
with him nearly every day, and the two were
becoming fast friends.

It had also been nearly a week since
Jessie's first visit to the hospital, and in that

time she had seen far more gruesome sights than a broken leg. Men with sticky tar covering the stump of a fresh amputation, others with an eye gouged out, part of an ear missing, all of them helpless and miserable and hopelessly mangled for the rest of their lives. Their whimpering pleas were awful to hear, the screams from the operating rooms enough to drive a person mad. And then there was Nurse Johnson, barking orders, forever complaining, always watching. Jessie was tired of her sour looks; there was never a word of gratitude or praise.

With great difficulty, Jessie shook off these images, fought off a wave of nausea. She had come home early; her mother wouldn't leave the hospital for another couple of hours. Jessie felt she deserved this peaceful time alone, soaking in the bath, and she wasn't about to allow her memories of the hospital to spoil it.

Garth was undoubtedly in the parlor, poring over the newspaper, as always. He was much better now; perhaps in another week he would be able to travel. Jessie still kept her distance from him, determinedly avoiding the chance of their being alone together. The feel of his lips on hers and the sensations they had brought on were still too fresh in her mind. Actually, she seldom thought of him as her enemy anymore. He was likable and engaging, had something fresh and boyish about him. She felt at ease with him, but only when her mother was present. Alone, he inspired emotions and thoughts she had never felt before, wondrous, conflicting emotions, emotions that had been denied for too long.

Annoyed at the wayward train of her thoughts, she rose from the tub and snatched a towel off the chair. She had dawdled too long; there was supper to think about for when her mother returned home. Jessie dried herself vigorously until her skin glowed pink and tingled, then wrapped the towel around her. With Garth safely ensconced in the overstuffed chair in the parlor, she had no compunctions about slipping down the hall and into her bedroom to fetch a clean dress.

But when she stepped into the room, she froze, her feet rooted to the floor. Garth stood before the mirror, shaving, his chest bare, wearing only a pair of trousers. Muscles like whipcord bulged across his shoulders; Jessie was acutely aware of his body, of its hardness and strength. His nearness was heavy and magnetic.

He glanced in the mirror and saw her reflection. There was an enigmatic smile on his lips, and his eyes were heavylidded. Jessie was drawn by his incredible male beauty and vibrant sexuality. She didn't turn to flee as she knew she should.

Garth turned and looked at her, his dark, liquid gaze meeting hers, his eyes suddenly aflame with desire. They held a magical promise, seemed to hold her captive, and she felt her pulse race unexpectedly. Jessie had an impulse to run, to flee from the stirring of passion within her, unfamiliar and somehow frightening, but she couldn't move. She felt the heat of his gaze, as warm as that of the sun, twin pools of desire, dark and smoldering, spreading an inner fire through her veins.

He wiped the lather from his face and crossed the room in three quick strides. His arm hooked out to catch her waist and haul her to him with an urgency that made her blood run quick. He kissed her, moving his mouth over her lips and parting them with gentle insistence. Jessie experienced a fleeting inclination to resist, to pound her fists against his chest and push him away, but her strength and stony self-control melted, and a wonderful weakness stole through her. All reserve, all restraint disappeared, and she kissed him with a wild, hungry response, curling her arms around his neck and pressing herself closer to his body.

Her lips parted, and his kiss became hungry; his tongue filled her mouth, teasing, exploring. Jessie's heartbeat quickened, her blood running sweet and fast. She stroked the back of his neck with her hands, ran her fingers through his rich, black hair.

When the kiss ended Garth drew back slightly, Jessie's hands resting lightly against his chest. His gaze warmly probed hers, a question flickering on his brow. "Jessie?"

He was giving her an opportunity to end it now, but she didn't want to. Deep down inside, she knew this was what she had wanted ever since she had first seen him.

Anticipation trembled through her; she was dazed and breathless, her eyes luminous and soft as she gazed at him. She caressed his cheek, traced a finger over his mustache and along the curve of his lower lip.

A slow, lazy smile crossed his face, and there was a warm glowing light in his eyes. With a quick, adroit motion, he drew the towel away from her body and flung it aside. His gaze was openly appraising, a smoldering flame of desire brightening his gray eyes.

One by one, he pulled the pins from her hair and let them drop to the floor, his eyes moving over her with frank appreciation. Long chestnut hair tumbled over her shoulders in loose falls. Jessie's head whirled, and she savored the delicious urgency that filled her. Garth touched her hair lightly, bunched up a handful and let his fingers glide through it. He gathered her to him and kissed her fervently, holding her so tightly she feared for a moment her ribs might crack. But she didn't care. She could feel his strong hands tremble with a fierce need for her, and now that the moment was here, she was filled with a sense of anticipation that was almost too much to bear.

Without any effort at all—as if his arm had never been injured—he picked her up and carried her over to the bed and carefully lowered her onto the quilt. She felt the warmth of his lips on hers in a wild, passionate kiss that aroused every nerve of her body. His hands caressed her shoulders,

the callused palms making her shiver in
ecstasy. His head bent, and his lips touched
her breast, his tongue softly cirling one rosy
bud. Jessie quivered in sudden longing,
trembling with the powerful force of her
feelings, new and exciting, and a delicious
weakness swept over her.

Garth stood up, began unbuckling his belt.
Jessie nestled back against the soft quilt, her
lids lowered, watching him. His body was
superbly hewn, radiating power and
authority. When he pulled the trousers down
over his long, muscular legs she blushed
furiously and dropped her gaze. But, in silent
fascination, she stole another glance at him.
Garth arched a brow, his mouth curving in
indulgent humor.

He lay down on the bed beside her, and
there was a feverish heat in his kiss. His
fingers seemed to leave fiery trails on her
skin wherever they went. She warmed to the
ardor of his caresses and felt a sweet,
hungering ache within her that yearned to be
satisfied. His mouth burned a fevered path to
the hollow of her throat, awakening her flesh.
She ran her hands over the smooth, hard skin
of his back and felt the strong muscles tense
beneath her fingertips. He bent his head
down and covered each breast with warm
kisses, firing her blood. The contact sent
pleasurable little vibrations throughout her
body, filled her with a silken languor.

She returned his passion, arched her body
under his and longed for his lips to cover hers
once more. His mouth moved upon hers with

a hunger that demanded a like response, and she gave it to him. The heat of his caresses set fire to every nerve, evoked fresh waves of desire. She gave herself freely to the passion that trembled through her body; she writhed under him, her hips urging.

But when he rose up on his knees a thin shiver of panic ran along her spine. Her breath was coming fast, and she wasn't certain she could speak.

Garth smiled reassuringly, his eyes warm and affectionate. "It's all right. I want you. I've always wanted you. And I know you want me too."

She caressed his chest, smiled into his eyes. She felt a quick, sharp stab of pain, but it gradually dulled with his rhythmic movements. She dug her fingers deeply into his back for a moment, then her hands began to move over the sculpted muscles of his back, exploring the width of his shoulders.

A fire swept through her that was magical and wondrous; it brought only pleasure, not pain. A honey sweet warmth spread through her. She felt the speeding rhythm of her heart, felt her deep demand grow and grow. His mouth held hers captive, smothering a little moan of ecstasy. The pleasure was intense; it was very nearly excrutiating, and she writhed beneath him.

He touched her cheek with the backs of his fingers, stretched out beside her and drew her into his arms. Jessie curled her body tightly against his, nestled against the comfort of his encircling arms. His breath near her ear was warm and ticklish, and she sighed contentedly. Still, she was slightly amazed at what had taken place and the wonder of it all.

"I'm not so sure I want to go back to Charleston in such a hurry now," he said.

His comment reminded Jessie painfully of who Garth Bodine really was. She felt a sudden, irrational annoyance at herself and him, but it was only a fleeting sensation. Regardless of the fact that he was a Reb, she liked him, and after today she knew for certain why she had been so strongly attracted to him. There was a subtle irony in it that she couldn't help but find missing.

He raised up on one elbow and studied her face intently, his fingers absently caressing her brow. "How do you feel?"

"A little sore." A soft smile touched her lips. "But I'll live. How's your arm?"

His mouth quirked into an amused grin, and he kissed her lightly. "What arm?"

# 7

Jessie stared into the pinched, scowling face of Nurse Johnson, and a flush of resentment colored her cheeks. "I can't help it! If you're running out of bandages, it's not my fault. I'd wager every spare sheet in Gettysburg has ended up in your hands."

Dorothy Johnson gave her a cold look of disapproval. "Miss Morgan, you needn't be cheeky with me."

"I'm not being cheeky. I just didn't misplace your bandages. What happened to that big shipment that came in on the train a few days ago?"

Nurse Johnson grunted, pivoted on her heel and marched away. Jessie stood amid a row of cots, fuming. It had been almost two weeks since she had first set foot in the hospital, and every day there was at least one confrontation with the woman.

"Don't mind her," a man in one of the beds

said. "She ain't much friendlier with the patients."

Jessie glanced at him, a middle-aged, balding man with severe powder burns on his face and neck. The wounds leaked a viscous fluid and were covered with a foul-smelling salve. She felt a hard knot of nausea in the pit of her stomach, but managed a faint smile for him. "With her around, it's a wonder any of you get well."

"I probably wouldn't be if it wasn't for Doc Tibbets."

Jessie nodded, checked to make sure the burned man's water pitcher and glass were full and left the ward. She loathed her duties at the hospital, even though she knew she was doing her part for the war effort as best she could. The place still stank, the men's conditions often turned her stomach, but at least she had only fainted twice. All the same, she was glad her stint for the day was over and was anxious to get home, eager to see Garth.

A dreamy, contented smile touched the corners of her mouth for an instant. Since that day over a week ago when they had first made love, Jessie found herself looking forward to returning home to his arms. He still remained a Reb in her eyes, but he was also a man. Garth had loosed a sensuality in her that she never knew existed. She wanted him to hold her, caress her, whisper to her in that low, lazy drawl she had hated so at first. The memory brought a flush of pleasure to her cheeks, and she smiled softly again.

She was brought abruptly out of her reverie when she saw her mother talking to Dr. Hollis Tibbets outside the alcove that served as his private office. He was the chief army surgeon in charge of the hospital, young, energetic and one of the staunchest pro-Union men she had ever met. Curly light blond hair capped his head, and he had rich, full sidewhiskers. His face was handsome, with sparkling blue eyes and a jaw angled almost square. If it hadn't been for her new-found relationship with Garth, she might have considered him attractive. Did, in fact—as he obviously did her—but Garth had managed to change Jessie overnight without her even being aware of it. The Confederacy remained her enemy, but Garth was her lover.

With a twinge of apprehension, she approached the two. Would her mother be sent home earlier than usual and spoil her tryst? A look of disappointment crept into Jessie's expression.

Hollis Tibbets turned his gaze on Jessie, and he eyed her slender form with almost insulting familiarity. "Our loveliest little helper."

Jessie's smile was slightly uncomfortable. "Thank you." She hoped Nurse Johnson hadn't been complaining about her. But then, the woman complained about everyone and everything.

Hattie turned, and her gaze sought Jessie's. "Dr. Tibbets needs me to stay a little later tonight."

"Two of our volunteers can't come in," Tibbets explained. "One has a sick child, and the other is ill herself."

"Do you need me too?" Jessie asked. She felt her excitement and enthusiasm drain from her with each passing second. Besides missing her opportunity to be alone with Garth, she knew he would undoubtedly wonder what had happened to his two benefactors. Perhaps worry too. He seemed to do that a lot lately. He was still in danger here, and there was really no reason for him to stay any longer. Except for what had begun between the two of them. She didn't know if she loved him or not—didn't know if she could ever love a Reb. But she didn't want him to leave her just yet. Two weeks ago that idea would have been absolutely preposterous.

"I don't think so," Tibbets said, interrupting Jessie's thoughts. She blinked and looked at him. "Nurse Johnson is staying behind as well."

"All right." Jessie threw a silent question at her mother.

Hattie gazed meaningfully at her. "You go on home and take care of things there. I'll probably be home a little after nine."

"What about supper?"

"I can eat something here."

Hollis Tibbits gave a lingering look at Jessie, then turned and vanished into his office.

"Just fix supper for you and Garth," Hattie said quietly. "I'll see you later."

As Jessie left the hospital, she noticed two guards lounging on the wide stone steps, their rifles leaning against a pillar. One of the men removed his slouch hat, and his lips drew back in an obscene smile. He was a big man, fat and bearlike, with greasy brown hair and a tobacco-stained beard. Jessie felt a shiver of repulsion race over her flesh. His companion hooted with raucous laughter at her reaction and passed an open canteen to his friend. Jessie caught the distinct, sour odor of whiskey.

She hurried on her way, anxious to be home. If the southern soldiers comported themselves like their Union counterparts, it was little wonder the Confederacy was in a shambles. Gettysburg was no better. Troops were bivouacked all over town, and they frequently were a rowdy, drunken bunch. Most of the injured had been taken away to better facilities, and, truthfully, Jessie was finding her chores at the hospital tedious and boring. In fact, after all the excitement of the battle—as much as she had been frightened then—much of her life seemed dull. Except when she was alone with Garth.

Garth stood at the sink and pumped water into a glass. He drank it slowly, absently gazing out the window. The chickens were pecking in the yard, Mrs. Purcell's cat alternately dozed and watched them from the shade of a bush.

He set down the glass and wandered aimlessly through the house, restless and on edge. How he longed to go outside for more than a few minutes at a time! The confinement of the place was beginning to take its toll on his nerves. He had ventured out several times to gather eggs with Jessie, but that was hardly satifying to a man used to being outdoors most of his life.

He wandered into the parlor and peered out the window onto Liberty Street. There were no soldiers in sight; only a woman pushing a baby carriage. Snorting in disgust, he let the curtain fall back into place and threw himself into the overstuffed chair.

This afternoon he would have to talk to Jessie, and tonight, to Hattie. He couldn't stay here any longer. His wound was healed, and only a puckered, pink, three-inch scar showed on his upper arm. He could purchase a horse and hopefully ride through Maryland into Virginia without being questioned. Once safely behind the Confederate lines, he could be back in South Carolina in no time, to join his regiment once more.

He pursed his lips thoughtfully, his eyes dark and distant. He had never met any Yankees before coming here, other than a few northern brokers at the bars in the Charleston hotels. They were mostly braggarts who drank and talked too much, but these people here weren't like that. Dr. Brooks and Mrs. Purcell were good, kind people, and he had no wish to fight with them. And Hattie and Jessie . . . He let out his breath in a quiet sigh. What to do about Jessie?

Garth was twenty-eight years old, and Jessie hadn't been the first woman in his life. There had been many before her, from lusty whores in the fancy bordellos on Tradd Street to the daughters of rich planters hoping to catch the son of Claiborne Bodine as a husband. But Jessie was different.

His thoughts fluttered back to her and the emptiness he felt when she was away. True, she had made no secret of her hatred of him in the past, and even now she occasionally showed signs of irritation at his place of birth. But there was something about her company that produced a warm ease in him, something he had never felt with any other woman. She was fresh and young, vibrant and beautiful, and he wanted her as he had never wanted any other woman.

The back door opened, and Garth could feel every muscle in his body tense with anticipation. He sprang from the chair and bounded into the kitchen. Jessie was standing by the table, unpinning her hair. She looked at him through the upward sweep of her dark lashes and smiled radiantly. She gave a little shake of her head, and long chestnut hair cascaded loosely, streaming behind her to her waist. He could smell her skin, the scent of soap, the fragrance of her hair, and the effect on him was magical. He became painfully aware of his growing desire.

She cast a provocative glance at him, small, perfect white teeth flashing in a teasing smile. "Mama's going to be later than usual tonight." There was an open invitation in her eyes, her head tilted back, almost challenging him.

Garth reached out and wrapped her in his arms, pressed her close to his chest. He could feel her smallness, the fragility of her shoulders. Her long hair was soft in his hands, and when he stroked it his fingers moved as if across silk. He could sense the trembling warmth of her, feel the contours of her breasts through the thin material of her dress.

He gave her a long, searching kiss, his lips lingering over hers as his arms drew her closer. Jessie wrapped her hands around his neck, her mouth warm and yielding, and Garth throbbed with a longing for release. Never had a woman had such power over him!

She drew back slightly and looked at him, a special excitement in her blue eyes. "We might be having a late supper tonight."

He lifted her chin and gazed into her eyes, a lazy smile on his lips. "I'm in no hurry."

"I reckon I'll see about getting a horse tomorrow."

Jessie was snuggled up against Garth, resting her head on his shoulder, her fingers twining in the mat of hair that covered his chest. But at his words, her eyes snapped open, and she stared at him.

"It's time I was on my way back home again," he went on. "I've taken your charity long enough, and I'm fit to travel."

Jessie felt her heart shrivel; he had finally spoken the words she had dreaded hearing. Now she despised him for saying them. "What about the soldiers in town?"

"I can talk like you folks if I have to. I can get a horse without any trouble, and then I can be on my way."

"Back to fight again, I suppose." There was a degree of annoyance in her voice.

"I suppose."

Jessie rolled away from him and sat up on the edge of the bed. She was hurt and angry with him. But it was what she had expected all along. No matter how she felt about him, she hadn't deluded herself. He was first and foremost a Reb.

She felt his hand lightly caress her back. "I'll come back after the war if you want."

"You might be dead by then."

"I might not."

She turned her head and looked at him with a trace of contempt. "I don't want you to come back. I haven't forgotten what you are."

"But you like me."

"I *tolerate* you."

One dark eyebrow quirked in cynical mockery. "Is that what it is between us?"

Her eyes flamed dangerously. "Don't patronize me!"

He reached out and gripped her arm, pulled her back into bed with him. She fell half across him, her hair spilling over his chest. She struggled to get up, but he put both arms around her and held her firm.

"I'm coming back whether you want me to

or not," he said.

A new rage began to boil inside her. "I bet you'll take all kinds of information back to your army about what we're doing here."

He uttered a deprecating chuckle. "Since the troops pulled out, this is hardly the high command."

Jessie tried hard to wriggle free again, but he kept her pinioned to his chest. "Would you let me go!"

"I don't want to." He made an exasperated noise deep in his throat. "Really, Jessie, I don't know why you're acting like this. Surely you didn't expect me to sit out the rest of the war here with you and your mother."

"Of course I didn't. It's just that I—"

"Look at me."

Jessie raised her head and looked into his face. She noted a softening in his eyes, affectionate and caring. She relaxed in his arms, felt her anger and indignation melt away.

"I don't *want* to go," he said. "I don't want to leave you."

Her eyes grew warm, and she reached out tentatively to stroke his cheek. "I don't want you to go either."

He curled a hand behind her neck and drew her head down to kiss her. It was a kiss so incredibly tender and sweet, it left her feeling breathless. She nestled against him, feeling safe and secure in his arms. She would miss him, but a defiant spark of pride within her refused to allow her to tell him so.

"Maybe I can get a desk job in Charleston,"

he said. "After all, I've been wounded."

"From what you tell me, your father would never allow it."

She felt his shrug. "So? He can send Loretta out in a uniform. She'd probably be only too happy to go. At least that way she'd get to meet lots of men."

Jessie smiled to herself. From what Garth had told her of his sister, Loretta Bodine was definitely one person she never wanted to meet. "You'll fight again."

"I don't know what I'll do." He stroked her hair, then pulled her body more tightly against him. "But whatever I do, I promise I'll be back to see you."

"Whether I want you to or not?"

"Whether you want me or not."

Hattie trudged down the steps of the hospital, a weariness in her bones. Darkness shrouded the area and there was barely a sliver of a moon in the sky. She took several more steps, then halted as a shape materialized out of the shadows. She peered into the gloom, but in that instant, there was the loud report of a gun, a bright flash of sparks.

Sudden pain came in great surging waves. The breath was driven from Hattie's body, and she crumpled to the ground. The pain was like a fire within her chest and shoulder. Her fingers touched thick, warm blood, and then all descended into sudden blackness.

Jessie wiped her hands on a napkin and

stared down at the plate of chicken bones before her. "You really plan to leave then?"

"I *have* to, Jessie. I'm going stir-crazy around here. I can't go anywhere, see anybody but you and Hattie and Mrs. Purcell."

"And her cat."

"Him too."

Jessie sighed, gathered up the dishes and took them to the sink. She dumped the bones in a tin cup, then washed the grease from her fingers. Despite her earlier agitation, she didn't want him to leave. Whether she loved him or not, it didn't matter. She was fond of him, and he had introduced her into a new world of sensual pleasure she had never known existed.

"I'm sorry I got angry with you earlier," she said.

"I know." He went over to the stove to pour himself another cup of coffee. "You were afraid I was just using you."

Jessie stared at him wonderingly. "I was?"

A wry smile flitted across his face. "Isn't that what most women think when a man beds them and then doesn't ask them to marry him?"

"I don't know. I've never been in a situation like this before. I guess I don't know what to expect."

He leaned down, and his lips brushed the side of her neck, moving up to touch the earlobe. "I can't very well ask you to marry me under the circumstances. I'll be away."

"And on different sides."

"Maybe not so very different."

She caught his hand and brought it to her cheek. "Just be careful. Don't end up in somebody else's cellar."

There was a knock at the front door. Jessie jumped away from Garth, and they exchanged puzzled, worried glances. Who would be calling at this hour?

"I'll go," she said.

"I'll come with you."

Jessie felt uncertainty fill her with a dull kind of dread as she walked through the parlor with Garth following behind. Had they finally come to get him? After all this time, after all the precautions, now that Garth was going home, was it too late?

As she opened the door, she felt the cold, clammy hand of terror close around her heart. A Federal soldier stood on the stoop, fidgeting uncomfortably with the slouch hat he held in his hands.

"Miss Morgan? Miss Jessie Morgan?"

Gradually, disquiet began to grow within her, a vague sense of wrongness. "Yes?"

The soldier's eyes flicked curiously to Garth, then settled back on Jessie. "There's been an accident at the hospital. I've come to get you. I'm afraid your mother's been shot."

Jessie straightened slowly, disbelief running through her. She reeled and staggered forward dizzily like a drunk, then her balance went, and she felt herself tumble away into a private fog.

Hattie lay on the cot in Dr. Hollis Tibbets' office, her breathing labored, her face a grimace of pain. Blood-soaked bandages covered her shoulder, but, thankfully, the blanket was drawn up to hide any other damage. It was a dreary little room, with coal oil lamps casting an eerie glow. Tibbets was checking her pulse; Nurse Johnson hovered just outside.

Garth stood behind Jessie, his hands on her shoulders, and he could feel them trembling. Her face was strained white, her eyes puffy and red from tears. The story had come out on the ride to the hospital in the wagon with the Yankee soldier. Hattie had been shot by a guard too drunk to discern male from female, friend from foe.

Tibbets straightened up and glanced with pity at Jessie. "I'll leave you alone with her for a few minutes."

As he passed, Garth sent him a silent, questioning look. The surgeon shook his head in despair and slipped through the open door.

Jessie hesitantly stepped forward, then knelt beside the cot and took her mother's hand. Hattie turned her head on the pillow and stared with glazed eyes at Jessie. A bitter twinge of sadness closed around Garth's heart, and he hung his head. He had an urge to leave, to give mother and daughter some privacy, but he couldn't bear to leave Jessie now. She was distraught, too upset, too numb from the shock.

"You'll get good care here, Mama." Jessie spoke in a hoarse, painful voice; tears welled in her eyes and she muffled a sob. "Look how many soldiers they saved."

Hattie's face was contorted in pain. "Not

for me." Her voice was thick, her lips moved slowly. "My mind's been drifting in and out, but I've been able to think clearly enough. There's no one here for you—no family."

"There's *you*!"

Hattie slowly shook her head from side to side. "Not anymore." She seemed to struggle for air for a moment, then relaxed. She gripped Jessie's hand more tightly. "If anything happens to me, I want you to go home with Garth."

"But—"

Hattie raised an arm limply in a weak gesture toward Garth. He stepped nearer to the bed, felt a lump in his throat and tried to swallow.

"Take her with you, back to Charleston. She has family there, however distant, and I know she'll be welcomed at least by Peggy Sue and your mother. Will you do that?"

Garth nodded solemnly. "Anything, Hattie. Just ask, and it's done."

"I know there's the war and all, but she'll be better off with kin. Here, she'd only be alone."

Jessie clutched desperately at her mother's hand, tears glimmering in her eyes. "Mama, don't talk like that!"

Hattie's head lolled to one side, and she closed her eyes.

Garth reached down and lifted Jessie to her feet. "She's gone, Jessie."

An explosion of sobs suddenly burst from her. She stood motionless, the stream of tears running down her face, her fist jammed into her mouth. Then she reached out for

Garth with trembling hands and clutched at him, burying her face against his chest and weeping uncontrollably. Garth gathered her close and soothed her, but a great hollow sadness pulsed within him.

He let her cry for a while, until her tears became occasional hitching gasps. Then he gently led her out of the room. Dr. Tibbets and Nurse Johnson stood stoically outside.

"Can you take care of—of the arrangements?" Garth asked.

Tibbets nodded curtly, and Garth continued to lead a shaking, trembling Jessie out of the hospital.

Dorothy Johnson turned to Dr. Tibbets, a hard gleam in her eyes. "Did you hear it?"

Tibbets inclined his head. "I heard."

"That man is a Reb. Charleston indeed!" Her face twisted into a mask of fury. "All the boys we've tended—*he's* part of their suffering. He should be arrested right now!"

Tibbets ran a hand distractedly through his blond hair. "Hattie Morgan and her daughter deserve better."

Nurse Johnson drew in a breath with a moan. "You're going to let him get away scot-free?"

"No. But he won't be going anywhere for a while. Let Jessie have her mourning and Hattie have a proper funeral."

"But—"

Tibbets waved her silent with a weary gesture. "The Reb won't get away, don't worry. Right now, I have an undertaker to summon."

# 8

Jessie sat hunched at the kitchen table, staring into a cold cup of coffee. Her eyes were red from tears, and there were salty streaks on her cheeks, but, for the time being, the sobs had turned inward. Frankly, Garth didn't think it would be possible for her to cry any more. Last night she had lain awake in his arms, alternately weeping, reminiscing, cursing the drunken soldier and the war itself. He had held her, comforting her as best he could, inordinately thankful he was here for her when she needed him, that he hadn't left for home a day or two earlier.

For himself, Garth felt a mournful heaviness in his chest. In the short span of time he had been in Gettysburg, he had become genuinely fond of Hattie. Now she was only a memory, an inert form lying in a closed, brass-bound casket in the parlor. The undertaker, a man named Dudley Pigg, had come by with the body early this morning. He was a solemn, obsequitous man in somber clothing. Jessie hadn't been able to speak to him, but he assured Garth all would be in readiness for a funeral tomorrow afternoon. Garth had also fended off neighbors and friends, explaining that Jessie was too distraught to greet callers. In justification of his presence and the drawl he couldn't quite conceal, he told them he was a cousin from West Virginia, unable to serve the Union because of the lung disease he had contracted in the coal mines. This seemed to appease their curiosity, and they left, leaving behind cakes and pies and hams and preserves, enough for an army.

Garth gazed across the table at Jessie. Her bottom lip was caught prettily between her teeth, but a frown knitted little lines in her forehead. She hadn't eaten much all day, and he felt a deep pang of concern. She needed her strength.

"How about a piece of pie?" he suggested.

She shook her head. "I can't."

"You're such a tiny little thing to begin with. You'll waste away to nothing."

"I don't care."

"My mother will be shocked if I show up with you looking like nothing but skin and bones."

She raised her head and gazed at him, a look of intense pain in her eyes. "I'm not sure I want to go with you."

"It's what your mother wanted."

"I know." She dropped her head and

resumed staring into the murky liquid in her cup.

Garth sighed inwardly. Taking Jessie with him would be no problem. In fact, it might make travel easier for him, make him seem less suspicious. But Claiborne Bodine would not be overjoyed having a Yankee in his house. Neither would Loretta.

Jessie groaned aloud as there was another knock at the back door. She didn't want to see anyone, couldn't see anyone. All day long they had been coming and going, but she couldn't bear to have to accept their sympathy at this point. There would be time enough for that tomorrow at the graveside—too much time.

She clenched her teeth and fought against the tumult of emotions. Since her father's death Hattie had become everything to her—friend, companion, mother. To think that she would never see her again, talk to her . . . Her eyes filled with scalding tears and a choking lump caught in her throat.

She rose from the table. "Get it, will you, Garth?"

He nodded, but at that instant the knock came again, this time a frantic pounding. Jessie darted down the hall just in time to hear Mary Purcell's voice, high-pitched and excited.

"They've found you out!" the woman exclaimed. "There's rumors all over town about the Reb living here."

Jessie stopped dead in her tracks, her mind

racing chaotically, her heart pounding in sudden fear.

"I don't understand," Garth said.

"Somebody learned your real identity —don't ask me who. But they're posting guards—even asked to use my house, but I refused. They plan to arrest you right after the funeral."

Jessie crept back into the kitchen, dread fluttering in her chest. Mary Purcell folded her into her ample embrace and patted her gently. "You poor child."

Jessie felt tears welling up and fought to control them. For the time being she pushed her grief to the back of her mind; right now she was more concerned about Garth's safety. She stepped out of Mrs. Purcell's encircling arms and looked at Garth, her eyes rolling in terror. "You'll have to go."

"I can't leave you now."

"You have to! They'll arrest you if you don't!"

Garth shook his head and swore under his breath. He glanced around, rubbing a finger nervously along the bridge of his nose.

Before he could answer, Mary spoke up again. "That's not the worst of it, I'm afraid." She put a hand comfortingly on Jessie's shoulder. "They suspect you of harboring the enemy. Garth isn't the only one they plan to arrest."

Jessie uttered a frightened little moan. She was clammy, trembling. For a moment waves of dizziness washed over her, and she found she couldn't speak.

Mary gazed at her with warm, kindly eyes. "It's all because of the battle. Tempers are hot, emotions are high. They want revenge for what the southerners did here, and anyone considered their friend is an enemy."

"But the women who came by today . . ." Jessie's voice sounded helpless and afraid. "If they suspected all this of me and Mama, why would they come?"

"Has anyone been to call in the last couple of hours?"

Jessie realized there hadn't been a soul, not since noon. A growing dread began to take hold of her senses.

"You should leave, for your own safety," Mary said. "I'll see to it that your mama has a fine funeral, and just let anyone dare call her a traitor to my face!"

Jessie's mind spun in an aimless, racing whirlwind. "I can't! I can't leave Mama like this!"

Mary gripped Jessie by the shoulders and turned her to face her. The woman looked hard at her. "You have to go. Listen to me. I don't want to see either of you young people in trouble."

"But how can we? You said yourself the soldiers are watching the house!"

"Garth isn't stupid. He'll think of something."

Jessie glanced helplessly at him. His mouth was pressed tightly shut, a frown of concentration on his forehead. Finally he released a long, weary sigh. "You're right, Mrs. Purcell. I can't endanger Jessie. We'll go."

"But how!" Jessie's voice rose to an hysterical pitch.

Garth took her hand and squeezed it. "We need to talk right now. We'll let you know our plans later, Mrs. Purcell. And thank you."

Jessie had composed herself, dried her tears and put on a suitable dress for mourning, a simple black bombazine with a full sweep skirt and jet buttons. Now, as she entered the bank, she felt a vague apprehension. It was nearly closing time, but it was still busy.

For an hour she and Garth had discussed various means of escape from Gettysburg—an escape that would be undetected and unsuspected by anyone. Garth's idea was the only one that seemed plausible, but it was also madness. And now that it was time to implement its beginnings, she felt tense inside, coiled more tightly than she had ever been before. Jessie knew it was a foolhardy plan that would never work and only bring disaster to them both. But she took a deep breath and closed her eyes a moment, willing herself to banish the panic inside.

She walked purposefully to a teller, a balding little man with thick spectacles perched on a rather bulbous nose, and took the family banking book from her reticule. "I wish to withdraw a thousand dollars."

The clerk lifted a brow in mild surprise. "A thousand, Miss Morgan? That's a great deal of money."

"I have to pay for my mother's funeral. Mr. Pigg doesn't come cheaply, and I want everything to be as perfect as can be." She drew in a breath, hoping the next lie would come out as smoothly. "Then I plan to visit relatives in New Hampshire—in several weeks."

The little man nodded sagaciously. "I understand, Miss Morgan. A terrible tragedy. And I want to express my deepest sympathy."

Jessie sniffed back genuine tears. "Thank you."

The teller began to move away, then turned back. "How do you want the funds?"

"Some in greenbacks, some in gold."

He moved away, and Jessie felt a wave of relief. At least she hadn't botched it so far. Her eyes whisked over the patrons in the bank. Several people were looking at her. The baker's wife gave her a look of pity, others merely stared. Some knew the rumors—she could feel it—but she made her face as expressionless as possible and waited patiently, though her heart was hammering against her rib cage.

When the clerk returned he counted out the sum and placed the bills in a brown envelope; the gold coins were in a small leather pouch. He handed over her book to her. "I'm afraid that doesn't leave much in your account."

"I may decide to sell the house and move away from so many memories."

The clerk nodded dutifully again, and Jessie turned to make her way out of the bank. Once on the sidewalk a shudder of relief went through her. At least this part was over, but the worst was yet to come.

She walked to the undertaker's parlor, a block away. Dudley Pigg greeted her effusively. "Any problems, Miss Morgan?"

"Not really. But I do have some questions I'd like to ask you."

"Anything, Miss Morgan."

She gazed disdainfully at the dreary little room with its dusty velvet drapes, knowing the only other room contained Mr. Pigg's display of coffins. "I wonder—could you come by my house around seven tonight? This place . . ." She made a small, helpless gesture with her hand.

"Of course, Miss Morgan."

"And could you bring the hearse with you? Having Mama in the house like she is makes me more upset than I already am. I'd like to get her to the church as early in the morning as possible."

Dudley Pigg looked a bit perplexed by this irregularity, but he smiled charitably, displaying ill-fitting dentures. "Seven o'clock sharp, Miss Morgan."

Jessie thanked the mortician and left the office with a silent sigh of relief. Poor Dudley Pigg wouldn't be so anxious if he only knew what was in store for him.


"I saw a soldier sitting on the stoop across the street." Jessie dropped her reticule on the bed and examined the array of supplies Garth had collected.

"Is the undertaker coming?"

"At seven."

"Good."

"I got the money without any trouble. Some people looked at me funny, but the man at the bank believed me."

"Then we've got a little over fourteen hundred dollars between us. My share should be more than enough to get us to Charleston in relative comfort."

"There's only about a hundred left in the account."

"You won't need it. If you do, you can send for it after the war."

Jessie said nothing, but stared at the food spread out on her bed. There were several wheels of cheese, jars of preserves, bread, a side of bacon, a small cured ham, coffee, apples, a canteen, and a bottle of whiskey. Garth's haversack was bulging with clothing that had once belonged to her father.

Fear mixed with sadness overtook her, and her eyes glistened with hot tears. Garth gathered her close and held her tightly for a few minutes. His shoulder was strong and muscular, and she leaned against it gratefully, his strength offering her silent comfort. His lips brushed her forehead lightly, then he held her at arm's length.

"You'd better start packing while I put this food into something."

Jessie nodded, and, with a sigh, turned to the task at hand.

Jessie dried and put away the last dish—for the last time. She glanced around the little kitchen sorrowfully. She had lived in this house all her life, and now she had eaten her final meal in it—a supper comprised of things neighbors and friends had brought by. The deed to the house was packed in her carpetbag, along with several other important papers, though she wasn't sure if the government would confiscate the property once she had gone.

Garth was peering out the window, and she went to stand next to him. Deep shadows were lengthening from the west, and the sky was a pure, pearl gray. The chickens were quiet, resting in their coop for the night. Jessie let out a pained sigh. "I hate doing this."

"I know." Garth turned his head and looked down at her, affection in his eyes. "But we'll both be better off once we get to Charleston."

"I wonder. I don't know how I'll feel in—in enemy country."

"You'll be with family."

"A pack of hot-headed Rebs. I won't be able to hide my feelings, you know. I still love the Union and the flag and Abe Lincoln."

Amusement lurked in Garth's gray eyes. "With a face like he's got, it's a wonder anybody could love him."

"Jeff Davis isn't exactly handsome."

"True." Garth turned his gaze back to the window. "This isnt going to be easy for you—at least till we're well beyond the town's limits. I have no idea where the Yankees have men picketed."

"Neither do I." She felt a sudden chill of dread. Jessie didn't even want to think of what she had to do in the next few hours. An overwhelming sense of doubt gripped her, and once again she realizd how insane this all was. Still, if they didn't leave, by this time tomorrow night she might well be sitting in the town's jail with God-knew-what as cellmates and Garth could be on his way to a Federal prison.

There were muffled sounds of restless, stamping hooves in the backyard.

"Here comes Mr. Pigg," Garth said, and he shot her a cautioning look. "Ready?"

"I guess as ready as I'll ever be." She glanced down at her olive green velvet riding skirt and smoothed it down before stepping to the back door and opening it. "In here, Mr. Pigg!"

Dudley Pigg alighted from the hearse. In the fading light, Jessie could see it was a fine conveyance, with etched glass sides and two strapping gray horses drawing it. A saddled horse was tethered to the rear, an unexpected bonus.

Dudley Pigg entered the kitchen, wearing the same somber black suit he always wore. He took off his flat, low-crowned hat and bowed low. "I'll put a feed bag on the horses before I leave tonight."

Jessie nodded, gesturing him to a chair at the table. "Coffee, sir?"

"Don't mind if I do."

He seated himself while Jessie poured a cup from the pot on the stove. She didn't want any herself, but she joined him at the table. Garth leaned idly against the work counter.

"There's plenty of flowers at the church and at the cemetery," Pigg said. "Roses, carnations, daisies, a veritable garden."

"That's fine, Mr. Pigg. Mama always liked flowers."

He ran a bony finger over the rim of his cup, glancing uncertainly at her. "I must admit, I've heard some disquieting rumors about you and Mr. Bodine."

Jessie ignored the implication, trying to look indignant. "I assure you, sir, Garth and I are cousins. There are no improprieties going on here."

Dudley Pigg hastily held out his hands to fend off her words. "That's not what I meant, Miss Morgan. But it seems that the authorities in the city believe Mr. Bodine is a Confederate spy or something to that effect." He turned to Garth curiously. "You did say you were a coal miner from West Virginia, didn't you?"

"I said that," Garth replied lazily. He reached behind him into the empty tea canister and withdrew his revolver. He aimed it at Dudley Pigg's head. The mortician's features contorted in sudden alarm. "That's what I said," Garth repeated. "Now, Jessie and I would like to request a little cooperation from you."

Pigg's eyes bulged in horror, sweat beads popping out on his forehead. "Cooperation?"

"We'll require the use of your hearse

tonight."

Dudley Pigg stammered incoherently. The fear in his eyes was sharper now. He swallowed hard, his adam's apple bobbing, and nodded his head quickly.

Jessie went into the parlor and slowly approached the coffin. She swallowed back a rush of tears as she placed her hand on the smooth mahogany. "I'm sorry it has to be this way, Mama. But you wanted me to go to Charleston with Garth, and this looks like the only way." Tears began to fill her eyes, and a sob caught in her throat. "I love you."

Garth had left his gun with Jessie. He wasn't entirely satisfied she would shoot Dudley Pigg if she was brought to that, but the poor man was so afraid and confused it was doubtful he would try anything. While the two waited in the kitchen, Garth unlatched the casket and lifted the lid. Hattie looked serene and peaceful in her best Sunday dress, and with a stab of remorse, Garth gently lifted her lifeless body out of the coffin. She seemed terribly heavy as he carried her down the hall to her bedroom and carefully placed her on the bed. Tenderly, he tucked the quilt around her; it was a warm night, but she would never notice it.

"Good-bye, Hattie. I'll take good care of Jessie for you."

Regaining his icy composure, he returned to the kitchen. Jessie held the gun on the mortician, now reduced to a mass of shaking nerves.

"Now what?" he asked.

"I'll need you to help me carry the coffin out to the hearse," Garth said. "But I warn you, try anything funny and I'll kill you."

Pigg nodded quickly in agreement, his eyes glazed with fear.

Garth turned to Jessie. "All right?"

She looked anything but pleased. "All right." She handed the revolver to Garth, which he tucked into his belt, and the three of them moved into the parlor.

With considerable apprehension, Jessie allowed Garth to lift her into the casket. He closed the lid and snapped the latches shut.

"She'll smother in there like that!" Pigg exclaimed. "There's maybe a half hour of air in there, if that."

"Don't worry."

"And where's Mrs. Morgan?"

"Quite comfortable, I assure you."

Garth took hold of two brass handles, indicating to Pigg to take the others. With no small effort, they carried the coffin through the house and out the back door. The moon was shining in a sky of tranquil stars. Garth set down his end and Pigg did the same.

"Open the hearse."

Pigg did as he was told. The saddled gelding snorted nervously and pawed the ground.

Across the street, two drowsy privates squinted into the night.

"What do you suppose is goin' on?"

"Dunno. I guess the undertaker's takin' the old lady somewhere. Don't rightly blame the girl for not wantin' a body in the house."

His companion chuckled and took a pull from a bottle of whiskey. "I wouldn't mind havin' the Morgan girl's body, though."

Jessie nearly cried aloud with relief when Garth opened the lid. It was terrible inside the casket. It was well padded with soft satin and actually quite comfortable, but it smelled of violets and some chemical, and was absolutely claustrophobic.

"I don't think I can stand it again, Garth!"

"It won't be for long. In the meantime, just lie here and be quiet while I finish with Mr. Pigg."

Dudley Pigg's face was filled with fear and uncertainty as Garth herded him back into the house.

"Wh-what are you going to do with me?" the undertaker stammered.

"Nothing much." Garth prodded him toward Jessie's bedroom. Once inside, Pigg turned, his eyes wild and confused. Garth was dryly amused; evidently the mortician feared he might soon end up in one of his own boxes. "Take off your clothes."

Pigg gaped in astonishment. "My clothes?"

Garth's humor faded, and impatience put a sharp edge on his reply. He gestured with his revolver. "Your clothes."

While Pigg undressed somewhat hesitantly, Garth did the same—trousers and shirt. He donned Pigg's somber attire, even the flat-crowned black hat, a trifle small but adequate.

Garth eyed the undertaker with interest. "One question before I leave you. Would you mind telling me why you're wearing woolen longjohns in the middle of July?"

"My wife. I'm a very modest person."

Garth suppressed a smile, then ordered Dudley Pigg to lie face down on the bed. With a short length of rope, he tied each of the mortician's ankles and wrists to the bedposts, then stuffed a gag in his mouth.

"I know it's not very comfortable, but I'm sure by morning someone will rescue you." He placed several gold pieces on the bedside table. "That's for the use of the hearse and Mrs. Morgan's funeral."

Pigg made a muffled sound of protest, but Garth ignored him. He gathered up the sack of food, his haversack and Jessie's carpetbag. Leaving the lights burning in the house as if nothing was amiss, he slipped out the back door into the night.

The two soldiers positioned across from the Morgan house watched apathetically as the undertaker loaded several items into the back of the hearse. Then the conveyance pulled out the drive and headed down the street.

"Mighty peculiar," one remarked, scratching his beard. "Takin' a corpse out in the night like that."

"Maybe not. I wouldn't want no dead

bodies lyin' around in my house at night."

"Think we ought to report it?"

"What for? The Reb didn't go nowhere." He reached for the bottle and peered at the lighted windows. "I reckon the gal didn't neither."

It was full dark as Garth turned the hearse onto the Emmitsburg Pike. Lights burned in homes, shop windows were dark. He drove casually, trying not to attract attention, but he could barely control the urge to whip the two grays into a gallop. Near the south end of town was a small village of tents. Campfires glowed, a harmonica played a sad song, voices were raised in laughter. The hearse moved past them, unnoticed.

Garth felt a pang of apprehension when he spied several sentries leaning against a fence. They stepped out into the road, one holding a lantern, three others carrying rifles poised to fire. The sight of their blue uniforms made his sweat suddenly turn clammy.

He halted the horses and smiled amicably down at the troopers, trying to conceal his mounting anxiety. "Evenin', gentlemen."

A burly corporal peered curiously up at him, then let his deep-set eyes sweep the hearse. "Strange time to be out with that."

"The family's request. The funeral's tomorrow morning in Frederick. I didn't get the body until late this afternoon, and it took me some time to prepare it." He flashed them an almost simpering smile. "You know how it is."

"Don't expect I do," the corporal said somewhat derisively. "I've seen lots of bodies in the last couple of weeks, an' nobody bothered fixin' *them* up." He squinted into the interior of the hearse through the glass sides. Apparently not satisfied, he walked to the rear, opened the back and held the lantern up for a better look.

Garth's palms were sweating as he held the reins in check, stilling his impulse to bolt the horses and make a run for it. He heard the rear doors click shut, and presently the corporal returned.

"Pass on."

Garth flicked the reins, and the horses broke into a trot. He let out a whistling sigh of relief, but worry flared in his mind for Jessie; this delay had taken up minutes of her precious supply of air.

Once well clear of the sentries, he pushed the horses into a gallop, rode for perhaps a mile, then turned off into a copse of trees. He scrambled down from the seat, ran around to the back of the hearse and flung open the doors. He climbed inside, then unlatched the casket.

Jessie struggled to sit up, sucking in huge lungfuls of air. Garth pulled a canteen from his haversack, but when he offered it to her, she glared at him mutinously.

"I thought you were going to leave me in here to suffocate!"

Moonlight streamed through the glass windows, gleamed on the perspiration on her face. Garth brushed back an errant wisp of her hair. "There were soldiers." He handed her the canteen, and she drank some water. "I couldn't do anything but stop."

"Where's Mr. Pigg?"

"In your bed—just like we planned. Mrs. Purcell will discover him in the morning."

Jessie gave him back the canteen. Her chin trembled slightly, her eyes dull and distant. "And Mama."

"I know how you feel, but we had no choice." He touched her cheek tenderly and gave her a soft smile. "For a little while at least, you can lay back and relax. Keep the lid open, but if I rap on the wall, close it—quick."

Jessie sighed and nodded, looking none too pleased about the prospect. Garth gave her another heartening smile, then climbed out of the hearse. He swung up on the seat, flicked the reins, and the horses broke into a fast trot. Once on the road again, he whipped them into a jarring run.

Hooves thundered on the road, pounding into the dirt. Jessie was being jostled about terribly in her satin-lined box. She cursed lustily at Garth for driving so fast as she bounced against the side of the casket, hitting her head. She sat up, gripping the brass rail to avoid being tossed about further.

Through the etched glass windows she could see trees whipping by in the moonlight, an occasional farm or outbuilding. The horses continued to move at a brisk gallop.

The hearse rocked alarmingly, threatening to fall apart.

Then they were slowing abruptly, and the force of the stop toppled Jessie backward into the coffin. She heard Garth's warning knock and fumbled to pull the casket lid down. It was pitch black inside and hot, stinking of the cloying scent of flowers.

Jessie had never been particularly fond of small, enclosed spaces, and her heart began to race. Beads of sweat popped out on her brow and she felt her muscles going limp with sheer terror. She could hear muted, muffled voices, but couldn't make out the words. The fear, the tension, the unknown all combined to push her dangerously close to exploding. She had to fight down the impulse to open the box, to breathe fresh air, to see what was going on. Panic began to set in, vibrating inside her, a wild thing pounding against her rib cage.

But then they were moving again, rocking away with a fierce jolt. Jessie opened the lid, wiped sweat from her face and breathed a fervent prayer. She couldn't bear being closed up in this dreadful house of death another time.

Garth swung toward the right at the sign-post indicating Hagerstown. He had driven for less than a mile when he came across a deep ravine edged by trees. He drew the horses to a halt, set the brake and climbed down to investigate. The gully was bordered by trees, a steep ditch, but still noticeable from the road. There wasn't a farm or house or town within miles. It was perfect.

He fetched Jessie from the casket, then unloaded the bags. The food sack and carpetbag were fastened to the saddle horse and the two grays were unhitched from the hearse after pulling the conveyance as close to the edge of the ravine as possible.

"I'll need your help, Jessie."

"Why are you doing this?"

"This is the road to Hagerstown. If we're followed, they'll think we dumped the hearse and went southwest."

"And we aren't?"

Garth shook his head, then put his shoulder to the rear of the hearse. "We're going to double back and head toward Frederick. Now, give me a hand."

Jessie placed both palms on the tailgate, and together they pushed with all their might. The hearse was heavy, and it moved slowly. The muscles in Garth's forearms stood out with the effort of pushing; he could hear Jessie's grunts of exertion. But finally the hearse began to roll forward. The front wheels went over the side, and the entire wagon went bouncing down the gully over rocks and tall grass, crashing and splintering at the bottom.

"I hope somebody finds that," Garth said, tossing the flat-crowned hat down into the ravine. It sailed through the air in the moonlight, coming to rest on a bush. He removed the long-tailed jacket and left it on the ground.

"Let's go." He helped Jessie mount the saddled horse, then slung his haversack over one of the grays and swung up onto its back. He fastened the reins of the other gray to his belt. Then he shot Jessie a quizzical glance. "I forgot to ask. Can you ride?"

Her chin lifted defiantly. "Of course I can ride!"

He smiled lazily across at her with a taunting gleam in his eyes. "Some gals can't, you know."

"I can do lots of things."

He caught a hint of pink thigh peeking from beneath her hitched-up skirt as she perched atop the brown gelding. He gave her a mock leer. "I know. And if I wasn't in such a hurry, I might be tempted to test you on one of them."

He kicked his heels into the flanks of the gray, and the horse broke into a trot. Jessie caught up with him, flashing him a challenging look. He wheeled the horse around, away from the road, and cantered through the trees, back toward the road to Frederick.

# 9

Dr. Hollis Tibbets sat on a bench along the wall of the schoolhouse, temporarily converted into the command post of the troops left behind in Gettysburg. Gathered inside the stifling little room were a badly shaken Dudley Pigg, a spiteful-looking Nurse Johnson, the two privates who had been watching the Morgan house, Mary Purcell, and Major Phineas Horton. The major, who had been left in charge of all the men stationed in town, was an aging, big, red-faced man with a wart on his nose and cold, hard eyes.

Tibbets took a handkerchief from his pocket and wiped perspiration from his brow. It had been a hot morning and promised to be an even warmer afternoon. And now all this trouble—the Reb and the Morgan girl gone in the stolen hearse, Pigg found gagged and bound and frightened out of his wits. For once, Tibbets thought dismally, he should have listened to the fiery Nurse Johnson. If Bodine had been arrested immediately, none of this would ever have happened. He had tried to be kind to Jessie—they all had—and now she had betrayed them. Anger and resentment smoldered hotly in his blood.

"Why didn't you report it?" Horton was addressing the two chagrined, slightly hungover privates.

"We didn't think nothin' of it. It just looked like the undertaker was loadin' up the body. How was we to know it was really the Reb?"

Major Horton flung up a hand contemptuously. "You two will be dealt with severely, perhaps even courtmartialed. Maybe that will teach a lesson to all you men who think there's nothing better to do than drink on duty." He turned to Mary Purcell, running a measuring, speculative eye over her. "What did you see or hear last night?"

"Just what I told you. I heard the hearse pull up, then a few minutes later Mr. Bodine and Mr. Pigg carried out the casket. I didn't think anything was wrong. I knew Jessie was uncomfortable with her mother's body in the house."

"And this Bodine—you knew him?"

"Only casually." She fluttered her hands, gazing innocently at the major. "I was told he was a cousin from West Virginia. I had no reason to suspect otherwise."

Major Horton's shoulders slumped in frustrated resignation. "Thank you, Mrs.

Purcell. You may go now."

She started to leave, then turned and glanced back at Dudley Pigg. "I'll be at the service—twelve o'clock sharp. You were paid, you know."

Pigg sighed, nodding his head. "Twelve o'clock it is."

After Mary Purcell had departed Tibbets rose and paced over to the window. Several children were playing in the schoolyard; a tall, thin man was approaching.

"You aren't going to let that rascal get away, are you?" Nurse Johnson demanded. "He's a Reb!" Digust curled her thin lips. "I might have known something was going on with those two. Hattie was too kind, the girl too pretty for her own good."

Dr. Tibbets silently agreed with Nurse Johnson's latter point. If given any encouragement, he would have tried to pursue Jessie Morgan.

"I can't let him get away," Horton said. "God knows what information he may have with him. But I can't spare any men to go after him. Washington wired me back immediately this morning. They want Bodine, but my men must stay here."

"Then he'll get away!"

"No, he won't."

Horton turned as the door opened, and the tall, lanky stranger entered. He had slicked-back brown hair, was clean-shaven with neat sidewhiskers. A patch covered his left eye; his right was black and hard and as shiny as a lump of coal. Tibbets judged him to be in his early thirties and briefly wondered why he wasn't in the service of the Union. Perhaps the loss of his eye.

"Mr. Coffin?" Horton inquired.

The man in civilian clothes gave a slight bow. "Jake Coffin, at your service."

"You understand what you're to do?"

Coffin's mouth lifted in a strangely sinister smile. "Bring back the Reb and the girl."

"Alive, I hope."

Coffin shrugged his thin shoulders. "If possible. I ain't seen the Reb, but I'd know the girl anywhere. Pretty little thing—with all that hair and them big blue eyes."

"I understand you've had experience in such matters?"

"I helped track down John Brown. He didn't get away, did he? I'll find 'em. I'm the best in the business."

Major Horton handed over an envelope of money. "That should be sufficient for your expenses. You'll receive your reward when you return with the prisoners."

A faint frown of perplexity furrowed Tibbets' brow. Jake Coffin was a bounty hunter, and, from the looks of him, none too scrupulous. "The girl. You won't harm her?"

Jake Coffin smiled, but it didn't quite reach his one good eye. "She's a little thing—ought to be easy to handle." He gave a half-mocking salute to Major Horton, turned, and slouched out of the schoolroom. Tibbets felt a sudden rush of apprehension, and his uneasiness gave way to an icy sense of foreboding.

\*   \*   \*

Jessie stifled a yawn as she gazed out the window onto the dusty street in the little town of Leesburg. They had ridden all night, and now here it was midmorning in a scruffy little room at a small hotel. She was bone-chilled and bleary-eyed, but she continued to stare out the window. This was Virginia—the Confederacy—yet it looked no different than Gettysburg before the battle. Women did their shopping, carrying market baskets and toddlers, the same as in Pennsylvania. Merchants sold what wares they had to offer, horses and wagons lumbered over the hard-packed earth that comprised the main street.

Sighing, Jessie turned away from the window and let her eyes come to rest on the bed. The brass headboard was tarnished and the mattress sagged in the middle. Still, it looked ever so inviting, and she sat down on it to remove her shoes.

Garth was out now, despite the fatigue he must be feeling, trying to sell one of the horses and purchase a wagon or buggy. They had both decided they would attract less attention if they traveled in some sort of conveyance.

They had passed through Frederick in the dead of night. The saloons, houses, and shops had all been dark, and no one had seen them, to their knowledge. Saddle-sore and weary, Jessie had wanted to stop for the night, but Garth had insisted they keep moving. And so they had, stopping only once not far from the Maryland town to partake of some of the food they had packed.

Jessie felt dirty, smelled of horses and clay

and longed for a bath. But the hotel had no such luxuries, and if she wanted to bathe, she would have to use the public facilities several blocks away. She was too tired to walk that far, and, besides, her heart was shrinking and twisting with sorrow for what she had left behind.

She lay back on the bed, finding it not nearly as uncomfortable as it looked. Soon, back in Gettysburg, they would be holding her mother's funeral, and she wasn't there to say her final farewell. Had Mary Purcell released Dudley Pigg? Was the town up in arms or had the authorities simply dismissed she and Garth as somewhat peculiar people who ran off in the night in a hearse?

But the funeral. Jessie wanted so much to be there for her mother, and instead here she was in this shabby hotel in Leesburg. A sad, distant look crept into her eyes; she felt an overwhelming sense of loss. Hot tears scalded her eyes, then the sorrow that had been trembling just below the surface broke into the open, and she began to cry, letting go with great, wracking sobs. She wept until sheer exhaustion caused her to sink into dreamless sleep.

Garth stood inside the livery stable, staring with some distaste at the proprietor. He was a small, dark, cadaverous man with a long horse face scarred by pockmarks. He stank of dung and urine, as did the stable.

"I'll give you forty dollars for the horse and the saddle," the man said, squinting at the gelding, then at Garth.

"That horse is worth twice that much!"

The man shrugged. "Times are hard. Folks ain't got much money to spare."

"And the buggy?"

"Over here."

Garth followed the weasel-like proprietor back into the bowels of the stable. He nearly choked on the stench and rubbed at his watering eyes, tearing either from the smell or his exhaustion.

"Here it is."

In the dim light from the wide double doors and what leaked in from the cracks in the walls, Garth studied the buggy. At one time it had been a fine little trap, but now the leather was cracking and the stuffing from the seats protruded. All the same, the axles looked sound, as did the tongue.

"How much?"

"With the horse and saddle—fifteen dollars. In greenbacks or gold." The proprietor spat a stream of tobacco juice into the hay at his feet. "Confederate money—make it a hundred."

Garth handed over the bills, wanting only to be rid of this disgusting creature and find welcome sleep back at the hotel. "I'll need to board the two grays here tonight."

"That'll be another dollar."

With no small amount of relief, Garth paid the stable owner and left the stinking building. Squinting into the sun, he trudged back toward the hotel, but first he stopped at a seedy-looking dry goods store to purchase a hat. In this blinding sun and heat, he would soon be needing one.

Jake Coffin let the undertaker's black coat fall to the ground and stared down at the broken pieces of the hearse in the ravine. It was shortly after noon, and he was perspiring heavily. Briefly, he wondered why he had ever offered his services for this job when he could be back in Gettysburg sipping a cool drink or sporting with one of the willing wenches at the tavern. But a thousand dollars was a lot of money for a man to turn down, and even if Bodine was clever, he would surely be slowed down by the girl.

Coffin removed his jacket and threw it over the rump of his black gelding. He rolled up his shirtsleeves, studying the road to Hagerstown. It had rained intermittantly for the last couple of weeks; the dirt was dry now, but fresh hoofprints would be clearly evident. There were none.

He rubbed a hand across his mouth in a thoughtful fashion. If Bodine and the Morgan girl had indeed gone southwest, that would eventually lead them into Union-occupied territory. Besides, the Reb had his family in South Carolina. At least—from the reports he had received from those who had known Hattie Morgan—she had relatives in that state. It made no sense for Bodine to head toward West Virginia and Kentucky and Tennessee. There were too many Federal troops in that area.

He dismissed the idea with a vague shake of his head and began to pace over the terrain near the ravine. Coffin knew he was good at his job, even if the story he had fed the major about tracking down John Brown was a pack of lies. He had done his share of hunting humans, all right—but his prey had been runaway slaves. Before the war the blacks' owners had paid dearly to have them brought back and punished; now they seldom bothered, and few of them had the funds to pay well. Now Coffin's trade was in spies, but even that was a hit-and-miss game.

He seriously doubted that Garth Bodine was a spy, but if Washington wanted him and was willing to pay, Jake would find him. And for the girl, he would no doubt find her quite entertaining before he got her back to Gettysburg.

Coffin studied the high grass carefully, and his face twisted into a shrewd smile. There were definite hoofprints crushing the grass and depressing the still damp earth here. His hunch had been right, after all, and his mouth curved in smug contempt. Mounting his horse, he followed the trail through the woods, then finally broke out onto the road heading south.

Jessie's eyes fluttered for a second, then opened. The late afternoon sun was streaming through the curtains, and the hotel room was intolerably hot. Perspiration ran down between her breasts and made the waistband of her skirt cling like a corset.

Releasing a wavering sigh, she rolled over and found Garth sleeping beside her, his shirt off, sweat beading in the hairs of his chest. At rest, his face looked almost boyish, so different from the ruggedly lean, planed features she had grown to know so well.

She sat up on the edge of the bed, cradling her head in her hands and rubbing her eyes. She was still tired, but she was even more hungry. Heaving another sigh, she rose from the bed and padded over to the washstand. She poured tepid water into the basin, then began unfastening the buttons of her blouse. She drew down the straps of her camisole over her shoulders and sponged herself. The water felt wonderfully cool on her skin, and again she yearned for a bath. But this would have to do for now. Hopefully, in the next town they stopped at—wherever that might be—there would be a tub available for her use.

A slow wave of depression came over her. Her eyes were red from crying, and the water didn't seem to help. Her mind turned once more to the funeral and all the tragic events that had led up to it, but she pushed the memories away. She had to stop feeling sorry for herself. The past was past, and she must force herself to look forward to her future, whatever that might bring.

Regaining her composure, she rummaged through the carpetbag, finding pins and a hairbrush. It was too hot to wear her hair down, and she set about arranging it on top of her head.

"Quite a fetching picture."

She turned at the sound of Garth's voice. He was propped up in bed, watching, lazily admiring her with eyes full of smoldering emotion. She suddenly realized her state of undress, and, a faint blush rising to her cheeks, reached to pull up the top of her camisole.

Garth assumed a wounded look of disappointment. "Now why did you do that? I was enjoying myself immensely."

She frowned, not knowing what to say. "I don't know." Why *should* she become so modest all of a sudden? Back home . . . but it was different then.

Garth swung his legs over the bed, approaching her in his stockinged feet. The back of his hand caressed her cheek, traced over her collarbone and bare shoulder. She felt her body flush with warmth. "Why don't you take the rest off?"

She fought down the trembling sensations his mere presence could evoke and turned back to finish her hair. "Because it's hotter than an oven in here, and I'm hungry."

"Now that you mention it, I'm a little hungry myself." He bent to brush his lips against her shoulder; his mustache tickled delightfully, and Jessie had to suppress a shiver. "But after supper . . . ?" He let the question hang suggestively.

She looked at his reflection in the mirror, his dark head bent, nuzzling her neck. She reached up and ran her fingers through his hair. "After supper."

He straightened up and gently turned her around to face him. "After supper what?"

She caressed his cheek and smiled into his eyes, gazing at him with a smoky, seductive look. "I want you to make love to me."

Jake Coffin's frustration mounted as he paced down Frederick's main thoroughfare. He was hot and dusty; his brows gathered in an angry frown. He had spoken to every hotel proprietor and livery barn owner in the town, and at each place he had received the same answer: no. No one had seen a man and a woman stop here last night. But they all agreed on one thing—none of them would easily forget a girl fitting Jessie Morgan's description.

Jake paused outside a general store, removed his hat, and ran his fingers through his slick brown hair. Perhaps he had been wrong; perhaps the pair had indeed gone on to Hagerstown. He dismissed the notion immediately. He had seen the horses' prints, and they had led here—to Frederick.

Snorting derisively, he kicked at a pebble and continued to amble up the street. It didn't make sense. He was sure they would have stopped here for the night, especially with the girl along. He knew females well enough—they required certain comforts such as a soft bed, a pleasant meal, a toilet. Unless Jessie was a lot tougher than she appeared.

"Hey, mister."

Jake glanced up from his thoughts,

realizing he was practically face-to-face with a young man. His hair was disheveled and dirty, his beard needed combing and washing. His clothes were baggy and stained with every conceivable substance. One leg was gone at the knee, and he leaned heavily on a crutch.

"Got a few pennies to spare for a disabled soldier? I served my country proud."

The breath that hit Jake was fetid and sour, stinking of whiskey and vomit. Jake swallowed his nausea, feeling a strong rush of disgust. "Nothin' for you, lad."

The ex-soldier's face knotted into a frown. "Lookin' for somethin', are you?"

"Nothin' you could help me with."

"Jes' try me. Lem—that's me—don't miss much that goes on in this town. My leg pains me somethin' awful, an' I don't sleep much."

Jake studied Lem intently. The eyes were intelligent, though a bit bleary at the moment. "You see any strangers pass through here? A man and a woman on horseback maybe?"

Lem grinned, revealing crooked, yellowish teeth. "I surely did. 'Bout eleven or thereabouts last night. A feller and a gal. She was ridin' a brown horse, him a gray with no saddle, and towin' another 'un behind him."

Jake's face came alive with interest. "They didn't stop?"

"Not that I could see. I was sittin' right out in front of the saloon across the street yonder. Saw 'em go right by. Thought it peculiar. Pretty gal, she was, in the moonlight. All this long, dark hair flyin' out behind her in the wind."

Jake smiled ingratiatingly at the young man and clapped him on the shoulder. "Let me buy you a drink, Lem. You hungry?"

Garth could tell that Jessie was out of sorts—had been almost from the moment they had entered the small dining room in the hotel. The place was hardly elegant, with stained checkered tablecloths and silverware that looked none too clean. And eating hearty meals were perhaps a half dozen southern soldiers, laughing and drinking, eyeing Jessie with frank admiration.

She had been extremely quiet during their meal—plentiful but plain—and Garth had not failed to miss her irritation at the presence of the soldiers. Soon that annoyance had turned to sadness, a kind of melancholy introspection, and he had left her to her thoughts.

He supposed it was the grief she felt for her mother and would go on feeling until God knew when. Garth had never had to personally cope with the death of a close loved one and wasn't exactly sure how to deal with it. Perhaps the closest he had ever come to real sorrow was when, at the age of eight, his mammy had died of pneumonia. He had missed her coddling, her scolding, the strong black hands that could magically make dough into all sorts of delicious treats. In the war his unit had fought relatively unscathed until Gettysburg, and those who had died had only been acqaintances. For Garth, death was an alien thing, a mystery, and his faith was small enough that he had not even that to believe in.

He closed the hotel room door quietly, slipping the latch into place behind him. Jessie sat down on the bed, staring vacantly at the tattered rug on the floor. Her thick, dark lashes glistened with tears. Garth didn't know what to say or do. Looking at her like this made his heart ache so badly that he turned away from her, going to look out the window. The lowering sun turned the cloudbanks on the western horizon into brilliant shades of fiery reds and purples.

"If it wasn't for them, Mama would still be alive." Jessie sank her teeth into her lower lip to keep from crying.

"For who? Those soldiers downstairs?"

"Them—and you."

Garth turned and saw the bitter spark of anger and hurt in her eyes. "It was a Yankee who shot her."

"I know that." She wiped at her eyes and cheeks with her fingers. "But if your army hadn't come in the first place, there wouldn't have been any need for a hospital—or drunken guards."

Garth sighed despairingly. He didn't want to argue with her, not now. Looking at her, with the red hue of the setting sun turning her skin a golden tan, making auburn streaks in her hair, he only wanted to make love to her.

"I can't possibly know what you're feeling," he said. "But in a while, the hurt will pass."

"Maybe the hurt will, but what about the hate?" Her blue eyes sparked angrily at him. "I despised you Rebs before. Think how I feel now."

Garth sat down beside her on the bed. The mattress creaked and sagged. "The hate will go away too. You hated me at first."

Her eyes measured him doubtfully. "You're still a Reb."

Garth lightly traced a finger over her face. "I'm a man, Jessie. Flesh and blood, like anybody else. And there was something special between us. Has that died too?"

She looked at him keenly, then released a long-suffering sigh. "I don't know."

He sought the sweet taste of her lips with his own, kissed her gently, felt her stir beneath his touch. Her arms crept around his neck, and he held her tightly to him. Her full breasts were mounds of ripe flesh, pushing against his chest; he could feel her hands trembling ever so slightly as they caressed the back of his neck. Nothing had changed between them. Hattie might be gone and they were on the run, but the powerful attraction they felt for one another was still there, still as hot and demanding as ever.

He cradled her in his arms and nuzzled her neck, gently nibbling at an earlobe. Shivering with delight, she yielded to his touch, answered his kisses with a like response. He stroked her body with gentle, practiced hands until her little moan of pleasure reassured him, and Garth felt himself being swallowed up in the heat and passion she aroused in him.

Hot and dusty from his travels and inquiries, after nearly falling off his horse in a creek, Jake Coffin entered the Leesburg Hotel. It was his first stop in town. Jessie Morgan had withdrawn nearly all her funds from the bank. The Leesburg was hardly elegant, but it was the best the town had to offer. If the two fugitives had money, it was doubtful they would choose to stay in any of the other fleabags—if indeed they had stopped here at all.

He stepped up to a sleepy-eyed desk clerk, so old and wrinkled Jake wondered if he was a relic from the Revolution. "Did a couple check in here earlier?"

The old man blinked owlishly at him. "A couple of what?"

Jake scowled savagely. "A couple—a man and a woman. He's tall and dark, wears a mustache. She's short and pretty with dark hair—lots of it."

The clerk squinted, his leathery face tight with suspicion. "Why you be wantin' to know?"

"I'm a friend of theirs." Had Bodine used an alias? If he had, and Jake asked for him by name, he was lost. "I have good news for them."

"Looked like they could use it. Mr. and Mrs. Bodine."

Jake could barely suppress his glee. "In that case, I'll take a room for the night."

"Just one night?"

"Unless my friends stay longer." Jake pulled out a gold piece and handed it over to the clerk. "What room are they in?"

The old man appeared not to hear. He was scrutinizing the coin with great care. "Ain't seen one of these in over a year. 'Fraid your change'll be in Confederate notes, mister."

Jake shrugged. "Just as long as you make up for the depreciation." He fairly goggled at the wad of bills he was given in return; the currency in the south was evidently devaluating faster than he had heard.

"Room seven," the clerk said, handing over a well-worn key.

"And Mr. Bodine? His room?"

"Three."

Jake inclined his head in thanks, then turned to scan the dining room. It was busy, the food smelled enticing, and a buxom serving girl gave him the eye as she passed. Jake hefted his saddlebags and headed for the stairs. Bodine and the girl wouldn't be going anywhere until morning; they could wait. Right now what Jake wanted was a hot meal and maybe a tumble with the serving wench.

# 10

Jessie stirred at an unfamiliar sound, and her eyelids fluttered open. She turned her head on the pillow to see Garth entering the room, clumsily balancing a tray as he closed the door with his foot.

"Breakfast in bed, madame." He gallantly placed the tray on her lap as she scrambled up to lean against the pillows, pulling the sheet up over her bosom.

Her eyes widened as they swept the plate of eggs, hamsteak, fried potatoes, and toasted bread. There was a glass of milk, a steaming cup of coffee. She looked at Garth in wonder. "What's this for?"

"You fed me enough in bed while I was recuperating. I reckon it's time I did the same for you."

A soft smile curved her lips, and her eyes sparkled radiantly. Garth looked exceptionally handsome this morning. He had donned

clean brown trousers, forsaking the
mortician's too short, baggy black ones. He
was freshly shaven, and the new tan hat he
had purchased yesterday was perched atop
his head at a rakish angle.

"Is it enough?" he asked.

"Enough!" She laughed softly. "I'll get as
fat as a pig."

"Remember—we've got a long drive ahead
of us today."

A small frown touched her brow. "Yes, I
almost forgot. Not that I particularly want to
stay here."

Garth's eyes glowed with dark amusement.
"I didn't think you would."

"Have you eaten yet?"

He shook his head negatively. "I thought
I'd go downstairs and do that now. Maybe
buy a paper and see what's going on farther
south."

"You should have brought some breakfast
up for yourself."

A ribald twinkle lighted his eyes. "I might
be tempted to have dessert first." He leaned
down, kissed her forehead and turned to
leave the room. "Meet me outside in forty-
five minutes. I left my watch on the dresser
for you." He picked up his haversack and left
the room.

Jessie gazed at the closed door for several
moments, sipping her milk. For a Reb, Garth
Bodine wasn't so bad, after all. He was handsome, thoughtful, considerate and extremely
talented in bed. Of course, she had no one
with whom to compare him on that score, but

he never failed to bring her senses alive. Smiling contentedly, she picked up knife and fork and began to devour her meal like a woman on the brink of starvation.

Garth pushed his empty plate aside and drank some coffee. He noted from his seat at a corner table that the dining room was just as busy as ever. There were soldiers and civilians, all men. It was just as well Jessie had eaten in their room.

His eyes moved slowly over the other diners. No one seemed to take any special notice of him, except one man, seated alone at the far end of the room. As Garth's gaze came to rest on him, the man was staring pensively at him. He was tall and lean, neatly dressed, with a patch over one eye. Even from this distance, Garth felt a shudder of distaste. That one good eye was like an onyx mirror, malicious and almost evil.

Garth dropped his gaze and picked up the newspaper, but gooseflesh raced over his skin. There was something about that one-eyed man that bothered him—even frightened him a trifle. There was a malignancy about him, as sure as any cancer.

Garth dismissed him from his mind and studied the paper. There was scattered fighting around Richmond and Fredericksburg, a cavalry raid at Rocky Mount, North Carolina, another led by Morgan into Kentucky.

He sighed, paid for his meal and got up from the table. He fervently hoped he and

Jessie wouldn't encounter any of those skirmishes taking place on a near daily basis. He glanced casually at the one-eyed man as he passed, but the stranger was engrossed in his meal.

Jake Coffin belched loudly after swallowing the last of his potatoes. Thoughtfully, he rubbed his hand across his mouth in an absent manner. Bodine was tall and good-looking; so had the man in the tan hat been. But if that was Bodine, where was the girl? Doubt furrowed his brow. That man couldn't be Bodine!

He sent a considering glance around the dining room. Phoebe, the serving girl, wasn't in evidence this morning. Jake smirked to himself. He doubted she had ever had the kind of workout he had given her last night; she was probably still recuperating. For himself, he felt in fine fettle. Phoebe had been lusty and inventive, and Jake was completely sated. But he had learned several years ago to be careful with whores. One in Savannah had put his left eye out with a hat pin when he had become too demanding. Unfortunately, she hadn't lived to boast about it.

To hell with Phoebe and all the whores! The woman Jake wanted was Jessie Morgan, and he intended to give her all he had before returning her to Gettysburg. And, if his luck still held out, he might have her soon—perhaps in a matter of hours.

Cackling maliciously to himself, he rose from the table and headed up the stairs to get his revolver before visiting "Mr. and Mrs. Bodine" in room number three.

Jessie closed the door behind her and stepped out into the hall just as Jake Coffin was entering his room. Hauling her carpet-bag with her, she descended the stairs and made a hasty exit out the front door of the hotel, followed by a rude invitation from one of the soldiers calling after her.

She hated it here and knew it would only get worse as they traveled deeper into the heart of the Confederacy. Sometimes she doubted her own sanity at making this wild journey with Garth. She should have let him go on alone and stayed behind in Gettysburg. Surely the Federal authorities would do nothing to her. She and Hattie had been respected and well liked in the community. Her friends would stand by her—or would they? These were uncertain times, and nothing was guaranteed anymore. Not even friendship.

Garth pulled up in a dilapidated buggy, drawn by Dudley Pigg's two grays. Jessie heaved a sigh of disappointment. Still, it was better than riding horseback all the way to Charleston. Once again she wondered if they would ever get that far, and felt a sudden pang of apprehension.

Garth took the satchel from her, then reached over and gave her a hand up. "It's not much, I'm afraid. But I got a map."

Mocking amusement lighted her eyes. "That's helpful. At least we'll know where we're going."

Garth flicked the reins, and the buggy lurched forward, heading south out of town. Garth had decided to avoid anything even remotely close to Washington. Jessie glanced disinterestedly at Leesburg, not the least bit sorry to see the last of it. But where they were heading . . . A sudden foreboding descended upon her.

Jake's face was knotted in rage. He made an abrupt, angry gesture as he stood inside the foul-smelling livery barn. He examined the brown gelding with its white stockings, then turned to the stable owner, his face a dark, unhealthy crimson, almost glowing with fury.

"When did he take the buggy out?"

The proprietor stood with his eyes downcast, twisting an old, battered hat in his hands. "An hour ago—maybe less."

"Was there a woman with him?"

"Didn't see any. Just him."

Jake's brows drew together in a fierce scowl. "Did he say where he was going?"

"Nope. But he was a nice fella. Polite, well mannered."

Jake stormed out of the livery barn, striking his fist into his palm. He mounted his horse, swearing vehemently. Several people paused to stare, and he glared at them. Damn Bodine! And damn the girl! But he would find them; Jake Coffin seldom failed. But he had missed his opportunity.

Drumming his heels into the flanks of his

gelding, he thundered out of Leesburg, kicking up clouds of dust.

Jessie was almost dozing in the buggy. It was afternoon, warm and sunny but not too hot, and there had been very little traffic on the road. They had made good time, only stopping twice to water the horses and attend to the call of nature.

"I wonder if I'll get a bath tonight," she said wistfully.

"It's the horses working up a sweat—not you."

Jessie flashed him a quick smile, but her humor abruptly died as she heard an ear-piercing scream, a kind of Indian war whoop. Alarmed, she turned to Garth; his mouth was set in a grim line. "What . . . ?"

"The old familiar Rebel yell."

The scream—for that was what Jessie thought of it as—came again, and Garth whipped the horses into a gallop. The buggy rattled and rocked; Jessie had to hang on to keep from being thrown about. As they rounded a bend, she caught a glimpse of a large number of mounted men in gray cresting a hill. Down on a low-lying field was a smaller group of Union cavalry.

Jessie's stomach churned with horror. There was going to be a battle, and she and Garth were right in the middle of it. It was Gettysburg all over again, only this time there was no house in which to hide. A cord of panic tightened around her chest and throat.

The grays ran faster, their hooves pounding over the rutted dirt road. A wheel hit a bump; Jessie was lifted six inches off the seat. She clutched frantically at the dash and the side rail, struggling to quiet the shriek of utter panic that was building within her.

She turned back to see the two sides charging at each other, all the while the Confederates screeching that ghastly yell. She saw a lone rider on the road far behind them veering off into the trees for cover.

The buggy careened sharply to the right, and Jessie feared it would topple over. They were racing down a side road, a road in even worse condition than the one they had just left. Up ahead, surrounded by trees but still visible, Jessie could see buildings, and as they neared, she could make out a farmhouse and barn. They were in a deplorable state. The front porch canted, the sides were blistered from the heat and the chimney leaned precariously. The barn was even worse.

Gunshots in the distance rattled like a drum roll. Jessie's mouth had gone cottony and her heart was pounding. Garth drove the buggy through the gaping, sagging doors of the barn, then pulled hard on the reins. The little ramshackle trap came to a jolting halt.

"Get out and help me shut the doors!" he ordered.

Jessie swallowed convulsively as her fear grew, but she managed to force herself to climb down from the buggy, nearly stumbling in the process. Her shoes kicked up hay as she ran for one of the doors. It was heavy; the wood was warped and one of the hinges was caked with rust. The gunfire continued to grow louder.

She darted outside and pushed. The door wouldn't budge. She threw her shoulder against it and heaved all her weight at it. Hinges groaned, old wood crackled, but it moved several inches. Blind panic surging through her, she pushed again. Another few inches.

Then Garth was there, lending his weight. "Get inside and pull!" he barked, as if issuing orders to his unit.

There was nothing but a thick rope loop for a handle. Jessie tugged fiercely at it, her chest heaving with tension and exertion. The door began to swing shut, and she nearly lost her balance. Horses neighed, guns fired, shouts rose. Nearly sobbing, Jessie gave a mighty yank just as Garth pushed. The door closed within a foot.

Garth sidled around it, took hold of the rope handle and pulled it shut the rest of the way.

"Keep the horses quiet," he told her.

Jessie moved to the two grays, but they seemed unaffected by the rising commotion outside. Both were munching dry hay contentedly.

Jessie leaned against the wall and breathed deeply, looking over her surroundings. Sunlight seeped through wide cracks in the boards, making a kind of twilight world of the barn. A few harnesses, their leather rotten, hung on the walls. There were tubs and buckets, and a child's wagon with one wheel broken. Moldy bags of feed were piled in one corner.

Garth was at one of the cracks, peering out, his revolver drawn. There was a cold glint in his gray eyes, like chips of slate, and his expression was hardened with determination. Jessie crept over to one of the walls and squinted through another crack.

The two squads of mounted horsemen were in the yard now. Horses kicked up great clouds of dust and men charged around like a pack of wild Indians, making a terrible racket. Most of the soldiers wore beards and mustaches, giving them an added look of malice. Their wide-brimmed slouch hats covered most of their features. Never had Jessie seen such wild abandon, such violence.

She watched, fascinated and repelled, as a Union trooper fired his pistol at a Confederate rider not a yard away. The side of his face disappeared in a spray of blood and teeth.

She turned away from the macabre sight, a strangled moan coming from her lips. She covered her mouth with both hands, and felt Garth touch her shoulder.

"Get in the buggy—down on the floor. A bullet could break through this flimsy wood without any trouble."

When Jessie didn't move, he gave her a gentle shove. Slightly dazed, she moved slowly, as if in a dream. Then another shot shocked the adrenaline in her body awake, and she fairly jumped into the buggy.

She crouched on the floor, her heart pounding in her ears. She pressed her knuckles to her mouth, recoiling in stark horror. It seemed like hours, but it must only have been minutes until the gunshots and rumbling hooves receded.

Garth waited until the last of the riders was gone. Two bodies lay sprawled in the grass; a horse lay bleeding near a tree. He turned away, holstered his revolver and helped Jessie out of the buggy. He wrapped her in his arms and held her tightly to him. She was trembling, her thin shoulders shaking against his chest, and at that moment she was very dear to him.

After a few minutes he gently held her away from him. His eyes found hers and held them. They were steady; she was in control again. Her brief moment of fear and terror had passed.

"I'm going out for a minute," he said.

"What for? There might be more of them out there!"

He shook his head, looking into her eyes. "Not live ones, anyway."

Garth pushed open the door on the side that held the least resistance and strode briskly toward the two soldiers. The grass was trampled. A saber lay on the ground; not far away was a blue slouch hat.

He went first to the soldier in gray, lying on his back. Unseeing eyes bulged from a shattered, bloody face; his head was little more than a misshapen lump of bone and bloody flesh. The Union trooper was a few yards away, facedown. Garth rolled him over. His eyes were still wide with fright, his mouth gaping open in what must have been his final scream of pain and terror.

The horse was thrashing pitifully on the ground. Garth stepped over to it, unholstered his revolver and fired. The horse lay still. Grimly, he removed the blanket roll from behind the saddle, then returned to the dead Yankee. Lifting the corpse by the armpits, he dragged it over to where the faceless man lay. He unfolded the blanket and draped it over the bodies.

"Who won this skirmish, boys?"

For a moment, he stood staring expressionlessly down at the two corpses. Then, choking back bile as it surged up from his stomach, Garth turned away and returned to the barn.

Jake Coffin peered out from behind a large clump of thorn bushes. The cavalry was gone and, thankfully, they hadn't stumbled upon either him or his horse. Leading his mount behind him, he emerged from his shelter, surveying the scene before him.

There were perhaps a half dozen bodies scattered over an acre of land. He stopped at the first one he came upon, ignored the blood and gore seeping out of a chest wound, and knelt down. In the Federal soldier's pockets he found cash and a fine engraved gold watch. Depositing these items in his own pocket, he moved on to the next man. He wasn't dead.

"Help me, mister." The voice, with a pronounced drawl, was a hoarse whisper. Blood poured from a deep saber wound in the shoulder.

"I can't help you. I'm no doctor." Jake's smile was cruel and contemptuous. " 'Sides, we ain't nowhere near a hospital."

The man let out a low, whimpering cry. His breathing was shallow and obviously painful. He was too weak to put up any protest when Jake rummaged through his pockets. A few Confederates notes and a daguerreotype in a case were all he found.

Jake opened the leather case and studied the photograph. "Pretty girl," he remarked, tossing it onto the bloody grass beside the soldier. The man attempted to reach out for it. Jake started to move on.

"Mister . . . Please!"

Jake disregarded the miserable entreaty and continued to prowl through the pockets of the other dead. Another was alive but unconscious, congealed blood matting his blond hair and drying on his face; flies crawled into his nostrils and open mouth.

All in all, Jake collected a little over a hundred dollars, four good watches, an exquisite ivory-handled knife and an opal ring. This last he had to acquire by cutting off the finger of the unconscious blond soldier.

Jessie followed Garth up the front steps of the house; the old wood creaked, threatening to splinter under their weight. He pushed open the door and stepped inside.

"I reckon the owners lit out shortly after the war started," he said. "There's been fighting around here nearly all the time."

Jessie didn't care who owned the house or where they were. Even if it wasn't likely she would get her bath tonight, at least there might be a broom to sweep a clean spot on which to lay a blanket and sleep.

As they entered, a large rat scurried away from her, squealing, its long tail whipping behind it like a snake. She only had to take one look around her to make up her mind where the place to spend the night was. Rats darted over the mantel, along the baseboards, nested in an old chair with the stuffing out. Their droppings covered the bare board floor. So did cockroaches.

She turned and fled back outside, down the steps, her head spinning, feeling sick and confused. For a moment—between the vermin and the grisly cavalry fight—she was afraid she might vomit, but she swallowed back the bile.

Garth was beside her, his arm curved around her waist. "We can sleep in the buggy."

She nodded dazedly, still numb from all that had taken place today. "You'll be uncomfortable with your long legs."

"I'll manage just fine." He gave her a brief hug. "Why don't you see what we've got for supper? But no cookfire. I'll see if the well water's fit to drink."

Jessie trudged back into the barn, her face a study in despair. Yet she was touched by

Garth's concern and protectiveness. He
didn't need a crying, frightened female by his
side; he needed someone calm and self-
sufficient. And that was just what she
intended to be.

Forcing herself to hold her emotions in
check, she pulled out the sack containing
their food. There was enough for tonight and
tomorrow morning. At least they wouldn't
starve. Recalling Garth's map, she thought
they must be fairly close to Manassas. If the
town hadn't shut down completely after two
major battles, they could restock there. Then
they had only two more days of driving in
relatively unpopulated areas—another day to
Fredericksburg, and then on to Richmond.

On to Richmond—how many times had she
heard that slogan chanted in the streets of
Gettysburg? So far, the Union army hadn't
been able to accomplish that feat, but Jessie
Morgan would. She shuddered, and her
twisted smile more closely resembled a
sneer. She had no desire to visit the capital of
the Confederacy, the heart and lifeblood of
her enemies. Would she catch sight of Jeff
Davis or Jeb Stuart or Stonewall Jackson?
What a heroine she would be if she could put
a bullet between the eyes of one of those men.
A heroine postumously, she reflected grimly.

Garth returned with a bucket of water.
"It's fresh and tastes wonderful!" He poured
some into their tin cups. "This is the cleanest
pail I could find. I'll use one of these others to
water the horses." He picked up a bucket
from the discards in the barn and vanished

outside again.

Jessie saw that the feed for the grays was almost gone. She glanced dubiously at the sacks of grain in the corner but dismissed them immediately. They had been wet and dry too many times to count. The horses could eat hay tonight, with the feed saved for tomorrow.

She laid out a meager supper of cheese, bread and preserves; she couldn't even boil water for coffee. In the morning they could dine on apples and still more cheese. Her eyes darkened with resentment and suppressed rebellion. If it wasn't for the Rebs . . .

She shoved the thought roughly aside. There was no sense dwelling on the circumstances that had brought her to this; there was nothing she could do about it anyway. As Garth reentered the barn, she forced a cheery smile to her lips and beckoned him toward their supper.

# 11

Garth awoke feeling stiff and sore from sleeping in the cramped confines of the buggy. He turned to look at Jessie. She was breathing softly and rhythmically, her face as serene and lovely as ever. She had been through a lot in the past few days—far more personal turmoil and grief than many men could withstand. Unexpectedly, a surge of affection went through him. He admired a woman with spirit and intelligence, and she quite obviously had both of these qualities.

He climbed down from the buggy, stretched, and gave a yawn that cracked the hinges of his jaw. The horses, unhitched but tied securely to the side of the barn, were once again eating hay. Garth gave them the last of the feed.

"That's all you'll get for a while, fellas." He patted them, then picked up the bucket.

"Where are you going?"

He turned and saw that Jessie was awake and stirring. Dark, disarrayed hair flowed about her shoulders and framed a beautiful face, even fresh from sleep. "For water."

"Can we boil some for coffee?"

He smiled at the hopeful, almost childlike expression on her face. "Probably. If I don't see somebody else's cookfire."

She scrambled down from the buggy, combing her fingers through her hair. "I'm starved. I feel dirty, and I've got to . . ." She broke off, embarrassed.

He flashed her an indulgent smile. "So do I."

Garth pushed open the barn door, stepped out into the sunlight and froze. Beside him, he heard Jessie's sharp intake of breath, the small trembling cry that came from her lips.

Leaning against the well, his hat cocked jauntily to one side, was the one-eyed man Garth had seen in the dining room in Leesburg. He was toying negligently with his revolver, and when he saw Garth and Jessie, a smile broke across his craggy features.

"Mornin', folks. You must be Captain Garth Bodine. And you, little lady, are Jessie Morgan. No mistakin' you."

Garth tried to show some bravado, but waves of fear and nausea passed over him. "Who are you? What do you want?"

"Name's Jake Coffin. And what I want is you."

Garth's stomach twisted in knots. Coffin kept playing with his gun, but Garth didn't doubt he knew how to handle it. His own was still in its holster in the barn, and he silently cursed himself for a fool. Still, he thought with self-contempt, who am I to think I could get the drop on him?

"Government sent me to find you," Coffin went on conversationally, but his smile was positively eerie. "Both of you. Seems you left Gettysburg in a bit of a hurry."

Jessie moved nearer to Garth and clutched at his arm. She stared up at him, a look of stark terror in her eyes. He mustered a reasurring smile for her, then turned back to Coffin.

"You don't want us. I'm not this Captain . . . whoever."

Coffin still had that strange, twisted half-smile on his face. "You ain,'t huh? Too bad, 'cause I'm still takin' you back with me." His one eye moved to Jessie, and there was a faintly leering curl to his lip. "And the lady."

Jessie's face was as pale as chalk. Garth searched his mind frantically for a solution, and in spite of his rising panic, he tried to think clearly. He remained stiffly alert, not relaxing his guard. He hadn't liked the looks of Jake Coffin back in Leesburg; he liked him even less now.

His first impulse was to try to run at the man and overpower him, but the notion vanished as quickly as it came. Coffin was, after all, armed.

"I got a rope here," Coffin said. "And I want you to walk over here slow and easy. You, Jessie, stay put."

Garth could see no other choice. He took

one step, but Jessie's hand on his arm held him back.

"No, Garth!"

He shrugged off her hand, took another step.

"*Garth!*" Her voice had risen to a strangled, desperate stridency.

Garth ignored her. He was sweating, felt clammy. This man would take him back north and throw him in prison. But why? He was only one soldier out of thousands.

He stopped, his eyebrows gathering in a look of puzzlement. "Why do you want me?"

"General Horton thinks you're a spy. So does Dr. Tibbets. I reckon even Abe Lincoln does too."

"A spy! Me?"

"You were in Gettysburg a long time."

"I was never even out of the house."

Coffin shrugged. "Don't make no never mind to me. I only do what I get paid to do. Now hurry up. I got business with the lady."

Garth was appalled. Rage blazed up in him; a muscle twitched at the corner of his mouth. Once he—Garth—was bound and safely restrained, Coffin planned to have his way with Jessie. The fear left him, was replaced by a hot flash of anger that swept through him.

"Garth, look!"

It was Jessie's voice, high-pitched and excited. He turned his head and saw her pointing up at the sky.

"Won't work, little lady," Coffin said. "You figure I'll look up too, and then your friend here can rush me."

Garth had no idea what Jessie was pointing to—something real or imagined. He was too busy trying to figure out a way to save them both. Then it happened. A huge, monstrous dark shadow passed slowly over the ground, like a great dragon. Coffin did look up; Garth did not.

Jessie stepped back, put a hand to her mouth and bit down on her knuckles. Garth charged at Coffin just as the observation balloon passed overhead. Garth lunged for Coffin's arm, hit it hard, and the gun fell out of his hand. Jessie tried to catch her thoughts, tried to reason away her fear, and scramble after it. It was heavy, but with two hands to steady it, she kept it trained on Coffin.

He had staggered backward from the force of Garth's weight, but by now he had regained his balance. In a blur of motion, Coffin's right hand shot out and caught Garth square in the face. Garth's head snapped back, blood dribbling from the side of his mouth. A scream was ripped from Jessie's throat, a sound of strangled fear and dismay.

Undaunted, Garth once more launched himself at his adversary, growling in rage. His fist crashed into Coffin's cheekbone, splitting the skin and sending him to his knees. Garth hit him hard in the neck. Coffin fell to the ground, putting his hands to his throat, gagging and choking. Then he crumpled into a formless heap.

Jessie shivered with a sudden release of tension and ran to Garth's side. He was sucking in huge, rasping lungfuls of air, but the only damage he seemed to have sustained was a cut lip. He wiped the blood from his mouth and chin with a handkerchief.

"How did he find us?" Jessie's voice was breathless and uncertain. "We were so careful!"

Garth gave a disconsolate shake of his head, eyeing the revolver she still held in her hands. "I ought to finish him off."

Her eyes registered horror. "Just murder him?"

Hatred burned undisguised in Garth's eyes. "You know what he had planned for you, don't you?"

She lowered her eyes, bit her lip. "I know. But there's been so much killing already. The soldiers yesterday, all the men in Gettysburg. My mother." A wave of despair engulfed her.

"I know." Garth pursed his lips and blew out some air. He studied Jake Coffin's unmoving form, a look of thoughtful consideration on his face. "But I don't want him catching up to us again."

He walked over to the unconscious man, grasped him by the shoulders and dragged him over to the porch. With the rope Coffin had intended to use on his prisoners, Garth bound his hands together and secured them behind one of the wooden columns supporting the porch roof. He then went over to Coffin's horse, unlooped the bridle from a branch, and gave the animal a sound slap on the rump. The horse bolted and dashed off into a grove of trees.

"Now what?" Jessie asked.

"We start on our way for Manassas and some food for us and the grays. Him"—he jerked his thumb at Coffin—"we leave. Maybe somebody'll find him, maybe the buzzards will get him. Either way, we'll be long gone."

Some semblance of calm was returning to Jessie at last. Her heartbeat had slowed from a gallop to a fast trot; her hands had stopped trembling. She still held on to Coffin's gun.

"I'll hitch up the buggy," Garth told her. "You fill the canteens."

Jessie nodded listlessly and picked up the bucket Garth had dropped. As he passed her, she handed him Coffin's revolver.

In a matter of minutes, they were loaded up and ready to go. As they pulled out the drive, Jessie looked back at the one-eyed man, still unconscious. Far above to the south was the observation balloon, now only a mere dot in the clear blue sky.

Jake was sweating like a pig; perspiration ran over his face and stung his one good eye. The pain in his head was like sledgehammer blows pounding inside his temples. Occasionally, waves of dizziness attacked him, but he fought them off. He was powerfully thirsty, his throat as raw as sandpaper. The well, only a few yards away, looked ever so inviting, but he couldn't reach it.

Damn Bodine! Jake could feel his anger

make his blood run faster. He worked a little harder behind his back, causing even more sweat to run into his eye. Some time after he had come to, he had discovered a thick splinter in the beam to which he was tied. After considerable maneuvering, he was able to slip the rope into the crotch formed between the splinter and the post. By moving his hands gently, the rope caught and snagged. Now, after working this way for more than two hours, he could feel the fibers beginning to tear. But it was agonizing work, awkward and uncomfortable, and his shoulders ached from the tedious, careful effort.

Judging from the position of the sun, it was well past noon. By now his horse could be anywhere—so could Bodine and the girl. Renewed rage burst in his head like a bright, hot light. His revolver was gone; at least he didn't see it lying about anywhere. All he had were the clothes on his back, his money and the loot he had taken from the corpses yesterday.

A shudder of disgust ran through him. If he didn't soon free himself, he might well become one himself. The two dead soldiers and the horse were already beginning to decompose in the heat, and his stomach spasmed from the stench.

Why hadn't Bodine killed him? That was a question that had plagued him all morning. If it had been the other way around, Jake wouldn't have thought twice about wasting a bullet on the Reb. And the girl . . . Jake sighed in admiration. With her full-busted, petite figure and all that magnificent hair tumbling loose, she had looked more alluring than ever this morning.

Redoubling his efforts, Jake worked his hands some more, felt another few fibers snap. He gave a tentative tug, separating his wrists, and felt more of the rope give way. He sawed carefully for another five minutes, then gave a mighty pull. The rope broke in two; his hands were free.

Jake slumped forward and closed his eye in relief, wiping sweat from his face. He rolled and bunched his shoulders, trying to get the kinks out, then bent to untie his feet. He stood, but his vision blurred, and the landscape seemed to weave in front of him. When the vertigo passed he lurched toward the well in a staggering, drunken gait. He hauled up the bucket, gulped down several huge mouthfuls, then dumped its contents over his head. The water felt cool and refreshing, seemed to bring his senses back to order again.

He drank more water, this time slowly. It eased the rawness in his throat, but did nothing to stop the throbbing in his neck where Bodine had hit him. He rested for a while, cleaning the scrape on his cheek with a damp handkerchief. His revolver was nowhere to be found.

Picking up his hat and dusting it off, he set off down the lane. The smell from the corpses hit him first, and he recoiled, gagging. He glanced at the pistol on the Confederate body, but, after some speculation, dismissed the idea of taking it. The corpse stank, was covered with flies. It was a grotesque thing, with a gaping, twisted mouth. Despite his prior resolve, he couldn't help but hesitate. A man alone and unarmed in a war zone . . .

"To hell with it!"

Uttering a scornful grunt, Jake plodded on past the corpses. He could buy another gun if he had to; might even have to buy another horse unless he could steal one.

The next time, Bodine wouldn't get away so easily. And there *would* be a next time, he was sure of it. Jake's lips curled back in a snarl, and he swore loudly. There was no need to worry about taking him back alive; the government didn't care. It was the girl Jake wanted, and he vowed he would have her, even if he had to follow the pair all the way to Charleston.

# 12

Sunset stained the western sky scarlet. Jessie
stared wide-eyed as Garth drove the buggy
through the streets of Richmond. It was the
largest city that she had ever seen; its sheer
size dwarfed her, made her feel small and in-
significant. She gaped, awed by its magnificent churches, large hotels, stately banks, the
many mills and foundries belching smoke.

The cobbled avenues were busy. Fine
carriages vied with wagons loaded with
munitions; soldiers and civilians alike
cantered along the wide thoroughfares. The
sidewalks teemed with humanity, old and
young, black and white.

Slowly, almost imperceptibly, a feeling of
uneasiness crept over Jessie. This was the
capital of the Confederacy, a place that had
only existed in the newspapers until now.
And the city was full of them—Rebs—each
and every one her enemy.

The buggy halted in front of a five-story hotel on Main Street. It was a monstrous brick building with a wide veranda spanning its facade.

Two black youths scampered from the cover of the porch to hold the horses. "Welcome to de Spotswood," one called, grinning so broadly his teeth seemed to dominate his dusky face.

"What a peculiar name for a hotel," Jessie remarked.

Garth shrugged, alighted from the buggy and helped Jessie down. He flipped a coin to one of the boys. "One of you get the bags. Is there a place to board the horses?"

"Yessuh. Out back. I take de buggy fer you."

Garth nodded, and Jessie took his arm as they entered the hotel. She goggled at the opulence of the lobby—fine imported rugs, plush velvet settees, polished mahogany, gleaming brass spittoons and sparkling crystal chandeliers. But, upon closer inspection, she noted a worn appearance as well. The arms of the chairs were frayed, tassels were soiled, there were bare spots on the carpeting. From too many booted feet, she thought acidly, noting all the uniformed men in attendance.

As she and Garth were walking toward the desk, two Confederate cavalrymen in dashing gray tunics with bright yellow sashes nodded pleasantly to Garth. One made a chivalrous gesture to Jessie, sweeping off his plumed hat and bowing low.

"Ma'm."

She nodded curtly in silent reply, tried to smile but could only manage a sort of grimace. She was able to maintain a guise of cool politeness, but inside she was seething.

She stood close beside Garth as he rented a room. The rates were astounding. In fact, the farther south they traveled, the more expensive everything got. In Fredericksburg it had cost three dollars extra to have a bath sent to her room. But at least Jessie had gotten that long-awaited soaking and washed her hair.

Three imposing officers in gray emerged from the billiard room. They were laughing and chatting as if there was no war going on at all. Jessie's face pinched into angry lines. One of the men caught her eye and frowned quizzically. Jessie's hands were suddenly trembling badly; she dropped her gaze and moved closer to Garth. What would they all think if they knew she was a Yankee?

The clerk rang a bell on his desk, and a sheepish black boy in a red jacket made a hasty appearance. Without a word, he picked up the bags and started up the staircase. Jessie and Garth followed to the third floor.

The Negro unlocked the door and waited until Jessie and Garth entered before coming in with the bags. He turned to leave, still never having uttered a sound.

"Here, boy." Garth tossed a coin at the Negro.

He caught it deftly, and for the first time, a shy smile appeared on his face. "Thank you, masta." He left the room, closing the door behind him.

Jessie turned to Garth, staring at him frostily. "*Master!*"

"I didn't tell him to call me that."

"Oh yes you did. You and all the generations of your kind that came before you."

Garth held up a placating hand. "Jessie . . ."

She cut him off with an impatient gesture, paced over and leaned against the dresser. "I don't know if I can stand it here! All the Rebs—and the darkies bowing and scraping."

"Better here than in jail up north."

A look of dismay crept across her features. "They wouldn't have jailed me."

Garth shrugged. "If they were desperate enough to send that Coffin rascal after us, who knows what they might have done to you?"

At the mention of Jake Coffin's name, horror welled inside Jessie. He probably would have killed Garth and then raped her. Jessie had to fight back the waves of revulsion and fear that washed over her.

Garth came over to her and put his arm around her shoulder, drawing her close against his side. "I reckon I know how you feel. I had a bad case of the heebie-jeebies whenever I'd see those Yankees marching up Liberty Street. But you've got nothing to fear here. You might be a Yankee, but who's going to know that?"

"Because I keep sneering every time I see a Reb."

"You don't sneer at me."

She lifted her head, studying him carefully, an impish gleam dancing in her eyes. "Only when you snore."

He looked at her in mock surprise. "I don't snore."

"Not much you don't!"

He gave her a brief hug, kissed her temple. Somehow when Garth showed her these little displays of affection things never seemed quite so gloomy.

"Hungry?" he asked.

"The aroma coming from the dining room did smell inviting."

"Then let's go eat. Tomorrow, maybe we can gather more supplies for our own larder."

Jessie found her brush, combed out her hair. There hadn't been much in Manassas for them—only a little feed for the horses, a loaf of hard bread and some eggs. The situation in Fredericksburg had been much the same. Not only were the prices higher, there was less for sale.

"As far as the darkies are concerned," Garth said, "I can't expect you to get used to it or even understand it. But the majority are happy. They have no cares, no responsibilities. Everything is given to them in return for work."

"Everything except their freedom."

Garth's brows furrowed in a slight frown. "At Magnolia Hall, you'll see. My father treats them well; so does our overseer. They're like family.''

Jessie gave him a curious, skeptical look, but she put down her brush and followed him out the door.

The dining room of the Spotswood was elegant. Fine linen cloths covered the tables, engraved silver gleamed, crystal glassware shimmered in the light from the chandeliers. For the first time since joining the army Garth felt like he was home again. This reminded him of the impressive hotels and restaurants in Charleston, where polite conversation prevailed, black waiters did their jobs efficiently, and women laughed softly at witty comments their escorts made. And there were women here in Richmond, dining with men in uniform or in swallow-tailed coats just like before the war. They wore their hair in sausage rolls or piled atop their heads and showed just enough cleavage to make a man more than passably interested. But the jewelry was missing. There were no flashing earbobs, no diamond chokers, no bangle bracelets or oversized encrusted rings.

It had probably all gone to support the Confederacy, Garth thought glumly. To purchase the much needed supplies brought in from abroad on the blockade runners.

''Do you see these prices?'' Jessie asked, astounded.

''Mmm,'' he agreed, glancing once more at the menu. They were ridiculously high, crossed-out and raised four times. "It seems the south's currency isn't much good anymore."

"Thank God we've got gold."

"I think it would be wise to exchange some of our gold for shinplasters tomorrow."

Jessie arched a wondering brow. "Shinplasters?"

"Just a local term for Confederate money."

"I suppose I'll have to get used to your colloquialisms."

"Loretta'll teach 'em to you. And then some."

Jessie's smile was distant and forced.

Garth grinned and squeezed her hand. "My sister's really not so bad. A bitch, at times, but she *is* my sister. You'll get along."

"I wonder."

So did Garth.

They ordered their meals and even a bottle of wine. Garth watched Jessie as she sipped from her glass, her eyes moving with curiosity over the occupants of the dining room. Even though they had been traveling all day, she looked fresh and clean, her skin flawless, her cheeks pink from the sun. She was the essence of a man's dreams; Garth could feel pleasure and contentment run through him just at the sight of her.

But despite her beauty, every now and then a little frown of annoyance would settle on her brow. She was watching the men in their gray uniforms as they entered and left, scrutinizing the women with them carefully.

"You might as well get used to it, Jessie,"

he finally said. "You're in the south now. You'll not see any of your beloved Yankees unless they're prisoners."

Her nostrils flared in irritation. "I don't like it."

"I didn't expect you would." He followed her gaze as it settled on a strapping young Negro in a white jacket serving food at a nearby table. "Have you ever seen any darkies before?"

"Only in engravings in *Harper's Weekly*. And they were dressed in rags and picking cotton."

"That one probably has a pretty good life for himself. I'll wager he's even free."

At that moment, the waiter tripped over the large booted foot of a well-dressed man. The tray went flying, goblets of water and wine crashing onto the table, liberally splattering the patron and his female companion.

"Damn you, nigger!" The man's voice rose in unbridled fury. He jumped up from his seat, a sudden blaze of hatred flashing in his eyes. He reached for a short riding crop on the table and slashed cruelly at the black waiter. Red welts immediately formed on the young man's cheek. He held up his hands to ward off the blows, stumbled back several steps.

"Masta, I sorry. It were an accident." There was genuine terror in his voice; his eyes turned up to the white man in fearful supplication.

The gentleman brought the riding crop

down hard on the waiter's shoulder.

Jessie winced, looking at Garth with disgust. "And you said he was better off than the others. I wouldn't even beat a mule like that."

Garth glanced helplessly at Jessie, then back at the commotion. Several other waiters had gathered around, but they all kept a respectful distance. A paunchy white man with fluffy sidewhiskers hastened to the scene, full of apologies. Garth couldn't make out what was being said, but from the expression on the face of the newcomer—the manager, he supposed—he was probably fully agreeing with the distraught patron that black help was worthless and unreliable. It was the standard speech Garth had heard many times before.

He turned back to Jessie and tried to give her a smile. "Eat your supper and forget about it."

She looked at him with unmasked annoyance. "I'm not very hungry anymore."

"Eat. We're paying enough for it."

Jessie's eyes challenged him, but she picked up her knife and fork. She cut viciously into her meat.

Impatience rippled through Garth like an angry wind. If Jessie continued to behave so self-righteously, she was only going to draw attention to herself and him. When he looked back at the disgruntled diner his table was being cleared and new dishes being set before him. The waiter was nowhere to be seen.

"Are all white men like that?" Jessie asked.

"Some are. There's good and bad in all of us. But you won't find any of that in my family."

"Not even from your sister?"

"Well . . . She does have a tendency to order the servants around. But then, she orders everyone around." He refilled her wineglass, urging her to drink. "Don't look so mad, Jessie. It's just the way things are here, that's all."

She glared at him, daring him to argue. "And you're fighting to save this way of life?"

The rest of the meal was eaten in silence. Garth could feel a certain hostility on Jessie's part that he hadn't sensed since his first couple of days in the house in Gettysburg. But his worries vanished in the next moment when he recognized a young man in uniform leaving the dining room.

Garth hurriedly excused himself from the table, rushed across the room and caught the man's arm. "Matt. Matt Caldwell."

The soldier turned and looked at Garth, then recognition entered his eyes. White teeth gleamed behind a lopsided grin. "Captain Bodine, what are you doing here?"

"Just passing through. How are you?"

Matt Caldwell's face seemed to sag, and his eyes turned wistful. "How do I *look*?"

A tiny shockwave went through Garth. For the first time, he realized Matt Caldwell was leaning on crutches. One leg of his trousers was pinned up at the knee.

"I lost it in Gettysburg—when our

entrenchment was hit. A little present from the Yankees.''

"I got one too," Garth said, recovering his composure. Matt had been a good soldier. Garth had gone to school with him, had known the Caldwell family, even though their social status was considerably lower than that of the Bodines. "Join us for coffee or brandy or something."

"Us?"

"A young lady. Prettiest little thing you'll ever feast your eyes on."

Jessie managed a small, polite smile for Matt Caldwell when Garth introduced her to him. She scrutinized his ragged uniform and suppressed a shiver of distaste. But then she thought of the crutches and the missing leg, and she couldn't help but feel some pity for the man. His face was thin, his cheeks hollowed and shadowed, and his hair was the color of ripe corn. He was lean and wiry, almost skinny. He would probably never dance with a pretty girl again, never ride a horse, never run through a sweet field of clover. Still, regardless of his injury, he was a Reb. He talked like one; he acted like one.

"There wasn't many of us left after the Yankees attacked us," Caldwell said, sipping a brandy appreciatively. "I was unconscious for a little while, and when I came to, they were putting me in an old beat-up wagon they were using for an ambulance. Everybody figured you'd been blown to bits."

"Not quite." Garth drank some of his own

brandy, cradling the snifter in his hands to warm it. Jessie gazed speculatively at him, picturing in her mind what he must have looked like before the war. Much the same, she supposed, just as handsome and roguish-looking as ever, sitting on a shady veranda after supper, smoking cigars and drinking, watching the slaves trudge in from the fields. She covered her irritating thoughts with a heavy sigh. "I was lucky—just got a flesh wound. Jessie and her mama nursed me back to health."

Matt Caldwell studied Jessie with puzzled interest. "You're a Yankee?"

"A displaced Yankee for the present. My mother and Garth's father are cousins."

She was grateful Matt didn't pry further. She didn't want to relive that horrible night at the hospital by explaining her mother's death to this stranger. It was still too painful, too recent. Most of the time she simply shut it out of her mind.

"I spent three weeks at Chimborazo Hospital here in Richmond," Matt said. "Now they're sending me home." Scoffing amusement riddled his voice. "The army's most graciously given me a pass for the train—in a cattle car."

"Stop by the house and tell my folks I'm on my way home," Garth said. "And that I'm bringing my cousin Jessie with me."

Matt nodded, finished his brandy and rose clumsily. He got his crutches propped under his arms and bowed graciously to Jessie. "A pleasure, ma'm." He turned to Garth, and a boyish grin flashed across his features, a reckless gleam in his eyes. "We'll whip those Yankees yet."

Jessie watched him hobble away and out of the dining room, indignant color staining her cheeks. If the Rebs had as much guns as bluster, they might win, she thought derisively.

Garth turned a quizzical eye on her. "Don't you want your brandy?"

She shook her head, suddenly feeling tired and depressed. "You drink it."

He took the glass and helped himself. "I never let good brandy go to waste." He shook his head disconsolately. "I reckon I was the lucky one. I only got a ball through my arm. Poor Matt."

Jessie wondered how many men were walking the streets of New York and Boston and Chicago like Matt, but she didn't voice her thoughts. "I think I'll go up to our room."

The faint smile melted from Garth's face and was replaced by a look of concern. He finished his brandy in one huge swallow and paid for the meal. Jessie remained silent all the way up the stairs, only casually noticing a buxom woman with hennaed hair coming down on the arm of an officer.

She let Garth unlock the door, then entered, not caring whether he lit a lamp or not. She walked straight to the window and breathed in the night air, so refreshing compared to the heat of the day. Down on the street, the gas lamps were burning and she could see people still moving about. Rebs, in the capital of rebeldom.

A sad, distant look crept into her eyes, and a confused rush of feelings swept over her. She hated it here, this fine city with all its tattered glory and glitter. Its customs were strange, its people talked differently than she and nothing felt comfortable.

She chafed her arms, though the breeze was pleasantly warm. A wave of homesickness swept over her, and she bit down on her lower lip to keep from crying. She missed Mary Purcell and her cat, Dr. Cornelius Brooks, friends and neighbors, and most of all her mother. If it hadn't been for these damnable Rebs starting the war in the first place, she would still be living in Gettysburg, possibly might even be married by now.

Instead, she was on the run, feeling like a hunted criminal for nothing she had ever done. And she was with a man who both puzzled and captivated her. She trusted him to take care of her as best he could, but did she love him? He was, after all, a southerner, the heir to a large plantation and town house and a batch of slaves. He stood for everything she despised, yet he had a power over her that no other man had ever come close to matching. She sighed, trying to sort out all the conflicting thoughts running through her mind.

She felt Garth's arm around her waist; she was aware of his closeness, his maleness, but she couldn't allow her emotions to interfere with her thoughts. And, indeed, she did have a lot of thinking to do if she was going to be in the south for the duration of the war, perhaps even longer. How many years could the fighting go on? It had already been over two. Would there be two more? Or four? Or even ten?

"Do you want to go to bed?" he asked.

"I suppose so."

He brushed her hair away from her neck, bent down and let his lips linger on her throat. His breath was warm and smelled pleasantly of brandy, and she trembled inwardly, but forced her feelings to calm down.

"I don't think I want to make love tonight," she said. "I'm tired and confused." Why had she said that? She had never denied him before, and being with Garth was one way she felt deliciously alive and exhilarated. But it was true. She *was* tired and confused.

"All right."

She turned her head and looked up at him. In the moonlight his cheek bones looked more prominent and his jawline sharply angled. But he wore a faint, understanding smile, as if he could read her thoughts. In that instant, Jessie felt her heart swell in her breast. Perhaps she did love him, after all. Whatever her feelings for him were, they were as peculiar to her as this new land she had entered into.

She turned back to the window, following the progress of a horse-drawn caisson moving along Main Street. "I don't belong here, Garth."

# 13

Jessie felt better after a good night's sleep, a rousing tumble in bed with Garth in the morning and a hearty breakfast. But her dilemma hadn't been solved. She still didn't feel comfortable here in Richmond. In fact, of all the cities in the south, this was probably the last place she would have picked to stay. It was from here President Jefferson Davis directed his sham of a government, where generals met and discussed strategies, where armaments were shipped to maim and kill.

The morning sun was shining brilliantly, and things didn't seem quite as gloomy as they had last night. She and Garth stood in front of the hotel, trying to decide which way to go. Directly across the street was an imposing structure, where officers in full regalia entered and exited in a never-ending flow.

"What's that place?" Jessie asked.

Garth shrugged, waited for several wagons to pass, then took her arm and crossed Main. A brass plaque informed them that the building housed the War Department.

"I bet the one in Washington is bigger," she remarked.

"Probably is." Garth's voice was dryly mocking. "Your people have more money than we do."

A heavyset, elderly officer emerged from the building, brass buttons winking in the sunlight. His gray tunic stretched over a belly of awesome dimensions. Wattles of fat hung on his neck, and jowly cheeks couldn't be concealed by gray sidewhiskers. He squinted in a puzzled frown at Garth, eyeing his frock coat and silk cravat with skepticism.

"Bodine? Young Bodine?"

Garth smiled, extended his hand. "That's me, Ellsworth. Or should I call you *Colonel* Duncan?"

The older man clapped Garth heartily on the back, then shook his hand energetically. "What are you doing here in Richmond? And dressed like that? The last I heard you were in the army."

"I still am," Garth explained. "But I was wounded slightly in Gettysburg and separated from my unit. Now all I'm trying to do is get home." He turned to Jessie, smiling disarmingly. "Jessie, this is Colonel Ellsworth Duncan, an old friend of my father's. Colonel, I'd like to present my cousin, Jessie

Morgan."

The colonel took Jessie's hand and bowed low over it; she felt her flesh crawl at the touch of his thick lips. "What a beauty! The fairest flower of the Confederacy."

"The Union, Colonel. I'm from Pennsylvania."

He arched a hairy brow in surprise. "A Yankee?"

"Yes, sir." She didn't know why she was saying this, but something about the man irritated her, and she throttled more wrathful words that had come boiling up like acid in her throat.

Garth shot her a frowning look of warning, then turned back to the colonel. "I'm taking her home with me."

"You'll like Charleston," Duncan told her.

"I doubt it."

The colonel exchanged glances with Garth. "A real Yankee, it seems. And here in Richmond, of all places. I suggest you curb that sharp tongue of yours, young lady. The people here in Virginia don't take kindly to Yankees. Much of their land has been destroyed by your northern soldiers."

Jessie's blue eyes became hard as granite. "Gettysburg was a mess after your people finished with it."

Colonel Ellsworth Duncan frowned, and Jessie could feel his displeasure.

Garth offered him a tolerant, embarrassed smile. "We're staying at the Spotswood for a few days to rest up. If you have the chance, stop by and see us."

"I'm not sure the lady would welcome me. But I'm staying there myself. We'll have a drink some night." He turned to Jessie, clicked his heels smartly and bowed. "Miss Morgan."

Jessie's eyes were expressionless and cold. "Colonel."

She watched him move away down the street with a kind of waddling, flat-footed gait, her mouth pulled down at the corners, her face burning.

She felt Garth's hand tighten around her upper arm, nearly bruising the flesh. "God almighty, Jessie! What got into you? You damn near insulted him."

"I don't care. The man irked me."

Garth continued to hold onto her arm, though the pressure of his fingers lessened, and they started up Ninth Street. "He's one of my father's best friends. He raises horses here in Virginia. They used to trade and sell animals to each other."

"He struck me as a pompous bastard."

"Maybe he is. But from now on, keep your Union sentiments to yourself."

Jessie stared back at Garth a second, her lips tightly compressed, but she said no more about it. They walked a block until they came to green, parklike grounds surrounding an impressive stone and marble structure. The stars and bars fluttered gently in the breeze, suspended high above on a flagpole. Fine carriages and noble steeds moved through the wrought-iron gates in a constant flow.

"The capitol," Garth said.

Jessie crossed her arms, her blue eyes furious. "I suppose Jeff Davis is inside there right now, planning his next move." What would it feel like to march right up those steps and bang on his office door and give him the tongue-lashing he deserved? The idea was both appealing and frightening.

"I can see from the expression on your face this isn't your favorite spot in town," Garth said. "Calm down. Let's go back to the business district and see about replenishing our supplies. I have a feeling the sooner I get you out of Richmond, the better off we'll both be."

They returned to Main Street by walking down Tenth and stopped in at a bank where Garth traded some of the greenbacks for Confederate notes. The teller looked curiously at him but seemed pleased to get some real, honest-to-God money for a change.

In the bright light of day, Jessie was better able to see Richmond for what it was. It was run-down; buildings needed painting, some shops were out of business. Children begged on the streets; women wore faded, mended dresses. In comparison, Jessie's calico frock was in excellent shape. At a bakery women with youngsters in tow were lined up for nearly a block.

Garth paused to ask one slatternly female what was going on.

She looked at him resentfully, her lower lip thrust out in a pout. "Mister, apparently you ain't never tried gettin' bread in this town. It's rare, and it's dear!"

He glanced at Jessie, shaking his head with elaborate exasperation. "I guess we can forget about putting bread in our sack."

"If it tastes as bad as that coffee we had for breakfast, I don't want any." Her nose wrinkled in distaste. "I shudder to think what was in it! Certainly not coffee beans."

They crossed the street, avoiding the waiting line for the bread. Two rather handsome officers greeted Garth as they passed and doffed their slouch hats gallantly to Jessie. She almost spat at them, had an uncontrollable urge to jab a finger in their eyes. God, how she hated this city! It couldn't possibly get any worse as they moved farther south. At every corner, in every facet of speech, she was constantly reminded where she was and who she was.

Jake Coffin rolled over in bed, feeling the lumpy ticking of the mattress sag with his weight, and squinted at the sunshine pouring through the tattered curtains. Dust motes danced in the air, giving the room at the inn in Manassas a seedy, disreputable appearance.

"Shit!" He closed his eye, rolled over onto his back and stared up at the chipped plaster ceiling.

He had been here for two days—two precious days that Bodine and the girl could use to gain valuable time on him. But the blow to his head had evidently been more severe than he had originally thought. He had slept most of the time, only waking long enough to have a serving girl bring food to his room. A pretty little thing, she was, with flowing red hair and huge green eyes, but Jake was too sick to even consider taking up with her.

For a time he feared he might have to seek out a doctor, but he had sent the girl to the apothocary, and the powders she had returned with had helped. That, and strong whiskey.

He could taste it now, as sour and stale as bile in his throat. Rising stiffly, he padded naked over to the pitcher, drank a glass of water, then poured some over his head. He studied himself critically in the mirror. The patch was gone from his eye, and an ugly dark socket looked hollow and evil. His other eye was murky and bloodshot. His complexion was a pasty gray, his cheeks sunken and gaunt. Heavy, full brows gave him a sinister appearance; his sidewhiskers were scruffy.

"A fine picture you cut for yourself this morning." He snorted derisively, turning away from the washstand. "What woman would want you?"

Certainly not Jessie Morgan, he thought sullenly, pulling the chamberpot from beneath the bed and urinating carelessly in it. But whether Jessie wanted him or not, he would have her. To hell with Bodine! Jake might just kill him and take Jessie off someplace for himself, maybe out west. The bounty money was less important than Jessie. Besides, she had money.

He fastened the patch to his eye and began

dressing, working out his plans in his mind. He still didn't feel particularly well, but he could waste no more time here in Manassas. In only one respect had he been lucky thus far—five miles from the deserted farm he had found his horse grazing by the roadside. That had saved him another five from walking to town. Now all he had to do was replace his gun; a watch or two taken from the dead soldiers should be worth the price of a revolver in the pawnshop across the street.

Pulling on his boots, he got up from the bed, gathered up his belongings and left the room. First breakfast, then a stop at the barber shop and public bathhouse. Afterward he would find a gun and eventually Jessie. Jake's mouth twisted into a cruel, gloating smile at the thought.

Garth grimaced at the coffee as he swallowed. Jessie had been right: it was awful. Probably a concoction of peanuts, the main staple substitution for the brew that was in such short supply. In fact, supper tonight in the dining room of the Spotswood was not what would be considered tasty. The chicken was dry and stringy, the greens over-cooked, the hominy tasteless.

He glanced across the table at Jessie, who was picking listlessly at her meal. A tiny frown of displeasure creased her brow. Her eyes continuously darted over the other diners, her distaste at the display of Confederates readily evident on her lovely features.

"We'll leave tomorrow," he said.

She looked up at him, her expression brightening. "Do you mean it?"

"There's no sense staying here any longer." He shrugged fatalistically. "Richmond seems to be no better off than anyplace else in the south."

"Our blockade of your ports must be working."

"Oh, it's working, all right." His amusement was bitter. "But from now on you'll be getting a taste of your own medicine. If supplies are short for us, they will be for you too."

"But your family—they're wealthy. They must have things. Money can buy anything."

"Anything as long as its available. Last night's wine and brandy—I don't think we'll be seeing much more of that for a while."

"I can live without them."

Garth wondered how many more days it would take them to get to Charleston. By train, they could be home in three, but his inquiries at the station this afternoon had been a waste of time. Only military personnel, the wounded and munitions could ride. Garth had nothing to prove he was a soldier. Leaving Richmond would make Jessie happy, and, in turn, make him happy, but he dreaded the thought of what lay ahead of them in the open country.

"There's your friend the colonel," Jessie said.

Garth looked in the direction she indicated.

Colonel Ellsworth Duncan sat at the corner table with several other army cronies, eating and drinking. Garth caught his eye, and Duncan lifted a hand in greeting, then nodded. politely to Jessie. Her smile more closely resembled a sneer.

Garth sighed in frustration. "God, Jessie, do you have to be so damn obvious?"

Icy fire burned in the deep blue pools of her eyes. "I can't help it. For over two years I've been taught to hate you Rebs."

He reached across the table, squeezed her hand gently and smiled into her eyes. "Forget I'm a Reb." His lids drooped slightly over eyes filled with desire, dark and smoldering. "We're leaving Richmond tomorrow, and I think we should celebrate tonight."

She eyed him with a faintly provocative look. "And how do you suggest we do that?"

He smiled lazily at her, faintly leering. "I'm sure we'll think of something."


Jessie was glad to be away from the dining room and all its Confederate patrons. Once inside the privacy of their room, Garth took her in his arms. His lips found hers, and a gentle rush leapt through her body as his arms wound possessively about her, drawing her closer to him. Her lips parted eagerly, hungrily accepting his; she pressed herself wantonly against the length of his body.

They wasted no time in undressing, then tumbled onto the bed together. If there was any time Jessie could forgive Garth for his political beliefs, this was it. Her hand ran down over his lean ribs as his tongue traced little arabesques along her ear. She could feel her pulse begin to race, and a familiar warmth spread through her lower body. His hands were soft and gentle on her skin as he caressed her leisurely, a steady fire moving along her veins. His touch was sure and practiced and magical, and her body came alive with a fierce need.

His lips moved from her neck to her erect nipples, teasing and tormenting. His mouth trailed down over her belly; her fingers stroked his arching back. His lips found her inner thighs and spread liquid fire as they moved upward. Jessie felt as if every fiber, every nerve, all her senses were deliciously alive, and she couldn't suppress the little moan of pleasure that escaped her lips.

Colonel Ellsworth Duncan grunted sourly as he watched Garth and Jessie leave the dining room. The other men's eyes were admiringly on Jessie as well.

"Who is she?" one asked.

Duncan choked out a bitter laugh. "Some high-falutin' Yankee girl. Jessie Morgan."

"I didn't know Yankees were so good-looking."

"She's a bitch." Colonel Duncan snorted. "A little bitch. Makes it damn plain she doesn't like us. Acts kind of skittish too. Like maybe she's hiding something."

"Like what?" Major Lionel Fox leaned forward intently. The chief of Confederate intelligence in Richmond, he commanded the detention wards in Libby Prison and Belle Isle, both places now packed with captured Union officers and enlisted men.

Duncan shrugged his wide shoulders. "I don't know. But maybe you ought to have a talk with her."

"And the man with her?"

"I can vouch for him—known him since he was a boy. It's the girl I'm curious about. Very curious."

# 14

Jessie made a face as she swallowed her coffee at the breakfast table. "This is awful!"

"Don't drink it then."

She eyed Garth, the corners of her lips twitching with amusement. "I can't start the day without my coffee. Even if it is this rot."

She ate some eggs, nibbled at a piece of toast, feeling much better about their state of affairs. In a few hours she would see the last of Richmond and all its faded trappings. There would be Rebs, to be sure, all along their route, but not in such abundance as here, a little less show to remind her just where she was.

"If Matt keeps his promise, maybe by tonight he'll be telling Mother and Father we're on our way," Garth said.

"I wonder if they'll be pleased? About me, I mean."

"Mother will. Father might have to get to

know you better, though he never could resist a pretty face. Maybe by then you'll have learned to keep your mouth shut and your feelings to yourself."

"I doubt it."

A trace of dry amusement glittered briefly in his gray eyes. "I doubt it too."

Jessie glanced up as a shadow fell across the table. A Confederate soldier stood gazing somberly down at her. She bristled slightly under his close scrutiny.

"Jessie Morgan?"

She coolly eyed the man who had addressed her. "Yes?"

"I'm Colonel Isaac Scott, attached to the War Department. I'm afraid I'll have to ask you to come with me."

Jessie felt suddenly cold and uncomfortable. She swallowed dryly but didn't reply, eyeing the corporal suspiciously. He was an older man whose body was squat, distended by a sizable paunch. His graying hair and beard almost obscured his features.

"What for?" Garth demanded, his voice harsh.

"Just to ask some questions of the lady."

"Why?"

Corporal Scott shrugged. "I don't know, sir. I only have my orders from Major Fox. He wants to see the lady in his office this morning."

Jessie felt as if her intestines were turning to ice water. She looked wildly at Garth for help. What could the Rebs possibly want with her?

"Miss?"

Her eyes darted back to the corporal, came to rest on the huge revolver strapped to his hip, and goosebumps broke out on her arms. "What does he want me for?"

"Like I said, miss, I don't know. Now, if you'll please come along . . . ?"

She threw another frantic glance at Garth, then rose stiffly from her chair. She tried to hold her head high and her shoulders straight, but the network of fear that had been weaving itself around her began to strangle her. She was an enemy in the enemy's land. Jumbled, confused thoughts spun wildly around in her head.

Garth threw some shinplasters on the table and stood up. He grasped Jessie's hand for only the briefest of moments before Corporal Scott gave her a gentle nudge. People stared as the three of them walked out of the dining room—the corporal, Jessie and Garth. She tried to put as much pride into her step as possible, but she shivered involuntarily and her feet faltered.

Garth was still hurling one question after another at Corporal Scott as they entered the War Department building, but he got no answers. Colonel Duncan was waiting in the hallway with another officer, a young man with a strong, square jaw and a cleft chin. His hair was so black it shone.

Ellsworth Duncan gave Garth a hesitant smile. "Come into my office for some coffee while Major Fox and Miss Morgan have their chat."

Garth let out an enraged bellow. "I don't want any coffee, dammit! I want to know what this is all about!"

Duncan pursed his thick lips in annoyance, catching Garth by the arm. "I'll tell you in my office." Any friendliness had left the old man's eyes; they were hard and cold and unpleasant.

Jessie cast one final, helplessly imploring look at Garth before she was ushered inside Major Fox's office. It was a dreary little place, with a desk, two chairs, filing cabinets and maps. The major walked with a decided limp.

"Please sit," he said, gesturing to a chair.

Jessie hesitated, then sat down. Her legs felt rubbery. Major Fox seated himself at his desk, glanced over some papers, then lifted his head to study Jessie. His eyes were intensely blue, with an ugly glint in them. Jessie felt a shiver pass through her.

"Now, Miss Morgan, would you mind telling me why you're in our fair city?"

"We just stopped for a couple of days to rest. Garth—Captain Bodine—is taking me to his home in Charleston."

The major folded his hands in front of him on the desk, still gazing with unnerving intensity at her. "Why?"

In a rush of disconnected words, Jessie blurted out the story of finding Garth in the cellar, of hiding him, of her mother's death, of the bounty hunter Coffin.

Major Fox raised one dark brow in surprise. "A Yankee shot your mother?"

"Yes."

"Then you must hate them as well as us."

"No! You people started this damn war—not us! It's you that's in the wrong!"

Eyes flashing, Garth spun around in a rage. He stared coldly at his father's old friend. "What's this all about?"

"Your cousin has created quite a stir in the short time she's been here. We don't like to hear Yankee abolitionist talk."

"She's only a girl, for Christ's sake. A hot-headed young girl."

"A hot-headed Yankee, Garth."

"She can't help that."

"Ah—but Richmond holds all the secrets, does it not? There's plenty to see here, plenty to overhear, plenty to send back to the folks at home."

Garth was dumbfounded. "You think she's a spy?"

"That's for Major Fox to decide."

Garth flung his arms wide in a gesture of complete disgust, but there was a frown of anxiety on his face. Jessie had indeed let her feelings be widely known.

Corporal Scott knocked, then entered. He spoke quietly to Colonel Duncan, but Garth was unable to overhear.

Duncan turned to Garth with something akin to sympathy in his eyes. "Apparently your cousin wasn't able to answer Major Fox's questions satisfactorily. She will be detained in Libby Prison."

Garth felt a stab of anguish shudder

through his body. Jessie—in a filthy Confederate prison! In that instant any doubt he might have had about his feelings for her dissolved like a fine mist. He loved her. He would do anything for her.

Libby Prison was an old brick warehouse near the waterfront at Eighteenth and Cary streets. It was three stories high, with sentries posted all around. They eyed Jessie with no small curiosity as she alighted from Major Fox's carriage with the assistance of a young private. A coldness gripped Jessie's belly; fear reached deep inside her and squeezed.

"This way, Miss Morgan."

Major Fox took her arm and ushered her inside. There were closed doors on either side of the entryway; beyond were cots and pallets filled with injured Union soldiers.

She looked at the major in desperation. "How long will I be here?" She whimpered in stark panic; she was fast losing any control she had managed to sustain thus far.

"I don't know, Miss Morgan. Until we're satisfied with your story, I suppose." He beckoned to a sergeant, who approached with a shambling gait. "Room number two for the lady."

A room—not a cell! Jessie felt relief sweep through her, but it was quickly replaced by renewed fear as the sergeant pulled out a huge brass key ring. He unlocked a door. Jessie stood rooted to the floor, unable to move. Major Fox gave her a gentle shove, and she stumbled forward. The door closed behind her; she heard the lock turning and the tumblers falling into place.

Jessie was so terrified she could hardly breathe. It was dark, with only a dusty shaft of light coming from a small barred window, too small for even her tiny frame to crawl through. The air was stale and hot inside, rank with foul odors. As her eyesight adjusted to the murkiness, she scanned her surroundings. Waves of revulsion washed over her. Gritty dirt caked the floor. There was a wooden bench—perhaps meant to be a bed—and a bucket in the corner. The stench seemed to be eminating from there.

She sank down on the bench, head in hands, sobbing silent tears of fear, frustration and self-pity, feeling exposed and vulnerable without Garth to give her courage.

Garth's eyes fixed angrily on Major Fox's face. He glared at the shorter man, the muscles in his jaw tightening. "She doesn't belong here! She's a woman—a girl of nineteen! And she's done nothing!"

"She spoke up against the Cause."

Garth clenched his fists at his sides, holding onto his rage with only a thin edge of self control. He wanted so much to punch that smirking face. But if he did, he might well end up in jail himself, and then what good would he be to Jessie?

He exhaled slowly, willing himself to calm down. "How long do you plan to keep her here?"

The major shrugged. "Until she can fully explain herself."

Garth hit his open palm forcefully with his fist. "If she were a spy, would she be so stupid as to talk against the Confederacy? It's lunacy!" The cold, contemptuous voice lashed at Fox. "She's just a girl, and yes, she *is* a Yankee. But she can do you no harm."

"Women can be wily creatures at times."

A wild desperation surged through Garth. "Couldn't you just release her into my custody? I'm an officer of the Confederate army. I'll see that she behaves until we reach my home in Charleston."

Major Fox shook his head, started to turn away. "She stays here for the time being. I've sent a message concerning her to President Davis. If she is to remain in confinement, we'll have to send her to Hampton. There are no facilities for women prisoners in Richmond." He entered an office, shutting the door in Garth's face.

Garth's features twisted into a savage snarl; he had an urge to kick the door down. He fought the anger, closed his eyes briefly and willed himself to be calm. He glanced dispassionately over the Federal soldiers in the hospital ward, then turned and left the prison.

A brisk wind was blowing off the James River, but it was hot. Garth trembled with frustrated rage. What could he do? If he wired his father, would Claiborne Bodine help? And if he did, would Colonel Duncan help? The affair seemed to be left in the hands of the arrogant Major Fox and Jefferson Davis. Could Garth go to Davis and plead for her himself? The idea was absurd. Davis was the president.

Discouraged and miserable, he thrust his hands into his trouser pockets and began to walk slowly east on Cary Street, back toward the heart of town. He loved Jessie. He wanted her for his wife, to be the mother of his children. For all her quick temper and irritating, stubborn Yankee pride, she appealed to him. She brought gaiety and excitement into his life. He envisioned the beckoning warmth of her smile, then roughly pushed the image aside. He needed to act, not to think and dream.

He had wandered aimlessly to Capitol Square, gazed at a bronze statue of George Washington, stared intently at the steps of the capitol building. But he hadn't climbed them. Jefferson Davis would never agree to see him.

Now he stood at the corner of Seventh and Franklin, staring down at his feet, confusion etching deep lines in his face. Then he heard several young boys who had been rolling a hoop along the cobbles call out a shouted greeting.

"Gen'ral Lee! Howdy, Gen'ral Lee!"

Garth looked up, saw a well-built officer on a white horse stopping in front of a house directly across from him. The gray uniform, the yellow sash, the shining sword, the steel-gray beard—it *was* General Lee!

Garth watched in something akin to awe as the soldier dismounted, handed the reins to a black servant and mounted the steps to the house. He entered, then the door closed behind him.

Without thinking twice about what he was doing, Garth crossed the street, climbed the stairs and rapped on the door. General Lee had been his supreme commander at Gettysburg; from all he had heard, Garth thought him to be a kind and compassionate man. Perhaps he would help.

Presently, the door was opened by a young girl in her late teens or early twenties, wearing a simple blue dotted Swiss frock. Her hair was brown, her face plain, but she eyed Garth with curious interest.

"Yes?" she inquired politely.

"I wish to see General Lee."

"I'm afraid my father has just returned home from a long meeting with the president and his staff. He's tired."

"Please, miss. It's urgent. My name is Garth Bodine. I'm a captain in the Palmetto artillery. I served under the general at Gettysburg." Garth's voice had risen to a trembling plea. "It really is urgent."

The girl stepped aside, silently beckoning Garth inside. "Wait here, please."

Garth shifted nervously from foot to foot, fidgeting with the brim of his hat. The parlor was small and decorated sparsely, certainly not the kind of place he would expect a man of Robert E. Lee's stature to inhabit. A sudden coldness congealed in the pit of

Garth's stomach. Perhaps he had made a mistake. Perhaps the general would feel the same toward Jessie as Major Fox and Colonel Duncan.

The girl returned with a shy smile illuminating her features until she was almost pretty. "My father will see you, Captain Bodine. If you'll follow me into the study . . . ?"

Garth felt a combination of relief and apprehension as he trailed after the girl. Then he was entering a small room at the back of the house, a comfortable, homey-looking nest. General Lee was ensconced in a rocker, his tunic removed, a massive chest and broad shoulders strained against a white lawn shirt.

He stood, extended his hand, standing as tall as Garth. His grip was firm and dry. "Captain Bodine. My daughter tells me you have urgent business with me. Sit." He indicated a wooden chair with an embroidered pillow on the seat. "Mildred, bring the captain a glass of iced tea." Lee settled himself in his rocker, then picked up a frosty glass. "Mildred makes the tastiest iced tea in the world." Brown eyes came to rest on Garth with a question in them. "Now, Captain, what can I do for you?"

Garth swallowed, licking his lips nervously. "I need your help, sir. My cousin and I were on our way back to Charleston when all hell broke loose here. You see, I was wounded in Gettysburg. Jessie and her mother—my cousin and aunt—nursed me back to health. They're Yankees, but they helped me. Then Jessie's mother was shot by a Yankee picket and died. . . ."

Garth broke off as Mildred Lee reentered the room and handed him a glass. He drank gratefully, then wiped his sweating hands on his pants leg, his mouth as dry as a parched desert. Lee gave a loitering Mildred a stern look, and the girl left the room. Garth went on, telling the general everything, speaking nonstop for over half an hour.

"She does have a spirited mind of her own and isn't afraid to speak her views. But she isn't a spy and is certainly no threat to the Confederacy." Garth exhaled, looked hopefully at the general. "Can you help me get her released from prison? Will you?"

Lee had listened patiently throughout Garth's entire disconnected story, never interrupting, only nodding occasionally. Now he turned away from Garth, fixing his gaze out the window. "This is my favorite room. I can sit here for hours and watch the birds and the butterflies in the garden."

Garth gaped out the window at the trees and bushes, the lawn and flowers. Hadn't the man been listening at all? "General, about Jessie . . . ?"

Lee turned back to Garth, a faint smile flickering on his lips, his brown eyes softening. "I think, son, you and I should pay a visit to Major Fox."

"Then you'll help?"

Lee nodded without hesitation. "If this Jessie of yours is as strong in her convictions as you say, then she reminds me a bit of my dear wife. Mother wouldn't hold her tongue if she was in the north." He stood, reached for his gray tunic. "Come along, Captain Bodine. Libby Prison isn't a very pleasant place for a lady."

Jessie had been visited twice by Major Fox, and each time he seemed to grow more hostile. She had repeated her story about why she was here in Richmond, but that didn't satisfy him. He didn't ask for any kind of apology about her anti-southern opinions, nor would she have given him one if he had.

She had no idea how long she had been in this filthy little cell. It seemed like an eternity; more likely only a few hours had passed. Her eyes had become accustomed to the gloom, her ears attuned to the water of the James River lapping against the docks outside. It was intolerably hot; she perspired freely. At least the major had been human enough to bring her a glass of water both times he had come.

Another wave of hopelessness and depression settled over her. Would she rot away here in this God-forsaken place? Would they indeed send her on to Hampton? Perhaps she would even be put on trial. She had never felt more despondent, more helpless.

Sniffing back a tear, she turned her gaze upward about three feet from the ceiling where she had earlier been watching the progress of a spider. He was still there, suspended in space on his silken thread, doing whatever spiders do. No doubt waiting for some innocent prey to claim for his supper. An ant, a fly, a beetle. At this thought, Jessie's insides twisted with revulsion. She shuddered to think of what creepy, crawly things inhabited this cell with her. She had seen rat droppings, but no sign of the rodents themselves.

A terrible, hopeless shudder twisted through her, and a choked, angry sob caught in her throat. Then she heard booted feet outside the door—more than just one man. The key rattled in the lock, and she tensed, not knowing what to expect.

Then the door was flung open, and light flooded the cell. Jessie blinked and squinted, and shaded her eyes from this sudden intrusion. Her heart sank. It was only Major Fox, glaring at her, and behind him, she could see another gray uniform. They had come to take her away!

"Jessie? Jessie, are you all right?"

It was Garth's voice! Jessie's heart leaped in her breast. She pushed herself up from the bench and out the door. In the next second she was being gathered into his arms and crushed hard against his body. She pressed herself more fully to his length, hugged him tightly, wept in relief. She reached out tentatively to touch his cheek, to reassure herself he was really there, and in that moment she realized how fully and completely she loved him. She looked at him with adoration; he returned her gaze, full of unspoken love.

"It's over now, Jessie." Garth's voice was gentle, tender. "We can leave now."

Her eyes widened in dismay. Then her gaze fell on the stranger in the gray uniform, and shock went through her like a cold knife blade. It was General Robert E. Lee himself, in the flesh. She would recognize him anywhere, for how many times had she seen his image in *Harper's* and *Leslie's Weekly*?

She looked at the older man in confusion, unable to speak.

An easy smile played about the corners of Lee's mouth; there was genuine warmth and kindness in his brown eyes. "Everyone's entitled to speak his mind, my dear. It's just wiser to be careful who can hear you." He turned to Major Fox, and the charity left his eyes. "May we take leave of this place, Major Fox?"

There was a sullen curl on Fox's lips. "Of course, General."

Lee turned back to Jessie and offered his arm. She slipped hers through it and followed the big man out the door, her other hand still clutching tightly to Garth's.

"I don't understand," she finally managed to say when they were outside.

A twinkle leapt into Lee's eyes. "We southerners aren't all ogres, no matter what you might think."

Despite herself, Jessie was smiling.

"Not a very pleasant place to spend an afternoon." Lee withdrew a handkerchief from his pocket and wiped a smudge of grime off Jessie's cheek. "I suggest you two leave town as soon as possible. President Davis and I don't always agree on everything, and this may be one of them."

Garth shook the general's hand heartily. "I can't thank you enough, sir. I don't know what to say."

"Say nothing." He turned to Jessie and winked. "And that goes double for you, young lady." He extended his hand toward her.

Jessie hesitated only a moment before clasping it in her own. "Thank you, General Lee."

He smiled, but there was a faint sadness in his eyes. "Perhaps this makes up in some small way for the inconvenience I caused your hometown earlier in the month." He nodded, then turned and mounted his horse, lifting his hand in salute before veering the animal away and up Seventeenth Street alongside the canal.

Jessie watched him ride away, erect and proud. Her emotions were too muddled to allow her to even guess at her real feelings about the man. A Reb had actually saved her, and not just any Reb!

Garth put his arm around her waist. "Come on, Jessie. I think we'd better take the general's advice and get the hell out of Richmond."

Jessie closed her eyes and sank back into the tub. She could feel the hot water working on her muscles, loosening them, relaxing her body as well as her mind. She and Garth had gone only about twenty miles from Richmond when darkness began to set in. They had stopped in Petersburg and taken a room at Jarrott's Hotel. Now, after a good meal and the bath, some of the horrors of the day were beginning to fade. The filthy cell, the rank odors, the gritty barred window . . . She pushed these visions backward into some dark, empty chamber of her mind.

She glanced at the bed and saw Garth reclining on it. His shirt was unbuttoned to the waist and his feet were bare. He sipped slowly from a glass of whiskey, his eyes dark and brooding. He was angry with her; the tension in the air was almost electric. In his present mood she didn't feel it was the right time to tell him of her love for him; she doubted seriously if he could return the feeling.

And General Lee—how did she feel about him? Certainly he was not the monster she had believed him to be. He was gentle and considerate, and there had been just the slightest hint in his kindly brown eyes that perhaps he was weary of the war.

"You can rant and rave all you want about the Confederacy," Garth said, interrupting her thoughts. "But do it to me—not in front of other people."

"I'll try harder. I really will. It's just so—so . . ." She exhaled a gusty, frustrated sigh.

"I reckon I know how you feel. But just try to keep it to yourself."

"I will."

She heard the mattress springs protest and turned to see Garth rising from the bed. His shirt was open, and she could detect the muscles rippling just below the flesh. The strong, firm cut of his jaw, the determined set of his full lips, the way his tousled black hair fell over his forehead all combined to remind her of what a handsome man he was, exuding an aura of vitality.

He reached for the towel, held it open for her. "Enough time soaking in the tub."

Jessie rose, graceful and catlike. He smiled lazily in appreciation as his eyes roamed freely over her, darkening with desire. She was aware of nothing but his nearness, of her longing to touch and be touched in return.

"We've got our own opinions about this war," he said softly as she stepped into the circle of the towel and allowed him to dry her. His movements were slow, unhurried, and Jessie shivered with raw pleasure. His voice dropped even lower to a husky whisper. "But, dammit, Jessie, I love you."

She turned, and her heart gave a great, startled thud. Then she felt a strange warmth deep within her, and a gentle smile curved her lips. She swayed into him, her hands creeping up over his broad shoulders to lace around his neck. "I love you too, Garth. Reb or not."

Garth bent his head, and at the touch of his lips all differences between them vanished. Only the full-blown passion that raged between them remained. With a low moan of desire, she pressed the full length of her body against his and kissed him with renewed intensity. Easily, he lifted her off the floor and carried her to the bed. He explored every inch of her sensitive flesh with skillful fingers and lips. His insistent desire answered hers, his warmth filled her. Her mind whirled until she felt herself go beyond the bounds of passion to indescribable ecstasy.

Jake Coffin slouched out of Libby Prison, a dismayed look of disgust on his face. He had missed them again—by only a few hours! Mounting his horse, he cantered off toward the heart of town, still shaking his head in wonder.

He had tracked Bodine and the girl to Richmond, arriving late in the afternoon. At the third hotel at which he had stopped to inquire—the Spotswood—the place had been fairly buzzing about the Yankee spy who had been staying there. Jake had dashed off to the War Department immediately, then on to the prison itself. Jessie Morgan had been released with no explanation.

Rage flamed in his chest like a burning coal. Still, there was some advantage to the officials in Richmond thinking she was a spy, and Jake planned to use it somehow. The Federal government thought Bodine was a spy, the Rebs thought likewise of the Morgan girl. Frankly, Jake didn't believe either of them to be a threat to any government.

He dismounted in front of the Exchange Hotel, tossed the reins to a liveried black youth and entered. Crystal chandeliers glowed with a warm light and people milled about the lobby. A cloud of blue cigar smoke drifted heavily out of a room to the right, and Jake headed in that direction.

It was the saloon, a monstrous, gleaming remnant of a fading way of life. Confederate officers chatted with civilians, discussed the war, the blockade, the weather. Jake sidled up to the bar and ordered a whiskey.

"Where might I find Major Fox?" he asked.

The bartender pointed a stubby finger. "Playin' pool, mister. But he don't like bein' disturbed."

Jake ignored the warning, flipped a coin down on the bar and picked up his drink. He sauntered over to the billiard table and watched the game in progress between two officers for a few minutes. "Major Fox?"

The young man with black hair and steely blue eyes glanced up at him, his body leaning precariously over the table, his cue poised above the green felt. He glared sharply, his eyes narrowed.

"My name's Coffin. Jake Coffin. I understand you had a young lady by the name of Jessie Morgan in custody today. I've been after her for over a week."

Fox set his cue stick on the table, straightened up and looked at Jake with considerable interest. "You have?"

"Special orders," Jake said. "She's a sly one, she is. And dangerous."

Fox shook his head irascibly. He picked up a tumbler of gin, swallowed half of it and scowled savagely. "I knew it!"

"Where is she now?"

"Who the hell knows? General Lee himself had her released. I didn't want to let her go, but Lee, well . . . He's General Lee. You don't argue with him."

Jake clucked his tongue, then sipped slowly at his whiskey. "A mighty big mistake."

"That's what I told Lee. Give me a general like Forrest. *He* knows what to do with spies—women or not!" Fox ran a hand through his hair, his brows arched skeptically. "She's really dangerous?"

Jake nodded, enjoying his little charade. "So it's said. A beauty like her can come and go as she pleases and flirt with just about any officer, and he'd be willing to tell her his life story at the slightest bat of her eyes."

Fox grunted. "Figures." He finished his drink in another huge gulp. "I'll speak to President Davis immediately."

Jake held up a hand in protest. "No need. He's fully informed of the situation. I'll find her."

"I don't kow where she went. Probably back up north."

Not likely, Jake thought scornfully. I'd bet my other eye she and Bodine are on the road to Charleston right now. "Don't worry yourself, Major. Miss Morgan will be safely in my care within a day or two. Thank you for your time."

Jake set down his glass and left the bar, chuckling silently to himself. So old General Lee was as beguiled by the lady's looks as every other man. Interesting.

He went back outside into the warm night air, lit a cheroot and consulted his map under the streetlamp's illumination. It was unlikely the pair would head for the coast, to Newport News or Norfolk. It was a far better wager they had gone on south to Petersburg, then on farther. Jake could eat supper here, ride all night and be at the North Carolina line by morning.

He would find them. A lot of money was riding on Bodine's capture, and Jessie . . He gave a little grunt of pleasure. He lusted after her, and he would have her. He had coveted her since the very first time he had set his eye on her back on the streets of Gettysburg. Maybe tomorrow, maybe the next day. Soon, Jessie Morgan would be his.

# 15

A few miles out of Goldsboro in North
Carolina, Garth guided the buggy over a
rutted, wooden bridge spanning the Neuse
River. Jessie settled back comfortably in her
seat, gazing at the scenery. It was heavily
forrested country; there was a constant
rustle of leaves and a gentle soughing of the
breeze in the pine boughs. The sky was
blotted by a tangle of branches, heavy enough
to keep out the hot sun. The air was laden
with the pungent odors of lichen and bark.

Jessie sighed contentedly, then smiled over
at Garth. He returned the smile, one corner
of his mouth lifting his dark mustache in a
kind of rakish grin. Jessie's eyes glinted with
pleasure. There was no holding back of
feelings anymore; both had admitted as much
to the other. But there were still differences
between them that neither could deny. Their
love was contradictory and full of contrasts,
both elating and exasperating at times.

It had been three days since leaving Petersburg; four since that horrible day in Richmond. No one had come after them, not Jeff Davis, not even Rebel soldiers. Jessie had almost begun to forget the entire affair, though she doubted she would ever be able to blot those few frightful hours in that dreadful little cell out of her mind.

"If the weather holds, we'll make Wilmington tonight," Garth remarked.

"And then how far to Charleston?"

He shrugged. "A day and a half. Maybe two. I don't rightly know whether my folks will be in town or out at the plantation. Probably in town. We usually spend the summers there. Swamp fever gets bad in the country when it's hot."

"What's swamp fever?"

"Nobody really knows. Just a sickness. It doesn't seem to affect the darkies much, but the whites get it. Whole families have died of it. Why, I remember one year when I was about fifteen—" He broke off, cocking his head as if listening for something. He handed the reins to Jessie. "Take 'em for a minute."

Somewhat baffled, she did as she was told. Garth swiveled around in the cramped seat and peered out the broken window of the landau top.

"Rider coming behind us—fast," he said.

"A soldier?"

"I don't think so." Garth continued to watch. They rounded a bend, then broke onto a flat, straight stretch of road.

"Dammit! It's that son-of-bitch Coffin!"

Garth retrieved the reins from Jessie. She

shook her head in terrified disbelief; sudden fear rose within her. After all this time, Jake Coffin was still after them. How had he managed to find them?

Garth passed Jessie his revolver. "I'm going to make a run for it. Shoot."

Jessie gasped in horror. "Shoot?"

"That's right, my sweet. Shoot. I don't care if you hit him or not—just keep him busy."

Jessie turned around on the seat until she was on her knees, her skirts hopelessly tangled around her legs. Holding the revolver with both hands, she put it to the broken window and squeezed the trigger. The report was deafening. She trembled wildly. Coffin veered to the right but kept on coming.

Garth whipped the grays into a gallop, rattling and shaking the little buggy. Jessie fired again. Coffin's mount reared and shied for a moment, but the one-eyed man got the animal under control.

Jessie shot a panicky look at Garth. "He's still coming!"

"Keep firing! When you run out of bullets, use his gun. It's still in your carpetbag."

Jessie fired again. The buggy hurtled around a bend in the road, and she nearly lost her balance. For a moment Coffin disappeared from sight. Jessie tried to aim, but the buggy was jolting and bumping too much to keep a steady hand. She pulled the trigger again. Coffin continued after them, gaining steadily.

"We'll never outrun him!" she cried.

"Pray that we do!"

Jessie fired once more; a pine branch

splintered and snapped and fell to the ground. "Garth, I'm no shot. I'll *never* hit him!"

She fired again, but nothing happened; the revolver was empty.

"Get his gun!" Garth ordered.

Jessie nearly fell trying to turn around on the seat. She unstrapped the carpetbag at her feet and fumbled for Coffin's Colt. It was buried at the bottom, beneath all her things. Panic rose in the pit of her stomach, paralyzing her, and she moaned softly. Garth whipped the grays on faster.

When she managed to maneuver herself around in the seat again and looked out the back, Coffin was nowhere in sight. They were on a long straightaway, but he was gone!

"Garth, where is he?"

He swore softly; his eyes were ugly and cold. "The bastard's out there somewhere, you can be sure of that. He won't quit now. He wants you more than me."

Jake let out a long string of curses as his horse stumbled and nearly threw him. Still swearing, he sawed on the reins, dismounted and watched the gelding favor his right rear hoof. Jake walked through the tall, marshy grass and lifted the foot between his legs; the shoe was gone.

"Sonofabitch!" Jake's face twisted in rage; he raked his fingers through his thick, greasy thatch of brown hair. In the near fall he had lost his hat somewhere. "Stupid horse! You *would* throw a shoe now!"

He swore some more, stalked around in a

circle, bent to pick up his black hat. He
dusted it off against his thigh, then mashed it
down on his head. "I *had* them. Out here in
the middle of nowhere with no place to hide!
Bodine would be dead, and Jessie mine by
now!" The muscles in his face twitched,
tightened, and he gave the gelding a vicious
slap on its rump. The horse whickered
mournfully and moved restlessly, favoring its
rear leg.

"I don't give a shit!" Jake snatched a limb
from a tree and broke off some of the smaller
twigs. He swished it in the air, satisfied, then
shot a venemous look at the gelding. "You're
gonna catch 'em, even if I lame you for
good!"

With that statement, he mounted, dug his
heels into the horse's flanks and swatted it
with his makeshift switch. The animal
whinnied in pain, but broke into a trot. Jake
slashed at its rump again, and the gelding
bolted into a clumsy, labored gallop.

Garth spotted smoke from a chimney
beyond a tangle of trees. A rutted, dirt lane
swung off from the main road, and he veered
sharply to the left. The buggy careened
around the bend on two wheels. Jessie cried
out in alarm.

There were a number of shanties grouped
together in a clearing. Wash hung on the line;
four pickaninnies stopped their play to stare
wide-eyed at the racing buggy. Several blacks
came out on the porches, others stopped
hoeing their meager gardens to watch.

Garth pulled the buggy to a screeching

halt, nearly knocking Jessie off the seat. He alighted in a jump, wondering what kind of place he had driven into but not really caring. They were blacks, but they were people. All the same, he doubted Jake Coffin would stop at murder even in front of the two dozen witnesses who stared, curious and hesitant, at the white man. Blacks were considered subhuman; no court would validate their testimony.

"My wife and I—we've been chased by a highwayman!" Garth's voice was charged with excitement. "He means to kill me—take my wife! Can you help? Will you help?"

A tall, strapping Negro in tattered clothes stepped forward. He was a deep coppery brown with a close-cropped head; his nose was broad and flat, his lips large, but the brown eyes were intelligent and sharp.

"Who you be, mistuh? Why should we help white folks?"

"Because I'm a Yankee."

Garth turned to see Jessie stepping down from the buggy. Her dark chestnut hair was disheveled; her face was flushed. But even amidst this crowd of strangers, she kept her presence, her bearing. Garth felt a spark of pride.

"My people are fighting to free you," she said. "We're helping you. Won't you help us?"

The tall black seemed to consider, his heavy brows drawing together in a frown. Then a slightly sardonic smile crossed his lips. "We already free, missus. Been free since de war started." He gestured contemptuously to the cabins, the scraggly gardens, the shabbily clad people. "Dis freedom ain't all we heard it would be. But I reckon . . ." His voice trailed off; he seemed to drift back into thought once more for a moment, some private place in his mind. Then he cocked his head to one side. "Mebbe bein' free—*really* free—be better'n dis. If'n you say dis man's aimin' to kill you and take yer woman . . ." He glanced at several of the other men. They looked indecisively back at him, then shrugged.

The Negro turned to Jessie and Garth and smiled for the first time. "My name is Roscoe." He extended his hand.

Garth vacilated for only the briefest of seconds, then took the proffered hand. Never before in his life had he clasped the hand of a black as an equal. "I'm Mr. Smith. John Smith. And this is my wife Mary." If Coffin stumbled upon this shantytown and mentioned Garth's real name, would Roscoe be so inclined to help them? He doubted it.

"Dicey here, she take you inside my house," Roscoe said.

"And the buggy?"

"Don' worry. Got us a spot we hides de cows an' mules whenever dey's soljers nearby." Roscoe turned to the youngsters. "You, Josiah an' Aaron an' Skeeter—take dat buggy an' de hawses to de hidin' place. An' do it quick-like."

Jessie looked both confused and frightened. Garth put his arm around her and gave her waist a gentle squeeze. "It's all right. Don't be scared of them."

"It's not them. It's that disgusting Coffin I'm worried about."

Roscoe turned to a woman and gestured to her, then turned back to Garth and Jessie. "Dis be Dicey, my woman. She take you down to de root cellar an' hide you."

Dicey was a slim, petite woman—a girl, really—with skin the color of light chocolate. Her hair was hidden beneath a red and white kerchief, her calico dress was patched; she wore no shoes. She gave a wavering smile, held out her hand toward Jessie: "C'mon, missus. Ain't nothin' to be 'fraid of."

Jessie followed, Garth trailing after her. As he climbed the porch steps, made of split logs, he saw the youngsters leading the two grays and the buggy away into the woods.

The cabin was surprisingly clean but sparsely furnished, and what furniture there was looked handmade. Even the rug on the floor appeared to have been woven with loving attention. The only outstanding features were two framed portraits above the fireplace: one of Jesus, the other of Abraham Lincoln. Garth suppressed a bitterly amused smile. If this was freedom for the blacks, why did they want it? This little colony lived in far worse conditions than even the worst-treated slave. At his father's plantation and in town, the Bodine slaves lived in splendor compared to this.

Jessie seemed hesitant to descend the stairs to the basement. "There aren't any rats down there, are there?"

"Got us a cat—comes in an' out. Ain't no rats, missus. Jes' an ol' cat."

The cellar was dark. Dicey lit a stump of a candle and gestured to two barrels. "Set yourselves down. If'n you hungry, help yourselves to some apples." She disappeared back up the steps, leaving Jessie and Garth alone.

The color had drained from Jessie's face. "This reminds me of Libby Prison."

"Don't even think about it."

Jessie sat down cautiously. Garth reloaded his revolver.

"Do you think he'll find this place?" she asked.

"Coffin?" Garth's mouth twisted into a sardonic smile. "He will. He wants both of us." He glanced up, listening to the footsteps overhead, and his fingers tightened around the wooden grip of this pistol. He wants you most of all, Jessie, he thought with a sharp stab of fear.

Jake Coffin's horse limped into the yard. Several black faces stopped work and play to stare at him. "You seen any white folks? A man and a woman?"

A somewhat dignified Negro stepped forward. "No, suh."

Jake dismounted. Foam dribbled from the gelding's mouth; its eyes rolled dazedly. "Damn horse threw a shoe." At this statement, the animal collapsed. Jake stilled the urge to howl out his rage, kicking dirt at the miserable beast.

"Mistuh, dat hawse in bad shape."

"He's as good as dead." Jake glared around suspiciously. "You sure you ain't seen a man and a woman? They were in a buggy. His name's Bodine. Hers is Morgan. Jessie Morgan." Just saying her name aloud made Jake's loins throb with yearning. Damn, how he wanted her!

"Ain't nobody been here today."

"Maybe I'll just look around. Where's your master?"

"Ain't got none. We's all free."

Jake's lip curled in contempt. "Free niggers is the worst kind!" He spat, scowled at the writhing horse, then marched up the steps of the largest cabin. The Negro followed after him.

What a pesthole, Jake thought scornfully, looking around. He peered into the three rooms, his boots scraping, spurs clanking. There was no sign of Bodine and the girl. His anger and frustration mounting, he looked carefully through every shanty.

Back outside once more, he turned to the tall Negro. "You sure you didn't see them? They must have come by here."

"No white folks."

Jake glared at the some forty-odd former slaves. "Anybody here tell me you seen two white people, I'll give you two dollars."

No one stepped forward. Some shifted from foot to foot, others stared at the ground. Jake's hand curled into claws at his sides. "*I want that girl!*" His voice vibrated with malice.

Not one person dared look him in the eye. The suspicion grew in his mind that they were all lying. If he offered more money, would they speak? Jake grimaced with disgust. Dumb niggers! They'd never give him any information. They were all stupid, each and every one of them.

He breathed a huge sigh of exasperation. "You got a horse I can have? I'll give you this old nag and five dollars."

"No hawses, suh. Jes' a mule or two."

Jake let out a bitter sound faintly resembling laughter. He looked at his gelding, realizing the animal would travel no more.

"There be a town 'bout two miles away," the black offered. "Not a big town, but somebody bound to have some hawses fer sale."

Jake's one good eye brightened. "A town?"

"Yessuh. Cold Creek. Half a mile or so down de main road, jes' turn right. Cain't miss it."

Maybe Bodine and the girl had gone there. Dammit! He had been so close! He unstrapped his satchel, then stripped off the saddle, blanket, and bridle. The animal gazed pathetically at him. Jake snorted in mild derision. Damn horse! He wasn't even worth putting out of his misery. Let the bastard suffer!

Jake fixed the tall black with a jaundiced eye. "If I find you been lyin' to me, I'll be back to kill you."

The Negro didn't even flinch.

Swearing under his breath, Jake turned and started down the dusty lane, hauling his equipment with him.

Fear knotted Jessie's stomach as the trap door swung open. She exhaled sharply in relief; it was only Dicey.

"He gone now, folks. You kin come up now."

Jessie stood up, but her knees felt rubbery. He had been up there, jangling his spurs, stomping his booted feet. Back at the deserted farm in northern Virginia, she had thought she had seen the last of him. But he was still after them, still determined. Did he want Garth so badly? Or was it her? At this thought, her insides crawled with revulsion.

Garth reholstered his gun and took Jessie's arm. He guided her up the narrow steps to the homey confines of the cabin. It was a simple place, but Jessie almost longed to stay here for the remainder of the war. At least here—with these poor Negroes—she would never run the risk of meeting up with Jake Coffin again.

"He de meanest-lookin' white man I ever did see," Dicey remarked, closing the trap door and smoothing the rag rug over it. "Ya'll should see what he done to his hawse. Nearly kilt him, he did."

"Where is he now?" Garth asked.

"De hawse?"

"The man."

"Roscoe sent him off to Cold Creek, a couple of miles yonder fer a new hawse."

"What happened to his horse?" Jessie asked.

"Come an' see, missus." The girl shook her turbaned head in distress. "Jes' awful!"

Jessie went outside with Garth and Dicey. Most of the blacks were gathered around a prostrate brown horse; several were rubbing salve on a rear leg and hoof; a young boy was coaxing it to drink water from a pan.

"Hawse throwed a shoe," Roscoe said,

joining them. "Dat man ride him hard. 'Most daid, but I figure we kin save him. A little linament an' love an' food, an' he be a good hawse again."

Scorn was etched in the line of Garth's mouth. "The bastard."

"Jes' what I thought of him," Roscoe said. "You an' yer missus mightly lucky you found us. Had me an overseer jes' like him once. Beat you even if'n you was doin' yer work."

The boys were bringing the buggy back from the woods. Garth reached into his pocket and offered a twenty-dollar gold piece to Roscoe.

"No need fer dat, Mistuh Smith."

"Take it," Garth insisted.

Hesitantly, Roscoe accepted the coin and studied it reverently. "Truth is, I wouldn't have helped you if'n ya'll hadn't been Yankees. Never met up with a real Yankee before."

Jessie noticed a blush creeping over Garth's darkly tanned face. His expression betrayed an instant of confusion and discomfort. She held her hand out to Roscoe, hugged Dicey impulsively. "Thank you for everything."

Dicey ducked her head in embarrassment. "Ain't never been hugged by a white lady before. I 'members it fer a long time."

"Don't you worry," Jessie said. "Soon all your people will be free, and it'll be better for you than this. The government will help you." She flashed Garth a smug look of triumph and walked over to the buggy.

He followed, chagrined, and handed her in. Then he climbed in his own side and took the reins. "Thanks again. And I wish you all well."

He flicked the reins, turning the buggy around in the dusty yard.

"Don' go into Cold Creek!" Roscoe called after him.

"I won't!" Garth set the two grays into a trot and muttered to Jessie, "We're going straight to Wilmington."

She and Garth rode in silence until they had reached the main road and had passed the Cold Creek cutoff. Garth finally shook his head, amazed.

"I never thought a nigger would save my skin."

Jessie studied him, sniffing disapprovingly. "And you're fighting to keep them in bondage. If they knew what you really are, they'd probably have handed you over to Coffin on a platter."

"*And* you."

Jessie's arms and back broke out in great rashes of gooseflesh.

"Enough politics," he said, flashing her a rakish, lopsided smile. "Get out the bag of food and see what there is to eat."

"How can you even think of food now?"

"Would you rather I think of sex? Coffin might catch up to us again, and in a very compromising situation."

Jessie shuddered, her flesh crawling.

Garth reached over and ran a finger over her cheek and across her lips. "I love you."

Her eyes sparkled with unrestrained warmth. "And I love you, Garth Bodine. Even if you are a no-good Reb."

# 16

Jessie sat at the dressing table in the Wilmington hotel, clad in her shabby wrapper, brushing out her long chestnut tresses. From the open window came a breath of cool sea air with a salty tang. The grog shops along the waterfronts a few blocks away were evidently busy tonight, attested to by a faint chorus of male voices and the tinny tinkle of a piano. She longed to view the ocean for herself, a sight she had never before beheld. Garth had promised to show her tomorrow.

He was in the tub now, soaking in the bath-water she had already used herself. They had discussed their differing opinions on slavery and freedom at length and now held a truce. Absently, she wondered where Jake Coffin was now, but the mere thought of him made her blood curdle.

"I bet that twenty dollars was more money

than those darkies have ever seen before in
their lives."

Jessie looked up at the sound of Garth's
voice and caught his reflection in the mirror.
Soap lather covered his hair, his neck, his
broad shoulders and chest.

"And if they can get that horse well
again . . ." she offered.

"He'll always be lame. Then again, maybe
not." Garth rinsed the soap from his body,
then leaned back as comfortably as he could
in the cramped confines of the tub. "I've seen
slaves work miracles on sick animals
before."

"Free men. Remember?"

He held up his hands defensively and
flashed her a disarming smile. "I remember."

Jessie frowned slightly, ran the brush a few
more times through her hair and continued
watching Garth in the mirror. She devoured
him with her gaze, eyeing the hard muscles
playing beneath his skin; one wet black
cowlick of hair was plastered to his forehead.
He exuded a maleness that excited and
stirred her. He was a Reb and probably
always would be, but she loved him. Looking
at him now made her acutely aware of the
urgings of her body.

She set down her brush and rose languidly
from the little stool, walking slowly to the
bed. She felt Garth's gaze on her, but refused
to turn and meet it as she slipped down the
blankets. Unhurriedly, almost deliberately,
she took her time unfastening the sash and
then let her wrapper drop to the floor. She

kicked it aside, climbed into bed and stretched out on the cool sheets. Only then did she allow her gaze to meet Garth's.

He was studying her with almost insolent appraisal, admiring every curve, the fullness of her breasts, the way her dark hair fanned out on the pillow. A weakness swept through Jessie, born of desire, and a glow of heat suffused her. His nearness was intoxicating.

She watched through lowered lids as he got up from the tub and began to dry himself, never taking his eyes from her. His body was perfect, a male Adonis that even the scar on his arm couldn't mar. She could see his lust growing for her, and an enigmatic little smile turned up the corners of her mouth.

Jessie waited eagerly for him, her eyes aglow with anticipation, but Garth was taking his time now, teasing her, and doing a good job of it. This wasn't the first time she had felt this way. Somehow, their near catastrophies only made her want him more. After prison in Richmond, after the episode with Coffin and the free blacks today . . .

Her eyes traveled the length of his magnificent body, studying the sculpted muscles that rippled beneath his flesh, the trim leanness that exuded such pure masculinity. Finally, after what seemed an interminable length of time, he flung aside the towel. Then he was on the bed with her, his mouth capturing hers in a kiss that inflamed her. His hands cupped the rounded firmness of her breasts, ran down over her ribs to her thighs. His lips were hot and eager; it was a wild, passionate kiss that aroused every nerve in her body. Jessie felt the fires of desire begin to rise, and a flood of longing surged through her.

Garth let his eyes travel down the delicate curve of her throat and the fine line of her lips. "You may be the most stubborn, pig-headed Yankee I've ever met, but I can't help loving you."

She flicked a smile at him, sparkling and affectionate, and clasped her arms behind his neck, drawing his face down to kiss him once more. Her lips parted, and his tongue teased her into a dizzying excitement. His lips moved to her neck, to her shoulder, to her breasts. Jessie's fingers ran through his thick black hair as she sighed with delight.

"Sometimes I can forget you're a Reb."

He raised his head and gave her a lecherous grin. Her eyes gleamed with deviltry. She wriggled down so that they were face to face again and kissed him hungrily. Her mouth clung to his endlessly, hot and demanding. She urged him to roll over on his back. One hand ran down over his ribs and lean belly, then closed around him, gently at first, then more demandingly. Then her lips began to follow the path her hand had taken, and Garth groaned in pleasure. She liked the taste and feel of him, the heady sensation of his yearning.

He seemed to be touching her everywhere, his fingers warm and eager on her flesh, gently kissing her in the most sensitive places until she was lost in an all-consuming passion. His breath was a hot flame on her skin, and his caresses made her tremble with desire.

She arched up to meet him, molding her body to his. His mouth sought hers and kissed her with a savage intensity; her hands kneaded the hard muscles of his back, ran over his smooth flesh. His movements were sure, his thrusts powerful and deep; never before had she felt so helpless against the overwhelming desire that coursed through her. It was exquisite torture, intensifying and prolonging her ecstasy until they both crested together.

Jake glared at the stable owner holding the lantern beside him, then glanced back at the horses. They were two matched grays, the same grays that had once belonged to Dudley Pigg, the mortician. They were now owned by Captain Garth Bodine, late of the Confederate artillery.

"When did he bring them in?" Jake demanded.

The short, stocky livery man blinked, then looked at him stupidly. "I ain't sure. Before sundown, but late. Maybe six o'clock or thereabouts."

"I don't suppose he said where he was staying?"

"Nope. Didn't say, and I didn't ask."

"Was there a lady with him?"

"Nope. I'd remember that."

Jake gave a quick sidewise glance at the man. "He was tall and good-looking? Wore a mustache?''

The stable owner nodded. "That's the man."

Jake's face flamed crimson. Bodine and the girl were here in Wilmington—but where? This was a big city. He could look for days and never find them, and in that time they could be gone again.

The proprietor was looking curiously at Jake. "Will you be wantin' to board your horse, mister?"

Jake nodded distractedly. "For tonight, anyway. Where's the best hotel?"

"That'd be the River House, over on Market Street."

No doubt lovely Jessie would want the best room in the city. At least that was a place to start looking. Jake ambled toward the open doors of the livery barn, the proprietor scurrying after him. Jake eyed his horse contemptuously. It was a sorrel mare with saddle sores; she complained mightily every time he mounted her. Still, it was the only horse in Cold Creek anyone was willing to part with, and for the outrageous sum of sixty dollars in gold! Damn Bodine!

"Fifty cents, mister," the proprietor said, holding out an open palm. "That includes feed and water."

Jake paid the man, gathered up his saddlebags and started off down the street. It was actually little better than an alley, with grog shops and brothels lining its sides. Garbage rotted in the gutters and stank. Drunken sailors from the blockade runners tied up on the river tottered about.

Feeling a powerful thirst, Jake turned into one of these dubious establishments, then wished he hadn't. The foul air was over-powering, with the reek of cigar smoke and stale whiskey and the sour odor of sweat. Coarse laughter and ribald remarks filled the small room. A painted redhead draped herself over a bearded man in a striped jersey, but she looked up long enough to eye Jake appraisingly. He stifled a shudder. Even that was beyond his taste.

He stepped up to the bar and ordered rum. The glass was dirty. Jake slugged the drink back in one huge gulp. It burned his throat and created a ball of fire in his belly.

"You seen a good-lookin' man in here earlier?" he asked the bartender. "Tall, black hair, a mustache?"

"Mister, I see so many men in one night I can't count 'em all, let alone describe 'em." The bartender squinted at him. "Want another one?"

Jake shook his head, then pushed his way out of the saloon. He stood in the alley, grateful to be breathing fresh air, rank though it was. A deep, hot rage was bubbling inside him. It was after ten. He was tired and hungry, and it was all Bodine's fault.

Snorting in disgust, he started off once more. He had done enough walking for one day. The hike to Cold Creek had not been an easy one, lugging his saddle and belongings with him. No one there had seen Bodine or the girl. Jake's eye smoldered with contempt. He might have known those niggers would lie, lead him on. Free niggers were a sly lot; a man couldn't trust one. Maybe when he finished his business with Bodine he would go back and deal with them properly. A few bullets in their black hides would do them good, teach them a lesson that white men were not to be trifled with.

But if Jessie was with them . . . Jake let out a lusty sigh of longing. Once he had Jessie, he wouldn't care about the niggers, wouldn't even care about the bounty money. He could take her out west, start a new life. Maybe even sail to Europe or some exotic island. Jessie was all Jake wanted anymore. Jessie, with her ripe young body and beautiful face. She could please a man well in bed, he was sure. And even if she was unwilling at first, Jake was confident of his powers of persuasion.

He entered the lobby of the River House. It was deserted at this hour, but voices drifted out from the bar. Jake walked over to the desk and let his saddlebags drop to the floor with a low thud.

"You on duty around six o'clock tonight?" he asked the clerk.

A cadaverous, aging man peered back at him through thick spectacles. "Yes, sir."

"Did a man and a woman check in here?" Jake described Garth, then Jessie, unable to keep the admiration out of his voice. "She's short. Blue eyes. Dark hair. *Long* dark hair. You wouldn't forget a beauty like her."

"Their names, sir?"

"Bodine. Garth Bodine. But they might have used any name." Jake gave the old man

a knowing smile and a wink. "They ain't
married."

The clerk raised one hoary eyebrow. "You
wouldn't be wanting to start any trouble,
would you?"

"*Me?*" Jake looked innocently at the man.
"I'm her brother. I only want to try to talk
her out of this foolishness. It's breakin' our
dear mother's heart."

"I really don't recall anyone fitting that
description. No couples checked in on my
shift. As a matter of fact, only one man
booked a room since I came on duty, and he
was an elderly gentleman."

Jake ground his teeth in frustration. This
ancient fart was probably too old to
recognize a pretty girl when he saw one.

"You're positive about that?"

"Quite."

Heaving a disgruntled sigh, Jake hefted his
saddlebags and trudged outside. Across the
street was another hotel; a block down,
another. He made the same inquiries, all to
no avail, at the first. At the corner hostelry,
weary and fretful, he had no definite answer.

The youthful clerk seemed eager enough to
help, but none of his replies were
satisfactory. "I just came on at eight, mister.
I don't know 'bout who checked in before
that."

Jake snatched the register, spinning it
around to scan the names. There was only
one couple registered: a Mr. and Mrs. John
Smith. The names cast a sudden cloud of
suspicion over him. He eyed the boy

curiously. "This Smith. You didn't see him—or his wife?"

"No. But they did order a tub of water and towels. The nigger boys took 'em up."

"Can I talk to them?"

"The niggers? They went home at nine."

Jake let out his breath in an explosive sigh.

"They'll be back at six sharp tomorrow morning," the boy offered. "You can talk to them then."

Jake's lip curled in a sneer. Not until tomorrow morning! Tiredness was weakening every fiber in his body, numbing his mind; his stomach growled loudly from hunger. Mr. and Mrs. Smith might or might not be Bodine and the girl, but Jake had to stop for the night; it had been a long day and could very possibly be an even longer one tomorrow.

He pulled a handful of Confederate notes from his pocket. "I'll take a room."

The young clerk brightened and handed him a pen to sign the register. "I'm afraid you'll have to take your own bags up."

Jake shrugged dismissively, signed his name and paid the boy. Then he turned and headed for the saloon, lugging his saddlebags with him. The hotel's restaurant was closed for the night, but, as he might have guessed, sandwiches and hard-boiled eggs and pickles were available in the bar.

He sank into a chair and lit a cheroot. An elderly black man in an apron appeared at his table. "Yessuh?"

Jake studied him with scorn. "A pitcher of

beer and two sandwiches—any kind of meat. I don't care. And be fast about it, boy!"

The Negro paused to speak to the bartender, then disappeared behind a swinging door. Jake sat and smoked and brooded, his gaze moving slowly over the patrons. Most were men—ship captains from the look of their garb. But there were a few women in attendance. Jake's eye settled on one of them with her back to him, and he held his breath. Her dark hair was piled artfully atop her head, but there was lots of it, so it was obviously long. A pale yellow silk dress molded to her shapely body, and as she laughed, her voice tinkled like musical chimes.

Jake stared intently at her for several minutes until she finally turned. Disappointment carved harsh lines on his features. It wasn't Jessie. The woman's eyes were brown, her nose too large, her cheek bones not as well defined. And, upon closer inspection, Jake realized it had only been his hopes that had made him see Jessie. This woman was at least ten years older, taller and plumper.

He scowled savagely when the waiter returned with his food and beer. "This better not be stale, boy!"

The Negro looked askance. "Jes' made it fresh, suh. An' de beer come in on de blockade runner jes' today. Real German beer, dey say."

Jake took a sip, swished it around in his mouth and swallowed. It was smooth and light and ice cold. He drank again, pleasantly surprised.

"Dat be eleven dollars, suh."

Jake goggled at the Negro, then fairly exploded. "Eleven dollars! For this?" His voice was loud, carrying an implied threat behind the words.

Several people turned to stare. The white bartender—a burly fellow with a solid jaw and powerful forearms—shot a sharp look at Jake. "This is Wilmington, mister. North Carolina, not Delaware."

Jake glared a moment, then finally handed over the money to the waiter. Evidently satisfied there would be no further trouble, the bartender went back to his duties, the patrons to their various conversations.

Jake bit into his sandwich and chewed with a vengeance, working out all his pent-up anger and frustration on the roast beef. But it wasn't bad. In fact, it was one of the better meals he had eaten since leaving Gettysburg.

His gaze returned to the dark-haired woman, and a thoughtful frown creased his forehead. He wanted Jessie—more than he had ever wanted any woman in his life. Unconsciously, his hand moved to the revolver strapped to his thigh, his fingers caressing the wooden grip. If Jake Coffin couldn't have her, then no man would ever again, he vowed. After all, the government didn't care how she was returned. The reward money would be his whether she was alive or dead.

# 17

Jessie and Garth strolled along Front Street, staring at all the people gathered there. The avenue ran alongside the Cape Fear River, where a half dozen blockade runners were tied up at the docks. Despite the fact that these craft defied the Union patrols, slipping past the Federal navy in the dead of night, Jessie couldn't help but admire their sleek lines. They were long, resting low to the water, and gave the impression of speed and maneuverability. One had landed last night, and it seemed all the citizens of Wilmington had come down to view her cargo.

Surgeons and aides, from both the Confederate army and the civilian population, were hauling away crates of much needed medicine. More soldiers were carting off boxes of rifles from England.

"It's not much, is it?" Garth remarked dryly. "To supply all of the South."

Jessie rubbed her arms in agitation. "If your people hadn't started this war in the first place, there'd be no need for any of it."

"Of course." His lips curved into a smile of pure mockery. "The bounty of the North will provide for all."

Jessie's eyes shot daggers at him, but she had to hurry to step out of the way as four dour-faced privates jostled about to load a crate of canisters of grapeshot into a wagon.

The citizens were ragged, thin and weary-looking; most were women, with hollow-eyed, sallow-faced children in tow. There were a few merchants bargaining for goods, but even they looked haggard and tired. And then there were the former soldiers, limping about on crutches, some blinded, some scarred, some with empty sleeves pinned to their chests.

"My mother and little sisters are hungry," one young man in a tattered uniform said to a sailor. He was gaunt, with deep-set eyes, his fair, tousled hair streaked by the sun; a livid red stump was at the end of his arm, where a hand had once been. "I've got a little money, and we've corn to trade."

The burly sailor laughed derisively. "What need do we have of corn on our ship? Eat it yourselves. 'Sides, we brought no food in on this boat."

The handless lad turned away dejected, and slouched away through the crowd. Jessie cast a pitying glance after him.

Standing atop a crate of perfumed soap was a middle-aged man in a swallow-tailed coat. He wore neatly barbered sidewhiskers and a silk cravat; diamond rings sparkled on the little fingers of each hand. "Step right up, ladies, and hear the most generous offer of your lives! The women of France will pay dearly for wigs made of human hair." He brandished a pair of shears in the air, the blades winking in the sunlight. "I'm willing to pay one dollar for each inch, ladies. Just think—one gold dollar for every inch of your hair."

Garth nudged Jessie in the side, making a dry, clacking sound of amusement. "There you go. I bet you could make a fortune if you cut yours."

"I'll keep it, thank you." Her eyes glimmered with mischief. "But I know where I can come if I get desperate for money."

"Don't you dare!" He ran his fingers lightly through the soft tresses hanging to her waist, bunched up a handful and tugged playfully at it. "If you ever cut this . . ."

"You'll what?" she challenged.

He leaned close, his breath warm on her cheek. "I won't have anything to play with when we're in bed."

An eyebrow quirked teasingly at him. "Nothing?"

"Well . . ." Amusement deepened the corners of his mouth and his eyes were openly lascivious. "I just like your hair." He took her arm and led her past a haggling pair of women, each trying to vie for the first snip of the shears.

An ancient Negro was selling oysters, and

Jessie noticed the young soldier trying to barter away some of his corn for a keg of them.

"It's worse than I had imagined," she remarked.

"The blockade? Oh, it's working. But we still manage to get by the patrols."

"But the people. These women and children! Look at them, Garth. They're so skinny, and they wear rags for clothes and most have no shoes."

"Are you changing your attitude about the war?"

"No." She was quiet a thoughtful moment before speaking again. "The soldiers are one thing. But it's not fair to make the women and children starve."

Garth looked mildly surprised. "I do believe you're seeing things as they are for the first time since leaving Pennsylvania."

"Maybe I am. But that doesn't mean I've deserted my side."

Farther down, another well-dressed man was selling bolts of cloth. Merchants argued, snatching up whatever they could afford. A woman in a frayed, torn calico frock watched almost painfully as every bolt of material was displayed. She was terribly thin, had a pale, drawn face and a sickly, decaying look to her. Two small children with pinched, frightened faces clutched at her skirts. Both were barefoot, and the little girl's dress was made from an old flour sack; the boy's trousers were made from another sack.

"Twenty dollars for this calico!" the vendor called out.

Three of the merchants scoffed. "It ain't worth half that!" one jeered. "It's a little bitty roll, and poor quality. I'll give you five."

"Twenty, and no less!"

The merchants turned away, waiting for the next bolt to be shown.

The thin woman stepped forward timidly. "Couldn't you just cut off a few yards, sir?"

"It *all* goes. The whole thing. Do you have twenty dollars, lady?"

She shook her head evasively, glanced helplessly at her youngsters, then turned back to the man. "But I've got my grandmother's cameo." She unfastened a ribbon from her neck and held the piece of jewelry out for the man's inspection. "It's valuable."

The man grunted, lit a cigar. "Ain't worth nothin' to me, lady. Now move on, so I can get on with my sale."

The woman retrieved the cameo and turned away, her face clouded with despair. Jessie felt a sharp stab of pity. Impulsively, she reached into her reticule and pulled out a gold eagle. She pressed the coin into the woman's hand.

"Buy it, and make some decent clothing for yourself and your children."

The woman looked at the coin, then at Jessie, her brown eyes wide with disbelief. "I can't accept this."

"Yes, you can. Offer the bastard fifteen dollars, then get some food with the rest." She took Garth's arm and hurried away before the woman could protest any further.

Garth was chuckling softly. "So you're a softy, after all."

Jessie tossed him a glare, then smiled sheepishly and shrugged. "I guess I am."

"Well, you've done your good deed for the day, at least. And since there's no food to be had until the ship that's expected comes in tonight, I might as well show you what the Atlantic Ocean looks like."

Jessie clapped her hands in gleeful expectation. "Really?"

"I promised, if we had the time, didn't I?"

"Yes, you did. Besides, this old river smells."

"So does the ocean, my love."

Garth stared off into the blueness of the tranquil sea. A few hundred yards out was a small boat carying two Negroes. The sand sparkled, strewn here and there with seaweed and shells, and the waves foamed with white peaks. Gulls swooped overhead. Off to the right was a gun emplacement, its Howitzer manned by three soldiers. The same artillery was to the left and on along the beach as far as he could see in either direction.

"What's that smoke up there?" Jessie asked.

Garth followed her pointing finger with his eyes to a fairly high hill. There was indeed smoke. "A signal fire, I reckon. So the blockade runners can sight land or something. I'm not sure."

"Yes, that's right. You were in the army, weren't you?" There was the slightest edge of bitterness in her voice.

"I still am."

"I know."

He turned to look at her. The sun gilded her dark hair as it blew gently in the breeze, brought out the color in her cheeks. Her blue cotton gown matched the color of her eyes and the sea, and fit her form to bring out all its glorious curves. There was a kind of natural grace in the relaxed posture of her body, short and slim and supple. He watched her gently tense face, the soft curve of her bosom, and longed for her. The sight of her always had the power to stir a hungry response in him while at the same time evoke feelings that were profoundly tender.

He thought back to last night, and, looking at her now, it seemed almost like a dream. Such intense passion from a woman had been unknown to him.

She had been delighted at first with the ocean, but the sight of the artillery had put a damper on her enthusiasm. Now she was quiet, almost brooding, as she watched the waves.

"Tomorrow we'll be on our way," he said. "Whether I can replenish our supplies or not."

"And then to your home." Her voice fell to a quivering whisper.

"*Your* home now too."

"My home is in Gettysburg. So is my heart."

He had an urge to take her in his arms and crush her to him; the nearby soldiers stopped him. Instead, he took her arm and started walking back toward the buggy parked on a little bluff.

"Jessie . . ." He faltered, felt suddenly like a tongue-tied teenager. "When we get to Charleston, I want to marry you. I love you."

She stopped halfway up the path and looked at him, her eyes glowing with happiness. But the sparkle dimmed almost immediately, and she began walking slowly once more. "I want to, Garth. But the war."

"What about the war?"

She uttered a soft, bitter laugh. "You can't very well forget that it's going on. And who knows when it will end?"

"Who cares?"

She stopped by the buggy and absently ran her hand over the neck of one of the grays. Her face was solemn, her blue eyes grave. "You care. And I care. It's something that's here and can't be avoided. Besides, you'll rejoin your unit and probably fight again."

"I won't fight again—not against your people."

"How can you *not* fight? The Confederate army's so desperate they're taking boys, for God's sake."

"I promise you, Jessie, I won't fight. Not ever again."

He expected mockery from her, but there was none. Only the sober, calm face, hesitant and a trifle confused. "I'll do something," he admitted. "But not on the battlefield."

"And then there's your family. They'll hate me—I know it."

"They won't hate you. It'll just take them a

little time to get used to you. Especially Father and Loretta."

Now the mockery came, in the form of a short, sneering laugh. "Especially your father and sister. I'm sure they'd just *love* having a Yankee for an in-law."

"Forget about them. All that matters is you and me." He gathered her close within his arms, folding her into his embrace. He tipped her chin up, and his eyes searched her face. "I love you. I won't take no for an answer."

She studied him with a slow, measuring look. "I couldn't give you an answer now if I wanted to." There was a soft glow in her eyes, and a shadow of a smile crept across her lips. "Let's just wait and see what happens when we get to Charleston." She slipped her hand behind his neck and drew his face down to hers.

Jake Coffin slouched out of a saloon, disgusted and weary. He had spent all morning and the better part of the afternoon looking for Bodine and the girl. Now it was after three, and all he wanted was a good stiff drink and a soft bed to lie on. He had been up bright and early this morning, but the two Negroes who had delivered the bathwater to the Smiths' room last night could tell him nothing. Mr. Smith had been a white man; Mrs. Smith had been behind the screen in the room. Could they describe him? No. All white men looked alike to them.

Jake chuckled hoarsely and mounted his sorrel mare. Bodine was probably gone by now. Jake was resigned to spending the night here in Wilmington and moving on to Charleston in the morning. If necessary, he would catch them there. They would have to come out sometime, and Jake would be waiting for them. The Reb could be planted in the family plot, and Jessie would be his at last.

The proprietor of the livery barn was in the process of supervising the unloading of hay when Jake rode up. He dismounted and handed the reins over to the squat little man.

"Keep the nag for tonight, will you?"

"Sure, mister." The proprietor assessed Jake with keen interest. "That buggy and them two grays you was so interested in last night. They're gone."

Jake swallowed back his rage. "I might have guessed."

"They'll be back, though."

Jake gaped in dismay. "Back?"

"Yup." The proprietor nodded and spat a stream of tobacco juice into the dirt. "The man and the lady took it out earlier. Said they'd be back."

"Was she small and pretty?"

"Prettiest little thing I ever laid eyes on."

Jake's spine prickled with sudden alarm. "You didn't mention me? Tell them I'd been around asking questions?"

The proprietor's round face broke with a sly smile. "Didn't say a word. I figured it might be worth somethin' to you if I kept my mouth shut."

Jake's glance was dark with suspicion and mistrust. "How much?"

The proprietor flashed him another furtive smile, displaying yellowed, broken teeth. "Say ten—in gold."

Jake swore loudly, but reached into his pocket anyway.

The buggy returned in less than half an hour. Jake watched from an empty stall as Bodine left it and the horses and paid the proprietor. Chuckling silently, Jake followed a block behind, ducking into a doorway once when Garth turned around.

It was a short walk to the hotel—the same hotel, Jake noted mirthlessly—where Mr. and Mrs. Smith were registered.

Garth paused at the desk. The young clerk was not on duty; an older, unfriendly looking man was. "The blockade runner *Sunshine* is due in tonight. Do you know when?"

The clerk shrugged. "About ten or thereafter. Maybe as late as midnight. Depends on what the Yankees are doing."

Bodine nodded his thanks and headed for the staircase. Jake followed at a safe distance, then crept along the hallway to room thirteen. An unlucky number if you ever had one, Bodine, Jake thought carelessly. He bent his ear to the door and could hear low voices coming from inside.

"The clerk isn't sure exactly when the ship will come in," Garth was saying. "But I'll leave around nine-thirty for the docks. I want to get there and get us some fresh supplies so we can get out of here early tomorrow."

"How long will you be gone?" Jessie's voice sounded like sweet, hot honey to Jake's ear.

"Who can say? But we'll need food to keep us going till we get home. There's never been much in the way of inns between here and Charleston, and I imagined it's worse now."

There was a long minute of silence, then Jessie spoke again, her voice husky and low and inviting. "Then make love to me now so I won't be lonely tonight."

Jake's face went livid with jealous anger. He listened, a spasm of rage working his facial muscles, but there was no more talk coming from the room, only the mattress springs squeaking in protest.

He turned away, jamming his hands into his pockets, and stood panting in hot anger. But a smile of lusty anticipation replaced his scowl. Tonight Jessie would be his for the taking while Garth was at the river. When the Reb returned the girl would be gone. And in a few days she would be speaking those same words to him.

Grinning coldly, Jake left the hotel to fetch his horse and belongings.

# 18

"If we're lucky and get an early start tomorrow, we might make Myrtle Beach by nightfall." Garth stood by the foot of the bed, buckling on his holster.

"Is there a place to stay there?" Jessie asked.

Garth shrugged, pulling on his jacket. "I don't know anymore. There used to be a few places. There was a lot of fishing done from there. But with the war . . ." His shoulders lifted in another shrug as his voice trailed off.

Jessie reclined against the pillow in her nightgown, pleasantly sated from the magic of Garth's lovemaking and a hearty supper. She watched him as he carelessly ran a comb through his black hair; just the sight of him had the power to arouse her. But, as the day of their arrival in Charleston grew nearer, she became more anxious. What *would* Claiborne and Della Bodine think of their Yankee cousin? What would Loretta think? And how would Jessie adjust to being waited on by slaves? The prospect made her feel strangely unsettled.

"Don't wait up for me," Garth said. "I don't know what time I'll be back."

"I hope you can find some supplies."

"So do I." He came around the side of the bed and bent to kiss her. His lips were light at first upon hers, almost teasing, then they became almost bruising in their intensity. Jessie's pulse quickened; she felt the first quiver of desire.

Reluctantly, Garth drew away from her and straightened up. He made a leisurely study of her from head to toe, his eyes lingering at the soft rise and fall of her breasts. "On second thought, I might wake you."

Jessie's lips curved into a sultry little smile. "Be careful."

"I will, don't worry." He put on his tan hat, pocketed the key and left the room. Jessie stared for a few moments at the wooden paneling of the closed door, a soft, dreamy smile lurking at the corners of her mouth, then she snuggled down against the soft pillow.

Garth closed the door, thinking of Jessie— the strong beauty of her features and that anticipatory look in her eyes. The thought of the softness of her voice and the fragrance of all that glorious dark hair made him nearly groan aloud.

He fervently hoped the *Sunshine* would
dock early—maybe even earlier than
planned. He wanted to get back to those
magnificent curves and warm lips as soon as
possible.

So engrossed was he in his thoughts, he
walked away from the room and down the
stairs, completely forgetting to lock the door.

Jake sat in a lumpy, uncomfortable chair in
the lobby, pretending to read the *Wilmington
Courier*. He was daydreaming and half
dozing when he heard footsteps on the stairs.

He peered around the newspaper; his smile
spread into a wolfish, self-satisfied grin.
Garth Bodine was crossing the lobby, his hat
perched on his head at a jaunty angle, the
lower part of his holster showing under his
jacket. He went out the door without even
glancing in Jake's direction.

Jake stirred in anticipation. He would wait
a few minutes, then head for the stairs.

Jessie was in that strange netherworld
between sleeping and waking when she heard
the doorknob rattle. Her eyelids fluttered
open and she realized she had drifted off with
the lamp still lit. It didn't seem possible that
she had been asleep for long, but if Garth was
returning . . .

The door was flung open, and a shriek of
pure horror caught in her throat. Fear filled
her eyes at the sight of the man standing in
the doorway, and she brought her fisted
hands up to her mouth in disbelief. The lean,

lanky frame, the slicked-down brown hair, that loathesome black patch over the left eye.

Jessie scrambled to sit up, terror gathering in her. She pulled the sheet up over her bosom. "*You!*" Her voice came out as an eerie whine.

Jake Coffin closed the door, his thin lips curling into a triumphant, sinister smile. "Well, little missy. So we finally meet again."

Jessie had remained motionless, feeling the beating of her pulse hammering at her temples, but she tried to muster some false bravado. She met his gaze with cool contempt. "Get out!"

His brow lifted in amused surprise, but the humor didn't reach his eye. "I have business with you."

"Garth will be back any minute." The fear was like a knife in her throat, but somehow she managed to get the words out. "And if he finds you here, you're as good as dead."

"Your friend won't be back for quite some time." Jake's smile was as mirthless as the grin of a skull without flesh. "He's gone down to the river to meet the blockade runner *Sunshine.*"

Waves of revulsion and terror broke within Jessie. How did Coffin know? How on earth could he know? How had he found them? Now—when they were so close to Charleston! A surge of sheer panic rushed through her.

"Now," he said slowly, still smiling that ghastly smile. "Just be nice."

An unwelcome memory intruded into

Jessie's jumbled thoughts. Back at the deserted farmhouse in Virginia, this disgusting creature had planned to . . . She couldn't complete the thought; it sickened her.

He took a few steps toward the bed. Panic assailed her, a wild, crazy fear that sent her heart drumming in her ears and strangled the breath in her throat. The gun—Coffin's own gun—was still in her carpetbag. She scrambled from the bed, but his look stopped her cold. His gloating gaze traveled her length, roaming insolently over her body.

Jessie glared at him with undisguised hatred. He seemed to find this amusing, for he only laughed harshly and continued to stare. His glance slid suggestively downward to the rounded curves of her hips.

"I knew beneath all them petticoats there was a body any man could worship."

Jessie's thoughts flew wildly. She took a tentative step, then halted. The revolver was there, and she knew how to use it. She had to reach her carpetbag—or the door. But Coffin was blocking both.

Gathering her courage, Jessie made a dash for the door. With lightning speed, Coffin's arm snaked out, and his hand closed tightly around her upper arm. His fingers dug into the soft flesh, and she cried out.

"Easy, missy," he warned, and his voice had taken on a low, threatening quality. "You just do like I say and you won't get hurt."

Struggling to retain some composure, she forced herself to look at him. "Why do you want us?"

"I don't want Bodine." There was a lewd gleam in his coal black eye; Jessie felt her flesh shrink away from his touch. "You're the one I want."

Jessie tried to pull away, the fear returning like a dash of cold water. She wanted to scream, but no sound would come from her suddenly dry throat.

Without warning, Jake pulled her into a brutally hard embrace. He tried to kiss her. She turned her head away; his lips only grazed her cheek. He increased his pressure on her until she felt her ribs might be crushed, but she fought him. She writhed, kicked, bit at his arms. His hands groped over her body; he seemed all the more excited by her struggle.

"You're a real wildcat, missy!"

Jessie felt sick at her stomach and wished she could vomit, hoping it would discourage him. Desperately, she reached out, clawing for his eye patch. It was the wrong thing to do.

The first blow with the flat of his hand did little more than send her flying against the wall. The second, with the back of his hand, cracked her jaw. Jessie cried out miserably, sprawled onto the bed. The pain was instant and intense, a bright flare of agony.

Through tear-filled eyes she glanced up at him, and her heart leapt in her chest, beginning to bang so hard between her ribs that she saw spots before her eyes. He glared back at her with that one malevolent eye, an eye that held a glimmer of something mad.

Despite the pain in her jaw and the metallic taste of blood in her mouth where her teeth had bitten into her lower lip, Jessie tried to scramble away. Before she could get very far Coffin seized her ankle with furious strength. She tried to pull free, but his grip was too strong. She flailed out, kicking with her free foot, aiming for his groin. She missed, kicking him in the stomach instead. He let out an agonized groan, clutching his belly.

Jessie made another effort to get off the bed and away from him. With an inarticulate sound of rage, he grabbed a fistful of her hair and twisted it viciously. Jessie felt a white-hot blaze of pain consume her scalp, her entire head. The sound that came from her throat was something between a gasp and a sob. He was grinning at her madly, like a dog.

But she continued to struggle. She squirmed frantically under him, kicked and clawed with her nails, and sank her teeth into his hand.

His good eye fixed cruelly on her, full of malice. He had her pinioned beneath him; no amount of movement on her part was enough to wriggle free.

"Now, missy, I'll take what I want." His voice grated harshly, filled with malicious triumph. "Any more shenanigans out of you and I'll take my pleasure with you while you're unconscious."

Jessie didn't doubt his threat; the man was crazy. Revulsion and fear attacked her; her breath caught and bile crawled up into her

throat. She squeezed her eyes shut, praying
that it would at least be over quickly.

But then, suddenly, the door burst open.
Coffin released his pressure for an instant.
Jessie peered around him and wept in relief.
Coffin uttered a grunt of sheer dismay and
disbelief.

Garth was standing in the doorway. Anger
locked his jaws, his teeth were clenched and
the muscles in his neck bulged. His gray eyes
shone with a rage so intense, so inhuman,
that it sent a chill up Jessie's spine. He
emitted a growling shriek, dropped the sack
of food and whipped the revolver from his
holster.

Coffin acted quickly. He pulled Jessie
around in front of him, using her as a shield.
Her arm was twisted behind her back, and
she grimaced as a rush of pain washed over
her.

"You'll hit her before you hit me, Bodine."
Coffin's voice was brittle, laced with
cynicism. "You wouldn't want that, would
you?"

Garth's eyes flickered with uncertainty,
but Jessie had regained some of her courage.
"Go on, Garth! Shoot him now!"

Coffin gave her arm a vicious wrench. She
uttered a weak, moaning sob.

"Move, missy! And stay in front of me."

Jessie had an overwhelming urge to try to
break free, but Coffin's grip on her arm was
unbearable. Besides, the man was mad,
totally, utterly mad. He would do anything to
save his own rotten skin.

Garth was still aiming the gun, following Coffin's every slow, calculated move with the barrel. But he didn't fire. Jessie knew it was because of her. Despite her smallness, she provided a more than adequate shield for Coffin. She hated herself for her vulnerability, her ineffectiveness to do anything.

Then it happened. Coffin let go of her. In a blur of motion, he reached for the haversack and hurled it at Garth. It hit him square in the chest. The shot went wild, striking the window and shattering the pane. Garth lost his balance and toppled backward into the washstand, upsetting the pitcher. The revolver came loose from his grasp and skittered across the floor, out of his reach.

Coffin was off the bed and out the door, laughing maniacally. Jessie and Garth both scrambled after the gun. Garth reached it first. Jessie's arm throbbed; her jaw felt broken.

Garth got to his feet and ran out the door, colliding with curious guests who had gathered after hearing the shot. "Stop that man!"

Jessie got slowly to her feet, disregarding her torn nightdress, rubbing her sore arm. She heard Garth's exasperated curses and frantic, high-pitched questions from a man.

Garth returned, grimacing with disgust. "He's gone." His eyes blazed; there was an angry curve to his lips. "But this time I'll find the bastard."

Jessie's knees felt weak; she was on the verge of tears. She threw her arms around

Garth and buried her head against his chest. His hands came up to stroke her hair. His voice was quiet, soothing, speaking her name over and over again as if she were a child just awakened from a horrible nightmare. He continued to hold her, and Jessie drew comfort from his closeness.

"He didn't . . . ?" Garth swallowed, unable to finish the question.

"No. You came just in time." She could hear voices in the hall, excited and curious. She ignored them, continuing to cling to Garth.

"Are you all right?"

Jessie wasn't exactly sure; her whole body seemed to ache. "I think so."

Garth turned as the manager entered the room, a stocky little man with wispy white hair falling over his forehead. His wife followed, a plump, rosy-cheeked woman with bright blue eyes. She took the blanket from the bed and wrapped it around Jessie's shoulders.

"What happened here?" The manager, Ezra Phipps, was the one Jessie had heard with the high, nasal voice.

"That man was attempting to rape my wife," Garth said, and anger raged through his low tone.

"I'll send for the sheriff."

"Never mind." Garth turned to Jessie, and his eyes softened. "You'll be all right now. Maybe Mrs. Phipps will stay with you for a while."

The woman nodded quickly. "Of course, Mr. Smith."

"Where are you going?" Jessie asked; it hurt her jaw to talk.

"After him."

Jessie nodded in resignation. She knew it had to end here—one way or another. There would be no sense in arguing with Garth. She squeezed his hand. "Be careful. Come back to me."

He mustered a reassuring smile for her benefit. "I will."

With that, he was out the door, shouldering his way through the milling group of people.

"Get in bed, dear," Mrs. Phipps said gently, then turned to her husband. "Ezra, go down and get her a glass of brandy—a big one. And a fresh pitcher of water and clean towels."

Phipps shrugged in surrender. "Yes, Winnie. But I still think I should let the sheriff know about this."

"That young man seemed perfectly capable of handling this himself. Besides, the sheriff is a buffoon."

Phipps left the room, closing the door behind him. Jessie could hear him speaking to the guests, sending them back to their rooms.

She climbed into bed and allowed Winnie Phipps to tuck the blanket around her. Her whole body seemed to shriek in agony; she would be grateful for the brandy.

"You've got a bruise on your jaw," Mrs. Phipps remarked. "Not a bad one, but it's there."

"I don't doubt it." Jessie closed her eyes and said a silent prayer for Garth. She hoped he returned with nothing more serious than a bruise himself. Suddenly her pent-up emotions burst like a dam, and she had to stifle her sobs with both hands pressed to her mouth.

As Garth clattered down the stairs and into the lobby, his rage began to grow. He was aware of his own pulse throbbing at his temples, of the heat in his flushed face. The knots in his stomach had drawn painfully tight. If the *Sunshine* hadn't made port earlier than expected . . .

He shook his head to banish the thought. The very idea of that slimy creature Coffin with his hands on Jessie sickened him. A chill rippled through him, and he found that his body was suddenly clammy.

Out on the street the night air turned Garth's sweat cold. He looked up one side of the avenue, then down the other. Which way had Coffin gone? After laming his horse Garth didn't even know what kind of animal—if any—Coffin was riding.

A skinny black boy stepped up to him, eyeing him curiously. "You need help, mistuh? 'Shore do look riled to me."

Startled, Garth turned to the youth. "Did you see a man run out of here a few minutes ago?"

The boy nodded eagerly. "I did indeed, suh. White man wid a patch on one eye. Dat be his hawse." He pointed to a weary sorrel tied at the railing. "He jes' lit out a-runnin'. Forgot all 'bout his hawse."

"Which way?"

"Towards the docks."

Garth waved his hand in thanks and took off down Market, his long legs pumping hard. He ran with the speed of desperation. Coffin wouldn't get away this time. Garth realized he should have killed him back in Virginia.

Madly, blindly, he pushed on, feeling as if his lungs were going to explode, his heart about to burst open. Rounding Front Street, he collided with a drunken sailor. The seaman fell into the stinking gutter, hurling curses after Garth.

The docks were dark and quiet. Most of the men from the *Sunshine* had departed for a night's entertainment. Garth slowed his pace to a walk, feeling exposed, keeping to the shadows. It was dark here, the moon obscured by a heavy layer of clouds. It was unnaturally quiet; only the river lapping at the pilings made any sound. A chill crawled up Garth's spine to the base of his neck.

A shot exploded, as loud as a cannonade. Wood splintered on a stack of kegs not a foot away from him. Garth ducked behind them and drew his own revolver. It was Coffin who had fired at him—Garth knew it as surely as he knew his own name. But where was he? The shot could have come from anywhere.

A can toppled over behind him, making a loud, metallic crash. Garth spun around, his gun at the ready. A tan cat darted from the shadows and streaked into an alley.

Garth exhaled slowly, letting his heartbeat decelerate. He turned back, cautiously peering around one of the kegs. For a full five minutes he watched and waited, then he saw the thin sliver of the moon as it passed beneath a cloud reflecting on the barrel of a revolver. Coffin was near the water, holed up behind bales of cotton ready to be loaded on the next ship bound for England.

Garth tried to analyze the situation objectively. Somehow, he had to get around Coffin, get behind him. The moon had disappeared behind the thick clouds once more; darkness enveloped the docks again. Garth picked up a broken piece of wood and tossed it up on the roof of an empty warehouse. Sparks flashed as Coffin fired again, this time at the rooftop.

Garth quickly tugged off his boots and darted a few yards closer behind a tall stack of crates. In fact, here, crates of everything imaginable lined the backs of the warehouse, and there was just enough room between them and the buildings for a man to squeeze through.

He picked up several oyster shells and tossed them upward. They hit the roof with a skittering, sliding sound. Coffin fired again.

Garth sidled along behind the crates until he felt he was directly opposite Coffin. He hurled a broken horseshoe up; it struck the roof ten feet to his rear. Coffin's revolver boomed again. Garth's mouth curved with satisfaction in the velvety darkness. Coffin believed his adversary was moving along the roof, just as Garth wanted.

Still crouching behind the crates, he sidled farther down, then threw more debris up on the warehouse. Coffin fired once more. Garth had kept track of the shots: five. His own pistol held only five rounds; perhaps Coffin's did as well. And there was always the possibility that Coffin had reloaded the chamber.

Garth was a man accustomed to taking chances, though it was a role he didn't relish. He hurled another batch of shells up. Coffin fired. Garth leaped out from behind his shelter. Coffin fired again. The revolver made only a loud click.

Garth hurtled over the bales of cotton and knocked Coffin to the ground. Jake flailed out with the butt of his gun, striking Garth on the side of the head. The blow jarred him, blurring his vision. But Coffin had been overwhelmed by the speed and surprise of the assault. Garth fought back the pain and struck out again.

He drove the heel of his hand square into Jake's face. Coffin's head rocked back on his shoulders and he stumbled and fell. For some perverse reason, Garth reholstered his gun. In his heart and mind, he knew he should simply finish the job efficiently and painlessly. But he wanted to beat Coffin, to take out all his frustration and anger on this slimy, one-eyed creature. For what he had done to Jessie, Jake Coffin deserved some pain before the end.

Jake lurched to his feet and rushed at Garth like a man possessed, lashing out wildly with his fists. Garth's hand went up mechanically to ward off the blows, but one connected with his right eye. Garth saw stars explode in his vision; he reeled back, colliding with the bales of cotton.

Coffin charged again. Shaking his head to clear it, Garth turned with catlike fluidity and swung his fist. Coffin grunted like a cannonball had just hit him in the gut; he fell backward into a wooden piling. He reached into his boot and pulled something out. Garth saw the ten-inch blade flash in the hazy moonlight.

Coffin lurched to his feet and staggered toward him. Garth reached for his revolver. It wasn't in his holster. It must have fallen out when he slammed into the cotton.

Coffin held the knife well balanced in front of him as he advanced. Garth scuttled backward. Coffin lunged. There was a flash of brittle steel through the air. Garth heard it whisper as it sliced within inches of his face.

Garth did a kind of pirouette on his toes, spun around and slipped out of the way. The blade went into a cotton bale to the hilt. But Garth stumbled to his knees, scraping the palms of his hands.

"You smartass Rebel sonofabitch!" Coffin hissed.

Garth turned. Jake was pulling the knife free of the cotton. The cruel smile died on Coffin's lips, and his face became something almost inhuman. His expression made Garth's throat constrict with fear.

"I'll have your woman," Coffin said in a furious whisper. "That soft, ripe body'll be mine."

Garth's hand groped out and closed around something hard and smooth and heavy: a belaying pin, cast aside by some careless sailor. "You'll have to kill me first."

"I intend to do just that, Bodine."

Coffin advanced slowly, like a wolf stalking his prey. Garth rose cautiously, warily watching his adversary. Jake lunged with the knife. Garth sidestepped with feline agility.

With a vicious, sidewise swipe of his hand, Garth laid Coffin's head open with the belaying pin. The side of his face exploded like a ripe melon. His hair was splattered with blood; tissue and brain matter oozed down his cheek like a hideous flow of lava. Coffin emitted a horrible, gutteral scream. The knife fell from his grip and clattered against the wooden planks.

Coffin staggered a few moments, reeling senselessly. He bumped into a piling, spun around, then collapsed. His body hit the water with a loud splash.

Garth crept shakily to the edge of the dock, breathing hard. There was no flailing, no kicking, no cries for help. One hand reached clawlike up out of the oily black water, then disappeared. Bubbles broke the surface for a few seconds, then the river was still. The silence was oppressive and terrifying.

Garth shuddered with relief. But he didn't feel happy; neither was he sad. If he had killed anyone in the past, they had been unknown to him, faceless Yankees, his enemies. Jake Coffin, for all his corruption and wickedness, had been, after all, a man.

With a heavy sigh, Garth turned away, searching for his revolver and boots. He picked them up, pulled on his boots and jammed the gun into his holster. Coffin's saddlebags were lying on the planking. Garth tossed them into the water, watched them sink and turned away.

His eye stung, watered, ached. He trudged back through the streets of Wilmington, head bowed, his hands thrust deep in his pockets. The clouds had cleared; a sliver of moon was shining in a sky of tranquil stars.

At the hotel, the young black boy approached Garth. "Find him, mistuh?"

Garth nodded. "He decided to take a little voyage. He won't be back."

"What about the hawse?"

"You keep him."

The boy's eyes widened in disbelief. "*Me?*"

"Sure. You ever owned a horse before?"

"Nossuh." The youth stepped into the street, put his thin arms around the mare's neck and hugged her.

Smiling faintly, Garth entered the hotel. The lobby was deserted, and he trudged wearily up the stairs and unlocked the door. A low lamp burned by the bedside. Jessie was sleeping. Mrs. Phipps woke from a doze in a chair.

"You're back, Mr. Smith."

Garth gave a lame nod. "How's my wife?"

"Been sleeping like a baby for an hour. The brandy, I think."

Garth handed the woman a ten-dollar Confederate note. "Thank you for your concern, ma'm. We'll be leaving in the morning. Tell your husband I'll pay for the broken window."

"And that scoundrel?"

"Gone. Left the state." And this world.

She nodded approvingly, then bid him good night and left the room.

Garth felt drained, exhausted, shaky. He poured brandy from the bottle into a glass and drank it down quickly in one gulp. Then he walked over to the washstand and grimaced at his image in the mirror. His eye was swollen shut in shadowy purple.

He dampened a cloth and held it to the livid eye; for a moment waves of dizziness descended over him. Then he stripped off his sweat-soaked shirt and sponged himself off. He sat down, removed his boots and socks, then stood and pulled down his trousers. A great weariness theatened to overwhelm him.

He went over to the bed and gazed at Jessie. Her faint, even breathing told him she was asleep. He reached for her hands; they were small and delicate. The fragility of them, the vulnerability of this lovely nineteen-year-old woman-child made his heart ache.

# 19

It was hot and humid and sticky; the buggy rattled over the cobbles of Meeting Street. Jessie's gaze roved over the city. Palmettos lining the avenue looked as wilted as she felt; people moved about sluggishly. At the court house, they turned right onto Broad Street.

"Just a little farther," Garth said.

Jessie could hardly believe they were in Charleston. After all they had gone through they were finally here! A mild panic seized her at this realization. How would the Bodines react to her?

She looked over at Garth; one eye was an angry purplish mass of livid flesh. "You look terrible."

"I know. At least that bruise on your chin hardly shows."

"But I can still feel it." A chill rippled through her, and she found her hands were suddenly clammy as she recalled her encounter with the fiend Coffin. "Is he really dead?"

Garth nodded grimly. "He's dead. He'd have to be some kind of a wizard to survive that crack on the head and the fall in the river."

"I'm not sorry you killed him."

"Neither am I." His mouth twisted with bitter amusement. "It was either him or me."

The buggy swerved left on Legare Street and stopped in front of the third house from the corner.

"Is this it?" Jessie asked.

"This is it." The lean planes of Garth's face were transformed by a youthful grin. "Home at last."

Jessie goggled. It was a two-story house painted a light blue with white shutters. A white wrought-iron balcony ran around the second floor. There was lattice work festooned with sweet peas at one end of the veranda and the brick walkway was bordered with pansies on either side. Everything sparkled and shined. Compared to this, her own home back in Gettysburg looked like a shack. The houses on the block were similar, though all were painted different colors. Some looked abandoned, however, overgrown with weeds, with rusted gates and closed shutters.

Garth handed her down from the buggy, swung open the gate and beckoned her to precede him up to the porch. He rapped lightly on the knocker, a huge brass thing molded into the shape of a horse's head.

"What if they don't like me?" she asked, her stomach flutering wildly.

"They will." Garth slipped his arm around her waist, giving her a brief squeeze. "Who wouldn't?"

Presently, the door was opened by a Negro wearing black trousers and a crisp white shirt. He was tall and lean and stood almost rigidly erect. There was a fringe of fuzzy white hair around his skull; his face was worn and wrinkled.

His eyes flew open in surprised disbelief, then this self-composure broke, and his face cracked with a broad, gold-toothed grin. "Mistuh Garth!" He turned around and shouted into the bowels of the house. "Mistuh Garth be home at last!"

Garth ushered Jessie inside the foyer. It was cooler than outside, but still warm. It smelled of beeswax polish and fresh flowers.

"How are you, Sam?" Garth asked the black man.

"Jes' fine, suh. But you don' look so good. What happened to yer eye?"

Before Garth could answer, a woman hurried into the hall, bustling with excitement. She threw her arms around Garth and hugged him fiercely. "I'm so glad you're home!" There was a misting of tears in her eyes. She drew back and studied him, then frowned. "What on earth did you do to your eye?"

"Nothing, Mother. Just a little accident." Garth turned to Jessie and took her hand. "Mother, this is Jessie. Your cousin."

Della Bodine hugged her. "Welcome to Charleston. Matt told us you were coming. I'm so sorry about your mother."

Jessie nodded woodenly. Della Bodine was as straight and supple as a reed and her blue eyes glittered with lively intelligence. Her long, straight brown hair, threaded with some gray, was coiled in a knot atop her head, emphasizing a gentle dignity in her features.

In stark contrast, Claiborne Bodine was nothing like his wife. He shook Garth's hand as if he were a business acquaintance and bowed stiffly to Jessie. Probably sixty, she judged, with a broad face and heavy jowls, he had silver hair and muttonchop side-whiskers. The skin around his eyes seemed drawn down by invisible weights, and there were lines deeply etched in his face. His once powerful shoulders were slightly stooped; he had a little round pot belly that bulged his vest.

"It took you long enough to get here." His voice was raspy, with a heavy drawl.

"We had some delays."

Claiborne Bodine turned to Sam, still hovering nearby. "Get their bags." He peered curiously at Garth. "You do have bags, don't you?"

"Not much. They're in the buggy."

The older man pushed aside a curtain at one of the tall, narrow windows on either side of the door. He grunted in disapproval. "You call that broken-down thing a buggy?"

"It got us here, didn't it?" Garth turned to Jessie and winked, taking her hand in his.

"Let's go sit down where it's comfortable. And I'm thirsty."

"I'll tell Violet Mae," Della said. She turned to Jessie with a question in her eyes. "Iced tea? Lemonade? Perhaps some sherry?"

"Lemonade would be fine, ma'm."

"Call me Della." And she vanished in a swirl of crinolines and taffeta.

Jessie followed Garth into the drawing room and seated herself next to him on the settee, gazing around her in wonder. Ornate silver sconces sat on a polished oak table; the lamps were of the finest cut crystal. Chairs and sofas, covered with silk and brocade, were arranged tastefully amid Chippendale tables and sideboards. A pianoforte sat in one corner, covered with a lace cloth and framed tintypes. This was only the Bodines' town house; Jessie had heard the plantations in the South were even more opulent.

Claiborne Bodine poured whiskey for himself and handed a glass to his son. He sat heavily in a maroon chair with hundreds of tassels. His glance at Jessie was cool and appraising. "I was sorry to hear about Hattie. She was a sweet little thing when I knew her."

Jessie managed a half-hearted smile. She shook off the melancholy and depressing thoughts, determined not to indulge in self-pity. But she felt uncomfortable under the older man's close scrutiny. He didn't like her; she could feel it clear down to the marrow of her bones.

"Where's Loretta?" Garth asked.

Before his father could answer a female

voice spoke from the hallway. "Here I am."

Jessie looked up as a young woman swept into the parlor with an unhurried, gliding walk. She wore a beautiful gown of lime green festooned with silver lace, but unfortunately it only seemed to emphasize her rather flat bosom. She looked nothing like Garth—nothing like Jessie had expected. Blond curls and ringlets were atumble about her shoulders. Her features were sharp and aristocratic, her face dominated by cynical gray eyes and a sullen mouth that drooped at the corners.

She came over to Garth, placed a perfunctory kiss on his forehead, then turned to Jessie. Her gaze was cold and impersonal. "You must be our Yankee cousin."

Jessie held out her hand, but Loretta flounced away in a rustle of skirts and sank into a chair. She eyed Garth critically. "Where'd you get that shiner?"

Jessie tensed, wondering what he would say.

"We were waylaid by some army deserters."

She raised a brow in surprise. "Not ours, I hope."

Garth shrugged. "I don't know who they were. I didn't bother to ask questions."

Jessie was grateful to Garth. She didn't want to hear about Coffin, didn't know how Loretta and her father would react. She wanted to reach out and squeeze his arm in thanks, but the way father and daughter were looking at her—as if she were some newly discovered species of insect—she didn't dare.

"Well . . ." Loretta drawled, wearing a slightly sardonic smile. "You botched up your part for the war, didn't you?"

Garth regarded her with a frown. "I didn't ask to get shot. Thank God for Jessie and her mama."

"Yes, thank God." Della reappeared, smiling, followed by a heavyset black woman in a brown bombazine dress and white apron.

The Negro offered a silver tray to Jessie. "Lemonade, miss?"

Jessie took a frosty glass and sipped gratefully.

"How are you, Violet Mae?" Garth inquired.

"Jes' fine, mistuh Garth." Her grin was wide; several teeth were missing. Her dark eyes sparkled with pleasure. "Shore am glad dem Yankees didn't hurt you any worse than they did."

Garth introduced Jessie to the black woman. She turned a beaming, moon face on her. "Never met up wid a real Yankee before."

"Let's hope it's the last you do," Loretta muttered.

A scowl flickered briefly across Violet Mae's face before she turned and offered refreshments to Loretta and Della. Her duties done, she disappeared silently from the room.

"Well . . ." Loretta sighed, taking a drink from her glass. "Brother's home." One eyebrow arched in sharp query, and a lopsided smirk settled on her lips. "Did you kill any Yankees?"

Jessie shuddered. These people made her uncomfortable in a way she couldn't pin down. She wished someone would show her to her room so she could lie down and think. She felt an immediate dislike for Loretta; she was positive the feeling was mutual.

"I don't know."

Loretta's head snapped up in surprise, curls bobbing. "You don't know! That's what you went away to do!"

"Yes. But I'm sorry I went. It's not a pretty sight to see out there on the battlefield."

Loretta lifted her hands in a wild gesture of disgust. "The only good Yankee is a dead Yankee." She glanced at Jessie, and her mouth quirked in a semblence of a smile. "Present company excluded, of course."

Jessie met the woman's comment with a brooding silence. She felt as if Loretta was patronizing her, even laughing at her.

"Enough talk of the war for now," Della said. "Jessie and Garth must be tired."

"I am." Jessie threw a look of gratitude at Della. "It's been a long drive—too long."

"I'll have Flobelle show you to your room." The older woman rose and tugged on an embroidered bell cord.

But instead of the maid Jessie expected, an exceptionally handsome black man entered the room. He had dark, coppery skin, and the duskiness of his complexion enhanced the whiteness of his teeth. Possibly in his middle twenties, he wore brown breeches tucked into shiny black boots and a loose-sleeved cream-colored shirt. His shoulders were broad above narrow hips and his black eyes were alert. "Mistuh Bodine, suh, I done put de two grays in de stable. But dey ain't no room fer dat buggy."

"Give it away," Claiborne muttered.

"To who?"

"I don't care."

The Negro squinted in a puzzled frown, but he nodded. He turned to Garth, and white teeth flashed in a broad grin. "Welcome home, suh."

"Thank you, Apollo."

The black bowed politely to Jessie, then backed out of the parlor.

"Our stableman," Claiborne said. "And worth every penny I paid for him."

Jessie winced. This was all so strange! She knew she was going to hate it here. What she wouldn't give to turn back the clock a month—back before the battle in Gettysburg, when things were normal. Then she looked at Garth, saw his lean, handsome face with its finely chiseled nose and cheekbones, and knew she didn't regret coming here. But if only he could have remained in Pennsylvania! She stifled a sigh.

Flobelle was a petite young woman with a shy but friendly smile. She ushered Jessie into a bedroom that was surprisingly cool. A rosewood bed dominated the room and a huge armoire stood in one corner; Jessie wondered what she would ever put in it.

"I help you unpack," Flobelle said.

"I can do it myself. Besides, there isn't

much." Her nightgown was still in shreds from Coffin's rough handling. She wondered carefully, measuring her size. "Do you have a nightdress I could borrow until I can get a new one?"

The girl looked absolutely scandalized. "Lordy, miss! White ladies don' wear niggers' clothes. You borry from Mis Della or Miz Loretta. They got plenty."

Jessie didn't argue, nor did she intend to ask either woman. Tonight she would sleep nude if she had to.

"You jes' lay down an' rest," Flobelle said, unstrapping Jessie's carpetbag. "I hang up yer clothes. You want somethin', you jes' ask me."

Jessie nodded distractedly, sat down on the bed and took off her shoes. She wasn't used to people waiting on her, and certainly not anyone bought off the auction block.

The dining room was huge, with a monstrous crystal chandelier suspended above the table. Silver platters gleamed on the sideboard; there was gilt-edged Wedgwood china and Waterford crystal. Jessie glanced at Garth out of the corner of her eye, seated beside her; he no longer resembled the bloodied soldier in the Morgans' basement, the fugitive on the run. He was wearing black trousers, a ruffled white lawn shirt and a white swallow-tailed jacket. He was freshly shaven except for the drooping mustache, though his black hair needed trimming at the collar. She had never seen him look so handsome, so male. His sexuality was potent; she could feel it radiating through her. Being so near to him was disconcerting when others were present. She wanted him to take her in his arms, whisper how much he loved her. Here—in Charleston, miles away from home—he was her only link to the past.

With Flobelle's help—insistence, actually—Jessie had freshened up for supper. She had put on her best frock, a simple white gown with a yellow silk sash. Still, she felt woefully underdressed. Loretta, seated across the table with an air of lofty assurance, was still wearing the lime green gown. Della had changed into a peach taffeta, much too young looking for her forty-six years. Claiborne, presiding at the head of the table, had donned a brocade vest threaded with gold, a gaudy maroon neckcloth and a black jacket.

Sam had poured wine for them all, then silently departed through the doors leading to the kitchen.

"I think a toast is in order," Claiborne said, raising his glass. "To Garth's return home."

"And our dear little Jessie coming with him," Della put in.

Jessie meekly lifted her glass to her lips and drank. Her eyes met Loretta's briefly across the table; the two women looked at one another in perfect understanding. Jessie managed a vaguely polite smile. If she was going to survive in this place, she had best be on her guard. Loretta was a woman accustomed to having her own way, a woman whose every word and gesture seemed calculated to impart a sense of her own importance. To be a Yankee in this household, Jessie knew she was going to have to be Loretta's equal. Loretta had to have a flaw—everyone did. Jessie intended to discover what it was, or she knew she would never be at peace here.

"My mother wrote to Peggy Sue often, but she hadn't heard back from her in ages," Jessie said. "I'd like to see her."

Della looked visibly distressed. "Didn't you know? We lost her last sumer—to swamp fever."

Jessie's heart sank. One more possible ally was gone. Would Garth revert to his old ways? Could she depend on him, now that he was home? She peered at him out of the corner of her eye; he gave her a faint, reassuring smile.

"Her husband died early in the war," Della explained.

"Of measles!" Loretta exclaimed with a dismissive wave of her hand. "Of all things!"

"She sold the town house, moved out to the country."

"Your climate doesn't exactly sound healthy," Jessie remarked.

"Better than freezing to death in the winter," Loretta said, sipping her wine and giving an exaggerated shudder. "I've never seen snow."

"You probably wouldn't like it."

Loretta smiled thinly. "I'm sure I wouldn't."

Jessie ground her teeth and twisted the napkin on her lap. Only a few hours in this house, and already she disliked Loretta intensely.

To Jessie's relief, Violet Mae waddled in from the kitchen, balancing a tray precariously. She first served Claiborne, then Della. She placed a plate of crisp, cold greens in front of Jessie, and Jessie smiled up at the Negress. "Thank you."

Loretta regarded Jessie with obvious disgust. "You don't thank niggers!"

Jessie met Loretta's gaze without faltering. "*I* do."

"What for? They don't expect it! Why, most of them are nothing but shiftless trash!"

Jessie eyed her with a curious, probing look. "If you consider them shiftless trash, then why are you fighting so hard to keep them in bondage?"

Claiborne coughed into his napkin. Loretta's mouth drooped open in astonishment. Violet Mae grinned as she left the room.

Garth gave Jessie a warning nudge under the table. She shot him a withering look.

"Actually," he said, trying to make his voice casually conversational, "some of that shiftless trash, as you're so fond of calling them, Loretta, saved our necks." He tasted his salad, chewed for a moment, then took a sip of wine. He related their experience in North Carolina, of Roscoe hiding them in the root cellar from the highwayman who was after them.

A sudden coldness crept over Jessie's body and settled in the pit of her stomach. She pictured in her mind Jake Coffin, his lecherous, mad grin, that ugly black patch over his eye, the way his hands had felt on her flesh, the strong scent of whiskey on his breath. Her skin crawled with revulsion. Was he actually out of her life for good? Or would he return to haunt her forevermore?

Loretta's nose wrinkled disdainfully as she studied her brother with a critical eye. "I think, dear Garth, you've become a bit of a Yankee yourself."

"Let's just say I've seen the war first-hand. I've seen men die, and on my travels, I began to see how the South was dying."

"Nonsense!" Claiborne stifled a belch, then refilled his glass from the decanter. "Yes, I'll admit we're suffering. There are privations, to be sure. But it's all for a great and noble cause—our independence!"

With a shuddering sigh, Jessie finished her salad in silence.

"We're still doing all right," Claiborne said.

"Are we?" Garth asked.

His father shrugged as Violet Mae removed the salad plates and returned with a platter of roast duck and bowls of vegetables and rice. "We're not starving, as you can see. I did sell off a few slaves from the plantation. I might sell off a few more, maybe even let our overseer go."

Garth arched a brow, his gray eyes full of surprise. "Fire Tyler?"

Claiborne nodded absently, helping himself to the food. "There's hardly any horses left, anyway. I gave most of them to the army. Leroy can handle things."

Loretta chuckled scornfully. "If he doesn't take a notion to run off himself."

Claiborne seemed amused. "And do what? He's better off with us than if he was free."

Tiny frown lines appeared on Jessie's forehead. She nibbled at her meal, but suddenly she wasn't very hungry anymore.

The house was silent, save for the ticking of the clock, as Garth sat with his father in the library. It was a comfortable room, its shelves lined with books and a few ship models displayed in glass cases. It smelled pleasantly of leather and tobacco.

Garth had removed his jacket and unfastened the top three buttons of his shirt. He reclined in an overstuffed chair, his feet propped negligently on an ottoman. Idly, he swirled brandy in a cut-glass snifter and studied his father covertly.

Claiborne Bodine had aged considerably in the year and a half since Garth had last seen him. His hair was whiter and sparser, his face more deeply lined. An extra ten pounds made him look older than his sixty years.

A cooling breeze wafted in through the open window, bringing with it the salt tang of the ocean, not far away. It felt good to be home, but Garth couldn't forget what he had seen all along his route. The Confederacy was falling to pieces like a giant house of cards.

Even General Lee, with all his infinite wisdom and goodness, had seemed to impart that feeling of doom.

Garth's thoughts drifted away from the war, back to Jessie. No doubt she was upstairs now, settled in her new bed. Was she as uncomfortable as he supposed she must be? She was a stranger here. Even Garth—though this was his home—felt ill at ease. The war had changed him; so had Jessie. His family had remained the same.

"Are we really all right?" he asked. "Financially, I mean?"

"I still have some cash, but most of our resources are in property. The plantations, this house, the slaves, our china and silver and furniture."

"Is the money in gold or Confederate bonds?"

"Bonds, of course."

Garth blew air out through clenched teeth in an expression of sheer frustration. "Do you have any idea what they're worth now?"

"I know they're devaluating a little." Claiborne swirled his brandy, sipped it, then smacked his lips appreciatively. "They'll come back, like our army will. We'll win, despite the few setbacks we've had recently."

"I wonder."

Claiborne's face knotted into a disapproving frown. "Loretta's never given up. Neither should you, son. After all, you're a soldier."

Not by choice, Garth thought derisively, and finished his brandy. While Garth could seldom do anything right in his father's view,

Loretta could do no wrong. She was the apple of his eye, a woman for whom he had big plans. With the right husband to guide her, Loretta could live like royalty.

"I'm not going back to my regiment."

Dismay and shock flashed across his father's face. "*What!*"

"I said I'm not going back. There's nothing left of it anyway but a few cripples."

"But you're a healthy boy. Just a little scratch. Join another regiment. Go out and fight for your country!"

"I promised Jessie I wouldn't."

"Jessie." Claiborne pursed his lips and blew out some air. He tipped the brandy bottle to his glass. "She's just a girl. And a Yankee at that."

"I'll do something for the war, but I won't fight. Not ever again."

His father peered at him with undisguised suspicion. "Just what does this Jessie mean to you? How close *are* you?"

"I love her. I've asked her to marry me."

A glint of anger shone in Claiborne's eyes; he flushed slightly but remained controlled. "How can you even consider living with yourself and a Yankee at the same time? A Yankee sworn to see the South brought to its knees! Where's your conscience, boy?"

"I knew you wouldn't be pleased." Garth rose and set his empty snifter on the table. "But you'd better begin to accept the facts as they are. I'll do what I can for the Confederacy, but not at the risk of losing Jessie."

Garth pivoted on his heel and departed the library, leaving his father sputtering in speechless outrage.

Jessie stood at the open window of her room, clad in her wrapper, staring out at the rooftops. A few of the other houses had lights burning, but most were dark. The faint tang of sea air was carried on the breeze; occasionally a horse or carriage would rattle up Legare Street. The sky was clear; a shining spray of stars surrounded a half moon. Below, in the garden, a fountain tinkled musically as water splashed and bubbled. The jasmine was in bloom, and it smelled delightful.

Jessie released a long, desolate sigh. Where was Garth? Since their arrival in Charleston, they hadn't had a minute alone together. She needed him now, needed someone she loved in this land of strangers. Unfriendly strangers at that. Only Della seemed genuinely pleased that Jessie was here.

A wave of homesickness swept over her; her shoulders slumped, and she felt the sting of tears behind her eyes. This place was nothing like home. The people talked with their oddly lazy drawls, they lived in a dream world of opulence, ordered their slaves about like trained monkeys. Jessie felt like an outsider instead of family, an intrusion into a way of life that was as doomed as the poor boys on the battlefields.

Tomorrow, she would write to Mary Purcell, tell her she had arrived safely. At least that might make Jessie feel better. If the mail was still able to get through, she could start up a regular correspondence with her old friend.

Feeling slightly comforted, Jessie was about to turn away from the window when she saw movement in the garden. She peered closely and saw blond hair shining under the faint glow of the moon. It was Loretta, moving swiftly and silently along the path. Then she disappeared around the carriage shed and vanished from sight.

Shaking her head in puzzlement, Jessie vented another long sigh and turned away. She unbelted her wrapper and slipped nude between the sheets. Maybe Garth would come later. With this thought, a little smile touched her lips, and she drifted off into a dreamless, peaceful sleep.

Loretta crept into the carriage house, closed the door and locked it behind her. A lantern was burning in one of the far stalls, and she could hear Apollo's deep, rumbling voice as he spoke to one of the animals.

Hay stirred beneath her feet, making a dry, whispering sound as she walked. Apollo straightened up, turned as she approached.

"It be late, Miz Loretta," he said, and resumed brushing one of the grays Garth had brought in with that deplorable buggy this afternoon.

"It's not late at all."

Loretta leaned against the stall, her arms folded across her breasts, watching Apollo as he worked. He was shirtless, and a thin sheen of perspiration gilded his coppery flesh;

muscles bunched and rippled beneath the skin of his arms and shoulders. He wasn't bad looking for a nigger, she told herself. His nose was straight, his lips were thin, his brow smooth. Unlike most of his kind, he possessed features that could almost be considered white. In fact, no doubt somewhere back in his line he did indeed have a drop or two of white blood in him. Besides, with all the men of Charleston off fighting in the war, the only males left behind were either too young, too old or crippled.

Loretta's hand snaked out, ran along the solid flesh of Apollo's shoulder. "You've worked enough for today."

"Got to finish," he muttered, casting an uneasy glance at her. "Your pappy say he kind o' like dese hawses. I don' want to make him mad."

Loretta snatched the curry comb from his hand and tossed it aside. "You don't want to make me mad either, do you?"

"No'm." He turned to face her, though he refused to meet her eyes, his arms hanging limp at his sides.

Exasperated, Loretta took his hands and wrapped them around her waist. She slipped her arms around his thickly muscled back, arching her body close to him. "You know what I want, Apollo. You know what I always want."

# 20

Jessie crept down the stairs, refreshed from a good night's sleep. It had been fairly cool last night, but already the house felt sticky. Hearing voices coming from the dining room, she entered. Garth, his father and his mother were seated at the table. Garth rose and pulled out a chair for her. Their eyes met briefly. Jessie's look must have conveyed her feelings of estrangement, for his gray eyes were grave and compassionate.

"Did you sleep well?" Della inquired.

"Yes, thank you." Jessie allowed Garth to pour her a cup of coffee. She swallowed and realized that even the Bodines' money couldn't buy the real brew; this was the same bitter-tasting liquid she had been served ever since entering the South. She smothered a grimace with her napkin, wondering if she would ever get used to the stuff.

Claiborne eyed her with cool speculation. "My son tells me he's not planning to rejoin the army." The words were almost an accusation.

Jessie's surprise turned to something like amazement.

One corner of Garth's mouth lifted in a faint smile that crooked the line of his mustache. "I promised you. Didn't you believe me?"

Truly, she hadn't. "Not really."

"You'd just give it all up because you think you're in love with a Yankee?" Claiborne's tone became deliberately patient, as if he were dealing with a cranky child.

"I don't think, Father. I know. Besides, that's not the only reason."

A shadow of irritation crossed Claiborne's florid features. "Then what is the real reason? The Confederacy needs men like you. Healthy, strong, well trained, seasoned in battle."

Della held up her hands in a placating gesture. "Claiborne, don't bark so. I'm happy for Garth that he's found someone. Jessie seems like a sweet little thing."

"But a Yankee."

"Enough!" Della flashed a meaningful look at her husband. "Frankly, I don't want to see my only son go back to fight. He was injured once. I couldn't bear to have him . . ." She broke off abruptly, leaving the sentence unfinished.

Garth reached over and took his mother's hand as Violet Mae appeared with a plate of toasted bread. Jessie glanced at the black woman with a friendly smile, but held her thanks on the tip of her tongue.

Claiborne helped himself to three thick slices and spread them liberally with butter and jam. His white hair was mussed, his eyes so bloodshot they seemed almost red. Jessie suspected he had been imbibing rather heavily last night. She had indeed created a rift, and she didn't know how to mend it.

"I've been in the field, and once is enough for me," Garth said, offering Jessie some toast, then serving himself. "I haven't given up my ideals. I still believe in the Confederacy. But I'll find some way to help here in town. Maybe in the quartermasters' department."

"Sounds exciting, brother dear." Loretta flounced into the room and settled herself in a mass of ribbons and lace at the table. "Just pray those mules they feed our soldiers don't bite you on the bottom."

Claiborne muttered to himself as he chewed, shaking his head in confused amazement. "A few weeks in the North, and my son has turned into a spineless Yankee-lover."

Jessie felt like crawling under the table.

"The next thing," the older man said, brandishing his toast as if it were a lethal weapon, "You'll be wanting to free all our darkies."

Loretta lifted a brow, studying Jessie over the rim of her cup. "Has our dear little cousin been putting abolitionist ideas in Garth's head?"

Jessie met Loretta's eyes defiantly. "Garth has a mind of his own. I can't change it."

Claiborne's gaze grew intent on Jessie. "But you'd like to try, wouldn't you?"

Before Jessie could answer, Garth spoke up in her defense. "If you don't stop picking on her, we'll move out, take a room at a hotel."

"Yes," Della agreed. "Do leave the girl alone. After all, she *is* family."

Claiborne wiped his lips, then tossed down his napkin. "I'm going out." His eyes fell on Garth. "Join me at the Planters' House for lunch. We'll talk some more."

"I thought I'd show Jessie the city today."

"Jessie's going shopping with me," Loretta told him. "I can show her the sights. I'm sure she's absolutely *dying* to see Fort Sumter." She turned a sweetly simpering smile on her father. "If I see something pretty . . . ?"

With a resigned sigh, Claiborne handed over some Confederate notes to his daughter. Then he walked ponderously out of the room.

Garth sat next to Jessie on the settee, drinking his third cup of coffee, while Loretta finished her breakfast and dressed for the day's outing. He studied Jessie's tense profile, the curve of her lips, the sweep of her dark lashes. She twisted her hands fretfully, her eyes distant and haunted.

"You don't like it here, do you?" he finally said; it was a statement, not a question.

"I don't know. I feel . . . strange."

"It's not a happy place—being in the South now. That breakfast!" He shook his head in disbelief. "I've never eaten just plain toast for breakfast in my whole life."

"You seem to enjoy the coffee."

"It's hot, at least." He finished the last of it

and set the cup and saucer on a marble-topped table. His hands touched Jessie's shoulders, gently turning her around to face him. "I missed you last night."

"I missed you too. Why didn't you come to my room?"

His brow furrowed. "I didn't think it was wise."

Her nostrils flared in indignation. "Because of your father."

"Partly. Partly I was tired. I figured you were too."

"He hates me."

"He doesn't hate you. You're just . . . Well, you're something new to him."

"A Yankee, you mean."

A disarming smile tugged at the corners of his mouth. He caught her in his arms and held her against him. She clung to him with a tenacity that revealed her uncertainty. She felt fragile and tiny and soft. Her nearness was intoxicating, but his lust abruptly died as he thought once again of his father. It would take more than a little persuasion to gain Claiborne Bodine's blessings on the marriage. Besides, Jessie hadn't said yes yet. She had wanted to wait and see how she was received in Charleston. So far, that reception hadn't been going too well. He fervently hoped Loretta minded her manners later today.

"I wish we'd never left Gettysburg," Jessie murmured, and her breath was warm and sweet against his neck.

"I know. But we did. We're here now, and we'll have to make the best of it."

She released a disgruntled sigh. "I'll try."
She raised her head and looked into his face,
her eyes an intense, deep blue. Garth kissed
her lightly at first, then curled his arms more
tightly around her and kissed her with
fervor. Her mouth clung to his endlessly,
warm and soft and passionate.

"Cheer up," he said, when he finally drew
away. "Mother likes you. So will Father, once
he gets to know you."

The corners of Jessie's mouth quivered
slightly, "I wonder."

Jessie felt infinitely relieved as she and
Loretta left the shop on King Street, Apollo
following after them, carrying several boxes.
Shopping with Garth's sister had been an un-
believable experience. Evidently every shop-
keeper in town knew Loretta Bodine, her
tastes, her whims and her temper.

Jessie had been fortunate at this last store;
a woman had ordered several gowns made
for her, then suddenly discovered her credit
was no longer good. By tomorrow, after a few
alterations, Jessie would have three new
dresses.

"There simply isn't any credit anymore,"
Loretta said as Apollo handed her into the
carriage. She broke open a painted fan and
cooled herself briskly; several strands of
blond hair had come loose from beneath her
bonnet and clung wetly to her forehead.
"You're lucky to have gold."

Jessie murmured agreement, settling herself on the cushioned seat next to Loretta.
Apollo stowed the boxes in the rear, then

mounted the driver's seat. He turned an uncertain, questioning glance at his mistress.

"Home," Loretta ordered. "It's too damn hot out here."

Jessie was relieved. She didn't want to spend any more time alone with Loretta than was absolutely necessary. It was clearly evident the two women disliked one another; they were polite but cold. Loretta fancied herself the belle of the city, refined, dignified, wealthy. Jessie felt her cousin thought her to be a northern hick, ready to stir up unrest among the slaves at her first opportunity.

Loretta's eyes narrowed in a wickedly speculative way as they came to rest on Jessie. "You and Garth seem, well . . . close."

Jessie didn't see any particular reason in mincing words. "I love him. And he loves me."

"A Yankee!" Loretta's laugh was totally mocking, totally disrespectful.

Jessie's cheeks flushed hot with indignation. She held back the malignant words forming in her throat and turned her heated gaze on the city. Charleston was still under seige; the many islands surrounding it were occupied by Union troops. Those residents who had gold were able to maintain a guise of their once grand life-style, with handsome carriages, liveried servants and fine silks. But food—here, as everywhere else—was scarce and expensive. Many restaurants had closed their doors. The soldiers' clothing was in tatters, and most wore anything they could find that vaguely resembled a uniform.

Houses needed painting, gardens needed tending. Spanish moss hung from the trees; palmettos blew in the gentle breeze. The air carried the salt-sharp tang of the ocean; gulls swooped and squawked overhead.

The carriage halted to wait for a squad of cadets from the nearby Citadel to march by.

Jessie felt Loretta's eyes on her and turned, arching a quizzical eyebrow. "Do you—are you affianced to anyone?"

Loretta grunted irritably. "All the men are fighting for the Cause. All the *good* ones, anyway. There's nobody left."

Out of the corner of her eye, Jessie noticed Apollo's back stiffen slightly. She thought it curious, but dismissed it from her mind. She didn't understand slaves, didn't understand anything about the South.

"I saw boys hardly out of short pants in uniform in Richmond," Jessie remarked.

Loretta's shrewd eyes gleamed knowingly, shining with evangelical fervor. "We won't give up. If necessary, I'll join!"

Jessie glanced away to hide her smile. At least that would be one way to get rid of Loretta.

Jessie's eyes swept the streets. Her face suddenly went white with shock, then she began to shudder helplessly and steadily, as if sick with a fever. Standing in front of a silversmith's shop was a tall, lanky man wearing civilian clothes and a black hat. A black patch covered his left eye.

Jessie was trying madly to catch her thoughts, trying to hold on to reason. It couldn't be! Garth said he was dead, his head smashed in at the bottom of the Cape Fear River. She felt terror rising within her, twisting her gut and clutching at her throat.

Then the man removed his hat, bowed politely, and smiled. His hair was a dirty blond, and his smile was genuine and warm. Jessie shook her head with relief and slumped back in the seat.

Loretta glanced at her oddly. "What's the matter with you? You look like you've just seen a ghost."

"For a minute, I thought I had." Jessie forced a nervous laugh. "It must be the heat and the humidity."

Loretta stared at her curiously for a moment, then shrugged as if to dismiss the matter, and began to fan herself once again.

"I could have sworn it was him."

It was late afternoon, and Garth was seated beside Jessie on the settee. Her face looked pinched and strained.

"He's dead, Jessie. Forget about him. Jake Coffin's out of our lives."

She sighed, unconvinced. Upstairs, Loretta's loud voice could be heard admonishing Flobelle for some minor infraction. Garth chuckled softly to himself.

"I think my sister's gotten even more bitchy since I went away, and I didn't think that was possible."

"She isn't very pleasant," Jessie conceded.

"Is she giving you a bad time?"

Jessie gave a vague shrug. "Not really. But I'd never choose her as a friend."

"Few people do. The only reason she's got any at all is because of her name."

A sobbing Flobelle rushed down the stairs and darted into the kitchen. Garth clucked his tongue, picked up his glass of lemonade and drank. Violet Mae had informed them that this batch had used the last of the lemons; there wasn't much sugar left either.

"Father's disappointed in me," Garth said, his voice low and troubled.

"Because you won't go back and fight?"

He nodded reflectively. "I've changed, Jessie. Maybe it's because of you, maybe it's because I've seen too much death already. It's probably a little bit of both. I just wish the war would end."

She tilted her head to look quizzically at him. "Even if the Confederacy loses?"

He responded with a thoughtful nod. "I think it will—no matter how much longer the war lasts. But I'd never dare tell Father. He'd likely have a stroke."

"Stubborn pride."

There was a teasing sparkle in his eyes. "You've got a little of that yourself, you know."

Her smile was tinged with guilt, and she looked for all the world like a little girl. "I suppose I do." Her smile widened, her eyes softened and she brushed back an errant lock of dark hair falling over his forehead. Her hand caressed his cheek; one finger ran down to the point of his chin. "Thank you."

He covered her hand with his, held it to his face. "For what?"

"For being you. For caring. For understanding. For standing up to your father."

God, she was beautiful! He longed to bury his hands in all that ravishing hair, bury his face between those lovely breasts. He leaned forward, then his mouth was upon hers, savoring the sweetness of her lips.

Loretta let loose with another stream of high-pitched explectives. Garth drew back and shook his head in mock exasperation. Jessie's face broke into a grin, and she let out a sudden rich laugh, then dissolved into a fit of giggling.

It was late, but the heat hadn't abated as it had last night. Jessie was positioned by the window again with the curtains drawn back, trying to catch the breezes coming in from either the Ashley or Cooper rivers, maybe even the Atlantic Ocean. But the air was still, moist and humid. The night-blooming jasmine in the garden below was occasionally obscured by a foul reek, undoubtedly from the gutters.

She allowed herself a sigh, wishing Garth was here with her. But for the past two nights he had been closeted in the study, no doubt still trying to make his father understand that he really and truly did not want to return to active service in the Confederate army.

She admired him for that, loved him all the more. God knew, the Confederacy needed every able-bodied man it could recruit. Everything she had seen in the South screamed the fact at her—the Rebels were losing. Finally, after all their early losses, the

Union had turned the tide.

Jessie supposed she should be elated, but, curiously, she wasn't. The politicians, she didn't care about. They could blow and bluster until hell froze over. But it was the people who were suffering the most. The wounded soldiers, their wives and children deprived of even the most essential of the necessities of life. Garth had changed; Jessie realized she had as well. The war was a senseless massacre of young men's lives, and the Confederacy had faint hope of winning.

She smoothed down her gauzy silk nightgown, purchased this afternoon at a ridiculously high cost. But at least now she had something in which to sleep; if she were going to sleep nude, she preferred Garth by her side.

Wishing once more to hear his tread in the hallway outside, she caught movement on the garden path below. She peered more closely. It was Loretta again, taking the same furtive route to the carriage house as she had last night. With growing dismay, Jessie watched until the honey-haired woman had vanished; then she turned away, shaking her head in puzzlement. Blinking, her mind a riot of confusion, she fell onto the bed, hoping that sleep would come swiftly. Loretta was an enigma to Jessie, as was so much else here. There were so many questions and so few answers.

# 21

The stars dotting the night sky were twinkling gems piercing a shroud of black; the moon was full. Jessie sat snuggled beside Garth on a wrought-iron bench in the garden. The wind whispered through the camelia bushes, tickled the moss hanging from a tree. Crickets chirped; water splashed in the fountain; the fireflies flickered a bright gold. It was pleasant outside, but inside, the house was stifling and damp. The heat had not let up in the ten days Jessie had been in Charleston.

"Does it ever cool off here?" she asked.

"In the winter."

Jessie groaned in mock frustration. But it *was* a pretty town. Garth had shown her the sights—St. Michael's Episcopal Church, with its tall spire on King Street. The City Hall, the Customs House, the Dock Street Theater, closed now due to the lack of performers.

Battery Park faced the rivers, but Fort Sumter was too far from shore for Jessie to see. The slave mart on Chalmers Street had not pleased her, nor had Cabbage Row, the run-down Negro district with its open-air stalls of vegetables and fish for sale.

For the past five evenings Garth had returned home in uniform—the gray Jessie so despised. True to his promise, he was working for the quartermasters' department, trying desperately to secure food and medicine for the troops in the field.

Garth's lips brushed her temple, grazed her hair. "I think Father's mellowing toward you a little bit."

"A little. Maybe. But he still gives me a look every once in a while."

"What kind of look?"

She made a weak gesture with her hands. "You know—like I'm a Yankee."

"You are. But I'll bet the prettiest Yankee he's ever seen."

For Jessie, Loretta was another story altogether. When she wasn't bellowing at the slaves, she was complaining endlessly: the lack of luxuries, no social functions to attend except bandage-rolling sessions. She was absolutely impossible, arrogant, spoiled, in love with only herself.

Jessie wasn't wanted here. The thought should have depressed her, sent her reeling back to the despair she had felt when her mother had been killed, when she was in the hearse running away from Gettysburg. But it didn't. She might be a Yankee, but somehow she was determined to win these Rebs over.

Della was kind and considerate. The three house slaves seemed to find Jessie something of a curiosity, a celebrity. Only Apollo remained aloof. He seldom spoke, seemed forever in a dull state of fear. Yet so far—other than Loretta's frequent outbursts—Jessie had detected no signs of cruelty to the blacks.

"You've been a good girl." The tone in Garth's voice was mocking, almost bantering. "I guess you learned your lesson in Richmond."

Jessie's head snapped around, a hard gleam in her eyes. "You thought my acid tongue would cause me problems, didn't you?"

"Frankly, yes."

"I'll keep my views about the Union to myself—for the sake of harmony."

Garth tipped her chin toward him, his gray eyes intent, sincere. "I've missed you. The way your kisses taste, the feel of your body."

"You haven't exactly been beating down my door."

"I know." He shrugged his embarrassment. "I've never been in a situation like this—with the most desirable woman in the world under the same roof as me."

"I think," she said slowly, running a forefinger over his lower lip, "that should change soon."

Instantly her arms were around his neck, her tongue hungrily seeking his. His kiss was fierce and gentle at the same time, spreading delicious, tingling sensations throughout her body.

Loretta stood in the shadows of the porch, covertly watching her brother and Jessie embrace. She curled her lip in well-practiced disgust. God, how she hated and envied the Yankee! Jessie, with her big blue eyes, her thick, luxurious hair and her slender and graceful figure. She was soft-spoken and well mannered, all the attributes Loretta herself wished she possessed.

Besides, she thought sullenly, Jessie had Garth, a white man, a handsome man, the heir to a small fortune if the damn war didn't wipe it out first. All Loretta could boast for herself was the Bodine name and a black lover. The former, she proudly proclaimed; the latter would create the biggest scandal Charleston had seen in years.

She scowled intensely; there was a grimness to her mouth. She had had her share of beaux before the war, but Loretta wasn't so dull-witted as to not know what they were after. They wanted a link with the family's prominence, not her. It wasn't that she was unattractive. In fact, until Jessie showed up, Loretta thought herself quite beautiful. But now—in comparison to her cousin's radiance—she felt absolutely dowdy. A knot of loathing and jealousy burned in her stomach.

She trembled, but refused to give rein to her anger. She could force herself to marry without love if the man was well placed in society. She could always take Apollo along to amuse her. But the truth was, her temper drove off all but the most doltish suitors. But when the war was over, when the South had finally won its independence, she would be as sweet as spun sugar, win herself a husband, perhaps even a hero cited by Jefferson Davis for his loyalty and bravery.

In the meantime, she had to be content with Apollo. And content she was. He was a magnificent lover, like some great black stallion, never failing to arouse her to a fever pitch. It was his reticence that bothered her most, his apprehensions, his fears. He well knew what the consequences of his dallying with a white woman would be; so did Loretta. But she was, after all, his mistress, and he her slave. He did what he was told. And until the troops returned to parade the streets in triumph, Apollo would simply have to do.

A slow smile of wicked anticipation spread across Loretta's lips. Apollo was more than adequate to fill the void left when the soldiers had departed.

Jessie stared dully up at the darkened ceiling, listening to the crickets outside, perspiration gathering between her breasts and trickling over her belly. It was an oppressively hot night, the air thick and wet.

Unable to lie there any longer, she got out of bed and padded over to the window, waving the front of her gauzy nightdress before her like a fan. Her lips spread into a tight, disdainful line of scorn. The sticky heat was bad enough, but Garth's sister was making Jessie's stay almost unbearable.

She pushed aside the lace curtain and gazed outside. Overhead, the sky was a canopy of stars, the moon white and full. It cast its glow on the garden below; the marble fountain with its cupids was silent now, but in the daytime they spewed forth refreshing cool water. Out on the street, she could hear footsteps. Idly, she wondered if it was another soldier; the Rebs seemed to be all over the city. Then she remembered Coffin, and an unreasoning chill passed through her body.

Her heavy sigh was long and wistful. She wasn't happy here. She felt like an outsider, an alien. She loved Garth with all her heart, but his sister and father persisted in treating her like a Yankee instead of a member of their family.

She heard a sound at the door, and a quick tremor of alarm raced through her. She turned, saw the knob move, then the door pushed open. Garth, clad in a robe, was briefly silhouetted by the dim light from the hall. Then the door closed gently, and she was in darkness again. Jessie glided toward him, saw his teeth flash in a smile in the moonlight.

She lazily curled her arms around his neck. He gathered her close and bent to kiss her. Their lips moved hungrily together; his mouth was soft and searching, and her lips parted beneath his. His fingers twined beneath the mass of hair at the nape of her neck, ran lightly down her back. His hands caressed the delicate curve of her spine and rounded shape of her hips. She thrilled to his touch, forgot about everything but the two of them. He was here now—at last. He held her more closely, pressed against the length of his body, and she could feel his excitement growing as he strained against her.

He lifted her hair, pressed fevered kisses along her throat. The silky brush of his mustache against her skin touched off a quickening in her pulse. "I didn't think you'd come," she whispered.

"I couldn't sleep without you another night." His fingers deftly untied the ribbon at the throat of her nightgown, and when she let her arms drop away from him, it fell to the floor in a filmy pool around her ankles. She stepped out of it and kicked it aside. The moonlight cast a satiny sheen over her skin. His eyes glowed with a warm light as his gaze roamed freely over her.

He caressed the soft flesh of her shoulders, his hands trailing down her sides to her waist, and drew her to him. His lips moved softly against hers in a light, feathery grazing, then they were pressing hers with a sweet, hot insistence. A need began to grow in her, a hollowness that demanded to be filled; Garth never failed to arouse her. She felt breathless and weak and wanted only to experience again all the mutual demands of their flesh and the heights of ecstasy he could bring to her.

His arm hooked under her knees and she

was lifted off the ground and swept into his strong arms. She locked her hands around his neck, nipping at his earlobe as he carried her to the bed. He lay her down gently and kissed her for a very long time, lazily savoring her lips. She returned his kiss with an ardor that matched his.

His head drew back, and his eyes were dark with need. His gaze lingered over her hair fanning out on the pillow, the creamy globes of her breasts.

The intense look in his eyes made her catch her breath. "Your family might hear us."

His finger outlined her lips and traced across her cheek. "Let them. I want you."

She cupped his face between her hands and gazed deeply into his eyes. "I want you too." Her eyes sparkled teasingly at him. "But we'll have to be quiet."

The quirk on his lips deepened to an amused grin. "I'll be as quiet as a mouse—I promise."

She couldn't help but giggle softly, but his lips claimed hers in another kiss, sweet and hungry. Her hot tongue was quick, but the kiss was long and slow, leaving her breathless and incapable of thought.

He slipped off the bed for an instant, only long enough to remove his robe. Her eyes wandered idly across the sculpted muscles of his body, then he was back on the bed with her, his lips seeking hers. His kiss explored her parted lips, lingered over her temples and ears. Her arms went around him, her fingers gliding over the hard flesh of his back and shoulders. His hands slowly caressed the swell of her breasts, felt the hardening nipples. She was conscious of the uneven beat of her heart, the trembling weakness in her limbs.

He pulled her hair aside and kissed her throat, leaving a chain of kisses along the smooth, sweet skin. His lips moved to her breasts, and he delicately ran the tip of his tongue lightly over one jutting peak. Little tremors of pleasure wracked her body.

His hands would not remain still; they moved over her in gentle, lazy exploration, and she felt his tantalizing caresses draining her will. Not that she had any will anymore, only a burning need to experience all of him.

Her hands moved over his body, its hardness, its strength, capturing new excitement for herself. As he caressed her thighs, her senses erupted in a fiery blaze. His fingers slid into her inner, quivering warmth. His touch brought a feeling that every sense was deliciously alive, an urgency that would not be denied. She nuzzled the corded muscles in his neck, let her hands roam over his body, eager to satisfy him and find her own satisfaction.

His warm lips slid over her stomach to the hot, moist flesh between her thighs. Jessie trembled, quivering with exquisite torment, moaning softly deep in her throat. He kissed and caressed all the tender, secret places of her body until she shivered under the assault on her senses. She writhed under him, her hips urging, until at last he raised above her and entered her. Her nails pressed into his back, drawing him nearer. His movements were strong and steady, and she arched up to meet his every thrust.

Wondrous feelings raced through her body, the emotions passing in a blur of delight, and she responded to his lovemaking with open, exuberant rapture. She thought she would gladly drown in the intensity of all the sensations that filled her, until, her body sated with delicious pleasure, she was wracked by spasms of welcome fullfillment.

After their passion was spent, Garth stretched out beside her. Jessie curled up next to him in a delicious daze of contentment. She was no longer aware of the muggy heat, but she felt a coating of perspiration on both their bodies. A whisper of a sigh escaped her lips, and she smiled softly into the darkness.

"Happy?" His voice was low and hoarse, slightly breathless.

"What do you think?"

He rolled over onto his side. His eyes studied her while his finger traced a slow circle from her cheek bone to her jaw. "Marry me."

She felt an unexpected glow light up inside her, and reached for his hand and brought it to her lips. But a feeling of melancholy stole over her. "Your family doesn't like me."

"That's because of the war."

"The war!" Her voice had an edge of impatience. "I'm sick and tired of the war. It's senseless."

His mouth made a gently exploring caress of her lips. "Forget about the war. Just think about you and me. That's all that matters. I love you. I want you to be my wife."

Jessie's heart seemed to swell in her breast, and a great tenderness washed over her. She linked her hands behind his neck, drew his face down to hers. "That's what I want too."

Garth's mouth moved upon hers with a strong yet gentle pressure. Her lips clung to his the instant they touched, yielding and soft, and the kiss turned wild and passionate, a kiss that excited every nerve in her body. His hands roamed over her naked flesh, heating her skin wherever they touched. His caresses reawakened a blazing need, and Jessie's excitement spiraled to an almost unbearable crescendo once again.

# 22

"Damn!"

Jessie dropped her wicker basket and clippers to the grass, gazing at the blood welling from her thumb, then sucked at it.

Several yards away, Apollo looked up from where he knelt, weeding. "You hurt, Miz Jessie?"

"No." She sucked again at her thumb, then examined it. A small bubble of red oozed from the flesh. "It's just a scratch."

"You sure? I kin git Flobelle or Violet Mae if'n you wants."

The bleeding had stopped. Jessie smiled over at the striking, rugged black man, touched by his concern. "It's all right, Apollo. I just got into a thorn."

He studied her a moment longer with a frown, worry drawing his brows together, then turned back to his work.

Jessie retrieved the clippers and snipped

off another rose. The garden was a riot of colors this early September day. The heat of August had turned to the crisper days of the coming autumn. A high blue sky seemed to go on forever.

Jessie realized she had more than enough roses to fill every room in the house, but, not wanting to deprive herself of this fine day, she settled on one of the benches. Garth was working at the quartermasters' office on East Battery Street and Claiborne was in his study; Loretta and Della had gone shopping for groceries.

Jessie inhaled deeply; damp earth smells mingled with the perfumed scents that drifted from the flowers. In a few weeks would the leaves on the trees here start to change their color as they had back home? Would families make apple cider, slaughter pigs for sausage? Somehow, she doubted it. There were few hogs in Charleston, and what were available sold at ridiculously high prices. A wistful sigh of remembered pleasure broke from her. She would miss Pennsylvania this fall. Autumn was her favorite time of the year, the last chance to enjoy the sun before the snow came.

She watched Apollo as he crawled around, pulling weeds from here and there, regarding him thoughtfully, completely mystified by his bashfulness.

"Apollo, are you afraid of me?"

"Afraid? No, miss. I ain't afraid of you."

"Then why don't you ever talk to me?"

"Tain't my place to speak to a white lady."

"Why? Flobelle and Voilet Mae and Sam talk to me. They're happy to talk to me."

'It ain't fittin', dat's all." He turned away, going back to his work.

Jessie gave a small, bewildered shake of her head. Perhaps she would never understand these black people. Apollo seemed intelligent enough . . . She sighed, then bit her lip in frustration as she watched him gather up his things and disappear out the gate to the alleyway.

When the Union finally had its victory men like Apollo would be free. But what would he do with that freedom? If the Federal government wasn't here to help him make the adjustment, he might well be worse off than he was now.

Strange, she thought, picking up her basket and going into the house, for a man so vigorous and strapping as Apollo to be so timid.

Violet Mae was kneading bread in the kitchen, her sleeves rolled up, stout forearms coated with white flour.

"You leave any roses in dat garden?" the woman asked.

"Plenty. And they all smell delightful. Where are the vases?"

"In de cupboard—over there." Violet Mae nodded with her head. "I help you when I through here."

"Don't bother. I need something to do."

Violet Mae snorted softly. "Ya'll don' sound like Miz Loretta. If'n she had de choice, she jes' lay around de house all day givin' orders."

Jessie smothered a malicious grin and selected several cut-glass vases from the cupboard, placing them on the sink. She was glad someone other than herself held the same opinion of Loretta. Loretta was Garth's sister, and Jessie felt the two women should be close. But try as she might, she couldn't bridge the distance between them.

She snipped off a few stems and arranged the roses in one of the vases, squinting, standing back, rearranging again.

"It be nice havin' you here, Miz Jessie," Violet Mae said. "Ain't never heard you yellin' and carryin' on. I don' know if'n Miz Loretta's tantrums is worse now or before de war. Back then, she fussed over party dresses an' such-like. Now she fusses 'cause dey ain't no parties."

"I'm glad you like me." Jessie was genuinely pleased by the black woman's honesty. "I like you too. Besides Garth and his mother, you and the other servants are my only friends here."

"Ya'll gwine to marry up wid Mistuh Garth?"

Jessie shrugged noncommitally. "I expect so. I hope so. If his father and sister ever accept me." Her eyes became sharp and probing, inquisitive. "Why is Apollo so shy and quiet all the time?"

There was a touch of surprise on the broad, dusky face. "Dat boy ain't quiet. He talk yer ear off."

"Yours maybe. Not mine."

Violet Mae was silent for a moment, obviously deep in thought. "I reckon I know what ya'll mean. He been actin' funny wid de white folks fer 'bout a year now. Didn't used to be dat way."

"Do you have any idea why?"

Violet Mae plopped the bread dough into two pans and gave an airy shrug to her shoulders. "Mebbe it be he's thinkin' 'bout de Yankees. Thinkin' 'bout mebbe bein' free someday."

Jessie studied her appraisingly. "Do you want your freedom?"

Violet Mae's pensive pause was long, seeming to go on forever. The two women stared at one another across the kitchen. At length, Violet Mae sighed. "If'n I had my druthers—yessum. I'd like to be free. These folks been mighty good to me, but they still own me, an' I got to call dem mastah."

"You'd be a fine cook and housekeeper for anyone who hired you."

Violet Mae regarded Jessie with a slight frown. "Trouble is, Miz Jessie, if de South loses, ain't nobody gwine to have no money left to pay fer help."

Jessie hadn't thought of that, but it seemed a very real possibility.

When she entered the drawing room she was surprised to find Claiborne pouring himself a whiskey at the sideboard. He turned, rather bleary-eyed, and managed a wan smile. "Lovely flowers, Jessie. I wish Della and Loretta would take an interest in the garden."

"It's something to do." She set the vase down on a Pembroke table by the window.

Claiborne waved an empty, delicate goblet to her. "A drop of sherry?"

"Just a drop." Jessie settled herself on a chair and accepted the wine from her cousin. His face was flushed, his jowls seemed to sag more and there was that ever present look of bored indifference on his face. He had been drinking more and more every day since she and Garth had arrived. His son had disappointed him, and she knew he was worried about the changing tide in the war, the shift in favor of the Union.

He sat heavily in an overstuffed chair, drank from his glass and ran his fingers through his thick silver hair. "I think I owe you an apology."

Jessie pursed her lips and her brows knit together in puzzlement.

"You've kept your Yankee sentiments to yourself. I feared you might upset our slaves, put notions in their heads."

Jessie dropped her gaze and took a sip of sherry. If he had just overheard her conversation with Violet Mae . . .

He drank again, this time with dedicated abandon, as if he was in a contest of some sort and expected a prize. "I suppose you'll want a large wedding?"

Her eyes bulged in disbelief. "You mean you don't object to my marrying Garth?"

He shrugged, rolled to his feet and returned to the sideboard. "I have . . . reservations." He waved the bottle as if he were batting away pesky flies. "But you aren't a trouble maker. No flag-waving, no praise for that oaf Abe Lincoln . . ." He belched, then returned to his chair. "And Garth says he loves you."

"I believe he does."

Claiborne's pouchy eyes narrowed in thoughtfulness. "I'd like to see some grand-children before I die." He looked deliberately at her. "You *will* have children, won't you?"

"I expect so, if God's willing."

"Good." He nodded, his chin drooping onto his chest. He lifted his glass to her in a giggling toast. "Perhaps spring then. By then, the war should be settled, things back to normal. A nice Carolina-style spring wedding."

Jessie forced a quick, tight smile. She didn't want to wait that long. The nights Garth crept into her room, he didn't stay, fearing one of the family members might discover their tryst. Jessie longed to fall asleep in his arms and awaken the same way in the morning.

Claiborne erupted with another loud belch. "How does that sound?"

"The wedding? It sounds fine. Although I would like it to be a little sooner. Garth probably would too."

"We like to take our time about doing things here in Carolina." He drained his glass in one tremendous gulp and belched again. "Besides, there's always the possibility Garth might be forced back into active service. Things aren't looking well for us out in

Tennessee right now." He rose clumsily, snatched the bottle off the sideboard and disappeared into his study.

Active service! The words sent chills rippling up Jessie's spine. Setting aside her goblet of sherry, she stood and paced the room, rubbing her arms in agitation. Her eyes flashed with all the fury and frustration pent up inside her. Was her cousin drinking merely to tolerate her presence here more easily, or was he genuinely distressed over the news of the war? Probably a little bit of both, she decided.

But if a wedding was definitely in the future, there was little sense in keeping the property in Gettysburg. She could write to Dr. Brooks, instruct him to handle the sale of the land, the house, the furnishings.

She ambled over to the window and stood for a moment staring out at the traffic on Legare Street. There wasn't much activity. A youngster was pulling a rickety wooden wagon that appeared to be filled with rags; several young girls hurried by with skirts flying and bonnet strings whipping behind them. Apollo was trimming back a hedge.

Jessie let out her breath in a long sigh. Maybe she should return to Gettysburg. True, Claiborne had mellowed to some degree, but he was still a bit of a pompous ass, filled with notions of the Confederacy's invincibility. It wouldn't happen for him. There was considerable trouble near Chattanooga, and once it fell into the hands of the Federals, the gateway would be open for the Union army to move into Georgia.

But she couldn't return to Gettysburg without Garth. He was the one person in this world she loved. She belonged to him, he to her. And he would never come with her.

A thin man in a business suit paused on the walk across the street, lighting a cheroot. He gazed at the houses, then turned to look toward the Bodine home. Jessie swallowed, found it difficult, then swallowed again, trying to regain control of her half-paralyzed throat. He wore a black patch over one eye!

Her heart, already beating fast, now thundered. Jessie continued to stare at him until he sauntered on toward Tradd Street. Jessie's soft laugh had an edge of hysteria to it. The patch covered the man's right eye; Coffin's had been over his left. Or had it? An ominous uneasiness nagged at the back of her mind. Would that man continue to haunt her?

Garth stared with disgust at the pile of requisition forms heaped on his desk. There was no way they could all be filled. Food was scarce, medicine almost nonexistant, uniforms, blankets, and shoes in short supply.

The air was close in the office, stale with old cigar smoke. Garth rose, stretched, trying to get the kinks out of his back muscles. Supper tonight had been biscuits with thin gravy, served at the officers' mess.

Heaving a disgruntled sigh, he walked over to the window, and, with some difficulty,

forced it all the way up. At least the air was
fresh. He was disappointed in his job.
Granted, he wasn't out in the field of battle,
but the responsibilities were just as great.
And he worried a lot. There simply wasn't
enough of anything to take care of the
fighting troops. The paperwork never
stopped, he fretted constantly, and he seldom
got home before ten o'clock.

Jessie didn't seem to mind. He had defied
his father's wishes, and for that she was
grateful. But Garth wasn't a man suited to
indoor work. He longed to be free, back at the
plantation, pampering his horses, idling a
day away fishing, watching the sunset from
the veranda with Jessie at his side.

Jessie . . . Garth's lips parted with a hint of
a smile. If he closed his eyes, he could see
her now. Her blue eyes bright, her face
glowing with the vigor of youth, her lips full
and soft, her teeth a dazzling white. The
curves of her hips swaying beneath her frock,
the firm fullness of her bosom. All those dark
chestnut tresses that hung in luxuriant waves
that spilled over her shoulders to her waist.

An almost inaudible groan came from deep
in his throat. The fragrance of her, the soft,
supple feel of her body in his arms returned
to torment him. He could picture her now,
her lips shining a silent invitation that
knotted an ache in his loins.

Annoyed by his fantasies, he abruptly
turned away from the window. If he wanted
her at all tonight, he had work to finish—at
least some. The rest he could do tomorrow,

even though it was Sunday and normally his day off.

Jessie found herself restless again. The house was dark and quiet, save for the ticking of the little clock on the bedstand. It was after nine; Garth wasn't home from work yet. Claiborne had fallen asleep in his chair immediately after supper; Loretta had made a cutting remark about her father's drinking. Della had Sam help him up to his room. The three women had played whist for a while, but Loretta cheated. Jessie retired early to her room.

A spring wedding! The thought upset Jessie. It was only September now. That could mean seven or eight months yet! She would have to talk to Garth, try to make him convince his father an earlier marriage was what the couple wanted. Jessie was eager to be Garth's wife, to have his children—even if they would grow up to speak with a drawl.

Fretful, she paced over to the window. She wasn't surprised to see Loretta's slim figure darting along the path in the garden. Where did she go every night? The mystery was beginning to intrigue Jessie. It was really none of her business, but curiosity overcoming her good sense, she slipped on her robe and crept quietly out of her room.

There was a dim lamp burning in the hall for Garth when he returned. Jessie padded barefoot along the passageway and descended the staircase. Another low light burned in the entryway; the rest of the house was dark.

The tile floor in the kitchen felt like a sheet of ice, and she wished she had stopped to put on her slippers. Ignoring her brief discomfort, she passed quickly through the cavernous scullery, opened the door and went outside.

The breeze was cool and fragrant except when the river's stench wafted toward town. The moon had just risen over the treetops; the stars twinkled brilliantly. Jessie followed the same brick path that Loretta took on her nocturnal wanderings. It led to the carriage house and out to the alleyway.

Jessie stood near the corner of the stable, suddenly feeling very foolish. Whatever Loretta did every night was none of her concern. Besides, the alley was deserted; wherever Garth's sister had gone, she was out of sight now. Jessie couldn't free herself from the memory of the one-eyed man she had seen in the street today, and she felt a dull, slow, churning sensation in the pit of her stomach. If by some wild happenstance Jake Coffin was still alive, she would make easy prey standing out here looking into a darkened alley.

Shuddering at the thought, she turned abruptly to retreat to the house, then noticed that one of the doors to the stable was ajar and weak, pallid light spilled outside. Jessie paused, took a step toward the door, then backed up. Her heart was suddenly hammering; she felt frozen by indecision. Biting her lip, determined not to behave like a frightened child, she inched toward the door and squeezed inside, careful to not make any noise. The straw on the floor was brittle beneath her bare feet, but she made no sound as she stole forward a few yards.

The light was coming from an oil lamp hung on a peg in an open stall. Jessie stopped. She heard Loretta's voice, breathless and almost inaudible. Jessie cocked her head, listening. Straw rustled in the stall.

Creeping forward a few more tentative steps, Jessie came in full view of the open stall. She caught her breath, blinked and staggered backward several paces.

Pale legs were clasped firmly around the sweat-coated black body of Apollo. The lamp cast a satin sheen over the whiteness of Loretta's naked flesh and turned her blond hair to a fiery orange. Lost in the throes of shameless, abandoned ecstasy, little sounds of pleasure escaping her, Loretta was oblivious to anyone else's presence.

Jessie wanted to turn and flee, but she gaped in slack-jawed horror and fascination. Apollo moved with the sureness of a sleek black panther, letting his fingers lose themselves in Loretta's silken hair as he thrust into her. Loretta's voice was muffled beneath his kisses; her body melted against his; her hips arched up to meet him, grinding, pounding. He attacked her with a sexual vigor that was wild and primitive, and Loretta matched his enthusiasm with her own.

Swallowing a sudden bubble of bile, Jessie moved with awkward haste, backing out of the stable and into the alley, her hands nervously clutching and twisting the fabric of her robe. She crouched low and darted back into the garden, then broke into a full run, stumbling once and nearly losing her balance. Her mind raced in a frantic search for logic, but reason had deserted her.

# 23

"What?"

Jessie was distracted; she hadn't been listening to Garth. Now she turned her gaze away from the cold, empty fireplace and looked at him. "I'm sorry. I wasn't listening."

A glint of amusement struck his gray eyes. "Obviously."

Jessie's mind kept going back to last night, to the scene she had witnessed in the carriage shed. The more she tried to block the images out, the more intense they became. Yet this morning, seated beside Loretta in the pew at church, Jessie could see no indication that Garth's sister was anything but the overbearing, imperious woman she had always been.

"I suppose it was church this morning," Garth said. "I know how the minister always talks about the glory and righteousness of the Confederacy in his sermons."

"Yes, he does." But that wasn't Jessie's reason for her preoccupation. Garth hadn't attended church this morning but had gone to work instead. Now he was home—and out of that dreadful uniform—while his father was visiting his cronies at one of the local saloons. Della and Loretta had gone to call on a recent widow whose husband had been killed in some obscure little town in Tennessee.

An unexpected wind had come up shortly after noon and rattled the windowpanes, wheezed under a crack at the front door. From the kitchen, Jessie could hear Violet Mae humming tunelessly and occasional low voices from either Sam or Flobelle.

"It was after midnight when I got in last night," Garth was saying. "I didn't want to wake you." He ran the tip of one finger over the outline of her lower lip, his eyes moving along her delicate profile, then dipping lower to the fullness of her breasts. "But I suppose we could always sneak upstairs and make up for lost time now."

"What about the darkies?"

"What about them? They'd keep their mouths shut. They might like to gossip among themselves, but they stay out of our business."

Did Violet Mae or Flobelle or Sam know what was going on between Loretta and Apollo? Somehow, Jessie doubted it. Probably no one knew but the two of them—and now her. She cursed silently to herself, wishing she had stayed in her room last night.

Garth kissed her, his lips warm and moist, soft and yet firmly insistent. "Well?"

Jessie attempted a brave smile. "In a minute. I don't want to be too obvious to the servants."

Sharp disappointment showed on Garth's face for a second, then he grinned at her. "I wish I could figure out a way to change Father's mind about a spring wedding."

"At least he agreed. That's something, anyway."

"I don't want to wait till spring." He traced the ridge of her collar bone with his fingertips, brushed his lips against her cheek, then settled back on the settee, stretching out his long legs before him. "Give him another week or two. I'll convince him. Right now, he's worried about money. He invested so heavily in Confederate bonds . . ." He shook his head, bemused. "He's thinking about selling off some of the land at the plantation—maybe even a few slaves, if anybody'll buy them. Slaves aren't a very good investment anymore."

Jessie saw a slight opening and threw him a quizzical look. "Is it common for slaves to . . . well, to be intimate with their masters?"

Garth quirked a dark brow at her. "That's a strange question."

"This is a strange place, a strange way of life to me." And getting stranger all the time, she had come to realize.

Garth shrugged casually. "It's not unusual for a man to take a wench for a mistress."

"And a white woman? What if she had a

black lover?"

Garth looked at her as if she had taken leave of her senses. "It's simply not done. Ladies don't carry on with black bucks. If it was found out, he'd most likely be shot or hanged."

"What would happen to the woman?"

"God only knows. I suppose she'd be an outcast, probably end up begging in the streets. I doubt even a brothel would take her on. Not a respectable one, anyway."

Deep inside, Jessie had known the liaison between Loretta and Apollo was strictly taboo. She involuntarily averted her eyes, evoking a curious, skeptical glance from Garth.

"What brought all that on?" he asked.

"Nothing really. I just wondered. If I'm going to live in this society, I figured I'd better learn all I can about it, that's all."

Garth tugged at his mustache, the corners of his mouth twitching with amusement. "If Mother knew we were having this discussion, she'd swoon."

Jessie wondered what Loretta would do. She turned to Garth with a seductive little smile and tugged on his hand. "Let's go upstairs."

Jessie wished the memory of Loretta and Apollo would go away. She lay alone on her bed, holding an embroidered pillow to her stomach, alternately staring at the ceiling and out the window, where the sunset flamed in a bank of clouds.

The aroma of roast ham drifted up from downstairs; idly, she wondered how much it had cost. In the time she had been in Charleston, she had watched the Bodines' larder diminish every day. Sugar and salt were rare and expensive, meat almost non-existant. Fish seemed to be the staple of her diet, and she was even beginning to learn to tolerate—if not enjoy—the strange brew that passed for coffee.

Suddenly, irrationally annoyed, she threw the pillow across the room. It struck the armoire with a little puff of dust and fell to the floor. Damn Loretta! It was little wonder Apollo acted so timid, so fearful. Loretta had put his life in danger. If he were ever found out . . . Jessie didn't even want to complete the thought.

Who had been the instigator of their sordid little affair? She didn't have to think very hard to decide. Apollo wasn't stupid. None of the blacks were, despite all their bowing and scraping and yessuhs and nossuhs. He had been born here in the South; he knew the consequences of something this improper.

And Loretta was hardly discreet. If Jessie could discover them, anyone could. Unless the possibility was so unthinkable, no one would even consider it.

She could confront Loretta, she supposed. But Loretta would only deny it. Still, it might give her pause to think, to change her behavior before it was too late.

No. Loretta was Loretta. If she wanted something, she got it. She was a woman used to having her own way. And besides, she cared nothing for the slaves. To her, they were chattel, less than human, something to be bought and sold on a whim.

A soft knock on the door interrupted Jessie's thoughts. Flobelle poked her turbaned head inside. "Supper's ready, Miz Jessie. 'Lessen ya'll wants a tray up here."

Jessie sat up. "I'll come down. Thank you, Flobelle."

The girl nodded with a smile and disappeared from sight.

At the supper table Jessie didn't have much of an appetite. She picked at her food and stole glances across the table at Loretta. Dressed in a lace-edged yellow gown that gave her a sallow look, Garth's sister ate voraciously. But for all her apparent hunger, she managed to keep up a veneer of refinement.

Della chattered incessantly, as was her usual evening custom; Claiborne drank heavily from a decanter of wine that smelled like a combination of kerosene and overripe grapes. Once Loretta looked up, and her eyes locked with Jessie's. Loretta's petulant mouth quirked into something resembling a smile, but Jessie detected behind that smile a rippling of disdain.

"Is there pie?" Claiborne asked, wiping his lips with his napkin and stifling a belch.

"If we had any sugar, we'd have pie." Loretta compressed her lips and glared. "You should have grown cane on the plantation instead of raising horses. We can't eat horses."

"You look no worse for wear, my dear." Claiborne refilled his glass. "As a matter of fact, I think you've put on a little weight."

Loretta gave an indignant snort. "Thank you. That's just what I needed to hear. Now I'm getting fat! The next thing you'll tell me is my hair's going gray and I've got bags under my eyes!"

"Now, Loretta . . ." Della smiled placatingly, speaking in a soothing, motherly voice. "You look just as bright and lovely as always."

Loretta stifled an obscenity and forked up a bite of mashed potatoes.

Garth's knee nudged Jessie's under the table, and he winked at her.

"Can't you snitch something from the quartermasters' department?" Loretta suddenly asked him.

"What did you have in mind? We got in some rubber ponchos the other day. I'm sure you'd look fetching in one of those."

Jessie hid a giggle behind her napkin. Loretta scowled savagely at her brother.

"I'm going out to the plantation tomorrow," Claiborne said, turning to Jessie. "Would you care to come along?"

She glanced quickly at Garth, then shrugged. "I guess so."

"We won't be long. I just want to see which parcels of land I want to put on the market."

"I'll go too," Loretta announced. "It's been ages since I've been out of the city."

"What about our meeting?" Della reminded her. "We have to roll bandages, then visit the hospital."

Loretta's lips curled in disdain. "I hate the hospitals. All those sick men!"

"They're our soldiers."

Loretta grunted, then drank from a crystal goblet of water. She darted an inquisitive look at her father. "When will we be moving back to the country?"

"Not this winter. I can't afford to keep up two houses."

"But, Daddy!" Loretta's voice became a wheedling whine; it grated on Jessie's nerves like fingernails on a blackboard.

Claiborne turned a rueful smile on his daughter. "I know how you feel. But we simply can't spend the money. You'll have to make plans for the holiday season right here in Charleston."

Loretta thrust out her lower lip in a pout; then she balled up her napkin and tossed it on the table. Without another word, she rose and stalked from the dining room.

Della smiled helplessly at Jessie and spread her hands in a hopeless gesture. Garth nudged her again under the table.

Garth stood with Jessie outside her bedroom door, one hand propped against the wall. She had come upstairs immediately after a distressing supper, and her face was grave, her eyes melancholy.

"It's Loretta." His voice was gentle with understanding.

Jessie gave him a lame shrug.

"I know she's not the easiest person to get along with. I just ignore her most of the time."

"It's not just Loretta. It's—" She swallowed the rest of the sentence. She couldn't tell him about Apollo and his sister. Besides, that wasn't all that was troubling her. "Today I was looking out the window. I saw a one-eyed man standing across the street, looking over here."

Garth frowned in helpless frustration. "Coffin's dead."

"I know." She heaved a sigh of acceptance. "I've got to stop thinking about him. I don't feel this way when I see an amputee or a blind man. It's just that damn eye patch!"

A flicker of a smile crossed Garth's face. The palm of his hand caressed her cheek, stroked her long hair. "Just try to forget Coffin. Go with Father tomorrow and enjoy yourself in the country."

She gazed into the warm depths of his gray eyes. "I wish you were coming with us."

"So do I." He brushed her lips with his, covered her mouth, tasted the sweetness of her tongue. "So do I."

Loretta gave an impatient toss of her head and flung down the cards on the table, glaring over at her mother plunking on the pianoforte. The woman couldn't play. None of them could, but they had bought the instrument years ago as yet another sign of their prosperity.

Prosperity! Disgust kindled up inside her. The Yankees were putting up a much tougher battle than anyone had suspected they would. What had become of all the Confederacy's excellent horsemen, their highly skilled youths trained in the southern military academies? Dead, most likely, by now.

All the dreams of freedom from the North's hated repression seemed to be going up in a puff of smoke. They had unlimited manpower, unlimited weapons, unlimited *everything*! Charleston looked like a town full of beggars. And now even her father was beginning to talk like a pauper.

She gave a short, contemptuous sniff. Garth could do more if it wasn't for Jessie. Jessie and her sweet smile and petite figure and gorgeous long hair. She had been quiet so far, but Loretta felt she would be nothing but trouble once Garth married her. Thank God the men were all off fighting, else Loretta might find her cousin's competition too stiff for even a belle with the name of Bodine.

"Stop it!" She glared at her mother. Della looked up, aghast. Loretta managed an apologetic smile. "I'm sorry. It's the news of the war. None of it's good."

"I know. It has your father upset too."

Upset and drunk most of the time, Loretta thought sourly. He did more drinking than anything else these days.

"Garth says we're losing," Della said.

Loretta's eyes narrowed murderously.

"That little Yankee vixen of his has turned his head so far around that he doesn't know whether he's coming or going anymore."

"I don't know." Della smoothed back a lock of graying brown hair. "She hasn't spoken against us."

"She hasn't spoken *for* us, either."

"She's harmless, and Garth loves her."

Loretta's lips curled with contempt. Love! How in the hell would she know what love was? Before the war, she had been too busy playing the coquette to let herself become serious over any one man. Now all she had was Apollo, a reluctant slave, a nigger!

Still, why should she complain? He satisfied her needs well enough. More than adequately. He wanted her, he desired her, even though she had to practically threaten him every time he made love to her.

Just thinking about him caused a delicious ache inside her. She gave her mother a hard, impatient look. She wished the woman would go up to bed and soon, so Loretta could sneak out to the carriage shed. Releasing an exasperated breath, she picked up the cards and dealt herself another hand.

# 24

It had been a pleasant drive along the Ashley River. The sun was warm, the air was fresh, the countryside beautiful. The scent of pine lingered on the breeze; flowers grew in wild, multicolored profusion.

Jessie glanced over at Claiborne, seated beside her in the surrey. He was wearing a white suit, a white, flat-brimmed hat and a flamboyant red stock that hid his double chin. He looked very inch the proud southern gentleman. And he had indeed been a gentleman, politely making conversation, showing her points of interest, only once tippling from the silver flask he kept in his jacket pocket.

Apollo turned the surrey down a long lane bordered by ancient magnolia trees.

"This is it," Claiborne announced. "Magnolia Hall."

It seemed to Jessie they must have traveled at least a mile before the house came into sight. Two stories tall, with stately columns supporting the veranda, it was the ideal picture of a southern mansion. It was huge—Jessie couldn't even conceive of the size of the rooms inside.

But as they drew nearer, its majesty seemed to fade. The house was badly in need of paint, several shutters were loose and hung crookedly, the windows were dirty. The grass was dry and brown, withered from the hot summer sun.

Jessie slid a sidewise glance at Claiborne. There was a melancholy look in his eyes, a faint, sad smile on his lips.

"It used to be a showplace," he remarked wistfully. "But the war . . ." He lapsed into silence for a moment. "There just isn't enough money to keep the place up anymore."

Jessie expected him to dig out his flask and take a big swill. But he didn't. He just continued to stare sentimentally at the fine old house with its peeling paint. Jessie felt an ache of pity for the old man. The war had been hard on Claiborne Bodine and his family. And even though his side had started the whole thing, she couldn't help but feel sorry for him. Gently, she placed her hand over his and gave him a faint, encouraging smile.

"Once the war's over you'll see this place like it once was," he said.

Apollo halted the surrey. Several pickaninnies appeared, exclaimed in surprise, then raced back toward a line of cabins to the rear of the house.

Jessie allowed Apollo to hand her down from the surrey. Claiborne alighted and stood scowling at the house. Once again Jessie felt in awe of the sheer dimensions of it, of the thousands of acres surrounding it.

A tall, burly man in patched breeches and a loose, baggy shirt appeared. His hat was pulled low over his forehead, concealing his features; he walked with a long, bow-legged stride. Several blacks followed him.

"Mr. Bodine, it's good to see you again. It's been a long time." The man extended his hand, and Claiborne shook it.

"This is Jessie Morgan, Calvin," Claiborne said. "Garth's fiancee. Our overseer, Jessie. Calvin Tyler."

Calvin swept off his hat, revealing riotous blond curls spilling over his brow. He had a ruddy complexion, and his beard needed combing. Jessie judged him to be in his middle thirties. "A pleasure to meet you, ma'm. I'll have Jewel take the dust covers off some of the furniture and fix you something to eat and drink."

Jewel looked remarkably like Violet Mae, except she was perhaps even plumper. She smiled, shooed away some of the children, then ushered Jessie up the wide steps and into the house.

The entry hall was immense, with an ornately carved staircase curving up to the second floor. Jessie only caught a glimpse of the dining room, but the parlor dwarfed the one at the Bodine's town house. Jessie stood in the middle of the room, gaping at the fire-place, the lovely paintings and tapestries, the draperies, the exquisite carpeting.

"Sit," Jewel ordered, shaking out a sheet covering a velvet settee. "I jes' squeezed oranges dis mawnin'. Ya'll want a glass o' juice?"

"That would be fine."

Jewel vanished into another part of the house. Jessie glanced out a rain- and dust-smeared window. Claiborne was talking to Calvin Tyler and several black men. Apollo leaned against the surrey, his arms folded across his massive chest, the sun glistening on the perspiration that had gathered in the tight curls of his hair.

Tyler carried no whip, no gun. He seemed friendly and pleasant. Perhaps all the stories Jessie had heard about the cruelty of the overseers to the slaves had been exaggerated.

Jewel reappeared with a frosty glass of orange juice. Jessie accepted it and sank down into the soft cushions of the settee. "Are you and Violet Mae related?"

"She be my sister. Gots us other brothers an' sisters, but they had different pappies. We both born here at Magnolia Hall, when Mistuh Claiborne 'bout eighteen. He be a good mastah." Her gaze slid curiously over Jessie. "Folks is sayin' you be a Yankee. Dat so?"

Jessie nodded. "I'm from Pennsylvania."

Jewel cast a surreptitious glance around her, then peered slyly back at Jessie. "It be true Mistuh Linkum really wants to free us?"

"It's true."

A faint frown of perplexity crossed her face. "*Then* what we do? Who take care of us?"

"You can take care of yourselves."

Jewel cackled mockingly. "Wid no schoolin'? Cain't read nor write nor cipher."

"I'm sure the government would help you. Send teachers down here." Jessie heard the front door open and flashed Jewel a look of warning. "Enough said on the subject."

Jewel nodded in understanding as Claiborne and Tyler entered the house.

"Fix us some juleps," Claiborne told the woman. "We're going in to look at the ledgers. Jessie, make yourself comfortable. We'll eat in a little while."

Jessie settled back on the settee, listening to a fly buzzing somewhere in the room. It smelled musty and unused. She drank her juice, wondering about this place, how it must have been before the war. Would it be the same grand country manor after the war? She supposed that depended entirely on which side was victorious. As the situation looked now, it wouldn't be the South.

Somehow, that thought didn't please her as much as it might have a month or two ago. She didn't believe in slavery, but could she really complain about it? In her limited sphere of knowledge, the blacks she had met seemed relatively content with their lot in life. The idea of freedom was more of a novelty than a desire for them.

Jessie found herself dozing until the men's

voices disturbed her. Claiborne stuck his head into the drawing room. "I'm going riding with Mr. Tyler. Jewel's frying a chicken. I'll be back in about an hour."

Jessie wished she had worn her riding clothes instead of a dress, but she hadn't. Restless, she prowled through the house, upstairs and down, marveling at the finery she found in every room. At length, her curiosity appeased, she wandered out onto the front veranda and settled herself on a swing. Apollo was sitting on the steps, flipping a jacknife into the dirt. He turned, glanced politely at Jessie, then went back to his game.

Jessie's mind triggered suddenly, and it all came back to her in a flood of ugly images—Loretta and Apollo locked in each others arms. Then she recalled what Garth had told her. If Apollo's liaison with Loretta was discovered, this faithful slave would surely forfeit his life. And for what? One of Loretta's whims? Jessie could hardly believe Loretta loved him.

Jessie watched him flip the knife into the dirt several more times, studied his broad shoulders a long moment, then finally inhaled deeply. "Apollo, how long have you and Loretta been carrying on?"

His back stiffened. The knife spun out of his hand. "Don' rightly know what you mean, Miz Jessie."

Jessie self-consciously bit her lower lip. She was butting into something that was not her affair. But now that she had begun she had to finish. "In the carriage shed. At night."

Apollo retrieved his knife. "Miz Jessie, I don' know nothin' 'bout what ya'll talkin' 'bout."

"I saw you. I see Loretta go out almost every night. I followed her once."

Apollo's entire body seemed to fold up. He hung his head and hunched his shoulders. A sudden silence hung in the air. Jessie could feel the tension radiating from him.

She floundered about in her mind for the right words; she didn't want Apollo to think she was blaming him. "Do you want to tell me about it?"

"No'm."

"Look, Apollo. I'm new to this part of the country. I don't know your ways. But I *do* know you could get into a lot of trouble if you're found out. I want to help you."

"How kin you help me? I ain't nothin' but a dumb nigger. Got to do what he's told."

"You're not dumb!" Jessie's voice was sharper than she had intended it to be. She lowered her tone, spoke slowly. "You just *think* you are because that's what everybody expects you to be."

Apollo folded his knife and put it in his pocket. He ran his fingers through his wiry hair, staring off in the direction of the stables. "Miss Loretta—it were all her idea. Said she was sick an' tired of havin' no decent white men around to pay court to her. Said if'n I didn't do what she wanted, she tell Mistuh Claiborne I try to rape her. Either way, I knowed I'd be de deadest nigger in

Charleston."

Jessie's breath came out in an exasperated sigh. "You see? I told you that you weren't dumb."

"Coupla times I figured to run off. But where could I go? Mistuh Claiborne, he jes' send de slave catchers after me."

"Slave catchers?"

Apollo nodded, still gazing off at the immense barn. "They like bounty hunters. Not so many of dem since de war. But fer a price they'll run down a slave an' catch him. Usually beat him good 'fore they bring him home."

Just like Jake Coffin, Jessie thought. A chill crawled over her flesh and made her shiver.

"Apollo, I think I can help you."

Finally, he turned and looked at her, his eyes wide with fear and doubt. "How kin you help me? What kin you do? I'm a slave. I belong to de Bodines."

"Do you want to continue your . . . your affair with Loretta?"

His eyes bulged, his jaw trembled; he shook his head in firm denial. "I don' want to end up in a pine box six feet in de ground."

An idea formed so suddenly in Jessie's mind, it made her catch her breath. Her head filled with the memory of her escape from the Yankees in her mother's casket. Could something like that be arranged for Apollo? It seemed unlikely, but right now she had no better plan.

"Are there many free blacks in Charleston?"

Apollo nodded reflectively. "Got a whole little town of their own. Cabbage Row."

"I remember seeing it. Garth drove me by." She tried to recall the neighborhood, the buildings, the businesses; her mind was blank. "Who buries a slave when he dies?"

Apollo regarded her with suspicion, his eyes tinged with apprehension. "On de plantation, it be de other slaves. In town, ol' Zeph does it."

"Zeph?"

"He be de undertaker. No white undertaker do it."

"Do you know this Zeph?"

He hesitated, then nodded reluctantly. "Had to see him last year when Blossom took sick an' died. Zeph, he has a son Luke—he 'bout my age. Sometimes when Miz Della or Miz Loretta shoppin', I visit wid him. Drink a little 'shine, tell some stories."

Jessie saw Claiborne, Calvin Tyler and Leroy riding in from the fields. She shot a warning look at Apollo. "We'll talk more, when we have the chance."

He eyed her with some misgivings.

"Apollo, do you trust me?"

His broad shoulders lifted in a shrug of surrender. "I reckon so, m'am. Yer not like de others—yer a Yankee."

A small, amused smile curved her lips. "Indeed I am. And if all this gets out, we'll *both* end up with our heads in a noose."

Apollo allowed a faint smile to touch his lips, then turned back to watch the approach of his master.

Leroy was leading a foal with him, a beautiful little caramel-colored horse with white stockings. Claiborne dismounted his stallion ponderously and took the foal from Leroy. "Jessie, come here, girl."

Jessie stepped around Apollo and went down the stairs. She patted the young horse's neck and received an affectionate nuzzle of its head in return.

"She's yours, Jessie. Garth tells me you ride well."

Jessie looked at him in dumbfounded surprise. "Mine?"

Claiborne's smile was slight but kindly. "You're practically part of the family now. What are you going to call her?"

"I don't know." Jessie was genuinely touched. A few weeks ago she would have believed this gesture from Claiborne impossible. "Thank you, Claiborne."

"My pleasure." The smile vanished as he turned to Leroy. "Feed the hands and have them gather in front of the cabins in an hour. Apollo, stable the mare and give her an extra helping of oats."

Apollo took the rope from Jessie's hands and began to lead the foal away. Jessie trailed after him.

"Why does he want all the slaves together?" she asked quietly.

"Gwine to pick out some to sell. Cain't afford all the niggers he's got here."

"Will he sell you?"

"Wish he would," Apollo muttered sourly. "No. Jes' de field niggers. Probably de chilluns, mostly, an' women."

"Remember, Apollo, we have to get you away before all this business with Loretta comes out."

His short laugh burned with bitterness. "Might as well ask me to turn white overnight."

Jessie shared a decent meal of fried chicken with Calvin Tyler and Claiborne. The two men did nothing but talk business, excluding her entirely from their conversation. This was fine with her. She was deep in thought, picking listlessly at her food. How was she going to get poor Apollo out of the mess he was in? The casket trick had worked once, but would it work again? And would Garth catch on? Jessie closed her eyes and rubbed her forehead with her fingertips in frustration. Maybe she should have stayed out of it, let Loretta continue her little game with the slave.

A frown narrowed her eyes and darkened her expression, and she abruptly rejected the idea. Apollo would be the one to lose the most if they were discovered. Loretta might even live down the shame. Lord knew, she had enough audacity to talk her way out of anything.

Jessie frowned unhappily again. She disliked Loretta intensely; she knew the feeling was mutual. Whatever Loretta would get from this messy little affair, she had earned. Apollo deserved his chance for a life of freedom.

"Are you finished?"

Claiborne's voice interrupted Jessie's depressing thoughts. She looked up at him, trying to compose her features into a mask that would give none of her jumbled emotions away. "I'm sorry. What?"

"I wondered if you were finished. You haven't eaten much."

"Yes, I'm through." Jessie had lost her appetite back on the front porch. Evidently Claiborne hadn't. He had eaten heartily and consumed the better part of a bottle of wine.

His jowly cheeks were flushed, making his hair appear a stark white. "Mr. Tyler and I have some business with the slaves. Would you care to come along?"

Jessie shrugged. She didn't especially want to stay alone in this cavernous mansion with its draped furniture. Sipping the last of her water, she placed her napkin beside her nearly untouched plate and allowed Tyler to pull out her chair.

"Pardon my boldness, Miss Morgan," he said. "But Garth found himself a mighty pretty woman in you—even if you *are* a Yankee."

Jessie winced, glancing surreptitiously at Claiborne. He was polishing off the last of the wine, seeming to find his overseer's statement amusing.

She managed a small smile for Calvin. "Thank you, Mr. Tyler."

Gallantly, he offered her his arm. She slipped hers through it, following him out through the back of the house. She rather liked this bearded, big-boned blond giant. There was a gentleness about him that bespoke of kindness, something—she had heard—that was unknown among overseers.

Jewel was scouring out several pans as they passed through the kitchen. Jessie heard Claiborne's chair scrape in the dining room, punctuated by a low, rolling belch.

"Tell me," Calvin said quietly. "How's Miss Loretta?"

Jessie felt a small jolt go through her. The tone in Tyler's voice startled her. Was he one of her lovers too? "Fine," she replied evasively, and sent him a mildly curious look. "Why?"

He blushed furiously and lowered his eyes. 'I've always admired her. Even her temper don't bother me. I like a woman with spunk."

Jewel coughed into her hand as Tyler opened the back door. Jessie threw a look over her shoulder and saw the black woman rolling her eyes.

Jessie subdued the amused smile that threatened as she stepped out into the bright sunlight. "Spunk? Yes, I suppose that's as good a word as any to describe Loretta."

A pity Calvin Tyler was just a lowly overseer. He seemed genuinely taken by Loretta. But somehow, Jessie couldn't quite picture the regal Loretta Bodine married to any man as poorly placed as Calvin.

He rang a heavy brass bell suspended from a wooden pole; its peal echoed loudly through the peaceful tranquility of the yard.

By the time Claiborne joined them, some

forty or more adult slaves and half as many children had gathered in front of a line of cabins. The small homes were made of logs, chinked with mortar, each supporting a chimney, and most of them had a small patch of garden.

Tyler released his hold on Jessie's arm and stepped forward. Claiborne came to stand beside her.

She threw him a quizzical look. "What's going on?"

"I've got to sell some of my people. They aren't needed anymore. They're only extra mouths to feed."

Jessie's features darkened into a frown as she turned to watch Tyler and Leroy talking quietly together. The blacks seemed openly distressed. Chattel, Jessie thought angrily, and a spark of that old pride in the Union and all its good came back to her with a vengeance.

"I reckon you all know why you're here," Tyler said. "I know there ain't no foolin' none of you niggers. You all know what's goin' on here as well as me and Mr. Bodine."

The slaves shifted about uncomfortably. Most of the adults kept their gazes downcast; the children—ranging from babies to near adults—stared with wide eyes.

Methodically, as if choosing unfit produce from a vegetable stand, Tyler selected slaves. Several older men stepped out of line, their faces drawn, expressions anguished. More were taken—women and children, young and old—until only half the original group remained.

A young boy of about six looked totally bewildered. A woman, perhaps Jessie's age, lifted her eyes in a plea of understanding. She took several lurching steps forward, casting wild, beseeching eyes at Tyler, then at Claiborne.

"Don' take my boy from me! He all I got!"

"He's young," Claiborne said. "He can't work yet, can't earn his keep."

"He kin hoe and run errands."

"There's nothing to hoe anymore."

The woman dropped to her knees, clasped her hands together in prayerful desperation and looked at the white man in despondency. "Please, mastah! My boy don' eat much. Ain't no trouble. Don' take him from me!"

Jessie turned and stalked back into the house. Apollo was sitting at the large kitchen table eating cold yams and talking to Jewel. Both fell silent as Jessie entered.

"Does this happen often?" she asked.

Jewel peered sheepishly at her. "Mistuh Claiborne ain't never sold off a slave in his life, 'lessen he bad. He ain't hisself no more."

"Nothing is." Jessie flopped down in a wooden chair at the table. Apollo started to rise, but she waved him back down. "This place—the South. It's mad."

Neither Jewel nor Apollo spoke; they just stared at her with more than mild curiosity and surprise.

Apollo kept the surrey at a slower pace so that the foal, tied to the tailgate, could keep up on the drive back to town. Jessie was silent for the most part; so was Claiborne.

At length, she glanced over at the older man. He appeared to be dozing, but she knew he wasn't.

"How many slaves will you sell?"

"Twenty-three." His voice was stiffly controlled, but there was a note of sadness in it, and he gave a slow shake to his head. "I doubt they'll bring a quarter of their worth."

Jessie wasn't moved by his melancholy; he was still thinking of them only as an investment. "The woman? What did you do about her and her son?"

"I couldn't keep him. I agreed to sell her as well."

"Together?"

"Possibly." His shrug was noncommital. "Perhaps they'll be bought together. Tyler's going to try for that when he brings them in to town Thursday for auction."

Auction! Jessie grimaced.

Claiborne eyed her intently. "I wonder if you'll ever get used to our way of life here."

It's a *dying* way of life, Jessie reflected morosely. The South is dying, as well as its men. But too late for that woman and her son. Jessie vowed it wouldn't be too late for Apollo.

Loretta made a ghastly parody of a sweet smile for a wounded man lying on a cot. A bandage was fastened about his head, the white linen stained a deep pink; tufts of oily dark brown hair stuck up from the wrappings.

"Water?" she asked. "It's fresh and cool."

He peered at her with one eye; the other was covered with a black patch, evidently the result of some old injury. "Got any whiskey?"

"There's some in the dispensary. But it's only being used for surgery now."

He grunted and closed his eye. Loretta stifled a disgruntled sigh and let her gaze flick around her at all the other men laid out on cots. Some moaned, some cried, some were silent. All of them stank, all of them had vermin. An icy shudder went through her body.

Once this had been the basement of St. Michael's Church; now it was a hospital. The army surgeons had too many men for them to administer to; civilian doctors helped in the operating theater, a section severed from the ward only by blankets hanging on a rope.

A scream, high and despairing, floated out from the curtained alcove. A bubble of nausea rose in Loretta's stomach. She despised sickness, despised its smell, thought sometimes she could even taste it. Besides, she hadn't been feeling too well herself lately. All Jessie's fault, she decided with acid resentment. Having that little Yankee snit in the house made her feel like a traitor to the Cause.

Her eyes swept the cots and pallets once more, the blood-soaked bandages, the putrefying flesh, the disfigured men. What are our soldiers doing? All they seem able to do anymore is get killed or wounded. And the Yankees—Loretta's teeth clenched in rage—*they* were winning battle after battle, skirmish after skirmish. Every day another precious inch of southern soil was being gobbled up by the Union hordes.

"Miss?"

Loretta glanced down at the one-eyed man, trying to soften the hard features of her expression into something resembling kindness. "What?"

"I'll take that water now."

Grimacing at the smell emanating from the man's wounds and clothing, Loretta helped him sit up and held a cup to his lips. He slumped back against the soiled pillow and seemed to drift into a deep slumber.

Loretta moved away with her pitcher of water, searching for her mother. She wanted to go home, to fall into bed and sleep until General Lee and his army were victorious. Della was nowhere in sight—only row after row of pathetic, maimed soldiers.

"Damn!"

Loretta's comment drew a giggling response from a young boy with a broken leg on the cot next to her. "That's just what I said when I seen them Yankees comin' at me, lady."

Loretta gave him fresh water with a puckered, sweet smile, then hurried off toward the stairs leading up to the church. She had to get out of here! Another minute, and she was sure she would lose her lunch. Ignoring the pleading calls of the sick, she hastened past their cots, wanting only fresh air to fill her lungs once again.

She nearly collided with four privates hauling wooden crates down the steps. Pressing herself against the wall, she allowed them to pass, then looked up in surprise to see her brother descending the dim stairway.

"Nursing doesn't agree with you?" he inquired.

Her eyes glittered with malicious pleasure. "Not any more than soldiering did with you."

His mouth became hard under his full mustache. "Don't start in on me again, Loretta. Those boxes those men had contain morphine and laudanum and quinine and sulfur. That's of more use to the Confederacy than any dozen Yankees I might shoot down."

"Where'd you get it?"

His mouth twisted with cynical amusement. "From the Yankees."

Loretta whistled softly in surprise. "The *Yankees*?"

"On Folly Island. A party of our men surprised them last night."

She peered doubtfully at him. "I don't suppose you were with them?"

"No. But I helped plan the whole thing." He gave her a taunting grin. "You see, sister dear, I didn't desert the Cause. I just changed my tactics."

Loretta shot a malevolent look at him. "So that little bitch of a Yankee you profess to love won't leave you?"

Garth's mouth tightened with anger, and corded muscles stood out on his neck. He stared at her with a hard, cold squint of warning. "You may be my sister, Loretta, and a woman. But if you ever call Jessie a name like that again, I won't hesitate to strike you."

She eyed him with a cool, challenging lift of a brow. "Garth Bodine, the grand gentleman, threatening a lady."

"You're no lady, Loretta. You never have been." He brushed past her and strode down the steps.

Loretta stood staring after him, a raging storm brewing in her gray eyes.

When the wild fires of passion had slowly subsided until there was only a tingly, sated feeling flowing through Garth, he gathered Jessie close and nestled her in his arms. One hand ran absently over her shoulder down her slim arm, felt the smooth warmth of her skin. Their lovemaking had been mutual, unhurried, pleasurable. He was content, and her soft hair against his chest felt like silken threads. He closed his eyes, secure in the knowledge that everything was as close to perfect as he could have ever wanted it to be.

Only one thing still stood between them—the differences in their upbringings. She had told him about his father's selling the slaves, separating families. He understood her feelings, but there was nothing he could do about it. Slaves and their acquisition and sale were a way of life he had known for as long as he could remember.

"Something tells me that foal Father gave you was a kind of wedding present," he said.

Soft laughter came from her throat. "Is

that a custom I haven't heard of yet?"

"No. I think it was just his way of saying he accepts you."

"Then maybe we won't have to wait till spring."

"We won't." He shifted on the bed, leaning on his elbow to study her features in the dim light. She was truly beautiful, her face perfection, her eyes sometimes playful, sometimes seductive and mysterious. "I'll bet before Christmas."

"That's still a long way off."

"I'll keep nagging him. He's just worried about the way the war's going, the way his money's disappearing. You may end up married to a penniless pauper."

"I don't care." Her fingertips touched his brow, stroking gently. They traced his cheek, his jawline. Beneath his chin, a light touch. Behind his ears, his neck. Her touch was magical.

"It won't be long." Lying on his stomach now, he traced the smooth valley between her breasts, ran his hand lightly over her belly. "Chattanooga's gone. Now all of Tennessee is lost to us. Soon your army will be in Georgia. The war's all but finished for us."

"Then *all* the slaves will be free."

"And you and I will be married." His lips caressed hers with a feathery touch and moved down to her ear, her neck. His mouth leisurely savored hers, the sweetness of her lips and the hotness of her tongue. Jessie sighed and closed her eyes, returning his kiss hungrily.

# 25

Loretta's head swam as she hauled herself to her feet. Her stomach churned; her mouth was sour. She jerkily turned away from the steaming, foul contents of the chamber pot. She thought she was going to pass out and briefly welcomed the idea. Sweat beaded her forehead, yet the morning was cool. Unsteadily, she tottered over to the washstand, dampened a cloth and patted it over her face and neck.

God, she felt horrible! She peered at herself in the mirror. Her eyes looked a little puffy, her blond hair was tangled and straggled limply about her shoulders and over her forehead. She sank down on the chair in front of her dressing table and took several deep breaths, nausea gripping her intestines and turning her color to a milky white pallor.

It must have been spoiled meat at supper

last night. If the others weren't sick, she could blame it on the stench she had been forced to breathe most of the day at the hospital. Whatever it was, she had barely gotten out of bed when the retching hit her.

A jay landed on the sill of her window, scolded her, then flittered away. Loretta scowled, picked up her brush and ran it listlessly through her hair. She had no idea what time it was. Everyone else had most likely eaten and gone out about their various tasks for the day. Breakfast! The mere thought of food sent her stomach raging again.

Perhaps later—if she felt better—she would take a drive down by the river, get some fresh air, watch the gulls. Shopping was out of the question, though buying pretty new things always made her feel better. The only trouble was that the shops never had anything new anymore, and her father didn't have the money to spend.

Poor Daddy. She gave a martyr's sigh, but she could barely contain her annoyance and impatience. Those damn Yankees and their blockade were preventing everything from coming into the city and driving up prices astronomically high. But after the auction her father would have more cash from the sale of the slaves. If anybody was buying these days . . .

Releasing another disgruntled sigh, Loretta rose slowly and walked over to the French doors, threw them wide and went out onto the balcony. Morning sunlight warmed her face, seeped through the thin material of her nightgown. But fall was actually here; she could feel it, she could smell it. The miserable heat of the summer was gone at last, the flies, the mosquitoes, the humidity.

She gave a little start when she saw Jessie emerge from the house below. Dressed in a billowy muslin frock with a smart little blue hat perched on all that hair pinned and coiled on her head and carrying her reticule, she made her way along the path toward the carriage shed. No woman had the right to look so lovely, so confident, so pert. With a little gesture of her fingers, Loretta dismissed the matter of Jessie's looks.

But her irritation grew even more when she saw Apollo leading the carriage out of the stable. Jessie paused to pat the horses, speak to the slave. She looked so trim and tiny standing next to Apollo's tall, rugged frame. Loretta's eyes flickered with sudden suspicion. Did Jessie have designs of her own on Apollo?

No, Loretta decided. Not even a Yankee would stoop that low. Only she—desperate and miserable. The thought of how unfullfilled her life was brought a touch of self-pity to Loretta, but it was quickly replaced by the cramping pain in her gut and the bile rising to her throat. She turned and lurched inside, bending over the chamber pot and vomiting so hard her head spun and tears streamed from her eyes.

Jessie felt extremely uncomfortable as the carriage stopped on a narrow street in

Cabbage Row. A small wooden building, with the word UNDERTAKER crudely painted on a signboard, greeted her. Several blacks, walking along the boardwalk, paused briefly to stare curiously as Apollo handed her down. They moved on, whispering among themselves.

Apollo wore a pained expression and wrung his hands in anguish. "Won't work, Miz Jessie. They come after me. Chase me down. Send de slave catchers after me."

Jessie stared at him intently. "Not if they think you're dead."

Apollo shook his head doubtfully, but pushed open the door to the undertaking parlor. Jessie took a deep breath to reinforce her waning confidence and stepped inside.

The place was nothing like Dudley Pigg's thriving establishment back in Gettysburg. There was only one room, a crude imitation of an office, with obviously handmade chairs, a desk, a dented pot-bellied stove, and what appeared to be some sort of filing system made out of old wooden crates. Above the desk hung a list of prices, ranging from a simple pine box to a more sturdy oak with a lining. Services at graveside were provided at an extra cost.

A wizened old black man with a fluffy cap of white hair looked up from his desk. When he saw Jessie, his eyes flew wide with surprise and alarm, and he nearly toppled over his chair as he quickly got to his feet.

"Missus?" His voice was hesitant, bewildered. "What kin I do fer you?" His gaze darted curiously to Apollo, but he didn't speak to the Bodines' coachman.

Jessie approached the old man—probably as old as Claiborne himself, and it was indeed a feat for a black to live so many years. There were small creases in his face, dug by a lifetime of hard work and desolation. He was cadaverously thin and wore a rumpled frock coat with a patch on the sleeve, no doubt purchased from one of the many secondhand stores Jessie had seen in the black district.

She cleared her throat, fidgeting with her reticule. "Apollo tells me he's a friend of yours. And your son."

The undertaker nodded. "Yessum."

"Your name is Zeph?"

Another nod. "Ya'll got business wid me, ma'm? One o' yer slaves die?"

"I don't own slaves. I'm from the North. My cousin is Claiborne Bodine."

Zeph's eyes grew so large, all Jessie could see was the whites. "You be a Yankee, miss?"

"That's right. And I *do* have business with you. Business that could very well save Apollo's life."

A hint of fear shone in Zeph's eyes, but he quickly recovered himself. Taking a tattered handkerchief from his pocket, he dusted off one of the chairs. "Set, miss. I best go out back an' git my boy."

As the old man vanished through a door to the rear, Jessie seated herself on the splayed-back chair. Perspiration beaded her upper lip, and she dabbed at it nervously with a hankie. The faint sound of hammering coming from outside abruptly stopped. A fly buzzed by and settled on a shelf containing bottles of various colors. Embalming fluid, Jessie presumed, and she swallowed the lump that had suddenly formed in her throat.

Apollo wandered around in a circle, then finally leaned against the wall next to a dog-eared calendar, folding his arms across his massive chest. A long sigh slipped from him.

Jessie was beginning to feel as hopeless as Apollo looked, and every bit as nervous. If she were caught . . . She couldn't complete the thought. She knew it would be the end of her plans to marry Garth. Claiborne would forbid it, and she doubted even Garth would understand. Unless she told him the reason why she was in fear for Apollo's life, and she knew she would never do that. If Garth even believed her, it would only make things worse for Apollo.

Zeph returned, followed by a much younger man. Unlike Apollo, Luke had the wide nose and broad, low forehead of his race. He was short but powerfully built, his filthy leather carpenter's apron stretching across a broad chest. The sleeves of his shirt were rolled up to reveal meaty forearms and bulging biceps.

His grin was hesitant when he greeted Apollo, then he turned dark, curious eyes on Jessie.

"My name is Jessica Morgan," she said. "As I told your father, I have need of his services, but not in the usual way."

All the black men stood staring pensively at

her. Jittery, she waved them to chairs. "Sit! You're making me more nervous than a cat!"

"Cain't set, miss," Luke said. "Tain't proper."

Jessie made an impatient gesture. "Damn proprieties! I'm a Yankee. Now sit!"

The three men hastily took chairs, but continued to stare.

Jessie turned to Luke. "Apollo is in trouble. I have a plan I think can save his life—with your help. I understand you're his friends, he can trust you?"

Luke nodded. "He kin trust us."

Zeph agreed with a solemn nod of his fuzzy white head.

"You're a free man, I'm told," Jessie went on. "I'd like to see your papers."

Zeph raised brooding, doubtful eyes to her but opened a desk drawer. He took out a folded paper, carefully tied with a faded red ribbon. Jessie took it, opened it and scanned the words. Instead of an elaborate document, the words were simple: "I hereby free my slave Zeph on this day January 14, 1835." It was signed by a Lemuel Jones of Claredon County."

"This is all there is to it?" she asked, amazed. "Just a piece of paper like this—no judge or anything?"

"Dat's it, ma'm." Zeph's gnarled hand reached out gingerly for the paper, as if it were as precious as gold. To him, Jessie supposed, it was. She handed it back to him, and he refolded it carefully. "Now if'n ya'll don' mind, ma'm . . . What dis be all about?"

"I'm going to free Apollo."

Zeph looked mildly staggered. "But he ain't yourn to free!"

Apollo made a low, groaning sound of despair deep in his throat. "We knows dat. But I got myself in a heap o' trouble. Big trouble."

Luke quirked a curious brow at him. "What you do, boy?"

Jessie thought she detected a blush creep into Apollo's dusky complexion—if such a thing was possible—as he leaned over and whispered to Luke.

Luke's eyes widened with shock and fear. "You a daid man, boy!"

Jessie nodded grimly. "That's precisely why we need your help."

She outlined every detail, while the three black men looked at her as if she were as crazy as a jackass. At length, she leaned back in her chair, studying Zeph with an air of expectancy. "Will you do it? *Can* you do it?"

"I kin do it, all right, ma'm."

"*Will* you?"

Zeph rubbed his chin reflectively. Finally, he nodded. "Dis be a dirty business 'Pollo got hisself into."

"Tweren't my fault," Apollo said indignantly. "Who needs a white woman anyway? I kin git me lotsa fine-lookin' wenches." He glanced sheepishly at Jessie with a faint, apologetic smile. "Beggin' yer pardon, Miz Jessie."

"It take some money," Zeph said.

"I have it." Jessie opened her reticule and

handed over a wad of Confederate notes to Zeph. "This should be enough for your part. I have more for Apollo."

Zeph goggled at the money, jammed it into his desk drawer and locked it with a rusty key. "When we gwine to do dis?"

"Thursday. Loretta and Della will be at the hospital most of the day. Garth's at work. Claiborne will be at the auction of his slaves."

"Reckon Cletus kin help," Luke offered. "He has two fine hawses an' a wagon. Delivers beer to de saloons on Meeting Street. Drives it fast. Won't look suspicious."

"Will he want paid?"

"Fer dis? Not when he find out why he doin' it. No nigger—free or slave—want to see another one hung."

"Thursday it is, then." Jessie rose; the men hastily scrambled to their feet. "I'll be at the Palmetto Millinery on Meeting Street at two o'clock sharp. Apollo will be with the coach outside. See that Cletus has his horses whipped up good."

Zeph eyed her with reluctant respect, then bowed deeply.

# 26

Jessie sat back in the surrey as it rattled over
the cobbles up Meeting Street, her head
down, her fingers twisting at the front of a
woolen shawl draped over her shoulders.
People went about their business, not taking
any particular notice of her and Apollo. He
drove carefully and with assured confidence
as always, but this time there was something
different: next to him on the seat was a
bundle of some of his clothing. Besides that
was a strange-looking object. Some six feet
long, it was hay tied together, wrapped in a
blanket and secured with several lengths of
twine. Apollo's double, and a poor imitation
of him. But it was the only thing either of
them could come up with.

Jessie reached into her reticule and
withdrew a sheet of paper, neatly folded and
tied with a snip of ribbon—Apollo's freedom
paper, just like the one Zeph had showed to

her. She had scribbled, instead of using her usually neat, precise script, hoping it would appear that Mr. Thaddeus Smith had written out the document in careless haste, perhaps worried about his circumstances due to the war. John Smith was a free man, as of this September day in 1863.

A faint, nostalgic smile touched Jessie's lips for a moment. She had chosen that name for Apollo for purely sentimental reasons. Garth had used it to his advantage on their flight from Gettysburg; hopefully, it would serve Apollo as well on his journey to the North.

She passed the paper to him, along with a small pouch of gold and Confederate notes and two letters, one to Dr. Cornelius Brooks, the other to Mary Purcell. Of all the people Jessie had known back home, they were the only two she could trust anymore.

"Do you remember what to do, Apollo?"

He slipped the papers and the money inside his jacket. "Yessum. An' I cain't thank you enough, Miz Jessie. Never figured I'd be free."

"You'll make something of yourself, Apollo. Dr. Brooks will help you find work. You can even go to school and learn to read and write. Promise me you'll do that?"

"I don't know, Miz Jessie. I ain't so smart."

"You're very smart. You can learn if you try."

Apollo nodded obediently as he pulled the surrey to a halt in front of the Palmetto Millinery, just above Market Street. He alighted from the trap and came around to hand Jessie down. She gazed at him with a kind of feverish intensity, felt a lump form in her throat and bit her lip to keep her emotions under control.

She cast one last apprehensive look at the blanket-wrapped form, then turned back to Apollo and risked a slight smile. "Godspeed," she murmured, and hurried into the shop before her composure completely shattered.

Garth looked up from a stack of requisitions on his desk as a whispered buzz of excitement suddenly rippled through the quartermasters' office. He was surprised to see his sister sweeping through the door, wearing a gown of blue taffeta festooned with white satin bows, a regal lift to her chin. But for all her superior air, she seemed pale and drawn, as if she were a dozen years older than her twenty-two.

Garth waved her to a chair and leaned forward with curious interest, folding his hands on his desk before him. "What brings you here?"

She looked him over with a haughtily cocked brow. "Can't I visit my brother if I want to?"

Garth hid his smile with a polite cough. The converted warehouse on East Battery Street was hardly the type of neighborhood Loretta would frequent. There were grog shops, brothels, soldiers' barracks, a slaughterhouse, and various other unsavory places nearby.

"Of course," he said, flashing her a rakish grin. "But I figured you'd be at the hospital with Mother."

"I'm *sick* of that damn hospital! Every time I see one more wounded man, it reminds me there's one less soldier out there fighting the Yankees." She glanced surreptitiously around the office, its workers comprised mostly of recuperating soldiers and old men. Frowning, she leaned forward and spoke quietly but urgently. "Why don't you go back and fight? You don't belong here!"

"I belong close to home. Close to Jessie."

Loretta sat back and grunted irritably. "Jessie!" Her voice was like the hiss of a serpent.

Garth shot her a stern look of warning. "No more outbursts on the subject of Jessie, or one of these days I'll knock those pearly white teeth of yours right down your throat."

Loretta glared, her gray eyes shooting sparks of hatred.

"Have you seen her today?" he asked.

Loretta shrugged indifferently. "She's been spending a lot of time out in the stable with that foal Daddy gave her. Today she went out with Apollo—shopping!" Her eyes turned hard as stone. "Damn her for her Yankee money!"

"At least she's not taking anything away from you, Loretta. She pays her own way."

"Which reminds me . . ." Loretta's expression changed abruptly from one of veiled hostility to that of sisterly love. "I need to borrow ten dollars."

"Why?"

"I just need it. I'll pay you back."

"You mean Father will." Garth reached into his pocket and handed over a ten-dollar Confederate note to his sister.

Loretta left the quartermasters' department, annoyed at Garth. Somehow, he had made her feel as if she were begging. Which she was.

As she walked down East Battery, fear began to gnaw at the pit of her stomach. This was a horrible section of town. Before the war it had been quite pleasant, but now it seemed filled with all the riffraff of the city. Soldiers eyed her with open and frank appreciation and some called out lewd invitations. It reeked of rotten sewage, stale whiskey and the stench of the river.

She turned onto Atlantic Street, away from the military and back into civilian life. But it was a poor neighborhood. Shops sold used clothing, used furniture, used shoes. The display in a bakery window held absolutely the most unappetizing stuff she had ever beheld, as did the fish outside a market.

Loretta glanced up at the numbers on the buildings, mentally consulting one in particular she had stored in her mind. Downstairs was an apothocary; upstairs, a physician's office. Not the family doctor up on King Street, but a man by the name of Hiram Willoughby, a stranger.

Loretta swallowed dryly, and for a moment had an urge to bolt and run. Fear closed around her heart, twisting it, but she got herself under some kind of control. Squaring her shoulders, she pushed open the door to the apothocary shop and ascended the stairs to the second floor office.

Jessie stood by the window of the millinery shop, pretending to look at a variety of bonnets. She bit a trembling lip; the breath wheezed at the back of her throat; at one point, she nearly tore the red velvet ribbons off one of the brims. Fortunately, the store was busy at this hour, and the elderly woman who ran it was too preoccupied with other customers to notice Jessie's anxiety. Outside, she could see Apollo standing in the street by the surrey, idly stroking the horse's neck and chewing on a wooden matchstick.

Then she heard it: the thunder of hooves. She dropped a straw chapeau with ostrich feathers and strained to see out the window. Cletus' beer wagon careened around Market Street onto Meeting on two wheels. It crashed into the surrey, sideswiping it hard and causing the horse to rear. Wood splintered and shattered, kegs of beer rolled from the wagon and struck the cobbles. They split open, spilling their contents in a river of foam.

Cletus' two brown mares reared, pawed the air with their hooves, and came to a jolting halt. Other animals tethered nearby shied away and whickered with fright.

Jessie could hear the rising commotion as

people poured out of the buildings close to the accident. She exited hastily, her heart thudding, just in time to see Cletus bending over a shapeless form lying in the street. He covered it with a tattered blanket, then furtively reached inside his coat pocket. Quickly, he withdrew a pint bottle, uncorked it and liberally sprinkled chicken blood over the covered body in the street.

People were gathering around now, whispering excitedly to each other, some turning away from the grisly sight on the street. For her part, the only thing Jessie noticed was the stench of all that beer running into the gutters. Apollo was nowhere in sight.

Cletus stood up shakily, noticeably upset, and looked around with wide, frightened eyes.

Jessie took a tentative step forward, let her eyes graze the bloody heap. "Is that my driver?"

Cletus shuffled his feet, shrugged helplessly. "Don't know, ma'm."

Jessie crept out onto the street, bent, and lifted a tiny corner of the blanket. Stifling a gag, she let the blanket fall back in place and staggered backward several paces. She turned away, looking sick and pale.

"It's Apollo."

The people were gathering in little groups now, chattering, speculating. An old Negro bootblack nodded grimly. "I seen him jes' fore' de accident. It be Apollo. De Bodines' coachman."

Jessie's expression was visibly distressed. She clapped a hand to her forehead in a theatrical show of emotion and made a weak little moaning sound deep in her throat. Out of the corner of her eye, she saw several people watching her with compassion. She should have been an actress on the stage, she decided.

A burly, red-faced saloon owner stepped out into the street, gingerly avoiding the body, and grabbed Cletus by the collar. "Damn you, Cletus! How many times have I warned you to slow down!"

Cletus hung his head, backing away when the bartender released his grip. He stooped down, picked up the body, and, grunting with feigned exertion, deposited it in the back of the brewery wagon.

He turned to Jessie. "Ya'll best come wid me, miss."

Jessie shook her head in dismay, twisting her hands in nervous confusion. "Where?"

"To old Zeph, de undertaker. Elsewise, yer man be rottin' out here in de sun all day."

Indecisive, her face chalky, Jessie fluttered her hands uncontrollably. Finally, she turned to the husky saloon owner and the diminutive women who ran the millinery shop. "Keep an eye on the surrey for me, please. It doesn't look too badly damaged. I'll be back for it later."

The barkeep spat a stream of tobacco juice and grunted. "Just tell that damn fool Cletus to drive nice and easy, ma'm. You a Bodine?"

"A cousin of the family."

The saloon owner handed her up into the wagon next to Cletus. "Drive slow, boy."

Cletus nodded, flicking the reins. Jessie heard several snide whispered remarks about the Bodines as the brewery wagon pulled away. Evidently what little money and few slaves Claiborne still possessed were a source of envy.

She turned and glanced back at the blood stains on the cobbles, some of them mixed with the flood of beer. Jessie closed her eyes in relief and briefly said a silent prayer.

Apollo ran through an alley between the milliner's shop and the saloon, hauling his bundle of clothing with him. He could hear the commotion back on Meeting Street, but he ignored it. He ran until the breath in his lungs ached, hoping with all his heart that Jessie's scheme had worked.

He had done his part—thrown the hay-bundled body into the street the minute Cletus rounded the corner. Then he had darted around the surrey, snatched up his belongings and raced for the alley.

He broke out of the narrow passageway onto Church Street by the City Market. There, tied at the curb, was a black gelding with white stockings and a white blaze: the horse purchased and outfitted by Luke with Jessie's money.

Apollo strapped his belongings behind the saddle and mounted. The horse seemed frisky and full of spunk. He took one last glance around at the neighborhood, then rode off. In a peculiar sort of way, he was amost grateful to Loretta. And he would never forget Jessie until the day he died. Thanks to her, he was a free man now with a new life awaiting him in the magical, glorious land of the North.

# 27

A little group of Negroes began to gather around the undertaker's parlor as soon as Cletus pulled up in front. They shouted out questions and Cletus answered them the best he could, although vaguely.

"It be 'Pollo Bodine."

"What happened?"

Cletus helped Jessie down from the wagon, and she darted inside the building. Luke and Zeph stood abruptly, both staring expectantly at her, their eyes questioning.

"Is it done?" Zeph asked.

Jessie nodded jerkily. "Help Cletus in with the body."

Luke scurried out the door; Jessie could hear him shooing away the curious crowd. She collapsed onto a chair, heaved a heavy sigh and rubbed her forehead. There was a cold knot of nervous tension in her stomach. This little show wasn't over yet.

Presently, Cletus and Luke entered with the bloody bundle, acting as if it weighed as much as a man instead of a bunch of straw bound together.

"Everythin' went jes' fine," Cletus announced, dumping the thing on the floor. A string must have broken, for suddenly the form bulged in the middle.

Zeph drew the blinds, locked the door, then turned to Jessie. "You look poorly, ma'm. Ya'll want a tot o' whiskey?"

Without hesitation, Jessie nodded her head. Everything had gone smoothly so far, but what if Claiborne insisted on viewing the body? Her heart throbbed in sudden dread.

Zeph poured from a bottle into a tin cup and handed it to Jessie. "I got some real store-bought whiskey fer special occasions. Didn't figure you'd want 'shine."

Jessie drank from the tin cup. It went down like fire, searing the back of her throat and spreading its warm tendrils in her belly. But it calmed her nerves, made her feel less jittery.

"Luke's got a casket out back filled with sacks of rocks wired down so they won't rattle around," Zeph explained.

Jessie didn't reply, only took another sip of the fiery whiskey.

Zeph turned and nudged the blanket-shrouded hay with his foot. "Reckon we ought to put dis in too. Make fer extry paddin' in case some o' dem rocks come loose."

Luke hefted the hay bale and carried it out

the back door. Cletus and Zeph followed, leaving Jessie alone in the shabby little undertaking parlor.

She shivered suddenly, even though it was quite comfortable inside. She sipped slowly at the whiskey, her expression remote, preoccupied. She could hear hammering out back as Luke sealed Apollo's casket—and his fate—forever.


Loretta stumbled up the front steps and into the house, feeling dazed and sick and frightened. Violet Mae waddled out of the kitchen with a big smile and started to speak.

"Shut up!" Loretta's voice was high-pitched, trembling, furious; she waved the black woman away with an abrupt, angry gesture and went into the drawing room.

No one else was home, for her screech would surely have brought someone. Shakily, she poured sherry into a Waterford goblet and sank down on one of the chairs. She took a long drink, then sighed deeply.

Her face was pale; her fingers worked helplessly at the tassel on the arm of the chair. How could everything have gone wrong so completely, so quickly? Things could hardly be worse. She couldn't have imagined a more horrible fate to happen to her if she tried.

She drank again, using both hands to steady the glass. She got up, thought for a moment her knees were going to buckle, and refilled the goblet. She took a quick swallow, then leaned against the sideboard for support, her head bowed. She began to shake all over, felt her bowels turn to jelly.

The doctor down by the battery had confirmed her worst fears: she was pregnant. Pregnant by that black bastard Apollo! A cold rage shook her, making every nerve in her body scream.

She wouldn't be blamed. She would say Apollo raped her. Regardless of what he said in his defense, no one would believe him. He was a slave, a nigger.

Pivoting away from the sideboard and taking her goblet with her, she climbed the staircase. Flobelle was coming out of Garth's room with a stack of dirty linen held in front of her, humming a tuneless little song. Loretta growled with contempt and shoved the girl aside. Flobelle crashed into the wall with her shoulder, dropping the sheets and towels, uttering a little cry of pain and alarm.

Loretta stormed past the girl into her own bedroom, slamming the door behind her. The first object she saw was a Limoges vase. She hurled it against the wall and watched it scrape away a piece of wallpaper and shatter into a hundred pieces.

Breathing hard, almost panting now, Loretta tore off her bonnet and sent it sailing across the room. She finished the sherry in two huge gulps and tossed the goblet. It struck the armoire; crystal disintegrated, and there was a chunk of cherrywood splintered away from the cupboard door.

So upset she felt like tearing out her hair at the roots, she threw herself down on the bed and pounded the mattress with her fists. She began to sob convulsively as the first waves of inexpressible, haunting fear overtook her. Fresh tears rendered her incoherent; she couldn't think, she couldn't speak. All she could do was cry.

Then she heard male voices downstairs. She sat up quickly, fumbled for a hankie to dry her eyes and listened. It was her father and Calvin Tyler, come back from the auction. Her mind suddenly went blank with panic. If her father found her in this state, she could never explain it!

Scrambling off the bed, she darted over to the washstand and patted her face with a damp cloth. Her eyes were a little red, but otherwise she looked presentable. Tucking a stray lock of blond hair into place and straightening her dress, she left the room. Tomorrow there would be time enough to worry about what to do. Right now, all she wanted was another drink.

When Loretta entered the drawing room, she gave her father and Tyler a perfunctory greeting and headed straight for the sideboard. She poured herself another sherry and drank half of it before turning around. Claiborne's expression was dour, with a trace of annoyance in it. Calvin Tyler, on the other hand, beamed at her. He stood by his chair expectantly, one meaty, sunburned hand gripping a tumbler of whiskey.

"Afternoon, Miss Loretta. If I might be so bold, you're lookin' prettier than ever."

An unwilling smile twitched at the corners

of her mouth. "Thank you, Calvin." She waved her hand, indicating that he could sit back down. He did so, stretching his large, scuffed boots out before him.

Loretta finished her sherry the minute she seated herself. Tyler immediately offered to refill it for her, and she gladly accepted.

"Almost empty, Mr. Bodine," he remarked.

"There's several more full bottles under the cabinet there. Get one out." Claiborne rubbed at his pouchy eyes and let out a tired, exasperated sigh. "I could have *sworn* I filled that decanter only yesterday."

Loretta sipped more slowly this time; her head was beginning to buzz, but at least her hands had stopped shaking. "How much *did* you get at the auction?"

Claiborne waved the question aside with an impatient gesture. "Only a measly six thousand for over twenty slaves." He gulped down his whiskey and handed his glass to Tyler for more. "Six thousand!" He shook his head in complete disgust. "I should have gotten at least four times that much, and I *would* have before the war."

Calvin passed a full glass to his employer and cautiously took a seat closer to Loretta. She glanced briefly in his direction, and he gave her a lopsided, sheepish smile. A cowlick of straw-colored hair fell over his forehead. His face—what could be seen from beneath his beard—was tanned and lined from so much time spent in the sun.

"You've got to remember, Mr. Bodine," the overseer said. "Most of those niggers weren't in their prime. There were a lot of old ones and children. Only the women could bring in a decent price."

"Decent!" Claiborne snorted in disdain. "You call five hundred decent for a wench who can have maybe a half dozen children?"

A shiver of unease crossed Loretta's heart, left her breathless. Children! How she despised that word! She drank more sherry. What was she going to do? How could she explain her condition when it began to show? Besides, she hated the little brats to begin with. She didn't want one. Her thoughts settled on this new problem, a far more immediate concern than her father's present worries.

Her musings were broken when she heard a vehicle stop outside, its brakes squealing and grating. Her father rose stiffly and went to peer out the window. Loretta saw his back go rigid.

"It's old Zeph, the nigger undertaker." Then his cheeks flushed bright crimson, and he swore. He slammed his glass down on a table and stomped off toward the entryway. "And the surrey—with Jessie in it and some strange nigger driving!"

Loretta froze, holding her breath. Where was Apollo?

Jessie hurried inside, holding her skirts above her ankles. She took a deep breath, then slowly exhaled. "It's Apollo, Cousin Claiborne! There's been a *terrible* accident!"

Claiborne caught her by the shoulders and gave her a gentle but firm shake. "An accident? What do you mean, girl?"

Jessie's lip began to quiver, and she

fluttered her hands helplessly. "While I was shopping. A brewery wagon ran him down." She gave a tremendously loud sniff. "He's dead!" she wailed, and tears trickled down her cheeks. "I didn't know what to do! Someone told me about this undertaker for the slaves. I—"

"No!" Claiborne smacked his fist into his palm; his face turned a bright beet red. "No! No! *No!*"

Loretta sat staring stupidly toward the foyer, her goblet poised midway to her lips. Apollo dead? She shook her head in furious denial. It couldn't be!

"I'm sorry, Claiborne," Jessie was saying. "It was an accident. A terrible, terrible accident."

Tyler joined his employer and Jessie in the entryway. He gave Jessie's shoulder a little pat. "It's all right, Miss Morgan. You're not to blame."

Zeph stepped up on the porch. "I done de best I could fer him, Mistuh Bodine, suh. But dem hawses mangled him up pretty bad. Had my boy, Luke, nail down de lid. Ain't nobody want to see a mess like 'Pollo was."

Loretta snapped out of her daze and shook her head in disbelief. The black bastard! She was *glad* he was dead. Now she wouldn't have him around to deny her charge that he raped her. A malicious little smile curved her lips, and she took another sip of sherry. She might have been jealous of Jessie earlier for having the cash to go shopping; now she could have hugged her.

Jessie sat quietly in the parlor with an untouched glass of wine. The entire family was gathered together. Sam had gone to the quartermasters' department to summon Garth from work. Flobelle had fetched Della from the hospital. Zeph and Luke had taken Apollo's body to the slave cemetery and were attempting to find a minister for a hastily arranged service.

Garth sat next to Jessie on the settee, holding her hand. Della was visibly shaken; Loretta was half drunk.

Claiborne had partaken of his fair share of spirits as well. He paced around the drawing room, his face darkened ominously in rage.

"After the fiasco of the auction today that's another loss for me. Two-thousand dollars' worth of good black flesh!"

Jessie winced. Is that all Claiborne cared about—the loss of an investment?

"Calvin, tomorrow morning I want you to ride back to Magnolia Hill. Pick me out a good man to be my new driver." Claiborne drank; whiskey dribbled over his chin. "A man who can handle horses. Sam's too old."

Jessie stole a glance at Loretta. Oddly, she didn't seem to be the least bit distressed over the news of her lover's death.

The burial plot for the slaves of Charleston was a pathetic little place. Some owners had seen fit to erect marble and stone monuments in memory of their servants' dedication. But, for the most part, there were only crosses with crude inscriptions, over-grown with weeds and tangled underbrush.

Luke had dug the grave, and the pine box was lowered into it without ceremony. Reverend Washington Drake, a grizzled old Negro with a long white beard and fuzzy white hair, was giving a short eulogy. Jessie risked a glance at the others. Flobelle and Violet Mae were wailing like banshees; Sam had tears in his rheumy eyes. Beside her, Garth held Jessie's hand; he seemed genuinely sad. Della wiped away a tear with a lace-embroidered hankie. Claiborne, Loretta, and Tyler stood staring expressionlessly as the Baptist preacher gave entreaties to Jesus.

Jessie eyed Loretta with no small amount of curiosity. Either she was numb, or the woman had no feelings at all. Whatever the reason, Jessie was certain she had been right all along: Loretta had cared nothing for Apollo.

As the Reverend Washington Drake tossed a handful of dirt onto the casket, the family turned away toward the saddled horses and the carriage parked on the street. Jessie felt a sense of perverse joy and triumph as she heard Luke's shovel dumping more earth on the casket. With any luck at all, Apollo was probably somewhere between here and Florence by now, on his way north as a free man, away from his callous owners, away from Loretta's greedy clutches.

A chilly breeze was blowing briskly off the Cooper River; there was a faint glow to the west where the sun lingered just below the horizon. Garth sat on the swing on the front veranda beside Jessie; both were silent, pensive. From inside the house, Garth could hear his father talking endlessly to Tyler, bemoaning the loss of Apollo and the meager amount of revenue he had collected for his slaves at the auction.

Jessie pulled her shawl more closely about her shoulders, sighing in hopeless frustration.

"You're not to blame," he told her. "Accidents happen."

"Yes, I know." Anxiety grated in her voice. "But I feel so guilty. I should have taken a hansom instead of having Apollo drive me."

"Maybe he's better off where he is now."

Jessie turned her head and looked sharply at Garth. "What do you mean?"

"I always thought Apollo was too bright to be a slave. Now he's free."

A brief look of confusion came into Jessie's eyes, and she quickly glanced away. "Is death preferable to slavery?"

Garth stared at her in mute wonder. "You mean you've changed your mind about our . . . our peculiar institution?"

"Of course not!" Her mouth set in a stubborn, determined line. "Slavery's a horrid thing! It's absolutely deplorable. But is death any better?"

"Maybe for some." Garth lit a cheroot and tossed the match onto the stone floor of the porch. "Not for Apollo, though. It's only a matter of time before he would have been free."

"You think the war's going that badly for

you?"

Garth nodded reflectively. "The Yankees have us beat. It just depends on how much longer we can hold out."

"Why hold out at all?"

"Because few people in the South are as ready to believe in the inevitable as I am. I see it every day. There's just not enough guns and ammunition, not enough soldiers. We're running out of everything. The Confederacy is finished."

"You could be tried for treason for talking like that."

Garth's lips twitched with ill-suppressed amusement. "I don't say it to anyone but you."

Jessie tugged nervously at a tress of her hair, curling it around her finger. "I feel so guilty."

"Don't." Garth tossed the cheroot aside and turned her face toward him with a gentle touch of his fingertips on her chin. "You did everything you could—taking Apollo to Zeph, bringing him back here. You did the right thing."

"I did?" She fell silent a moment, then seemed to catch herself in some reverie and looked up. "I hope I did."

"You *did*! And no matter how Father feels right now, he'll come to appreciate it in a few days." His lips brushed hers with a teasing lightness, then took possession of her mouth. Garth couldn't see the sparkle of triumph that shimmered in her eyes.

Late that night, Loretta paced restlessly in

her bedroom, half tipsy from all the sherry
she had consumed. Apollo's death was of
little consequence to her; if anything, it got
him out of the way. But an overwhelming
feeling of despair came over her. She was
pregnant! How would she ever explain it?

Panic nibbled at the edges of her mind. She
needed a husband, and she needed one fast.
But all the men were off fighting in the war!
She couldn't bear the shame; her father and
mother would never understand.

The night seemed to mock her. She drained
the contents of her goblet and set it clumsily
on her dressing table. Then she had a sudden
flash of insight. It was an idea born of
desperation, but it just might work.

She peered in the mirror. A little bleary-
eyed, but she was certainly just as attractive
as ever. And there was one man in this house
tonight who had wanted her for years.

Summoning up her courage, she opened
the door and stepped out into the hall. The
house was quiet, unnaturally so. Silently, she
slipped down the hallway to the guest room,
put her hand on the knob and turned it.

Calvin Tyler sat up in bed with a startled,
mumbled question as Loretta entered the
room.

"Shhh!" she warned, holding a finger to
her lips.

"Miss Loretta?" Calvin's voice held a note
of disbelief.

"Yes, it's me." She padded over to the bed
and stood staring down at him. His sandy
hair was disheveled; his eyes were large with
surprise and confusion. In the faint light cast

from the moon, she could see he was wearing a pair of tattered white longjohns, unbuttoned at the neck.

"You oughtn't to be here," he said.

"Why not?"

He didn't speak for a moment, just stared like the gaping fool that he was as she slowly unbelted her robe.

"I want to be here, Calvin." Her voice was husky and low, carrying an implied invitation.

She pulled the robe apart, shrugged out of it and stood naked before him for several long seconds before kneeling on the bed. Calvin's eyes were as wide and large as saucers; his mouth drooped open ever so slightly.

Loretta let her hand run lightly over the mat of blond hair on his chest peeking out of his undershirt, then leaned forward. She kissed him teasingly, then kissed him again, this time hungrily. Calvin moaned hoarsely and wrapped his arms tightly about her.

# 28

It was two days after Apollo's pathetic little funeral. Jessie finished dressing, pinned up her hair and left her bedroom. Yesterday it had rained, but the storm passed quickly. This morning it was sunny and bright, and Jessie was humming to herself as she walked along the hallway.

She stopped abruptly in front of Loretta's room and listened to the sounds of retching. Vaguely alarmed, Jessie rapped lightly on the door. There was no answer from within, but the gagging had ceased. Hesitating only a moment, she pushed open the door.

Pale and sweating, Loretta was getting up from her knees in front of the chamber pot. She looked up at Jessie in surprise, then averted her eyes and anxiously bit her lip. Jessie could smell the hot, sour odor of fresh vomit.

"You're sick?"

Loretta nervously pushed a lock of hair away from her face, turning away from her cousin. "It must have been something I ate."

Jessie had eaten the same foods yesterday, and she felt fine. Then a thought struck her, one that took her breath away with the suddenness of its assault. It was wild and crazy, but it must be true. And Loretta's uneasiness at being discovered in such unladylike behavior only confirmed it: she was pregnant—pregnant by Apollo!

By all rights, Jessie should have felt the urge to laugh. But she didn't. Instead, she found herself feeling strangely compassionate toward Loretta. What a dreadful predicament!

"Loretta . . . ?" Jessie's voice was gentle and concerned as she crossed the room and touched her cousin's shoulder.

All of a sudden, Loretta cried out and threw up her arms in a wild gesture. She sagged onto the bed and erupted in a burst of bitter tears. Her shoulders shook violently; she rocked back and forth, practically collapsed with uncontrollable sobs.

Jessie stood gazing at her, a worried frown knitting her brows, until the weeping eventually trickled down to a ragged trembling.

Loretta finally looked up, her eyes red and puffy, and wiped her nose with the sleeve of her nightgown. "Jessie, I'm going to have a baby." She buried her face miserably in her hands. "A child! What can I do!"

"Who's the father?"

Loretta faltered; Jessie could almost see her mind racing and floundering. "A soldier," she stammered. "A soldier I met while he was on leave."

Jessie nodded gravely, pretending not to know who the father really was. "What's his name?"

"Joe somebody—from Georgia. Oh!" Loretta flung out her hands in exasperated dismay, then wrung them in fearful worry. "It was a foolish mistake!"

"Can you contact him? Tell him your . . . . your problem?"

"I don't even know his last name!" Loretta wailed, and a new flood of hot tears overtook her. "I don't know *where* in Georgia he's from. He could be dead for all I know. Oh, Daddy will absolutely *kill* me!"

By afternoon Loretta was back to feeling her old spiteful, nasty self again. In her distress this morning, she had been less than self-controlled. But at the time—upset, afraid, worried sick to death—she had desperately needed someone to confide in. Jessie could be discreet; at least Loretta hoped she would. And her cousin had believed her story of the soldier on leave. After all, why not? The city was full of men on their way to fight. It was as good as anything, she supposed. Certainly better than the truth.

Calvin Tyler had returned from Magnolia Hall with a new coachman, a young buck by the name of Jody. He didn't have the good looks of Apollo nor the intelligence; he was just another nigger. Right now, Claiborne was out in the carriage house with the new boy, showing him around.

Loretta primped in front of the mirror in the foyer, fluffing her blond hair and pinching her cheeks to bring out their color. Then she straightened her skirts, snugged down her bodice to display some cleavage, and wandered into the study.

Calvin dropped the newspaper he was reading and scrambled to his feet. He bowed in greeting, and gave her a shy but broad smile. "Miss Loretta. May I say you look as lovely as always?"

A knowing gleam danced in her eyes. "You may." A teasing smile playing on her lips and her eyes full of mischief, she glided toward him and ran a finger over the worn bottle green velvet of his lapel. "But you needn't call me *Miss* Loretta." She fluttered her lashes coquettishly. "After all, you haven't forgotten what happened the other night, have you? If I recall, you were there too."

"I haven't forgotten." He scrubbed nervously at his beard, peering sheepishly at her. "You were wonderful."

Loretta twined her fingers in his hair and tickled the back of his neck behind one sunburned ear. "*You* were wonderful." She leaned forward, tilted her face up to him, inviting his kiss.

He forced her lips apart in a fierce, hungry kiss. His large hands moved over her waist and hips to mold her closer to him. Loretta wantonly pressed her body next to his, wriggling her hips against him until he let out a little groan.

"Loretta." His breathing was harsh and fast as he buried his face in her hair. "Loretta, I love you. I've always loved you. I've always wanted you."

Loretta stared over his shoulder at the bookcase, her eyes gleaming shrewdly. "And I've always wanted *you*, Calvin."

He drew away, held her by the shoulders, raised a brow in disbelief. "You have?"

"Of course." She averted her gaze, trying to look coy. "But I was waiting for you to come to me. A *lady* doesn't chase after a man."

"How could I? I'm just your father's overseer. I'm not nearly good enough for you."

"Nonsense."

One rough, callused finger ran over her cheek. His sad brown eyes gazed at her with all the adoration of a faithful puppy. "Loretta, would you . . . ?" He broke off, swallowed and tried again. "Would you marry me?"

She clasped her hands around his neck and drew his face down to hers. "Yes," she whispered against his lips. "But you'll have to ask Daddy."

Calvin met her eager mouth with his. Loretta closed her eyes and sighed, but not from passion. At least her ploy had worked, and Calvin Tyler had taken the bait. But how degrading! Loretta Bodine—married to a lowly overseer, an uneducated bumpkin, a rube! But at least the baby would have a father.

Garth rubbed his forehead and stared at his feet, only half listening to his father. It was late afternoon, and normally Garth would still be at the quartermasters' department, but the office had shut down early this day. There were piles of requisitions from generals, cooks and surgeons from all regions of the South, but there was not one item of use left in the warehouse to send them. Garth had stumbled upon two hundred overcoats earlier in the day, and they had immediately been shipped to units in the Shenandoah. Ten vials of morphine and two dozen bottles of laudanum had gone to the surgeon in charge of the men stationed in Atlanta. Those pitiful supplies had been the last—until another blockade runner put in somewhere.

Garth sighed, staring intently into his brandy as if reading tea leaves. Absently, he wondered how much more liquor his father had stored in the cellar. Probably gallons of the stuff. A fleeting stab of guilt hit him; just one bottle would have several men ready for amputation from considerable pain.

"Tyler says he's good with horses—good with all animals."

Garth swung his gaze to his father and blinked. "What?"

"The new boy—Jody. He's young, but he's competent."

Garth nodded distractedly, sipping at his brandy. It was smooth and mellow and warmed his belly from the bite in the air.

Jessie was out in the carriage shed now, getting acquainted with Jody, probably sneaking an apple or a carrot to her mare. Privately, she had confessed the desire to name the foal Mary Lincoln. For harmony's sake, she had settled on Girlie.

"Damn, I hope he's half as good as Apollo." Claiborne released an impatient, exasperated sigh. He drank deeply from his own snifter of brandy.

"You don't blame her, do you"

"For Apollo's accident?" Claiborne looked momentarily surrprised, then shook his head. "No. Everybody in town knows how fast crazy Cletus drives that brewery wagon."

"Jessie feels terrible."

"I'll speak to her. It was just an unfortunate accident."

Movement in the garden caught Garth's eye. Loretta and Tyler were strolling among the last of the season's roses. As Garth watched, something very strange happened. Tyler bent down, kissed Loretta's cheek and strode away. Garth frowned in puzzlement and shook his head.

"I want you to know, son, I've grown very fond of Jessie."

Garth's face broke into an amused grin. "So have I."

"At first I feared . . . Well, you know what I feared. She's a Yankee, no matter if she *is* kin. I had visions of her stirring up unrest with our darkies as well as every other darkie she came across."

"She hasn't, has she? Garth swirled his brandy. "She doesn't hold with slavery, though."

"I'm well aware of that, son. Frankly, if things keep going the way they are with our army, there won't be any slaves by this time next year."

Garth's mouth curled in disbelief. Was it finally beginning to sink in? Did his father at last realize how poorly the Confederacy was faring in the field?

"My wedding, Father. Jessie's and mine. Does it have to be in the spring?"

A lewd grin twisted Claiborne's lips. "Can't wait, eh? You always were quite the ladies' man."

At that moment there was a tap on the library door. Claiborne sobered, and called for whoever it was to enter. Tyler stepped in with his bow-legged stride, holding his hat in his hands and crushing the brim.

He glanced at Garth, then turned his gaze on Claiborne. "I wonder if I could have a word with you, sir?"

"Of course, Mr. Tyler. Sit down. Have a drink."

"No thank you." He rocked back and forth on his heels, mopping his brow with a red bandana. "I—uh—Mr. Bodine, I've come to ask for your daughter's hand in marriage."

Garth grunted in bewildered astonishment. He choked on a sip of brandy and began to cough.

Claiborne's look was uncomprehending and blank. His eyes bulged; his face turned crimson. "*Loretta?*"

Tyler bowed his head sheepishly. "Yes, sir."

Claiborne swigged down the contents of his glass, refilled it immediately and drank again. He observed Calvin without expression. "What does my daughter have to say about this?"

"She loves me, sir. She wants to marry me."

Garth's brows knit in dismayed confusion. Loretta and Calvin Tyler? It was unthinkable, impossible! Tyler was just an overseer! Loretta was—Loretta. He set down his glass, excused himself and left the library, closing the door behind him. He guffawed in a short, loud burst.

Then he heard his father calling his name. "Garth, find Loretta and send her in here!"

Gritting his teeth to keep from laughing out loud, Garth practically ran through the house to the garden.

"Father wants to see you in his study."

Loretta glanced up from her perch on a bench, a woolen shawl pulled close around her shoulders. Her eyes narrowed; she threw him a smoldering, ugly glance. "What are you smirking at?"

"Nothing."

"Like hell, Garth! I'll thank you to mind your own business!" She rose, gave him a look of utter disdain and tossed her head back in a wild, flamboyant gesture of superiority.

Garth executed a mock bow, then stood watching her until she was inside the house. Then he threw back his head and burst into peals of rich, lusty laughter.

Calvin had been dismissed. Loretta sat across the desk from her father, watching him carefully. His face was dark with suppressed anger, his eyes like black glowing coals. The atmosphere crackled with tension.

"I forbid it!" he finally rasped through clenched teeth. "It's absurd. He's not in our social status. He's an overseer, for Christ's sake, Loretta! What's gotten into you?"

Loretta knew this was going to happen. Calvin Tyler was not the kind of man her father wanted for a son-in-law. He wasn't exactly what Loretta had dreamed of for a husband, but that was immaterial now. She *needed* Calvin.

Taking a deep breath, Loretta stared into her lap, trying to make her expression as contrite as possible. "Father, I'm going to have a child."

The silence expanded, filled the room. At length, she looked up. Claiborne was staring at her in hurt confusion.

"*His?*"

Loretta hung her head. "No."

Claiborne slammed his fist down on his desk in rage. "Whose, dammit!"

"A soldier's."

"A soldier! *What* soldier!"

"I don't know, Daddy. I met him while he was on leave. He was so handsome and charming, he just swept me right off my feet." She assumed a look of innocence. "I—I couldn't help myself."

Claiborne rubbed nervously at his mouth with the back of his hand. "Does your mother know?"

"No. Nobody knows but Jessie."

"Jessie?"

She nodded meekly. "I needed another woman to confide in."

"*God!*" Claiborne sputtered for a moment, then tossed down a huge mouthful of brandy.

"Calvin will never know it's not his."

"But if he finds out?"

"He won't care. He worships me, Daddy."

Claiborne lifted a hand helplessly and sighed deeply. "Oh, God, Loretta, I'm disappointed in you."

"I know." She sniffed and dabbed at her eyes with a hankie. "But you *must* let me marry Calvin. I don't want to bring shame to you and Mother. Or me either."

Claiborne drank again, closed his eyes and seemed to mutter a few words of silent prayer. "Very well. You and Mr. Tyler will have a quiet wedding—tomorrow. No guests, no parties. A very quiet wedding. Then you and he can live out at Magnolia Hall."

Loretta's head snapped up. "At Magnolia Hall! Just me and Calvin?"

"He'll be your husband."

"But why can't we live here?"

"Because, my dear, he's my overseer. Besides, the other evening you were in a snit because we wouldn't be moving out to the country this winter."

She went rigid before him, her head thrown back in defiance. "But that was *all* of us! I don't want to live way out there with Calvin and a handful of field niggers!"

He was staring at her intently, his gaze disconcerting. "You made your bed, Loretta. Now you'll have to lie in it."

Loretta looked as if she would spit on the floor in disgust.

"He *what!*" Jessie stared at Garth with numb disbelief. Her voice reverberated through the stable, frightening the foal. Jody looked up at her with bland curiosity, then went back to mending a harness.

Eyes sparkling with unbridled humor, Garth took Jessie by the arm and led her out of the carriage shed, into the garden. "I said Calvin Tyler asked Father if he could marry Loretta."

"I don't believe it!" Jessie shook her head, her mind unwilling to absorb the idea. "Calvin?"

Garth chuckled. "That's right, my love. Calvin Tyler, my father's overseer."

Jessie's head spun. What was Loretta up to now? The notion was preposterous! Loretta Bodine married to an overseer? A man who was either too afraid or too uncommitted to the Cause to join the Confederate army.

"He told Father she loves him. She *wants* to marry him."

An unsettling thought wormed its way into Jessie's mind. Of course. It all made sense now. Loretta needed a father for her unborn child—for Apollo's child. And Calvin Tyler was the only white male over sixteen and under sixty who was available.

Garth paused by a weather-beaten trellis where sweet peas had grown this past summer. "What's my damn sister trying to pull? She doesn't love Tyler!"

"I don't know. She's your sister."

Garth tugged at his mustache and ran a hand through his thick, black hair. "I think she's lost her mind, that's what. She'd no more marry Tyler than spit in public. He's nothing. He hasn't any money, no name for himself." Garth shook his head in dismay. "It's crazy."

"It seems that way."

Garth's eyebrows lifted suspiciously. "You don't know something *I* don't, do you?"

Jessie glanced away, making a show of picking a damp leaf off her rose. "No."

"Father will never agree. Whatever's going on around here, that's one thing you can bet on."

Jessie nodded dutifully, watching a bird pecking at the grass for seeds or worms. If Loretta had dared tell her father the same story she had fed Jessie—about the soldier on leave—all bets were off. Would Claiborne Bodine rather endure the shame of an unwed daughter giving birth or marrying his overseer? That was a question Jessie couldn't answer.

The Court House at Broad and Meeting streets was a dreary, ancient structure that might have been imposing before the war, but was now in need of polish and repair. The Justice of the Peace was equally as old, his skin sallow, stretched like parchment over sunken cheeks. His lined face was as somber as the rumpled black suit he wore.

Jessie stood next to Garth, her arm slipped through his, and gazed at Loretta. The wedding gown was in actuality a pre-war party frock of white satin festooned with tiny pink bows. The form-fitting bodice was cut daringly low, but instead of helping, it only served to display Loretta's rather flat bosom.

Beside her, Calvin Tyler wore a suit he had purchased at a secondhand store last night. The trousers were too short; the jacket looked as if it might tear at the seams from his broad back and shoulders. He appeared nervous and ill-at-ease, but that couldn't deter the grin lurking beneath his blond beard.

Della was already weeping into a hankie, even though the marriage vows had yet to be taken. Claiborne stood stiff and expressionless, staring, not at the couple, but at a framed portrait of Jefferson Davis.

The old judge's voice was high pitched and nasal, with a heavy drawl. Jessie paid little attention to what he was saying; her eyes were on Loretta. The tilt of her head conveyed a sense of regal superiority, even under these circumstances. She answered when she should with a clipped, sharp tone.

"The ring?"

Calvin slapped his forehead with the heel of his hand. "I plum forgot, Your Honor. I spent my last cent on this here suit."

Loretta's sidewise look shot daggers at her intended husband. Jessie raised a brow in amusement. The celebrated Loretta Bodine —without even a wedding ring to her name.

Garth knew his sister was pregnant—by the imaginary soldier. That much his father had told him, and Garth had passed this juicy tidbit on to Jessie. She had acted properly shocked. All Della knew was that her little girl was getting married to a man—albeit an overseer—who doted on her.

The ceremony finished, Calvin gave Loretta a blushing peck on the cheek, then turned to shake hands with Garth and Claiborne. Della embraced her daughter, sniffing and crying. Jessie gave Loretta a brief hug.

Unable to stop the words, Jessie whispered sarcastically, "I imagine you'll especially miss Apollo now."

Loretta drew away, her face pale, rasping in a sharp breath. Jessie's smile was full and sweet and charming, but at the same time unnervingly frigid. There were no more secrets: now Loretta knew that Jessie knew.

Composing herself, Loretta forced a laugh

of gaiety and took Calvin's arm. "Daddy's taken a room for us at the Planters' House. We mustn't let his money go to waste."

Calvin's face burned bright crimson, but he let Loretta practically drag him out of the Court House. Della let loose with another fresh burst of sobs.

Jessie turned thoughtful eyes to the portrait of Jefferson Davis, hanging just above the Stars and Bars. By now, Apollo should probably be in Virginia, heading for the Maryland border—and freedom.

# 29

Loretta stared bleakly into the cold stone fireplace, an empty goblet dangling from one hand. She briefly glanced beside her chair to the half bottle of wine on the table, then turned her gaze back to the hearth. A long, disgruntled sigh slipped from her.

Nippy gusts of wind wheezed through the cracks in the doors and windows, caught up swirls of dust and carried them around the huge drawing room. It was late October and had rained for three days straight, great, gushing sheets of water that refused to let up. Now the storm was over, but the sky was overcast with low, dark clouds. Little light entered the drawing room.

Loretta sighed and poured herself another glass of wine. She was glad the room was dark, glad she couldn't see more than mere outlines of the place where once couples had chattered and drank and danced at gay parties, where her father and his cronies had held forth on the power of the South and the swift end to the Yankees' tyranny.

No more parties, no more brave talk. Only memories.

Loretta drank, feeling the warmth spreading through her, but failing to calm the tension in the pit of her stomach. A banjo clock on the wall ticked off the seconds slowly; Jewel hummed softly in the kitchen, a barely audible whisper. The dust covers had been removed from all the furnishings in the downstairs rooms; the carpets had been beaten and rolled back into place. Upstairs, only one room had been restored—the bedroom she shared with Calvin Tyler, her husband.

Loretta's face twisted into a grimace. Granted, he was patient with her, doted on her, but he was such a bumpkin! She saw him only in the late afternoons and evenings; he was up and dressed and gone long before she ever awakened. But for one thing she was thankful: Calvin was overjoyed at the prospect of becoming a father in the spring.

Loretta drank more wine, clutching the goblet so tightly that her knuckles turned white. She hated it here! Hated the isolation, the loneliness. Calvin was the only white person for miles; the two nearest plantations had been abandoned. The only other people to talk to were the two dozen or so half-witted slaves that populated Magnolia Hall, and of all of them, only Jewel and Leroy could carry on a halfway intelligent conversation.

She heard the back door open, heard Calvin's voice as he spoke to Jewel. Loretta brushed back an errant lock of hair, but she didn't really care about her appearance anymore. Most days, she didn't even bother getting dressed. She spent her time either in the bedroom or the drawing room, sometimes reading, but mostly just dozing and daydreaming and drinking. At least the stock of bottles in the wine cellar ought to last through the winter.

"That chicken smells delicious," Calvin said, entering the room. He was bootless, but mud soiled his trousers up to his knees.

"All we ever eat is chicken! Chicken for dinner, chicken for supper!" Her eyes blazed with fury, her voice crackled with sarcasm.

"Now, honey, be thankful we have that." Calvin bent to kiss her; she turned her face so that his lips and beard only grazed her cheek.

He shrugged his broad shoulders and bent to light a fire. "It's cold in here. I don't want my pretty little bride to take sick. You got to be careful in your condition."

Loretta sneered at his back, watched him light a cut-glass lamp, then pour himself a whiskey. God, how she wished he would learn a little finesse in bed! His lovemaking was like tangling with a grunting, sweating old bear; his caresses were crude, his kisses sloppy and wet.

He stood by the hearth, smiling at her from beneath his tangled blond beard. "You're lookin' poorly, honey. You sure you're feelin' all right?"

"I'm just lonely out here. I wish we lived in

the city."

"If we did that, I wouldn't have a job. I'm your daddy's overseer, remember?"

*How could I forget?* She grunted, sipped at her wine and eyed him harshly. "Are you going to spend the rest of the evening in those dirty clothes?"

"I'll change in a minute. Just thought I'd visit with you for a spell. You know how proud I am to have you for my wife."

Loretta managed a twisted sort of smile for him.

"And me—a papa!" He gave a little laugh and shook his head in delighted amazement. "You make me mighty proud, honey."

She answered with a noncommital murmur.

"What do you want it to be, honey? A boy or a girl?"

Loretta shrugged. "I don't care."

Calvin gave her a wink and left the room, presumably to change out of his muddy clothing. Loretta stared gloomily at the ruby contents of her glass, a puzzled and angry frown creasing her forehead. *I don't give a damn what sex the little bastard is! I just hope and pray it doesn't come out black!*

Jessie sat beside Garth on the settee, her arm linked through his, her fingers straying over the gold cuff on his uniform sleeve. Della was perched on a chair at the small desk, almost too flustered and excited to write. Claiborne sipped a brandy and watched his wife with amusement.

"I don't know if we'll have *time* to do everything!" Della tapped her pen nervously against a bronze inkwell. "But it's *so* exciting!"

Garth glanced down at Jessie and winked. "Mother's never going to be the same."

A soft smile played across Jessie's lips, the color high in her cheeks, her eyes glowing lusterously.

"There's so much to do!" Della went on. "Invitations, a gown, the reception . . ." She fluttered her hands and heaved a tremendous sigh.

"Calm down, my dear," Claiborne told her. "There's time."

"Oh, Claiborne, you don't understand. Something like this means so much to a mother."

Claiborne chuckled dryly. "I suspect it means more to Garth and Jessie."

"But November! That only gives me a month!"

Jessie squeezed Garth's arm. November was in reality only a week away. In another four, she would be Mrs. Garth Bodine. Claiborne had finally relented. After the fiasco with Loretta, he was willing to grant Garth and Jessie anything. He only wanted to forget about his daughter's *faux pas* and see his son married before Thanksgiving.

"This is going to be the social event of the year for Charleston," Della said. "We'll have the biggest reception—right here. Bring in some of the slaves from the plantation to help cook and clean and serve."

Except for Della's enthusiastic babble, the house had been peaceful for the last six weeks—ever since Loretta's hasty marriage and departure. No more tantrums, no more yelling at Flobelle and Violet Mae and Sam. Jessie felt quite at home and content.

Even Claiborne had changed. He no longer treated Jessie like a Yankee but as a member of the family. The armies were settling down for the winter in Georgia and Tennessee and Virginia, and, though the news was still not good for the Confederacy, it wasn't bad either.

"I'll need Loretta to help," Della said, turning to Jessie. "She can write invitations, help with the planning. After all, she did miss out on all that for herself."

Jessie nodded sagaciously. So Loretta would be coming back for a while. No matter. Jessie was too happy to care about Loretta and her temper and her black moods. She had Garth, the man she loved. Loretta only had Calvin Tyler, a likable oaf who was not the father of the baby his wife was carrying.

Della turned to scribble something on her paper. Claiborne rose and left the room.

Jessie glanced at Garth out of the corner of her eye. "I really don't need such a fancy wedding."

"It's for Mother as much as it is for you. She couldn't very well do it for Loretta, now, could she?"

Jessie suppressed a tiny, malicious smile. She might not have saved herself for her wedding night, but at least she was marrying a man she adored and respected. And she wasn't pregnant either.

"I hate for them to go to all this expense," she said.

Garth leaned down and brushed her hair with his lips. "Let them. They might as well spend it before it devaluates anymore."

Jessie smiled at Garth enigmatically and leaned over for a kiss. His lips were soft, his kiss sweet, and Jessie's heart fluttered in her breast. Della, oblivious to everything around her, was busy at her interminable lists.

"I love you," Garth whispered.

Jessie's lips caressed his lightly. "I love you too."

Amusement twinkled in his gray eyes, brightening them to a vivid glow. "Even if I'm a Reb?"

Claiborne returned and handed Garth a small velvet box. "I've been saving this for you."

"What is it?"

"It belonged to my grandmother. When she was dying, she gave it to me to give to my son—if I had one. When you open it I'm sure you'll undertand what she meant."

Garth flipped open the lid of the box. Jessie peered over and caught her breath at the dazzling piece of jewelry, so brilliant it was almost blinding. Dainty, yet beautifully crafted, it was a gold ring set with a ruby surrounded by tiny diamonds.

"Grandmother intended that for your bride," Claiborne said, then turned to Jessie with a gentle smile. "And I'm sure it couldn't find a lovlier woman to wear it even if it had a mind of its own."

Jessie rose and impulsively threw her arms around Claiborne's ample form and hugged him. "Oh, thank you, Claiborne. It's beautiful!" Then a small frown marred her brow, and her smile faded. "But shouldn't it be Loretta's?"

Claiborne scowled. "My grandmother—rest her dear old soul—meant it to be for my son to give to his wife. Loretta . . ." He broke off and shook his head in grave disappointment. "Loretta has displeased me—deeply."

Jessie sat back down, watching Garth holding the ring up to the light. It sparkled like fire and ice. Loretta didn't even have a wedding ring; Calvin couldn't afford one. Jessie glanced at Claiborne and saw his little smile of pride as he gazed at her. At last, she finally knew she belonged to the family, even if she *was* a Yankee.

Jessie lazily watched three soldiers tottering down Legare Street, no doubt in search of another tavern to visit or a brothel in which to spend their pay. A chilly breeze blew off the Ashley River, but Garth's close presence beside her on the porch swing—and her shawl—kept her comfortably warm.

"When I first met your father, I would never have imagined him giving me such a gift," she mused aloud. "To him, I was just a northern troublemaker."

"You're *not* a troublemaker."

Jessie didn't answer, just stared across the

street where a woman was putting out a loudly protesting cat. Trouble? If Garth and Claiborne and Della only knew the mischief she had caused! But it was for a good cause, a noble cause, and the proof was in her pocket right now.

Earlier today, she had received a letter in the mail from Gettysburg, addressed in Dr. Brooks' scrawl. Inside was a sheet of paper with a few words printed in large, childlike block leters. A simple message: "Thank you. John Smith."

Jessie felt a swell of pride and accomplishment. Apollo was safely in Pennsylvania, had even learned to print, although it resembled the crude penmanship of a six-year-old. One slave was free—months, perhaps years—before others would be. And when that time came, she vowed to help them make the transition to freedom as easily as she could.

And Loretta—stuck out there in the country. Grim amusement twitched at the corners of Jessie's mouth. She could well imagine Loretta's indignation at helping plan a fancy wedding, a wedding she never had—and for a Yankee, of all people! Jessie suppressed a mirthless little laugh.

"Happy?" Garth's voice was low, his face close to hers, his breath warm against her cheek.

"Very." She turned her head, her eyes bright with blissful radiance. "We've come a long way from Mama's basement to here."

His fingers caressed her cheek and twined around a long tress of hair. "It's been an adventure, I must admit. The Yankees after me, the Rebs after you in Richmond, Jake Coffin . . .''

Jessie involuntarily shuddered at the mention of that scoundrel's name. Garth pulled her close, kissed her lightly and stroked her hair. "Once and for all, he's dead, Jessie. Forget the bad times." In the dim light, his gray eyes shone with love as he gazed at her. "There's nothing but happiness ahead for us now."

She looked at him steadily, her eyes unwavering, their glow warm and admiring as they probed his. "Yes. And we *will* be happy." His lips were warm, and the touch of them on hers started a turmoil in her blood that she knew only he could satisfy. They had the rest of their lives for that now.